The lilies thrust up bold yellow trumpets. Tiny crimson spots decorated their interior. He blinked. They seemed to follow him heliotropically as if he were the sun. He reached out. The trumpet flared, and the bloom dipped toward his hand. The image of jaws opening flashed across his mind. He jerked back, embarrassed at his reaction. It was only a flower, after all. . . .

Edited by
Charles L. Grant
The SeaHarp Hotel

The
Third Chronicle of
Greystone Bay

TOR ®
HORROR

A TOM DOHERTY ASSOCIATES BOOK
NEW YORK

THE SEAHARP HOTEL

Copyright © 1990 by Charles L. Grant

A Tor Book
Published by Tom Doherty Associates, Inc.
49 West 24th Street
New York, N.Y. 10010

Cover art by Mark and Stephanie Gerber

ISBN: 0-812-51870-5

First edition: June 1990

Printed in the United States of America

0 9 8 7 6 5 4 3 2 1

ACKNOWLEDGMENTS

Introduction, copyright © 1990 by Charles L. Grant.

Ex-Library, copyright © 1990 by Chet Williamson. By permission of the author.

The Coat, copyright © 1990 by Al Sarrantonio. By permission of the author.

Beauty, copyright © 1990 by Robert R. McCammon. By permission of the author.

Services Rendered, copyright © 1990 by Bryan Webb. By permission of the author.

Aquarium, copyright © 1990 by Steve Rasnic Tem. By permission of the author.

Three Doors in a Double Room, copyright © 1990 by Craig Shaw Gardner. By permission of the author.

CONTENTS

THE SEAHARP HOTEL
Introduction
by
Charles L. Grant

Greystone Bay   **17 July 1862**
The SeaHarp Hotel

My dear Jonathan,

Born here, died here. If you would be so kind as to put that on my tombstone, son, I would be grateful. Anything else would no doubt be blasphemous. And I doubt God has any patience left for me, being busy enough putting fools in high office who will, I no longer fear but know, soon have us all bearing arms against our own kind. Children in the park play at war. Those who claim to understand such things, as I do not, claim that conflict is unthinkable, that no man, no state, no country would dare wage open warfare against itself. As usual, those who claim to know, know nothing.

Would you were here, you would be shocked to see that even the Bay is afflicted. Aside from the arguments which rage nightly in the Gentleman's Lounge here at the hotel, each night, on the sand, a madman who claims to have fought with General Harrison shrieks his anti-abolitionist message to anyone who will listen, including the gulls and the tide.

The guests are disturbed. There is little I can do. Perhaps God, or an armed drunk, will put this fool out of his misery. I lose rooms because of him.

But perhaps I am too much the cynic these days.

Perhaps I am bitter because, after all these years, I still miss your mother.

Only time and the Rail-splitter will tell.

On a more important subject, in this package you will find the key. Do not lose it. Show it to no one, not even your lovely Lucinda. It is time.

I know. I understand. You protest, you deny, you may find yourself moved to return to the Bay and examine my senses for signs of deterioration. Do not bother yourself. Stay where you are. I assure you, Jon, the only deterioration is in my soul, and my body. I cannot rid myself of this cough. It prevents my sleep, it disturbs my guests, it has kept me a virtual prisoner in my apartments in order that I do not cause more to flee to other houses along the shore.

I cannot eat.

I can barely drink without spilling.

The men who pass for physicians tell me it is the climate. They tell me my constitution is not suited to the dampness of the sea air, the chill of even the summer night. The fog. It makes no difference to any of them that I was born in this very place, not a hundred paces from where my dream now stands. They blame the air.

We know what it is, you and I.

And perhaps it will permit me to see you before I die.

It is much too hot here.

There is too much noise.

I think it is time, perhaps for the last time. I visit the room. I think of your mother often when I am there, which makes it all bearable. She was so lovely, so fragile, one would never have guessed her age when she was taken. I, now, am fully aged.

Damn this hotel!

I have changed my mind. Come home. Without your mother's strength I am too much afraid.

Yours,
Howard Bolgran

Greystone Bay   *19 February 1889*
The SeaHarp Hotel

Walter,

Since you are determined to remain away from your home and your family, I have no choice but to inform you that I have made arrangements for the affairs of the SeaHarp to be administered by Graham Menzies after I am gone. He has already taken over most of the daily chores, sees to it that our guests are treated in the manner to which they have rightly become accustomed, and despite your no doubt drunken accusations, takes nothing out of it but the simplest of amenities.

I have also seen to it, through Mr. Thargood, that the stipend you now receive be terminated at my death. You will have no idea how much that pains me, but since you would rather enjoy the ''entertainments'' of New York than the comforts of your birthplace, I have no choice. You are now free to find other means by which to finance your debaucheries.

I thank God your grandfather, the founder of this respite from the horrors of the world, is not alive to see this.

However, should you see your way clear to return for my funeral, do at least one thing for me. A deathbed request if you will—take the key I enclose here and go into the room. What you find there will no doubt answer all your questions.

And I can assure you, it will solve whatever questions you have about your future as well.

Mr. Thargood knows nothing of this, nor does Mr. Menzies.

You need not respond to this correspondence.

Either you come or you do not.

I do not care.

As far as I am concerned, you have died before me.

Your Father

Greystone Bay   *11 October 1900*
The SeaHarp Hotel

Dear Mr. Thargood,

When I purchased the SeaHarp Hotel from Mr. Walter Bolgran three days before his unfortunate passing, it was with the understanding, in writing both from him and your firm, that this was a thriving establishment, well thought of by the genteel and the wealthy. As you have seen by the abrupt decline in bookings, this is not the case now, nor has it been for the past several years, long before I took possession. Even the improvements I made—the doubling of capacity by cutting the rooms in half, the paint, the gardens, the rates—have had no effect. Nothing seems to work.

If I were not a businessman, I might even go so far as to say that this place, this fog-damned village, has deliberately attempted to put me out of business. And I am one of them, for God's sake!

If I am to maintain my reputation in commercial circles, I must divest myself of this albatross. It would please me, then, if you made all the necessary arrangements. You may reach me at my hotel in Boston, certainly a more civilized place than this. I shall be leaving in the morning, after I am positive nothing has been overlooked, or pilfered, by this laughable staff.

I have come to suspect, by the way, that much of which has been reported lost and stolen by the handful of guests who have stayed here—none, by the way, more than a week through the past five months—has been stored in that locked room in the corridor just before the so-called Gentleman's Lounge. I will check it myself. I would not be surprised if there is something there I will be able to report to the police.

Until I hear from you then, I remain,

Yours truly,
Lamont Hews

Greystone Bay　　　　　　　　　　　　*1 November 1904*
The SeaHarp Hotel

Dearest Dorothy,

Just a quick note, on this the first anniversary of our assuming title to our dream, to tell you that I have, in the library, at last located the word "SeaHarp." It refers to an obscure form of oceanic life which used to thrive in our very own bay before the middle of the last century. It is so called because of its peculiar harp-like shape. Oddly, I can find no mention of whether it is fish or plant. I suspect the "scientists" of the day were, at least here, not much more than amateurs. No matter. There are times when I cannot be sure if this hotel is really a hotel, or a way-station for those fleeing from the law.

A jest, my love. Do not worry. We are on sound footing at last, and in only one year. I think we will make it.

Please give my best to your mother, and tell her that I trust she is recovering rapidly.

And do hurry home. I have a surprise for you. I cannot tell you what it is for that would spoil the surprise, but suffice to say, I have finally discovered which lock accepts that key you found in the attic last month.

You won't believe your eyes.

I love you.

Your loving husband,
Peter

Greystone Bay   **26 May 1955**
SeaHarp Hotel

Dear Father,

The redecoration of your and Mother's apartments on the top floor is now done. Both Simon and I urge you come home. Simon's children miss you terribly. Frankly, how he manages those dreadful little children I'll never know. They are horrid, and the longer you two are away, the worse they get.

One of these days, I'm going to put them in the room.

The weather is beautiful.

Wish you were here.

Simon sends his best wishes.

Love and kisses,
Elinor

Greystone Bay   *9 August 1988*
The SeaHarp Hotel

Dear Howard,

   Right now, while you're sweltering in the city, ducking
from one air conditioned office to another and catching pneu-
monia in the process, I am sitting quite comfortably at a
small table on the front porch, watching a fishing boat on the
bay, watching the shadow of the SeaHarp darken the water
(the tide is coming in), and waiting for that famous Greystone
fog to roll in. It's a little chilly for this time of year, but it
beats 100 in New York any day.

   Someone is playing Mozart on the lobby piano.

   To my left, in the garden, a young woman and her daughter
are chasing a gull that seems to have the kid's pink rubber
ball.

   And if someone brings out the hotel's croquet set and asks
me to play under the stars, damned if I won't do it. That's
the kind of place this is.

   I'm sending along photocopies of those letters and personal
reminiscences you asked for just so you can see that I'm
really not exaggerating when I say that this building has been
jinxed from the word go. The bizarre stuff that seems to go
on here beats all hell out of me, and yet they keep on coming
from all over with their suitcases and their families, on their
honeymoons and on their retirement, just as if nothing's ever
happened here and nothing ever will.

   It's as if we're talking about lemmings in human form or
something.

   I've even sent a couple of things over to Wes Martin, the
guy who took over for Abe in the Station, to see what he
makes of it. Talking to the police here is a small-town joke—
they have one of those it's-our-town-not-yours-so-what atti-

tudes. You know: "This is the way we've always done things, and it's worked so far, so why bother to change?"

Right. If it ain't broke, don't fix it.

Damn. There's the fog. Write five words and the damned thing sneaks up on you. Pretty impressive, actually. It's just about at the boardwalk, and you can't even catch a glimpse of the people who were on the beach a moment ago.

Spooky as hell, if you want to know the truth.

Speaking of spooky, I've finally gotten Victor Montgomery, grandson of the people who reopened the joint, to admit that I have in fact discovered the mysterious "room" that keeps popping up in all this correspondence. The trouble is, he won't let me in. And you can forget that brilliant idea of kissing up, as it were, to sister Noreen. She reminds me of Mrs. Bates, after Norman took care of her. No thanks. I'll think of something else.

Meanwhile, the fog rolls in every night like clockwork, the bar is well-stocked, and there are, I suppose, worse places in the world to put your feet up and forget about deadlines and stuff.

I just wish I knew what was in that room.

The streetlamps are on.

It's almost like London, before they cleaned up the factories.

But it's not so much the fog, not really.

It's the sounds *in* the fog.

Right now, I can barely see over the porch railing. But I can hear the water slapping at the pilings, I can hear someone in high heels walking on the sidewalk, I can hear what almost sounds like a carriage rattling over cobblestones in the street; someone is giggling in the garden; there are wings overhead, probably a large gull heading for home; the piano has stopped; the streetlamps are little more than blurs of lighter fog; a fish jumps, or something has been thrown into the water; a buoy rings unevenly, as if something has just passed it, tipping it in its wake; a match is struck, but I can't see the light; far down Harbor Road someone's whistling; someone kicks a pebble; a door opens, but I don't know where; footsteps on wood; wings; whistling; humming; a carriage; a woman laughs; and someone, out there, whispers my name.

Charles L. Grant

EX-LIBRARY
by
Chet Williamson

It was not, Kendall Harris thought, the ideal place for a family vacation, and he would damn well let Riggs know it when he got back to Boston. The SeaHarp Hotel, despite Riggs's paeans of praise, struck Harris as little cheerier than a mausoleum, and the town of Greystone Bay was not so much "charmingly caught in time," as Riggs had put it, as it was embalmed, like a long-dead insect trapped in amber.

Every face Harris had seen in the hotel, including his own in the mirror, had a pale, sickly cast that unerringly reflected the pallor of the sky. Was it ever blue over Greystone Bay? Harris wondered. And was there any haven in this great pile of a building where you could not hear that damned surf? The pounding of each wave on the strand seemed to mock the pounding of each worry, every concern that beat against the rickety seawall that was all that was left of his relationship with Maureen and David.

His wife. His son. He said those words to himself over and

over, trying to find in them something that moved him, some saving grace that would make things the way they had been before Deborah had come into his life, Deborah with her heart-shaped face, her willowy form, and her heart of oak that would brook no rival, not even a wife. She had refused to be a mistress, and for that Harris loved her all the more.

But his family was too important to him to give up, even for Deborah, and he told her that, and told her that it had to end between them. She had understood and had walked away, leaving his life emptier than it had been before, the memories of his happiness with her creating an abyss in which the small amount of affection he still had left for Maureen was totally swallowed up.

Maureen had known that he was having an affair. She was neither dumb nor blind, and her pain had lashed out at him, and he had returned word for word, curse for curse, until there was nothing left but legalities to bind them together. They had gone to a counselor, and the counselor had said to get away, go on a vacation together, escape the petty pressures of everyday life.

And so they had come to Greystone Bay, where the petty pressures vanished, making room for the huge and deeper pressures that Harris carried inescapably within him, the pressures that now boiled inside his brain as the foam boiled on the rocky strand.

They had arrived only that morning, and already the large, second-floor suite they occupied seemed tight and claustrophobic. Christ, Harris thought, the Superdome would have seemed claustrophobic if both he and Maureen had been in it. Her presence, smoldering with disgust toward him, filled the room, leaving him no air to breathe, and the way in which she sheltered David, as though his father were some brute who might devour him, both saddened and angered Harris. The worst of it was that the boy had begun to share his mother's aversion, and in the presence of his wife and child Harris now felt leprous, monstrous, murderous.

So much, he thought bitterly, for a fucking family vacation. And this was only the first evening. Ten more days to go. Jesus God, he wondered, grimacing inwardly at the absurd melodrama of the thought, will I be able to get through this vacation without killing somebody?

He shook his head at the idea, wondered if a third drink would be too many, decided that it would not, and ordered another Glenfiddich. He drank it in less time than he had taken with its two predecessors, and after it was gone he decided that he would drain his bladder before adding any more fluid to its contents. It was a long way to the door of the bar, but he made the trip easily, and just as easily found his way to the men's room beneath the staircase. No, he thought, not drunk yet. He sighed. Not drunk enough. Never drunk enough.

He urinated, washed his hands, splashed some water on his cheeks, and ran a comb through his graying hair, trying not to look at the haggard face that suddenly seemed so old and sad. Forty-two, he thought. Only forty-fucking-two and everything is over? He slipped the comb back into his pocket and listened for a moment.

It was there. The sound of the breakers. He had heard it in the bar, and could even now hear it in here, in a room with no windows. Maybe through the pipes, he thought. Jesus, was there any place you couldn't hear those goddamned waves crashing?

Harris went back into the hall and took a few steps toward the bar, but then stopped and looked to the right down the corridor. Was there someplace down there, he wondered, someplace quiet, where a man could stop thinking about those waves?

He crossed the corridor only to find a locked meeting room on the right, a locked ballroom on the left, and, further down

the hall and to the right, a room with a closed door marked
Club. "Not a member," Harris muttered to himself, and
went back the way he had come. At the cross-corridor, he
turned left, and heard the sharp sound of billiard balls striking one another. Not tonight, he thought. Not in the mood.
Then he noticed the door with the words *Reading Room* let-
tered on it. It was closed, but Harris could see a light beneath
the door. He walked up to it, turned the knob slowly, and
pushed it open.

An old man was sitting in a leather armchair against the
far wall, the only light in the room coming from the brass
floor lamp whose green shade hung over him like a censer.
When the man looked up, Harris thought for a moment that
he was staring at an egg, not so much for the shape of the
man's head as for its color—or lack of it. His hair was a
brilliant white, as was the well-trimmed beard that wreathed
his chin, and the pallor of his flesh was almost equal to that
of his hair and whiskers. Harris, frozen in the doorway, was
relieved as the apparition's face split in a friendly smile, and
blue eyes observed him from behind shining bifocals.

"Come in," the old man said warmly. "I had the door
closed to keep out the sounds of the billiards, not fellow
readers. Make yourself at home. The chairs are comfortable,
the ambience is pleasant, and the silence is delightful."

Harris smiled back and closed the door behind him. Peace
settled over the room like a shroud. He listened in pleasèd
surprise. "You can't hear the surf," he said.

"You're glad of that?"

"Well . . . yes."

The old man nodded and quoted:

" 'Sophocles long ago
Heard it on the Aegean, and it brought
Into his mind the turbid ebb and flow
Of human misery . . .' "

"Dover Beach," Harris said, happy to recognize the allusion.

"Ah!" the man said, delighted. "You *are* a reader."

"I, uh, remembered it from college, that's all."

"You agree with Matthew Arnold? The ebb and flow of human misery—the surf reminds you of it?"

"I . . . guess so. Sometimes."

"Well, you're safe from it for the little while you're here. But I'm being rude, I should introduce myself." He pushed himself to his feet with surprising agility, and thrust out a hand. "My name is Samuel. And you?"

Harris took the hand and shook it. It was warm and dry and gripped his own hand firmly and a bit longer than Harris thought necessary. "Harris," he said. "Kendall Harris."

"A pleasure, Mr. Harris. And to what tastes does your reading run? I know this room and its holdings quite well. Perhaps I can help you select a suitable volume?"

"Well . . . I don't know. I mean, I came in here mainly for a place to just sit and . . . and think," Harris finished weakly.

"Ah, and here I am chattering away." Samuel put his head to one side and frowned. "But are you sure, Mr. Harris," he went on more softly, "that you *want* to sit and think? You appear, if you don't mind my saying so, to be more than a little ill at ease. Perhaps some literary escapism would be more in order."

Jesus, it shows, Harris thought. He didn't know why he just didn't tell the old man to be quiet and sit down and finish his damn book, but there was something that stopped him. Perhaps it was the air of occupancy that Samuel possessed, as though this reading room was his private suite, and Harris was only there at his indulgence. "Look, I don't know . . ."

"Mr. Harris, have you ever read M.R. James?"

The name struck a chord, and Harris remembered a Dover paperback that he had bought when he was in college. A roommate had turned him on to LeFanu, and for several joy-ously chilly months he had immersed himself in English ghost stories whenever he was not doing the required reading for his classes. "I have, yes."

Samuel stepped up to one of the packed mahogany book-shelves that surrounded the room, and drew from it a small, thick volume bound in a dark red cloth which he handed to Harris. "Please, take this. There's a certain story I'd like you to read, if you have a half hour or so?"

Harris looked at the book, *Collected Ghost Stories* by M.R. James. He opened it to the title and copyright pages and saw that it was a British edition published by Edward Arnold Ltd. in 1931. The volume was dog-eared, and the front hinge had broken. As Harris turned to the back, he noticed a paper library pocket pasted in, and in it a yellowed card, covered with several signatures. "Greystone Bay Public Library," Harris read aloud.

"Yes. Destroys its collectors' value, but it also brings . . . another dimension, shall we say, to the book. Now the story I'd like for you to read is 'Oh, Whistle, and I'll Come to You, My Lad.' "

Harris sighed in exasperation. "Look, Mr. Samuel—"

"Just Samuel."

"All right. Samuel. Now I don't know why you want me to read this story, but—"

"An experiment," Samuel said, never losing his soft smile.

"An experiment," Harris repeated.

"To be explained when you finish the story."

Harris smiled thinly. "Samuel," he said, "what is it with you? Are you a retired high school English teacher who misses the old days or what?"

Samuel chuckled. "I assure you I'm not, Mr. Harris. What harm can it do? Do you have anything better to do with your time tonight?"

Harris thought of Maureen and David watching television

in the cavernous living room of their suite, and felt a hot flame of revulsion blaze through him. He shook his head. "No. No I don't."

"Then make yourself comfortable. What better way to pass an evening than to sit comfortably and read a thrilling tale?"

While Samuel resumed his own seat and volume, Harris stepped over to a chair twenty feet away, turned on the floor lamp, sat, and began to read. He dimly remembered having read the story years before, but was soon caught up in it enough to forget both the odd circumstances under which he was now rereading it and the old man seated several yards away.

It was, he thought, a truly eerie story, with an effective and terrifying ghost, and he blinked quickly several times at the story's end until he felt free of the false yet chilling reality of the tale. He looked over at Samuel, and closed the book with a loud enough report to make the old man look up.

"I'm finished," Harris said. "Do you want me to do a book report for you?"

Samuel grinned, and Harris was not surprised to find that his teeth were as startlingly white as his hair. "No, Mr. Harris," he said. "All I want is to ask you a question about the story. A single question."

"All right."

The old man stood up and crossed the room until he was next to Harris's chair. "What did you *see*?"

"What did I . . . see? What do you mean?"

"When the ghost . . . the malignant thing . . . forms itself out of the bedding." He held out a hand for the book. "Allow me." Harris placed the book in Samuel's hand, and the man opened it and read: " 'I gathered that what he chiefly remembers about it is a horrible, an intensely horrible, *face of crumpled linen*. What expression he read upon it he could not or would not tell, but that the fear of it went nigh to maddening him is certain.' " Samuel closed the book. "We all create mental images when we read. Now what I should like to know is what, specifically, was the image that you saw in your mind's eye when you just read that passage.''

Harris had no trouble remembering. For some reason the image had been extraordinarily vivid. Still, he was hesitant to allow the strange old man to share his thoughts.

"Well?" Samuel pressed.

Why not? Harris thought. It was certainly neither secret nor intimate. "It was . . . kind of silly, I guess. The sheet that made the image of the ghost had these waves of hair parted in the middle . . . there were bulging eyes, and the mouth was wide open with . . ." Harris had to chuckle. ". . . with linen teeth. Fangs, I suppose. And a beaked, pointy nose." He shrugged. "That's about it."

"And does that surprise you?" Samuel asked. "That you should create such a picture?"

Harris thought for a moment. "Yes. Yes, it does," he said slowly. "When I was halfway through the story, I remembered reading it before, and I remembered that there was an illustration—I don't know by who—but it was of this, this *sheet*-thing rising up over its victim. But when I came to the part in the story where it happened, I didn't see that, but instead got this *other* image."

Samuel reached into the pocket of his dark suit coat and withdrew a sealed envelope which he handed to Harris. It bore the return address of the SeaHarp Hotel. "Open it," Samuel said.

Harris tore it open and withdrew a sheet of hotel stationery on which was written in a spidery script, *Long wavy hair. Large eyes. Sharp nose. Fangs.* Harris read it twice, then looked up. "What is this?"

"Evidence that our little experiment worked."

Harris looked at the man, the book, the paper, and back at the man again. "Experiment? In what, ESP? You read my mind?"

Samuel shook his head. "No, no. That was in my pocket, sealed, before you even came in here. I would have to be precognitive to have done such a trick. No, Mr. Harris, there was no thought transmission between you and I while you read that story. But there *was* something between you . . ." He held up the book. ". . . and *this*."

Harris was confused, almost frightened. "Look, I don't know what you're trying to do, but—"

"Mr. Harris, please be calm. You have done this much at my request, will you do one thing more?"

"Do . . . what?"

"Read the story one more time. To prove that this paper is no coincidence."

"This is ridiculous," Harris muttered, starting to get to his feet.

"Please," Samuel said earnestly. "It is important. More important than you may guess."

Harris looked into the pale face and blue eyes for nearly a minute, then nodded curtly. "All right. All right, one more time, but then I'm leaving." He took the book, opened it once more, and reread the story. This time it took him only ten minutes, and when he had finished he looked up, puzzled.

"Yes?" Samuel said. "You have read it, and what did you see?"

"I saw . . ." Harris swallowed heavily. "I saw something different. It was more mature, more . . . fleshed out? The . . . contours of the face were lined and wrinkled, and there seemed to be traces of, of decay, or rotting on it." He looked at Samuel. "What is this all about? What is this book?"

"Look at the card in the back," the man said. "Read the first two names."

Harris turned to the back of the book and slipped the card from the pocket. The first name, Donald Lorcaster, was written in a childish scrawl, the second, Richard Williams, in a firm, adult hand.

"Notice the handwriting," Samuel said. "A child, and an adult. Now, remember the two images that you saw in your mind—the first a child's cartoon horror, the second a more developed adult vision."

"You're saying that this book is . . . a storage medium of some sort?"

Samuel nodded. "A battery, if you will, that stores not power, but images. A single, strong mental image of each person who has read this particular story. In this particular volume."

Harris barked a laugh that sounded unpleasantly loud in the quiet room. "That's ridiculous! How could something like that happen?"

"I can't explain, Mr. Harris. I can only tell you that it is so. And you can see for yourself. Read on, if you doubt me. There is a third borrower's name on the card."

Harris looked down at the book in his lap as though it was a rattlesnake poised to strike. The third name was S.T. Plummer, and the script in which it was written was artistic, even florid. What had Plummer seen, Harris wondered, and did he really want to see it for himself? Despite his fear, Harris opened the book to the story, and began to read it again.

This time, when the apparition manifested itself, there was nothing of the supernatural about it. Instead, Harris saw the mental image of a young man's face, a face unmistakably human, but filled with an inhuman hatred. It was a vicious, tortured mask, mindless and violent, with eyes that Harris knew would never close until whatever it saw was torn and destroyed, until the object of its fury and loathing lay dripping and lifeless on the floor.

"*Jesus* . . ." Harris whispered, and clapped the book shut. "Oh, *Jesus*."

"Plummer," the old man said softly. "His name was Plummer. And what you have just seen was his own face."

Harris looked at the old man and shivered.

"He was a poet," Samuel went on. "It was over fifty years ago. One summer night he murdered his wife and child and slashed his own wrists. He was saved, only to enter a madhouse, where he most certainly deserved to be." The old man stepped to Harris's side and took the card from the book. "The deaths occurred three days before the due date stamped here. A terrible thing. Unforgivable. I knew the family, you see." He sighed and shook his head. "It is not often that we get to view the world through a madman's eyes. It can be . . . instructive."

Harris sat, his gaze still on the book in front of him.

"Now. Since you have humored me with the gift of your time, might I repay you with a glass of sherry in the bar?"

Samuel strode to the door and opened it. Harris heard the sound of the waves. "No. No thank you. I'd just like to stay here for a while."

The old man nodded and walked through the door, which he left open. The billiard balls no longer clicked together, but Harris still heard the breakers on the shore. He picked up the book in his lap, weighed it in his hands, opened it, and read the tale.

This time, it was his own face that he saw.

He closed the book and sat trembling for several minutes. "Instructive," he whispered to himself.

Then he made up his mind, got up, walked out of the reading room and into the main lobby, where he asked the night clerk to call a taxicab for him. While he waited for it to arrive, he sat at one of the secretaries and wrote a brief letter:

Maureen—

There is no point to this. What we had has long been over, and any attempt to save it may lead to something far worse than divorce. I am leaving, and will have my attorney contact you when you return to Boston.

Ken

In the cab, traveling toward the western hills and the highway beyond, Harris felt, for the first time in many months, at peace. He could no longer hear the waves crashing on the strand.

A week later, a red-cheeked and heavy-set man, dressed richly if not tastefully, burst through the doors of the SeaHarp Hotel's reading room. "Now what the hell's this?" he loudly asked anyone who cared to listen.

Samuel looked up from his leather-bound volume of Milton and smiled. "The reading room, sir. Please come in."

"Reading room, huh? Great. You can't get dick on the TV, the bar is as dull as hell, and they won't let me in the goddam club room. I shoulda known the high point of this place'd be a library." The man walked in and looked around, a belligerent set to his shoulders. It was obvious that he had been drinking, even without the evidence of the reek of bourbon that surrounded him like a cloud. "So what've they got to read?"

"Well, they have a good many classics, and if you're interested in recent fiction, that shelf over there is filled with it. There are magazines and newspapers as well." Samuel paused. "But if I might make a suggestion?"

The man eyed him with bleary wariness. "Like what?"

"Have you ever read M.R. James?"

"Pal, I never even *heard* of M.R. James. They got that new Tom Clancy in here?"

"I'm afraid not. M.R. James is considered the dean of English ghost story writers, and—"

"*Ghost* stories? I don't have time to waste reading that kinda crap, buddy." The man swung his head back and forth one more time. "Shit, the hotel's a mausoleum, and this place is the crypt. See ya around."

"But, sir! . . ." said Samuel, rising to his feet. But it was too late. The man was gone.

Samuel sat down, the volume of Milton drifting closed as the memory came to his mind of the red-faced man, his timid, quiet wife, and their young daughter checking into the hotel that afternoon, of the man's quick, hot flare of temper when his wife did not remove the reservation confirmation swiftly enough from her purse, of his sharp and cruel command to his daughter to hurry up when she stopped to examine the oil painting of Captain Fletcher's ship that hung near the elevators.

Then Samuel closed his eyes and saw what the morning would bring, saw the sad-eyed woman and the shy little girl lying in their second-floor suite, lying and not moving, not even when the maid came in to make the beds, saw the red-faced man, exhausted and panting, his fury spent, his face far more red than before, with something more than his own blood coursing beneath his skin . . .

"Sir?"

Samuel opened his teary eyes and looked up. Frederick and Noreen Montgomery were standing in the doorway of the reading room. He smiled, as he smiled at most people, but with the Montgomerys it was more heartfelt. They had always been kind to him, and had never asked him to leave the hotel before it was time to close the public areas. He felt at home at the SeaHarp.

"We have to close the reading room now," Noreen said, her voice soft and apologetic.

"It's rather foggy," Frederick added. "Would you like me to call a cab for you?"

"No, thank you very much. I'll walk."

Samuel stood, adjusted his suit coat, nodded at the pair, and walked past them into the hall, toward the main entrance.

The thick carpet muffled his footfalls, and allowed him to hear snatches of the Montgomerys' conversation—

". . . such a kind man . . ."

". . . so gentle it's almost impossible to believe that . . ."

". . . when he was young . . ."

The old man had just stepped onto the porch when he heard rapid footsteps and Frederick Montgomery's voice calling his name. Samuel paused, holding the door open, and Frederick came up to him. The younger man was holding a small, red cloth-bound volume.

"This isn't from the SeaHarp's library," Frederick said, slightly out of breath. "I thought it might be yours."

The old man nodded. "Yes, it is. I forgot it. Thank you, Mr. Montgomery. I should hate to lose this book. I surely should."

Frederick Montgomery held out the book, and Samuel reached out a hand to take it. His right coat sleeve inched itself up with the motion, and, in the glow of the large globe overhead, the thin and ancient scar on his wrist shone as white as his hair, whiter than the pallor of his mortified flesh, nearly as white as the bright fire of his atoning soul.

"Goodnight, Mr. Plummer."

"Goodnight, Mr. Montgomery," the old man said, and walked off with his book into the fog and the night.

THE COAT
by
Al Sarrantonio

Here's what happens: Harry puts this coat on, he thinks, *God, I hate women.*

Not only that: he wants to kill them.

No kidding. He finds the coat neatly folded in a deep open box, tissue paper folded back, by the service entrance of the SeaHarp Hotel. Drunk as Harry is, nobody pays much attention to him anyway. Wandering Harbor Road, half in the world and half out, unshaved, unwashed, thinking about Noreen and hoping she'll come out of the SeaHarp and let him explain why he said all those terrible things to her, that it's not like when they were children, why he told her to go to hell, to leave him alone, to *stop loving* him . . .

It's a pretty nice coat, actually. New, good wool, not phony polyester crap, frays that tear like cardboard, wet snow and damp air from the Harbor coming in where the nylon stitching pulls out, flapping, ice cold on his back. This is good, long, down past his knees, deep warm pockets, big brown buttons that slip into their holes like hands into perfect gloves, hand-tailored, maybe.

Man, this coat is *warm*. He stumbles out onto Harbor Road, the late big sun on this winter day hitting him square in the eyes from between buildings. He squints like Dracula for a second, bringing his hand up to shield his eyes, and at that point this coat, which is so friggin' *comfortable*, talks into his head and says, *Get rid of the wine, Harry*.

He's startled, but only for a second because he's so damn zipped and the voice sounds so damned reasonable, smooth, cultured, and who cares if it's coming from the coat, he doesn't care if it makes him jump like a kangaroo he was so cold before he found it. He remembers shivering like mad, even the wine not helping, lurching from alley to alley, try-ing to forget the past four days, hoping Noreen would stay away, hoping at the same time he would see her, let him *ex-plain* . . .

Get rid of the wine, Harry.

The voice is gently insistent. Harry still shields his eyes with his right hand, doesn't know where the wine is, then looks down to see the Chablis bottle weighing down his left hand.

Get rid of it.

"Sure," Harry says, shrugging, and then he hoists the bottle up to his mouth, tilting it up. Down goes the wine, sour smooth. The bottle stays ass-up, dark green cheap glass in the orange sunlight, and then the white wine is gone and Harry turns abruptly and throws the fat bottle over the high wall of the SeaHarp and out into Birch Street.

"Home run!" Harry shouts as it shatters loudly. "We win!"

He laughs, and then he makes his way along the wall and walks out of the entrance of the SeaHarp and down the six steps to Harbor Road, walking down toward his part of town.

The girls are at it now. They're always at it. Early morning, bright noon, late afternoon, midnight, three in the morning. Ply the trade. He knows them, they know him, just like they know his buddies Jimmy and Wax, and all the other bums, they're all part of the landscape, like salt spray, tall brick, dogshit mashed into the curbs, sidewalks cracked up and down like snakeskin, dirty, boarded-up windows.

Here they are, ladies of night and day. Part of the terra-firma, just a "Hi, Harry" as he stumbles by, a lush's wave of his hand. "Hi, gal," too high to get it up if he wanted to, as if he'd rather spend what little he has on *that* instead of Chablis.

But he tracks in on the few of them out on day patrol, the coat wants him to watch, the skirts hiked up to *here*, a scant inch showing under leatherette jackets, Halloween hair, dark orange, frightful yellow, hoop earrings, skinny asses, puckering mouths, Marlboro stains on teeth. Shivering cold, most of them. Harry feels the wool-warmth of the coat, and laughs. "Sorry, gals," he says to himself, "but I got mine."

Let's go, Harry, the coat tells him.

Harry shrugs, turns away up Linwood Avenue. "Where we going, chief?" he says out loud, like any other drunk. Then he adds, "Wish I had some more wine."

Forget the wine. Walk.

They walk, up to Colony Avenue, over to Port Boulevard, turning left, passing cold faces, giving dirty Harry and his coat a wide berth, and then suddenly they're there.

Stop.

Somewhere over by the hospital. Wide, high store window, bright white and chrome inside. Rows of medical stuff. Stethoscopes, tongue depressors, wheelchairs. Old gent behind a glass-topped counter, telling a woman in a walker why she doesn't want to trade it in. Or why she does. The woman shakes her head vigorously, turns, walkers away from the counter. Harry hears the little bell over the door tinkle. The woman moves like a humping snail past him.

The old man in the store disappears through a small door into the back.

Look, the coat tells him. Harry's eyes roam over the store through the window. Little doodads with mirrors on the end, tiny picks and shovels, catheters, bloodbags.

That, the coat says.

There in one corner, glass shelves, rows of instruments, surgical masks, rollout leather cases, and a long scalpel.

Now, the coat orders.

He's in before he knows it. Holds the little tinker bell as he presses open the door, lets it go gently when he's in, over to the counter, reaching behind, hands steady—

The old man reappears from the back, his balding head ducking under the low eave of the doorway.

Quick, the coat says, and Harry is grabbing the scalpel, shoving it into the deep pocket of the coat, turning and walking quickly, tinkling the bell over the door as the bald man begins to shout, "You punks! Not again!", the coat pulling him like a hand tugging his lapels, three blocks away before it lets Harry stop, sure the old man's not following.

"Christ," Harry says, regaining his breath, and then he feels something clutched in his hand and looks down wanting to see a big green bottle but instead there's only this knife, half as long as his arm.

And then the coat says, *Let's go,* and Harry very much wants to have a drink that he knows the coat won't let him have.

Night now. The boardwalk. Not the tourist end, with the shrimp shops, gew-gaw stands, postcard racks, pay telescopes mounted on the railing for looking out at the foggy harbor that as often as not take your dime and either stay blind, or open their shutters to show the lenses so blotched with seagull droppings and dried salt as to be blind anyway. Not that end. The other end of the boardwalk, where the slats aren't swept and the railings are oiled black by the weather and bum piss. Where the ladies are.

The coat makes Harry study them again. They look like Martians to him: day-glow colors, shaking behinds, lipstick, dull eyes with dark painted blue circles—gum chewers, knees cocked away from each other, doing the walk, the lean, smoking, talking in twos and threes, walking, walking . . .

That one, the coat orders.

Alone, or about to be, two friends shuffling off to turn a corner. Classic lamplight pose. Harry's seen her around: blonde hair, up a little on top, shag cut, lips not as red as most, fishnet stockings. Young.

"I don't—" Harry begins.

Go, the coat insists.

She looks up slowly as he's up to her, then away. "Don't have any spare change, Harry," she says.

"Excuse me," Harry says, embarrassed, but then the coat takes over his mouth and he's smiling, saying it again with a rakish knowing edge in the voice.

"You hear me?" Still the cow eyes, the dim animal glow, gum in her cheek.

"Would you like an escort?" Harry asks, barely knowing the word.

It's obvious the word isn't too big with her, either.

"Would you like to go somewhere?" Harry says, still that suave manner coming through.

She looks him over more closely. He knows what he looks like, he hasn't had a bath in four days, but the swagger the coat has given him must come through because she doesn't walk away.

"Fifty, Harry," she says, testing him.

"Fine," he says.

The smile goes away, then comes back, wider. "You got that much? What about your wine, Harry?"

The coat makes him wink. "I'm thirsty for other things."

"Why, *Harry*." She puts her hand on his arm, her eyes and mouth smiling, her whole body loosening. She leans into him, rubbing at the fabric of the coat. "Got a lot of money in those pockets?" she asks coyly.

"Oh, I have lots in there," Harry says, the coat making him speak, and the way he says it is so assured she laughs, and he laughs too.

And then, up in the clapboard hotel room, with even the harbor outside smelling cheaper, dirtier here, the coat makes Harry kill her.

She takes him up there, the top floor, a crack in the ceiling so wide and deep he feels night air coming through the roof, off comes the jacket, the sweatshirt, nothing underneath, the silver boots, the short skirt, the fishnet stockings. The room is chilly but she doesn't show it except with little goosebumps all over her. "Want to take the panties off yourself?" she offers.

The coat makes Harry shrug and smile. "You do it."

She says, "You gonna pay me before?" and when the coat turns Harry around and he smiles, she smiles too, pushing herself up on her hands and arms, showing off her breasts. She puts all her weight on her back and one stiff arm, holding the other hand out. "That's fifty, Harry," she says, and the coat makes Harry put his hand gently on hers, leaving the long scalpel there.

"What—?" gets out of her mouth but the coat says *Now* and he closes her hand on the smooth cold handle of the scalpel and thrusts it toward her chest. She goes back with a huffing little gasp and her eyes go wide; then real pain reaches her and she starts to thrash, trying to scream through his hand over her mouth. Expertly, the coat makes Harry pin her back against the mattress, knees straddling her ribs. She fights, then a light pulls away from her eyes and she goes limp. He lets up his pressure but as he does so she rears up, nearly fighting out of his grasp. In a moment she is down again, and then the scalpel works and there's no doubt about it this time.

Harry's shaking, and what remains of the sour white wine in his stomach is boiling up into his throat, but the coat says, *Stop*. Harry stops. Not only that, but he finds himself tidying up, running his scalpel under the water from the tap in the bathroom, rusty and barely warm, cleaning the bloodstains from his clothes and himself.

Then the coat says, *Go*, and he's making his way out and down the back steps, newspaper sheets sleeping in the corners of the stairwell, the smell of cat crap, and out into the morning.

Wake up.

"Noreen?" Harry says, coming out of sleep, almost feeling her hand in his as he sits across from her at the little table on the porch of the SeaHarp, a candle flickering between them like faerie light, that first sober summer night enfolding them, the slight ocean chill, salt-smell, her telling him, as the wine he had soaked in for years evaporates out of him into the suddenly magical night, that she loves him and wants to help him, that she has loved him since they were children, that she knows, has always known, that he has greatness in him, how much pain it has caused her to see him this way, that he can still be great, that she will take care of him, that night, when, for just a while, it seemed it all might just work . . .

But that's dreamland, this is real, and he wakes up curled inside the concrete wall of the SeaHarp, and the coat says, *Get up.*

"No," Harry says out loud, suddenly scared, his head perfectly clear of wine and not liking the memories of last night flooding in on him. Suddenly he wants a *lot* of alcohol to make him forget, to make him forget *everything*, last night, Noreen, the whole enchilada.

In answer, there's laughter in his head and the coat commands, *Move*.

It's near night again. By the SeaHarp everything's quiet, and, as he struts down to the boardwalk, at the far end of Harbor Road, it's as if nothing ever happened the night before. He wonders where Jimmy and Wax are, his drinking buddies, maybe they've got some wine, then he wonders about the girl. Maybe they never found her. Maybe they did, and no one cares. Maybe right now she's feeding the sharks out at the mouth of the harbor, a hundred and twenty pounds of bloody fish food, too much paperwork for her pimp or the Greystone police to bother with . . .

Suddenly he goes stiff. Two Greystone policemen appear, walking toward him on the boardwalk. They must have found the girl after all. He freezes, the coat putting a semblance of a smile on his face, waiting for them to stop, search him, find the long scalpel in his pocket and club him to the ground, handcuffing him behind his back—

But they brush by him, not seeing Harry at all, one saying to the other, "Goddam garbage dump. You ever *see* anything like that before? Friggin' bums . . ." and then walking on.

And suddenly everything is back to normal, and the ladies of the night are walking, and the coat makes Harry look them over.

Her.

Older than the first. He knows this one, her name's Ginny, she's hit on him once or twice, even offering to do it for wine.

"Want to go someplace, Harry?" she asks, smiling. She runs her hands up around his neck, pulling his head down. He feels the tip of her tongue in his ear, touching, then running down and up his neck before her mouth stops by his ear again. "I'm *real* good," she says, and when he looks into her eyes something about them—the color, or maybe the pride in them, the absolute knowledge of herself, her mission in life, that she *is* good at what she does—reminds him of Noreen. He remembers Noreen's self-assurance, her absolute certainty that she could turn him from a walking wine bottle back into a man, her willingness to fight the alcohol for him, for both of them, to fight her brother Victor, manager of the SeaHarp Hotel, who thought she had lost her mind when she took him in, feeding him, letting him sleep his drunks off in a vacant guest room on the fourth floor. He remembered the first time she had taken him to her apartment in the attic, the tender way she had treated him, like a mother as much as a lover, the soft look of unasking love in her eyes . . .

"*Real* good," the hooker repeats, smiling, looking at him with those Noreen eyes of hers.

Harry tries to talk to the hooker, to yell at her to go away before something bad happens, but the coat cuts in, making his mouth say, in that cultured tone, full of fatherly playfulness, "I bet you are, my dear."

"We'll see, Harry," she says, and then she laughs and turns and leads him into the night.

In her room, in another weathered building overlooking the sea-dredged rot of Greystone Bay, Harry tries to fight the coat. There's a bottle of French wine she'd insisted on buying, looking up at him coyly in the dim light of the liquor store to tell him that it's her birthday and she feels like being nice to herself. And to him. The bottle sits on a table by the window, and Harry wants to run to it, tilt it back against his mouth and drown himself out. But the coat won't let him. "We'll save it for later," the coat makes him tell the girl.

"I'm flattered you think more of me than the wine, Harry."

The coat makes him smile. Harry wants to cry, because she's so much like Noreen. But the coat won't let tears come. He remembers now how much he hurt Noreen when he was with her, how he drove her away because he couldn't stand her looking so hurt anymore, couldn't stand her love for him, couldn't make her see that he was no longer a schoolboy with valentines and big dreams, and couldn't face the thing he'd turned into: a wine-sucking mouth with no feelings attached, no heart. He had driven her away because he couldn't stand himself . . .

"I won't kill her," Harry hisses at the coat.

"You say something, sweetie?" the girl says from the bed behind him.

You will kill her, the coat says to him, mildly, but there's anything but mildness behind the words.

"I won't!" Harry nearly shouts, turning around to see this innocent prostitute, this proto-Noreen, staring at him with real concern, the smile on her face turning to a question, parted legs angling closed as she sits up, nipples hard against the room's chill.

"You okay?" she asks.

Harry's mouth is forming the word "No," but even before he tries to say it, which he never does, the coat has made him thrust his hand into the long pocket of the long coat, drawing the scalpel out like a sabre.

She barely cries out, the knife drawing across at her, cutting her almost in two at the neck line.

Harry cries out, *"Noreen!"* and then Harry is gone, and the coat is hacking and cutting with strength and finesse, and the night turns red and wheels away from him.

This time when the coat tells him to wake up he is still on the bed in the room. He can barely lift his arms from exhaustion. By the weak light coming in the window it looks like dusk. On the table in front of the window, unopened, silhouetted in pale light, is the bottle of French wine and he feels an overwhelming need to rise and take the bottle like a nipple into his mouth.

He sits up and sees what he has done.

Harry loses whatever little is in his stomach, retching bile when there is nothing left. He's still vomiting when a sound comes on the stairs outside, and then a knock at the door.

"Dammit, Ginny, get up!" someone growls outside. "You gonna sleep all night, too? You got five minutes or I'll be back to kick your ass onto the street."

Footsteps retrace down the stairs.

Move, the coat commands.

He is up, cleaning the room, cleaning himself and his instrument. The water is cleaner here, and in no time the blade is shining like new, the coat scrubbed free of stains and brushed. He washes his hands and face and combs his hair, and then the coat makes him look into the mirror and smile the smile of a man ready to do again what he likes to do.

Fine, the coat says. *Walk.*

He walks out of the bathroom toward the door to the hotel room. But then, as he passes the table with the unopened bottle of wine on it, Harry, with supreme effort, stops walking.

I said walk.

"No," Harry says.

He puts his hand on the bottle. The coat gives a shriek of rage in his head but Harry holds on. Slowly, fighting for control of his own fingers, he peels the foil from the top of the bottle. His hands shake like he has the DTs. The coat is screaming at him, ordering him to put the bottle down, but he has actually pulled the cork out and is lifting the wine spastically to his lips when the knock comes again on the door.

"Ginny? What the hell are you doing in there?"

There is rough handling on the doorknob, and then banging.

The bottle drops from his hands, spilling wine into the worn rug, and in a second the coat has regained him and he is climbing over the table in front of the window, shoving it up and crawling out onto the fire escape. *Down*! the coat commands, and he descends the rusted, half-stuck ladders to the street. The coat makes him look coolly from right to left, smoothing his lapels, then makes him swagger away towards Port Boulevard, whistling a song he knew as a boy.

And then he sees Noreen.

She is just descending the stone steps of the SeaHarp to the pavement, leaving the walled fortress of the hotel behind. He is right in front of her, and though he tries to keep walking, their eyes meet.

She gasps, and Harry tries to walk by her but the coat stops him dead where he stands and smiles.

"Hello, Noreen," he says, and now the coat makes him bow.

She stand speechless, but the shock has left her face. There is something different about her, her clothes or her hair, and, looking into her eyes, Harry can't help thinking that his absence has only strengthened her resolve to save him.

"I've missed you, Noreen," the coat makes him say.

"What's happened to you, Harry?" she asks in her mild voice, smiling at his politeness—but, with horror, Harry sees that she likes the change in him, that she approves.

"I'm a different man," the coat makes him say, and then the coat makes him smile, and Noreen smiles too, looking as if she has stepped into a dream.

Noreen gives him a long look, and then she takes his arm, her hand brushing along the sleeve of the coat, and she says, "I've missed you too, Harry." She pauses, then turns to look at him, and says, "Harry, are you—?"

The coat, not missing a beat, gives her his most charming smile and says, "I no longer drink, Noreen."

* * *

To Harry, trapped deep within the coat, the evening pro-
gresses with horrible predictability. She takes him up the steps
to the porch of the SeaHarp, and, though it is cold, she insists
they sit at the same table they did that first night. She seems
to battle with herself and then, suddenly, with a bright smile,
she says, "Stay here, Harry," and she enters the hotel, returning with food from the kitchen, along with a candle. She
lights the candle, and there is faerie light between them once
more.

They eat, Noreen shivering, holding her coat tight about
her, but gazing through the candlelight at Harry as if he were
a god. As the meal is finished, a veal piccata with Harry's
favorite dessert, Boston creme pie, which the coat makes
him compliment extravagantly, there is a growing look of
promise fulfilled in her eyes. The coat makes Harry tell her
what she wants to hear, letting him see what it can do to
her.

In the glow of the candle, Noreen takes Harry's hand. "It's
cold out here," she says. She pauses, then adds softly, "I
want you to come to my room."

"Of course," the coat makes him answer, tenderly.

For a moment she loses her composure, and begins to cry.
But then she regains herself. "This is the dream I always had
for you," she says. "This is what I always knew you could
be."

The coat makes Harry lift her hand to his mouth, and kiss
it.

"I'm all I've ever wanted to be," it makes him say, sin-
cerely, and Harry knows it's speaking the truth.

Her attic apartment is as Harry remembers it. Big bed
neatly made, with the coverlet Noreen quilted herself, patch-
work pieces from all the worn covers and sheets she'd collected in her years at the hotel. A clean white bathroom,
unchipped tiles, pictures on the walls of the living room,

Edward Weston photographs, Renoir prints. Persian rugs. A polished mirror, before which, Harry remembers, she brushes her hair a hundred strokes each night before bed.

She stands before the mirror now, an aging young woman with a dream fulfilled, and she smiles, shivering, holding her coat tight around her neck. "I must have caught a chill outside, Harry," she says.

"My Noreen," The coat makes Harry put his hands lovingly on her shoulders and smile at her in the mirror.

"Oh, Harry," she sobs happily, and turns to let him hold her.

Deep inside, Harry is screaming, trying to claw his way to the surface and stop the inevitable. But he has lost. The coat has mastered him, and it makes Harry try to gently guide Noreen toward the bed.

"Wait." She puts the flats of her hands on his chest and stays him.

"Yes, my dear?" The coat makes him smile sweetly at her, though it really wants to pull the long sharp blade from its pocket now and cut her throat from ear to ear as she gazes adoringly up at him.

"I just want to tell you that you've made me the happiest woman in the world."

"Dear Noreen," he says, pressing her close to him, unable to wait for the bed, holding her tightly with one hand while the other slides into the pocket of the coat to feel the smooth cool handle of the scalpel—

—at the same moment he feels the deep cold cut of a blade into the back of his neck, the cold rush of air striking hot blood.

He staggers back away from her as she brings her scalpel neatly around to find the jugular. A bright wash of blood lifts out of Harry's open neck. He feels himself falling, then feels the vague thumping softness of the bed against his back. He hears from far off his own gurgling screams and, in his dimming vision, he sees the ceiling, then the silhouette of Noreen's form above him, raising the knife again to bring it down and . . .

She works on him leisurely, the door to her rooms locked tight, the long night ahead of her, a butcher's instinct guiding her expertly. She is better than Harry was, tidier, and the strong dark green plastic bags she scatters around, as she learned with the first two, serve her well with packing and disposal later on.

By the time the sun is climbing tentatively behind the drawn shades of her calico-curtained windows, she is finished, the room cleaned, the long scalpel glinting, the bags dropped into the disposal chute in the hallway, not to be discovered till they are hauled to the dump out beyond the whorehouses on the boardwalk.

It is chilly in the room, she really must get Victor to send up more heat to the family quarters. She shivers and hugs her coat around her as she puts the scalpel back into its long pocket.

She yawns, stretches, looking at the growing brightness of day on the window shade.

It is time to sleep.

She lifts the quilted coverlet of her bed, ignoring the pale dried red stains on it, and slides beneath.

As she lays staring at the ceiling for a moment before sleep, she lets Noreen come up from below. Shock has quieted her somewhat, and the crying that has broken through periodically will not be repeated. She is beaten. Her thoughts are revolving nightmares now, centering on the box she found by the service entrance to the SeaHarp four days ago, and the two new coats within. *Rich guests always throwing something valuable away,* she thought, taking the woman's coat on top out, daydreaming, as she tried it on, how nice it would be for Harry to have the other coat, if only Harry, dear Harry, love of her youth and forever, would come back to her . . .

Noreen begins to scream, and the coat, tired and longing for its own dreams, pushes her back down to the depths.

The coat makes her sleep then, thinking of the coming night, and remembering with pleasure its own thoughts while cutting the long bloody woollen strips from Harry's body, *God, I hate men.*

BEAUTY
by
Robert R. McCammon

Welcome, Beauty was what the sign said. It was right up in front of the SeaHarp Hotel, where everybody in the world could see it. What I didn't find out until later was that the sign had said *Welcome, Miss Greystone Bay Beauty* but the windstorm the night before had blown the rest of the letters to kingdom come. When my Momma and I saw that sign, she squeezed my hand and I felt like my heart was going to burst open. My Momma always called me Beauty, and now the SeaHarp was calling me Beauty too.

Oh, that was a wonderful day! My Momma used to tell me the story of Cinderella. I could never get enough of it. And when we took the curve in that fancy, long black car they'd sent for us, and I saw the SeaHarp Hotel up on the hill in front of us, I knew how Cinderella felt. If you were to take a dream and put sugar frosting on it, you'd have the SeaHarp. All those windows, that green grass, the blue sky over us . . . and that sign. It made my blood thrill, to think the SeaHarp knew my name. 'Course, my little sister Annie had to come along with us, and she was kicking a fuss because it was my day to get all the attention. But I didn't mind. Not much. I missed Daddy being there, but Mr. Teague wouldn't let him off from the mill not even for a day like this. Momma says things about Mr. Teague that I wouldn't tell a soul.

The driver pulled us on up to the front steps. Another man in a uniform came down and opened the door for us. We got out, and we went up to the porch and we didn't even have to carry our own bags. Then I stood at the open doors looking in at the SeaHarp like a frozen statue while Annie danced and raised Cain all around me. Momma told her to hush and not disgrace us, and the man in the uniform smiled and said, "It's our honor, Mrs. Guthrie," in a voice that let you know you'd gotten to where you were supposed to be. My Momma smiled, but her lips were tight; she was always ashamed of her teeth, the front one broken and all.

Before we went in, I turned toward the Bay. It was full of sunshine. And then I just let my head turn along the crescent of the water, and way off in the distance I saw a smudge of smoke against the sky. It was coming up from a long brown building that hardly had any windows. "My Daddy's there," I told the man at the door, and I pointed. I saw my Momma flinch just a little bit, but the doorman smiled real nice.

I won the contest, see. The Greystone Bay Beauty Contest, for young ladies sixteen to eighteen. The winner got a dozen roses, a hundred dollars and a weekend stay at the SeaHarp. And her picture in the paper too, of course. I'd just turned sixteen, on the second day of May. My Momma always had faith in me. She said I could sing up a storm, and my voice was okay I guess. She said, "Beauty, someday you're gonna go far. Gonna see and do things I never did. I wish I could go with you to those places."

I said, "You can, Momma! You can always go with me!"

She smiled, a little bit. "You're a beauty," she said, and she took my hands and held them. "Beauty outside, beauty inside. Me, I'm just a tired rag."

"No!" I told her. "Don't you say that!" Because my Momma was a pretty woman, and there's nobody better say she wasn't. Isn't, I mean.

The manager was waiting to meet us, in that big lobby bathed in light. He was a tall man, in a dark blue suit with pinstripes. He said how happy he was that the SeaHarp could host us for the weekend, but I hardly heard him. I was looking around that lobby, and trying to figure out how many of our house could fit in it. Maybe ten. We only had four rooms; they called where we lived a "shotgun shack," and the walls were gray. Not in the SeaHarp. The walls were white, like clouds. I'd never seen so many chairs, sofas and tables outside of a furniture store, and there were crystal vases full of fresh-cut flowers. I've always loved flowers. I used to pick daffodils in the Spring, where they grew along the cheekbed outside our back door.

"Hello," the manager said to me, and I said hello back. "Someone's wearing some nice perfume."

"That's violets," Momma said. "She always wears the scent of violets, because that's a right smell for a beauty like her."

"Yes," the manager agreed, "it certainly is." And then he snapped his fingers and you would've thought the carpet has sprouted bellboys like mushrooms.

It's strange, how you notice things. Like the pink dress my Momma and Daddy had bought for me to wear. It looked fine in the gray light of our house, but at the SeaHarp . . . it looked like the pink was old and faded. It looked like something that had been on a hanger for a long, long time. And the sheets of my bed in that room were so cool and crisp; they embraced you. They didn't want you to leave them. The windows were all so clean, and the sun was so bright, and you had hot water whenever you wanted it. Oh, that was a Cinderella dream come true.

Momma said Daddy was going to come visit the SeaHarp when he got off work, even if it was at nine o'clock at night. She said Daddy was so proud of me, just like she was. All Annie did, though, was prance around and make a mighty fool of herself. Momma said she was going to lie down and have a rest, and for me to watch Annie and keep her out of mischief. We went off together, through the white hallways, and we found the stairs.

Annie said she could dance better than me, and I said she couldn't. I was sixteen, but there was enough little girl in me to want to show her who was a better dancer. So we danced up and down those stairs, like that scene where Shirley Temple dances on the steps and she goes up three, down two, up four, down two, up five, down . . .

My head hurts.

Sometimes I get tired real easy. Sometimes day seems like night, and night seems like a long day when clocks won't move. I get tired, and I can't think right.

I leave my room, where the crisp cool sheets of that bed are always laid open like a blue wound, and I go to the elevator. I know the elevator man's name: Clancy. He's a black man with gray hair, and he knows me too. He brings the elevator to where I wait, and when he cranks the doors open I step in smooth as pink silk.

"Evenin', Beauty," Clancy says. I say hello to Mr. Clancy. "Mighty quiet in the SeaHarp tonight," he says: this is what he always says. Mr. Clancy only works during the quiet hours. He cranks the doors shut, pulls a lever and the old elevator begins its descent. I listen to the cables and gears turning above our heads. A gear needs oiling; it squeaks too loudly.

"What time is it?" I ask Mr. Clancy.

"Gloria's sister June is gonna have a baby," he answers. Oh, he can be a mean man! Sometimes he acts as if you have no voice at all! "Got the names all picked out. Third baby for her, shouldn't be no big thing."

"Is it springtime, Mr. Clancy?" I ask. "At least tell me that."

"Smithie got a raise. Seems like I oughta get a raise. You know, that Smithie's always complainin' 'bout one thing or another."

I want to scream, but that would be beneath me. To tell the truth, I like hearing Mr. Clancy talk to me. I like the sound of his voice, and the noise of the elevator. I don't care for the stairs.

The elevator arrives at the lobby. The doors open, and I see the lamps glowing and the beautiful walls and furniture; all there, all just the same as the first day. "You sure smell nice tonight, Beauty," Mr. Clancy says as I leave—he always says this—and I turn back and say thank you to his blind-eyed face. Then Mr. Clancy sits on his stool and rests awhile, waiting for me to return. I roam the lobby, between the walls of clouds. There are new, fresh-cut flowers in the crystal vases. I decide it must be springtime, after all. At the SeaHarp, it's always springtime.

This is my Cinderella dream. I can sing here, and dance across a carpet the color of sun on the Bay. Once I saw a young man walking here; he was a handsome young man, older than me. Maybe he was twenty. I walked beside him, but he had a newspaper under his arm and no time for beauty. I drift amid the vases, and some of the flowers rustle as I pass. Sometimes I hear other voices here: fragile voices, drifting in and out. Daddy used to have an old radio he kept in the front room, and Annie and I listened to it. That's what those voices are like: from faraway places, places that aren't nearly so beautiful as this.

I don't like the attic. They don't keep it clean enough, and the voices up there want you to do naughty things.

Once I was here, dancing and singing, and I saw the manager. The very same man. I recognized him by his walk, and the way he snapped his fingers at the people behind the front desk. They jumped like whipped dogs. I came up behind him and snapped my fingers at his ear, and he turned around real quick and for a second he looked right straight into my eyes.

Oh, no, I thought. Oh, no. This couldn't be the same man. I was wrong. This was an old man, with white hair and a wrinkled face. Oh, the man I was thinking about was a lot younger than this. But he must've smelled my violets, because he made a gasping sound and stepped back against the counter and his eyes were as big as silver dollars. "Talk to me," I said. "Somebody talk to me."

But the old man just gasped, and I went on.

What time is it? My head . . . sometimes it hurts so bad. Momma? I thought I heard—

I get tired, real easy.

Mr. Clancy takes me in the elevator, back up to the third floor. "Goodnight, Beauty," he says, and I wish him goodnight too. Momma always said being polite was a sign of good blood.

The door to Room 301 is open. It's always open. I wouldn't have it any other way, because if anyone wants to come in and talk to me, I want them to know they're welcome. I go inside—and there's a woman sitting in a chair, a lamp with a blue shade burning next to her. She looks up as soon as I come in, and her eyes widen. She shakes a little bit, as if she's about to get up and run for the door. But she settles down and sticks, and I drift past her toward the bed with blue sheets.

"You're there, aren't you?" the woman asks. Her voice is strained, but . . . I know that voice, from somewhere.

"You're there," she says, positive now. "It's Ann, Beauty. It's your sister Ann."

"I *know* who my sister is!" I say, turning toward the woman. "But you're not her!" This is an old woman sitting in my chair; an old woman with gray in her hair and deep lines on her face. "My sister's a little girl!"

"I . . . don't know if you can understand this or not." The old woman who's pretending to be my sister stands up, and she grips her hands in front of her as if she's afraid they're going to fly away like wrinkled birds. "I wanted you to know . . . that Momma died tonight. At the hospital. The cancer got her."

"Liar!" I shout. "You dirty old liar! Get out of my room!"

"Momma asked me to come tell you," the crazy old woman goes on. "I was right there when she died. Can you understand what I'm saying?"

"NO! NO! NO! NO!"

"Jesus, I must be a damn fool." The woman shakes her head. "I'm talking to the walls. I'm in a damn hotel room, talking to the walls."

"Get out!" I want to knock the stuffing out of the old woman. I want to pick her up like a scarecrow and throw her through the door. I want to drag her by the hair to the stairs and shove her down the . . .

My head. My head hurts. Oh, my head . . .

"It's better she passed on," the woman says. Why did such a crazy old fool think I'd believe she was Annie? "Momma had some pain. It's better this way." She looks at her hands, and I can see them too, in the lamplight. The fingernails are broken, and her hands are rough and cracked. They're the hands of my Momma. "I . . . came up the stairs, Beauty," she says. "I was going to take the elevator, but . . ." She shrugs. "I needed to walk up the stairs." Then she lifts her head, and I watch her look all around the room as if she's searching for a ghost. "Beauty," she says, in a very quiet voice, "I want to ask you something. It's been . . . tearing at me, for such a long time. Beauty, please tell me . . . I didn't make you fall down those stairs, did I?"

She's not my sister! My sister's a little girl! "YOU GET OUT!" I shout at her.

"Please tell me. It's been killing me, all these years. I didn't make you fall . . . did I?"

She waits. Annie, what happened to us? What happened, in an instant when balance failed? What time is it, and where is our Momma?

"Please . . . please," Annie says, and she lowers her head and begins to cry.

"No," I tell her. "Annie? You didn't make me fall. Okay?"

Annie keeps crying. She always did like attention.

"I'm all right now," I say. "See?"

She sobs, and runs a hand over her eyes. I remember something, now: here, in my room, Momma sitting on the bed and crying as she told me Daddy had died. An accident at the mill, she said. An accident . . . just like yours was an accident.

"Annie!" I say. "I'm all right! Stop crying!"

"I just wanted to tell you about Momma," Annie says. She blows her nose on a tissue and wads it up. An old stranger, she moves toward the door. Then she stops, on the threshold. "Beauty? I don't know why you stayed here. Maybe Momma did, but I didn't. Maybe you're here and maybe you're not, but . . . if you can, could you go be with Momma? I mean . . . it seems like it's time for you to leave here, Beauty. It's time for you to go on."

And then my sister goes through the door, and I follow her to the staircase. She descends, treading carefully, and I watch her out of sight.

"Annie?" I call down after her. "I love you!"

Momma? Are you here, Momma? Have you come to be with your Beauty?

No. Wherever Momma is, she's not at the SeaHarp. She's gone to a place I should have gone to first. She's already seen things I never have. But we can be together again! Can't we?

If I want to be with her, I have to leave the Cinderella dream. I don't think I'm ready for that yet. I'm afraid. I love the springtime, and I'm so afraid of winter.

But I have my answer now. I know what time it is. Annie told me: it's time to leave here. It's time to go on.

Maybe I will. Maybe. But if you were to take a dream and put sugar frosting on it, you'd have the SeaHarp. Do all dreams have to end at midnight? Do they?

My head hurts. I get tired real easy. I want to rest in the blue sheets, and I want to hear the Bay crash against the rocks. I want to dream of pink dresses, a dozen roses, and a sign that said *Welcome, Beauty*. Maybe my Momma will find me in that dream. Maybe she's waiting for me there, and if I hurry we can go together.

But the SeaHarp holds me. It's so full of light and beauty, so full of dreams. Can't I stay here, just a little while longer?

I need to rest. Mr. Clancy will be waiting, at the elevator. He is the master of his little square of the SeaHarp, just as I am the mistress of mine. Tomorrow is the first day of spring. I am sixteen years old, there will be fresh-cut flowers in the crystal vases, and all the world will be beautiful.

SERVICES RENDERED
by
Bryan Webb

The "Betty" caught the breeze. All hands looked aloft as the lines creaked and the square sails rustled and rose against the spars.

The lookout on the fore-mast called down, "A breeze, Captain, quartering abaft the starboard beam."

Captain Jeptha Collins had heard the lines moan, and watched the sails swell with the gentle breeze. He called back, "Aye, mate. Now, let's see if she'll move."

Not enough wind to move this scow, he thought. She's down to the mark. Last time out for this old relic, but by God her tanks were full of whale oil. He'd show those Boston bankers that a man with a good crew could still make money in an obsolete ship named for his wife.

Not that they cared. Not with the Depression in full swing. Not in 1937. He'd divide the shares among the hands, and pay the rest toward the note. Nothing for him. When was that new? Screw 'em. The ship was lost to the times, and some lines on a piece of paper. He'd known it to be a voyage of futility when they'd set sail fourteen months ago. Just one last time. To show 'em he still could.

"A hole in the fog, Captain. Ten degrees to port," called the lookout.

"Aye," he answered. Then softer, "Steer to port, ten degrees."

"Aye, Captain," answered the helmsman. The wheel eased left, but the "Betty" did not to respond. She needed more headway.

The dense autumn fog shrouded the New England coast like an undertaker's sheet, covering the living and the dead alike. They were closed in by the dank, smothering cloud with only a little slanting light from the coming sun. And less hope, he thought.

And so quiet. The sails rustled and the lines moaned softly, but no sound came of the hull moving through the water. The feet of unseen men moved across the deck in soft patters. The ship's cat purred beside the binnacle, licking its breakfast paws.

Nothing else. What had he expected of this last homecoming to Greystone Bay? A parade? Most likely the damned bankers in their black suits would be on the docks waiting, like so many vultures glaring down at a salt-sick cow.

"A whale. A whale! There she rolls, dead ahead." The lookout's cry caught the men up, but they were not prepared for it. The whaling was done. For them, and for the ship.

"A right whale. Full sixty feet. A big one, Captain."

Collins thought quickly. No need for this whale. And a right, not a sperm. But hell, what's one more to the sea?

"Longboat over the starboard side. Harpoon crew to stations," he called out through cupped hands.

The helmsman asked, "Where you gonna flense it, Skipper? We're close by home port as it is, and the tanks are already full."

The Captain pierced his seaman with a glare as sharp as his whaling lance. "We'll lash it alongside, and tow it in. If those old copper pots still hold oil we'll try out the blubber on the beach."

This one was for him. No harpoon cannon for this last whale. He'd take this one the old way, with longboat and lances. And the money from this oil would go into his account. To hell with the bankers.

The helmsman said, "Kinda risky in a longboat in this fog . . ."

Jeptha Collins did not answer as he walked forward. No. This one was for him. This was his whale.

The men lowered the longboat. They strained at the oars, and it surged through the water with each splashing. The "Betty" faded astern into the fogbank.

The right whale was just ahead, blowing softly at the surface.

"She's got a calf, Captain. There alongside her."

"I don't want its damned calf. Just the whale. Take the tiller, Mason, I'm going forward."

Collins stepped eagerly between the oarsmen's legs, and braced himself in the bow. He hoisted the old harpoon, and gazed into the dark water. There she was. An old right whale. Maybe as old as he. Maybe forty-four. And the faint outline of the young calf beyond, nudged into her side.

"Easy now, men. Don't bump her, but get close. We'll stick this last one for old time's sake."

He rose up, arms outstretched, and rammed the lance into the whale with all the strength born of his frustration and fear for tomorrow.

The giant, dark head reared back in pain and blew bloody water onto the men. It arched back under, and the flukes rose behind them like black sails on some devil ship. The line between his legs whizzed out, and gray smoke, heavy with the smell of burning hemp, flared his nostrils.

The whale's run was not deep, and short. The Nantucket sleighride ended when the dead whale neaped on the rocky shore of Blind Point. And the men cheered, "We're home. She brung us home."

At the tiller again, Captain Jeptha Collins looked back into the fog, and saw the water rise in a small, dark hump. The calf. It rolled, and turned aside. A low-fixed eye peered at him from just beneath the black water, and the young whale squalled.

"To hell with you," he muttered. And the bankers, too, he thought. This was his whale.

Peter Collins stopped the rental car in front of the SeaHarp Hotel, leaned back, and smiled. Just as he remembered it. But why not? The whole town was the same, except for a few more factories he'd passed on his way in, and a few more homes. Harbor Road—what he could see of it—seemed caught up by time, no different than the dim childhood memories of a seven-year-old.

How long had that been? 1940 when he and Mom had left Greystone Bay after Dad's death. Forty-eight years. And no changes . . .

"Help with your bags, sir?"

"Huh? Oh, yes." The words had been soft, but right in his ear. He was embarrassed by his startled reaction. Silly. But he'd drifted away for a moment, back to a time before World War II had begun, when mourning for Captain Jeptha Collins was still new and painful.

"They're in the trunk."

The intruder turned and walked toward the back of the car, but seemed to be looking at the ground, watching for snags that might snare his short steps. He was as thin as a reed. Peter looked down at the bellman's hand as he tendered the keys. It looked like a map with blue lines, the tendons extended ridges from wrist to knuckles. The old man's head and shoulders were stooped, his white hair hidden beneath a gray cap that matched the coat and trousers.

"Is that you, Mister Jim?" Peter asked.

"Yes, I always was. And how do you know me?" The old man leaned back so he could look up at this visitor. Pale blue eyes met Peter's, and scraggly white eyebrows shaded those eyes in puzzlement. Then, the eyebrows rose like two cresting waves.

"You're a Collins, aren't you? Jeptha Collins' boy? You're the spittin' image of him."

"Yes, I'm Peter. I haven't been back to Greystone Bay since Mom and I left when I was seven."

"Well, welcome home, Peter Collins. What brings you back to this washed-up old place?"

"I'm not sure, Mister Jim. I just had an urge to see it again." And that was the truth. He hadn't been able to explain to his wife the feeling that had come over him. To see it all one more time. To come back home? Maybe. But he knew he had to see this childhood place again, the mulberry bush he hid in when Jamie Barlowe was on the prowl, the elementary school where he'd learned to fight with his fists, and the small harbor that had greeted his father for the last time one foggy morning so long ago.

He was embarrassed to let the frail old man carry his suitcases up the steps to the hotel. But to deny him that would be to deny the old man himself. So he just smiled, and let Mister Jim lead the way while he fished in his billfold for three dollars. More than it's worth, but being recognized by the first person he'd talked to today was a bonus he hadn't expected. No homecoming parade, but it would do.

He lingered on the porch, gazing out at the bay, afternoon green water marked by a light chop from the breeze. The oak trees on the front lawn were a brilliant red. He hadn't forgotten the glories of fall in Greystone Bay.

He pulled open the door and stepped into the lobby, the

wall's rich paneling darkened by age. The faint aroma of a
man's pipe still lingered in the air as he walked to the registration desk. Oriental rugs muffled his steps, but the colored
designs were worn thin by a million crossings. Worn down
like this old hotel, and this old town.

The receptionist looked up from her papers. "Welcome
home, Mr. Collins. I'm Noreen Montgomery." She extended
her hand in friendship. "Welcome back to Greystone Bay."

She must have learned of his identity from the bellman.
His name had brought no hint of recognition from her when
he'd registered by phone.

"Thank you, Ms. Montgomery." Peter began filling out
the form she offered. Funny old family. Montgomerys had
operated the SeaHarp since the turn of the century. It was the
only thing they knew.

"Is Simon still running things?" he asked while filling in
the boxes.

"No, he passed away a few years ago. We children are
holding on. Don't know why." She looked up as the grandfather clock struck five, then glanced down at her wristwatch
to confirm the ancient timepiece. "Don't know what else to
do, I guess. How long will you be with us, Mr. Collins?"
She poised her pen to write.

"I'm not sure. Couple of days, maybe. Until I'm done."
Done with what? It wasn't as if he were here on business.
He had no business in Greystone Bay. How long? He didn't
know. Until it was over.

"Well, you stay as long as you like. I'm giving you room
202. It has a beautiful view of the bay. I think you'll like
that."

"Thank you, Ms. Montgomery. That's very nice."

Mister Jim was posted by the open elevator with Peter's
bags inside. Only one flight, but he'd already lugged them up
the front steps. The safety gate creaked behind Peter as he
stepped in.

"Be serving dinner in the dining room soon. It's quite good." The old man stood as straight as he could as he operated the elevator, his pride in the place, and his work, obvious.

Peter looked at a yellowing placard to his left, promoting the hotel's food. It said, "Our goal is to make you a most enjoyable dinner." For whom? he thought.

The old man opened the door to room 202, and dragged the luggage across the carpet to the closet. With a grunt he hoisted the largest bag onto a bench, and stationed the smaller suitcase alongside.

"Can I bring you some ice, or something from the bar, sir?"

"Yes. How about some Cutty Sark on the rocks?" He handed the tip to the bellman, and smiled.

"Very good, sir." Peter turned toward the windows, and heard the door close softly behind him as Mister Jim went on his errand.

He'd always liked that scotch. Not the best by any means. But it had a picture of a sailing ship on it. Sort of like his father's.

He stood at the window, leaning forward with his hands against the frames. He looked up at Harbor Road as far as he could see, and then out at the bay. There were four tall ships, berthed close together, hulls dark with age. Their masts pointed up at odd angles, lines dangled in disarray, and their sagging spars reminded him of empty crosses. Relics of a forgotten time. Tools for forgotten men.

He noticed that it was much darker now, but it was not late enough in the day for that. Then he saw the fogbank rolling in from the sea. Was it real? It had crept up on him while his back was turned. Just there the water mounded darkly, and a large, rounded shape pushed a small wave ahead of it. A chill ran through him, and he trembled. He shook his hand in the air as if to cast off the dark illusion. The black form disappeared beneath the surface, and its small wave angled toward the shore. He stared in wonder at the spot. Had he really seen something?

It rose again. Much closer this time, as if it rode the mist. Larger and blacker. A gigantic mouth parted the shape. The head rose higher above the wave, and he saw an eye, low alongside the strangely smiling mouth.

He heard a knocking and quickly turned away from the dark vision. He opened the door, and Mister Jim was smiling in the hallway, an old-fashioned glass balanced carefully on a small silver tray.

"Ah, that was quick," Peter said. The bellman stepped into the room. Peter took the drink off the little tray, and took a long swallow.

"Can you add this to my tab?"

"Of course, sir." The old man looked deep into Peter's eyes. A faint frown crossed his face and he said, "Is there anything else I can do for you?"

"Uh, I think I just saw a whale. Is that possible?"

The bellman raised an eyebrow. "Not really, sir. The whales have been gone from these waters for a long time. You should know. Your father sailed the last whaling ship out of Greystone Bay back before the war. That's her there." The old man went to the window and pointed. "The second one in that row of four. His ship's never moved since the day he lost it to the bank. Same with those others. Not much use now. All rotten. But the tourists like to take pictures."

Peter wondered what the old man remembered of his father's last voyage on the "Betty." About that last whale? He had heard the story, of course, from his mother. Often. But somehow he'd sensed that she had not told him everything, as if a seven-year-old boy could not understand such things.

He had been confused and frightened by his father's growing depressions. A dark gloom had consumed the man, and made him older. Times had been hard with his ship lost, but there seemed to be more to it than that, more than the loss of money.

Their little house enjoyed a wonderful view of the bay, but Jeptha Collins never looked out upon the sea again. He sat in the living room, slumped in his favorite chair, a bottle standing on the rug near his limp hand. The room was dimly lit by sunlight intruding through the drawn curtains.

Peter crossed to the front wall, pulled back a drape, then another. Light streamed into the room. He looked out beyond the front porch, and gazed at silver water dancing in the sunshine.

"Don't do that again." His father's voice was firm, but muffled, and the words came slowly. "Close the curtains."

The boy did as he was told. He stood for a while in the darkened room, and stared at the back of the unlined curtain. Outside there was light, and the bay. He knew it was all still there, just blotted out. His compulsion to see it again forced him to pull one curtain aside a little, and put his head into the gap. Just to look out, to see the bay.

His father's blow struck him from behind, the clenched fist hitting his shoulder with great force. Then the man sat down again, and stared at the floor.

Peter fought back the tears. He ran to the porch, then down the steps and onto the narrow footpath that led to the rocky shore. There he sat on his heels, and stared at the water for hours. He watched the boats moving across the harbor, and listened to their sounds. He watched crabs scurrying sideways just beneath the surface. The world around him slipped away as he was lost into another world of water, and salt, and strange creatures operating under different rules. He did not rise until he heard his mother's voice calling, "Dinner."

The old bellman coughed. He was saying something. What? Answering Peter's question.

"Town talk is all I know, Mr. Collins. Odd story. They were almost home when they spotted this whale in the fog.

They put a boat over the side and he speared it right outside the harbor. That whale pulled them right up onto the beach over there, near Blind Point.'' The old man pointed into the fog, as if he could see that distant spit of land and rocks through the fog.

"Is that all?'' Was there nothing else?

The bellman's brow furrowed. "Well, there was some talk that whale had a calf, but nobody mentioned it much. Maybe that part's not true. Just sailor's talk mixed with beer. Will that be all, sir? I must help in the dining room.''

"Thank you, Mister Jim.'' Peter handed the old man another dollar. The withered hand tucked it into a coat pocket as the ancient bellman left.

He stretched out on the bed to relax, and thought back to the day he had gone walking on the beach. It had been shortly after his father died, scarcely three months after he took the last whale. His mother had found him slumped in his chair in that darkened living room.

He had walked to Blind Point in search of adventure. He came upon an old shed, almost ready to collapse from the weatherings of wind, salt, and time. A row of large copper pots set on stones ran the length of the shed. The remains of a bleached skeleton lifted long, white ribs from the sand nearby.

He picked up some small rocks, threw them at the flat water, and counted their jumps. He sat on the warm sand, and listened to the small groundswell waves dying on the beach. He stared out over the vast gray ocean, and smelled the salt air. This was where he belonged. To the sea.

He rose without knowing why and gathered sticks and driftwood planks from the beach. He heaped them under the nearest pot. It seemed the thing to do.

His small hand pulled a clutch of kitchen matches from his pocket, and he started his fire with some dried seaweed. The fire caught, and soon the sticks were burning furiously, smoke leaping into the afternoon sky. He sat down beside the pot, and stared at his fire. It was, somehow, right and good.

His mother seized him from behind, and jerked him to his feet.

"No!" she screamed, "the sea can't have you." She grasped his collar, and walked him quickly back to town.

She kept him in the house, with the curtains drawn, until they left Greystone Bay a week later. She never spoke of that day again.

Peter woke with an uneasy start. Where was he? What was this place? He stared up from the bed, and recognition came as he focused on the ceiling fixture. Yes, the SeaHarp. He must have dozed off for a moment. He needed to think about going downstairs and sampling the cuisine. *Our goal is to make you a most enjoyable dinner.* He smiled at the thought.

He crossed the dim room and looked out the window again. It was not yet totally dark, but the fogbank had covered the town. Streetlights had come on, piercing the fog in fuzzy points. The oaks outside were no longer a brilliant red, but dark brown, their withered, dying leaves rustling in the breeze. A car passed below, leaving dark tracks in the black street made shiny by the damp fogfall.

As Peter looked out the chill came back suddenly, clutching his spine, moving into his belly. He trembled and stared at the floor, ashamed of the trembling, confused by the fear. Of what? What was here to be afraid of? Then he whimpered, softly, so his mother, dead for ten years, wouldn't hear.

He had to do something. Had to find out what it was. He raised the window and leaned forward, listening. There. A dinging bell. Buoy marker probably. Ringing for any poor sailors caught out on an evening like this.

The fog swirled and he could see the ships, the black ships

with their rotted sheets and lines, masts jutting up through the mist like markers for the dead.

He descended the wide stairway into the hotel's great hall. Nobody there. Sounds from inside the dining room told of meals being served. A large painting, browning with age like the leaves outside, showed a whaling scene, longboat rising over a black wave, a sailor in the bow hoisting a long harpoon as the gray whale looked up with fear. The lone, shielded lamp over the canvas cast a pale, yellow light that seemed to fall only on that red eye. Had that been there before? He couldn't remember.

He lit a cigarette, and pulled his jacket closer as he stepped down onto the sidewalk. It was cool, but the damp fog and light breeze made it seem colder. Or was it the fear again? He crossed the road and moved toward the docks, toward the old, tall ships. The second one, Mister Jim had said.

In the darkness he could barely make out the faint, gold-leafed outline of his mother's name painted on the bow. A lighter shade of wood showed where a carved maiden had once adorned the ship. Peter tested the ramp that led from the pier to the deck. Was it safe? Was anything safe?

He stepped down onto the deck, and felt the soft planks give under his feet. He walked aft, feeling his way along the railing he used both for guidance and support. He moved very slowly through the darkness that covered the three-masted ship.

He climbed four steps and ducked as a line brushed against his forehead. Here was where the wheel would be, and the binnacle. But they were gone to the same thieving salvagers who'd stolen the maiden. He crept to the high stern, and looked out into the dark fog. The buoy dinged again, swaying softly in the undulating water. It was so quiet. He could have been at sea, becalmed. Waiting for help, or salvation. Or understanding. So still.

He thought of his father, gone to sea too much of the time.

Now gone forever. He had wanted his father's hand on the rudder of his childhood. Had his father loved the sea more than him?

A great black shape rose up from the dark water. Peter jumped back, and a scream died in his throat. The black head spouted mist into the air. The air hole shut, but the dark shape did not move. Water oozed down its sides, flowing along old scars.

Peter stared down at the whaleshape in the darkness. The whale squeaked a low, sad sound that ended on a lower note. It squeaked again, louder. Then it shrieked a cry of pain that forced him back from the rail.

He stumbled over unseen debris as he ran back toward the gangplank. A board cracked beneath his foot, and he caught himself on the railing. The ramp sagged under his feet as he jumped from the ship.

He ran along Harbor Road through the dark fog, past the SeaHarp without noticing, and on along the waterfront. No cars passed. No voices. Not a soul, anywhere that he could see. A wind off the ocean freshened and blew against him.

The calf! That had been his father's crime. The whalechild had been too young to survive without its mother. He had killed it as surely as if he had speared it in the heart.

Peter slowed to a walk, caught his breath, and felt the freshening wind. A storm was coming. He had not noticed the last building where the sidewalk stopped, but he moved over to walk in the street. Only his soft footsteps, and the rising surf bothered the night.

It was as if no time passed. He walked on, trying to think, to shake off the chill that still held him like a cuttlefish gripping its victim, awful maw ready to devour. The pavement ended, and he continued along the dirt road that wound its way near the shore.

He heard the splashing of waves. The wind blew the fog apart, shredding it. His soul trembled. Oh, God, he thought, why was he here? He saw an irregular shape in the darkness ahead, and he ran toward it.

It was a fallen-down shed, the remains of old timbers sticking up out of the beach sand like the black skeleton of some great, dead animal. And a row of large, round pots. He moved closer, reached out slowly, and touched one. He stuck his clammy fingers into his mouth, and tasted the oxides of copper mixed with the metallic taste of fear.

Then he knew why he was here.

He knew why his mother had taken her seven-year-old son away. Away from all boats. Away from the bay. He knew why she had taken him far inland. Why she had settled him down in a small town far from the sea, and the whales.

He ripped a plank from its anchoring beam, and heaved it under the nearest great copper pot. He grunted as he worked, squinting in determination as he groped in the darkness for sticks of driftwood. Panting, he moved from one timber to the next, grabbing the smaller boards and ripping the half-rotted wood from the nails.

Lightning tore the black sky. Rain was coming. He had to hurry.

He threw off his jacket and added it to the fuel under the pot. His shoes were next. He tore at his shirt, and then his trousers and undergarments.

His lighter sputtered against the wind, but the sheltered fire caught. The flames danced under the pot, then leaped up its sides.

He stood naked in the darkness, thrust up his heaving chest, and tilted his head far back. When he lowered his head and opened his eyes he saw the great shape again, mounding above the surging black water.

The fire licked the huge pot. It was ready.

The first raindrop struck his face, slid down, sizzled against hot metal. He shouted against the gale that whipped the waves into frenzy, but his words were lost in the raging storm.

Another raindrop struck his shoulder. Glided down. And sizzled.

AQUARIUM
by
Steve Rasnic Tem

In the orphanage they'd had an aquarium. A wooden model of the ancient, sprawling orphanage itself, open at the top, had served as a frame for the ordinary glass aquarium inside.

The orphanage was always receiving unusual gifts like that—giant gingerbread men, dolls with some president's face, doll houses modeled after some famous building. There'd be an article in the paper each time with a picture of the donor and his gift, surrounded by dozens of children with practiced smiles.

Other benefactors hosted special events. The SeaHarp used to throw parties for the children of the orphanage every year, parties that sometimes lasted for days, with the children sleeping in the hotel. Michael knew he had attended several of them, but he had been so young at the time—not more than four or five—he really couldn't remember them.

The aquarium had had a little brass plaque: "Gift of Martin O'Brien." Michael had heard that the fellow had been some sort of fisherman, and himself an orphan. Many of the gifts were supposedly from former residents of the orphanage. But Michael never actually believed that there was such a thing as a former resident; the place marked you forever. Sometimes he would wonder what he would give to the orphanage when he got old and successful.

Sometimes the fish would swim up to the tiny model windows and look out. One of the older boys said that fish could barely see past their mouths, but they sure looked like they were peering out at you. As if you were a prospective parent and today was visitor's day. That's the way the children always looked on visitor's day, Michael thought: staring wide-eyed out the windows and moving their gills in and out nervously. Trying to look like whoever these prospective parents expected you to look like. Trying to look like you'd fit right in to their family. Sometimes when the light was right in the aquarium room you could see your own reflection in these windows, superimposed over the fish. Looking in, and looking out. Waiting.

In the orphanage Michael used to dream that he had no face. He was waiting for someone to choose a face for him. Until then, he had the open-mouthed, wide- and wet-eyed face of a fish.

Now, in Greystone Bay, Michael got into a green cab that said "Two Crazy Brothers Cab Co." on the door. He wondered if that meant there were two identical cabs, a brother driving each one, or perhaps only one cab with which they alternated shifts—Greystone Bay was, after all, a relatively small place. Or perhaps there were dozens of such cabs, and the brothers didn't drive anymore, being president and vice-president of the company, or perhaps co-vice-presidents, their mother or father taking the largely honorary presidential post. It was difficult to know exactly who his driver was, and what he expected from him.

"Not many go to the SeaHarp this time o' year," the driver said.

Michael glanced at the rear-view mirror and fixed on the driver's eyes. Seeing just the slice of face holding the eyes bothered him. He'd never been able to tell much from eyes—people's eyes had always seemed somewhat interchangeable. Seeing just that cut-out of someone's eyes led him to imagine that they were his own eyes, transplanted somehow into someone else's shadowy face. A social worker at the orphanage had once given him a toy that rearranged slices of faces like that, a chin, a mouth, a nose, eyes, hair, all from different characters mixed and matched. After a while the particular arrangement hadn't seemed to matter. It was the very act of changing which had been important.

"You must like a quiet holiday," the cab driver said.

Michael looked at the mirror eyes which might have been his own. He wondered what the driver's mouth was like, whether it conveyed a message different from that of the eyes. "Why do you say that?"

"Like I said. Before. Nobody much comes to the SeaHarp this time of year. Thanksgiving through Christmas, right up 'til the party on New Year's Eve. Then the whole town turns out. But up 'til then, that's their dead season. People are home with their families, not in some hotel."

"Well, I don't have a family, I'm afraid."

The driver was silent a moment. Then, "Didn't think you did."

Michael held himself stiff, eyes motionless. They always seem to know. How do they always know? Then he forced himself to relax, wondering what it was the cab driver might like to see. What kind of passenger he might like and admire. Just like a good orphan. He could feel the themes of independence and "good business" entering his relaxed facial muscles, his posture.

"Too busy building a career, I guess." He let slip a self-amused chuckle. "A fellow my age, his career takes up most of his time."

"Your age?"

"Twenty-five." He'd lied by twelve years, but he could see in the mirror eyes that the driver believed him, apparently not seeing all the age signs that made that unlikely. People believed a good orphan. "I'm an architect."

A sudden, new respect in those mirror eyes. "Really? They planning to expand up there at the SeaHarp? Maybe they know some things about money coming into the Bay us regular working folk don't?"

"I really couldn't say . . ."

"Or maybe they're going to remodel. You gonna give that old lady a facelift?"

"Really. I couldn't."

"Hey, I get ya. I understand." One of the mirror eyes half-winked.

The driver offered to carry his bags up the steps to the hotel, but Michael told him that wasn't necessary. "Travel light in my business." The driver nodded as if he knew exactly what Michael was talking about. Michael gave him a generous tip anyway; he had to. Walking up the steps he wondered if he had enough expense money left.

In the dark, the SeaHarp was magnificent. Its classical lines flowed sweetly into the shadows left and right; its silhouette climbed smoothly out of the porchlight with very few of the architectural afterthoughts that spoiled the proportions of so many of its type. Outside lighting had been kept to a minimum, forcing the night-time visitor to focus on the windows—so many windows—exaggerating the width of that first floor.

But then most old buildings looked impressive in the dark. He hoped it lived up to its promise in the less forgiving daylight. That's when you could tell just how much of the SeaHarp's budget had been alloted to maintenance and repair over the years. By mid-morning he'd be able to spot any dry-rot or sagging wood. He could already tell the SeaHarp had been fitted with Dutch gutters in spots—the downspouts went right up into the enclosed eaves—a real problem with water damage if they hadn't been refurbished recently.

Something bothered him about the windows. It was silly, and these little naggings he was prey to now and then made him angry; he didn't like to think of himself as irrational. Rationality had always meant safety. All the kids he'd grown up with in the orphanage and all their dreams—it had given them nothing but a crib of pain as far as he could see.

And yet he took the few steps up onto the porch and stopped, compelled to examine these windows before entering.

The glass was extraordinarily clean. A good omen. In fact the glass was so clean you'd hardly know it was there. It was an invisible barrier separating what was in—the contents, the atmosphere of the hotel—from what was out. Michael imagined the heavy pressure of that atmosphere—the accumulated breath and spirit of all those visitors over all those years—pushing mightily against that glass which had to be so strong, so finely crafted. Like an aquarium.

He stepped closer to the glass. Inside, the furniture and the carpets were of sea colors, blue and blue-green, the wallpaper a faded blue. The guests moved slowly from setting to setting. As if asleep. Or as if underwater. Their faces, blue and green, pumping the heavy, ancient hotel air. Michael wondered if they could see him outside the glass, peering into their underwater world, seeing his own face in the faces of all these fish.

He walked gingerly to the main door and opened it, took a deep breath. The moist air quickly escaped, pushing over the porch and wetting his face and hair. Stepping inside, he pulled the door tightly, sealing himself in.

He forced himself to remember who he was and the nature of the task he had been hired for.

He was pleased to see that much of the furniture in the lobby and other public areas dated back to the original construction of the hotel; whether it was original to the SeaHarp itself, of course, remained to be seen. And there was so *much* of it. On impulse he crouched as low as possible for a child's eye view, and peered along the floor at a sea of Victorian furniture legs: rosewood and black walnut with the characteristic cabriole carving and rudimentary feet supporting a Gallic ornateness of leaved, flowered, and fruited moldings and upholsteries. Here and there among the Victorian legs there were the occasional modern, straight-legged anachronisms, or, stranger still, legs of curly maple and cherry, spirally reeded or acanthus-leaf carved American Empire pieces, or, going back even further, Sheraton mahogany with satinwood. Michael wondered if the original builder—Bolgran he believed was the name—had brought some older, family pieces into the hotel when he moved in.

No one appeared to be watching, so Michael went down to his knees, lowering his head to scan the floor even better. And then he remembered: four years old, and all the legs and furniture had been trees and caves to him, as he raced across the lobby on hands and knees, so fast that Mr. Dobbins, the supervisor that day, had been unable to catch him. Every time Dobbins had gotten close Michael had hidden under a particularly well-stuffed item, sitting there trying not to giggle while Dobbins called and pleaded with increasing volume. Dobbins' tightly-panted gabardine legs—old, stiff, a bit crooked—seemed like all those other legs of the forest while he was still, and once he moved it was as if the whole forest of legs moved, and when other adult legs joined the search, it felt like a forest in a hurricane, legs sliding across the floor, crashing to the floor, old voices cracking with alarm. At the time he'd thought about staying in that forest forever, maybe grabbing a few of his friends and living there, but then Dobbins had lifted the chair from over him, there was daylight and thunder overhead, and Michael was lifted skyward.

He stood up, dusted off his pants, and headed toward the desk. Still looking around. No one had noticed. Good. He made himself look professional.

Numerous secretaries and writing desks lined the far wall of the lobby, including two excellent drop-fronts of the French *secrétaire à abattant* type, built all in one piece, which must have been brought up from New Orleans at no small expense. He couldn't wait to open them up and examine the insides.

He continued to the registration desk, his eyes alert for the odd detail, the surprise.

Victor Montgomery sat motionless on the other side of his desk. He seemed strangely out of place, and yet Michael could not imagine this man being anywhere else. Perhaps it was the clothes: all of them a size too large, including the collar. But the knot of the tie was firm and tight, and the suit wasn't particularly wrinkled from enclosing a body too small for it. It was as if Montgomery had shrunk after putting the suit on. The desk appeared too large for him, as well. As did the black phone, the blotter, the desk lamp with the green glass shade. They seemed huge to Michael. And Victor Montgomery seemed an infant, forcing his small wrinkled head out of the huge collar, his baby face glowing red from the exertion, his small eyes having difficulty focusing.

"There is quite a lot to catalogue," Montgomery said, his baby eyes straying. "The furniture in all the rooms, the public areas, the storage cellars. As well as all the art and accessory items, of course. You will not be inventorying the family's private quarters or the attics, however, nor will you be permitted access to a few odd rooms. But those are locked, in any case. If there is any question, I expect you to ask."

"I can assure you there will be no problem completing the

inventory in the allotted time. Perhaps even sooner." Michael permitted just a hint of laughter into his voice, thinking it might show enthusiasm.

Montgomery looked like a baby startled by a sudden noise. "I did not expect there would be."

"No, of course not. I just thought that if you were leaving the family quarters, the attics, or any other areas off my assignment for fear of the time they would take, I should reassure you that they would be no problem as well. I have done a number of these hotel inventories and have become quite efficient, I assure you."

"Any furniture in those off-limit areas I wanted inventoried has already been moved into rooms 312 and 313. You will evaluate each piece, make recommendations as to which should remain part of the Seaharp collection—whether because of historical interest, rarity, or to illustrate a particular theme, I do not care—and which might be sold at auction. Any marginal items of dubious functionality should be disposed of as quickly and inexpensively as possible. Most importantly, I want a complete record and evaluation of all items in the hotel. I am quite sure we have been pilfered in the past and am determined to put a stop to it."

Michael nodded, doodling in his pad as if he had recorded every word. The infant's head was frighteningly red. "May I start tonight?"

"If you wish. In fact I would suggest that you do much of your work at night. That will avoid distracting the help from their work, not to mention attracting their curiosity."

"And that would be a problem?"

"I do not want them to think I distrust them. Although, of course, I do. You will be eating Thanksgiving dinner here."

Michael didn't know if that was a question or an order. "I had planned on it, if possible."

"What of your family?"

"I have none. And no other place to go this holiday."

The infant looked vaguely distressed, as if it had filled its diapers. "I am sorry to hear that. A family is a great source of strength. It is important to belong." Michael waited for him to say something specific about his own family, but he did not.

"I feel I am a member of the family of man," Michael lied.

The infant looked confused. "An orphan?"

"Yes, in fact the children of the orphanage came here over a number of years for a kind of holiday. Even I . . ."

"I was away at school most of those years," Montgomery said.

"Yes, yes, of course."

"There are no more orphanages, are there? In the United States, I mean?" Montgomery said.

"No, I don't believe there are."

"Foster homes and such, I believe. The poor orphans get real families now," Montgomery said. Michael simply nodded. The infant Montgomery was suddenly struggling to his feet, lost in his clothes, his baby's head lost in the voluminous collar. The interview was over. "I will make sure the staff prepares a suitable Thanksgiving repast for you tomorrow. After that you will have the hotel essentially to yourself. The staff will be home with their families. We Montgomerys will remain in our quarters for the following two days, at the end of which time I expect to be able to review your full report."

"Certainly." Montgomery was moving slowly around his huge desk. He seemed to be extending one sleeve. For a panicked second Michael thought he was extending his hand to him, but the infant's arms were so short Michael would never be able to find the hand, lost in the huge folds of the coat sleeve.

"One more thing." The infant yawned and its eyes rolled. Up past his bedtime, Michael mused. "Any remaining furniture should *fit* the hotel. It is very important that things fit, find their proper place. I hired you because you supposedly know about such things.''

''I do, sir.''

The infant lolled its head in the huge collar, then waddled off to bed.

Michael took a long, rambling, post-midnight tour of the SeaHarp's floors to get a preliminary feel for the place. He didn't at all mind working at night. Most nights he was unable to get to sleep until three or four in the morning anyway. There never seemed to be any particular reason for his insomnia—his mind simply was not yet ready for sleep. And he had no wife or children to be bothered by his sleeplessness.

The walls of the SeaHarp's public areas were well-supplied with art. There was a number of pieces by British painters in the German Romantic style. Michael had a working familiarity with art but knew he'd have to call in someone else for a proper appraisal: Reynolds from Boston or perhaps J.P. Jacobs in Providence, although Jacobs was often a bit too optimistic in his appraisals for Michael's taste. And Montgomery would want a conservative appraisal, the more conservative the better. So maybe it would have to be Reynolds. Reynolds would have a field day: there were several excellent examples of the outline style, after Retzsch. Also some nice small sculptures he was sure Reynolds could identify—if the sculptors were worth identifying—the pieces looked nice enough but Michael was out of his area here. The themes seemed to be typically classical: Venus and Cupid, Venus and Mercury. The Death of Leander. And several small pieces of children. Cupid, no doubt. But the faces were so worn. Expressionless, as if left too long underwater.

Along one stretch of wall there were so many of these small, near-featureless sculptures, raised on pedestals or recessed in alcoves, that Michael was compelled to stop and

ponder. But there seemed to be no reason for it. He could
not understand the emphasis of these damaged, ill-colored
pieces. Literally ill-colored, he thought, for the stone was a
yellowish-white, like diseased flesh, like flesh kept half-wet
and half-dry for a long time. Even when he left this area he
could feel the sculptures clamoring for his attention, floating
into his peripheral vision like distorted embryos.

The door to room 312 creaked open. He pawed through a
fur of dust for the lightswitch, and when he finally got the
light on he discovered more dust hanging in strings from the
ceiling, and from antique furniture stacked almost to the ceiling, obscuring the glass fixture which itself appeared to have
been dipped into brown oil. Obviously, Montgomery had had
the furniture moved here some time ago. He wondered why
it had taken the man so long to finally decide on getting an
appraiser. Or maybe it was a matter of finding the *right* appraiser. That thought made him get out of the chill of the hall
and completely into the room, however dim and dusty. The
sound of the door shutting was muted by the thick skin of
dust over the jamb. Michael slipped the small tape recorder
out of his coat pocket.

A good deal of the furniture in the room predated the hotel, late eighteenth century to early nineteenth. Bought as
collectors' pieces, no doubt, by some past manager. Most of
them were chairs: Chippendale mahogany wing chairs and
armchairs of the Martha Washington type, late Sheraton side
chairs and a few Queen Anne wing and slippers. But they
varied widely in quality. Most of the Sheratons were too
heavy, with rather awkward carving on the center splat, but
there was one boasting a beautifully carved spread eagle and
fine leg lines, worth a good ten times more than the others.
The Chippendales were all too boxy and vertical in the back.
Most of the Martha Washingtons suffered from shapeless arms
or legs that were too short, seats often too heavy in relation
to the top part of the chair, but there were two genuine mas-

terpieces among those: finely scooped arms, serpentine crests, beautifully proportioned all around.

Some of the chairs had been virtually ruined by amateurish restoration efforts: the arms crudely embellished, mismatched replacement of a crest rail or stretcher, the legs shortened to give the chair an awkward stance. And something odd about one of the altered pieces. Michael clicked on his recorder:

"A metal rod has been added to the top of the chair, with leather straps attached." He brushed off the leather and leaned in for a closer look. "It appears to be some sort of chin strap. Another, wider leather strap has been attached to the seat. Like a seat belt, I'd say, but poorly designed. It would be much too tight, even for a child."

He gradually worked his way around the room, not trying to catalog everything, but simply trying to get a feel for the range of the pieces, highlighting anything that looked interesting. "An English Tall Clock, with a black japanned case embellished with colored portraits of both George III and George Washington. An excellent matching highboy and lowboy with cabriole legs. An early eighteenth-century high chest of drawers. Ruined because one of the cup turned legs has been lost and replaced at some point with a leg trumpet turned. A very nice India side chair with Flemish scrolls and feet . . ."

He stopped once he discovered he was standing by the window. A heavy fog had come in from the bay, had crept like steaming gray mud over the trees, and was now filling the yard to surround and isolate the SeaHarp. It seemed only fitting for such obsessive, lonely work. On the evening before his solitary Thanksgiving meal. It had been only recently that Michael realized he had no practical use for the antiques he valued so much. These were heirlooms, family icons and embodiments. Made for a family to use, for fathers and mothers to pass down to children and grandchildren. And he was someone who had no place to go for Thanksgiving. A wet fish trapped inside the aquarium. He was haunted by mothers and fathers, grandparents, generations of ancestors who—as far as he could tell—had never existed.

He had no fixed place. He was, forever, the rootless boy who cannot get along.

He got down on his hands and knees and rooted like a pig through the dust of ages. He pretended to be a professional. He examined the pieces of patina, wear, and tool marks. His fingers delicately traced the grain for the track of the jack plane. He crawled around and under the pieces, seeking out construction details. He made constant measurements, gauging proportion and dimension. "A sofa in the Louis XV style with a scroll-arched rail and a center crest of carved fruits and flowers with foliage," he chanted into the recorder held to his lips, like a singer making love to his microphone.

But in fact he was a dirty little boy, four or five, hiding in a forest of legs and upholstery. Now and then he would try out a chair or sofa, sitting the way he was supposed to sit, sitting like a grownup in uncomfortable furniture that broke the back and warped the legs and changed the body until it fit the furniture, and nothing was more important than fitting in however painful the process. "A Philadelphia walnut armchair, mid-eighteenth century, with a pierced back and early cresting." Yellow-pale, distorted children with featureless heads were strapping themselves into the chairs around him, trying to sit pretty with agreeable smiles so that visiting adults would choose them. "Three Victorian side chairs after the French style of Louis XV, both flower and fruit motifs, black walnut." Wet children with eyes bigger than their mouths pressed tighter and tighter against the glass. "Belter chair with a scroll-outlined concave back and central upholstered panel crowned by a crest of carved foliage, flowers and fruit."

He examined the wall nearer the floor. Letters were

scratched into the baseboard, by something sharp. Perhaps a
pocket knife. Perhaps a fingernail grown too long. V. I. He
imagined a child on his knees, scratching away at the baseboard with his torn and bleeding fingernail. V. I. C. T. O. R,
the baseboard cried.

The next morning he woke up from a series of strange
dreams he could not remember, in the rough chair with the
straps, the cracked leather chinstrap caressing his cheek like
a lover's dry hand.

The morning's disorientation continued throughout the day.
Thanksgiving dinner in the Dining Room was a solitary
affair; he quickly discovered that the last of the hotel's guests
had left that morning and, other than two or three staff members and the Montgomerys hidden away in their quarters at
the top of the hotel, he had been left to himself. An elderly
waiter poured the wine.

"Compliments of Mr. Montgomery, Suh," the old man
creaked out.

"Well, please tell Mr. Montgomery how much I appreciate
it."

"Mr. Montgomery feels badly that you should dine alone.
And on *Thanksgiving*."

"Well, I *do* appreciate his concern." Michael tried not to
look at the old man.

"Mr. Montgomery says a family is a very important thing
to a man. 'Families make us human,' he says."

"How interesting." Michael bolted his wine and held up
his glass for more. The elderly waiter obliged. "He is close
to his family, is he? And was he close to his father as well,
when he was alive?"

"Mr. Simon Montgomery had a strong *interest* in child-
rearing. He was always looking for ways to improve his
children, and read extensively on the subject. You can find
some of his reading material still in the library, in fact."

"Is that why he brought the children from the orphanage here over the years?" Again, Michael bolted his wine, and again the old waiter replenished his glass.

"I suppose. Did you enjoy yourselves?"

Michael stared up at the waiter. The old man's tired red eyes were watching him carefully. Michael wanted to reach up and break through the glass wall that had suddenly surrounded him, and throttle this ancient Peeping Tom. But he couldn't move. "I don't remember," he finally said.

After dinner Michael spent several hours in the library trying to sober up so that he could continue his cataloguing. He was particularly interested in the older books, of course, and in the course of his examinations discovered the German title *Kallipädie*, 1858, by a Dr. Daniel Schreber. Michael's German was rather rusty, but the book's illustrations were clear enough. A figure-eight shoulder band that tied the child's shoulders back so they wouldn't slump forward. A "Geradhalter"—a metal cross attached to the edge of a table—that prevented the child from leaning forward during meals or study. Chairs and beds with straps and halters to prevent "squirming" or "tossing and turning," guaranteed to keep the young body "straight."

Off in the distance, in some other room, Michael could hear the pounding of tiny knees on the carpet, the thunder of the old men trying to catch them.

Michael made his way down to the cellars via a door in the wall on the north side of the back porch. That door lead him to a descending staircase, and the cellars. The main part of these cellars consisted of the kitchen, laundry, furnace and supply rooms, and various rooms used by the gardeners and janitors. But hidden on one end, seldom-used, were the storage cellars.

In the cellars had been stored a treasure of miscellaneous household appurtenances: some of the most ornate andirons Michael had ever seen, with dogs and lions and elephants worked into their designs; shuttlecocks and beakers; finely painted bellows and ancient bottles and all manner of brass ware (ladles, skimmers, colanders, kettles, candlesticks and the like); twenty-two elaborately stenciled tin canisters and a chafing dish in the shape of a deer (necessary to keep the colonials' freshly slain venison suitably warm); dozens of rolls of carpet which had been ill-preserved and fell into rotted clumps when he tried to examine them; a half-dozen crocks, several filled with such odd hardware as teardrop handles, bat's-wing and willow mounts, rosette knobs and wrought-iron hinges, and the largest with an assortment of wall and furniture stencils; another half-dozen pieces of Delft ware from Holland (also called "counterfeit china"); a dripping pan and a dredging box; a variety of flesh hooks and graters and latten ware and patty pans, all artifacts from earlier versions of the SeaHarp's grand kitchen; a jack for removing some long-dead gentleman's boots; a finely-made milk keeler and several old jack mangles for smoothing the hotel's linen; a rotting bag full of crumbling pillow cases (sorting through these Michael liked to imagine all the young maids' hands which had smoothed them and fluffed their pillows—they would have been calling them "pillow bears" back then); skewers and skillets; trays and trenchers; and a great wealth of wooden ware, no doubt used by some past manager in an attempt to hold down costs.

He could spend a full week cataloguing it all, which wasn't really what he wanted to do during his time at the hotel. After seeing just these more common, day-to-day, bits and pieces, he was more anxious than ever to go through the other rooms. But he could tell from his finds in the cellars that there was quite a bit of antique wealth here. If the sales were handled properly they could bring the Montgomerys a fair amount of money. And the beauty of it, of course, was that these relics were now of little use in the actual running of the hotel.

That evening Michael began his inventories of the guest

rooms themselves. Most could be handled very quickly as
there was little of value or interest. The only thing that slowed
him was a continuation of the vague sense of disorientation
he'd felt since awakening that morning. Things—most rec-
ognizably the faceless cupid statues he'd encountered his first
night—hovered at the periphery of his vision, and then disappeared, much like the after-effects of some drug-induced
alertness. He began to wonder if there had been something
wrong with his Thanksgiving dinner—perhaps it had been the
wine the old waiter had delivered so freely—and he became
very careful of the things he ate, examining each glass of
beverage or piece of bread or meat minutely—for consis-
tency, pattern, tool-marks, style—before consumption.

"A tea-table with cabriole legs and slipper feet tapering
finely to the toe. Like some stylish grandmother dancing.
Perhaps my own, undiscovered, grandmother dancing. Second quarter of the eighteenth century, probably from Philadelphia."

The orphans squealed with delight, their tiny knees raw
and bleeding from carpet burns.

"This kettledrum base desk is obviously pregnant. A por-
trait of my mother bearing me? Its sides swell out greatly at
the bottom. A block front."

In two rooms he found painted Pennsylvania Dutch rocking
chairs. The pale yellow children rocked them so vigorously
he thought they might take off, fueled by their infant dreams.

When it finally came time to retire, Michael of course had
his choice of many beds. But many of the beds were of the
modern type and therefore of little interest to him. Where
there were antique beds they were usually Jenny Linds with
simple spool-turned posts or the occasional Belter bed with
its huge headboard carved with leaves and tendrils.

Michael finally settled for a bed with straps, so many straps
it was like sleeping in a cage. But he felt secure, accepted.
He began a dream about a forest full of children, tying one

another to the trees. The crackling noises in the walls of his bedroom jarred his nerves, but eventually he was able to fall asleep. That night, as always, he had a boy's dreams. No business or marital worries informed them.

It was only upon waking that Michael discovered this room had a stenciled wall. This was of course a surprise in a structure from the 1850s, with the number of manufactured wallpapers available, but he supposed it might have been done—no doubt using old stencils—for uniqueness, to preserve some individual effect. Michael was surprised to find that it had survived the many small repaintings and remodellings that had occurred over the years. Usually a later owner would find the slight imperfections normal to a stencilled wall irritating, and the patterns crude, as certainly they often were.

But Michael liked them; there was a lot to be said for the note of individuality they added to a room. He suspected the only reason this particular wall had been saved, however, was because the guests hadn't the opportunity to see it. Looking around the walls—at their shabbiness, and the crude nature of the furniture—he felt sure this room was not normally rented. So an owner would not be embarrassed.

The pattern was an unusual one. The border was standard enough: leaves and vines and pineapples, quite similar to the work of Moses Eaton, Jr. Some of the wall stencils Michael had found in the cellar matched these shapes. Within these borders, however, was a grove of trees. Most of them were large stencils of weeping willows, but still fairly standard, again derived from Eaton's work. But here and there among the willows was another sort of tree: an oak, perhaps, but he wasn't sure, tied or bound by a large rope, or maybe it was a snake wrapping around the trunk and through the branches. *Bound* was the proper description, because the branches seemed pulled down or otherwise diverted from their natural direction by the rope or snake, and the trunk *twisted* from the upright—a dramatic violation of the classical symmetry one usually found in wall designs.

The design of this particular tree was obviously too intricate to have been done with a single stencil. There had to have been several, overlapping. But the color was too faded and worn to make out much of the detail, as if some past cleaning woman had tried to remove the bound trees, though not the willows, with an abrasive.

He got down on his hands and knees. The baseboard was covered with scratches, the signatures of dozens of different children. He could hear a distant thundering in the hall outside, hundreds of orphan limbs, pounding out a protest that grew slowly in its articulateness. *Choose me. Me me me.* He began to doubt that Victor Montgomery had ever been away to school, that he had ever left this hotel, and his father's watchful eye, at all. The voices in the hall seemed strangely distorted. *Distorted embryos.* As if under water. The scratches in the baseboard tore at his fingertips.

Michael crawled out the door and down several flights of stairs. The faceless children all crowded him, jostled him, and yet he still kept his knees moving. He maneuvered through a mass of legs, odd items of furniture stacked and jammed wall-to-wall, all eager to grab him with their straps and wooden arms and bend him to their shape. He cried when their sharp legs kicked him, and covered his face when hurricanes swept through the woods and shouted like old men.

He stopped at the front windows and floated up to the glass. A crowd of people watched him, pointed, tapped the glass. Sweat drenched him and fogged the glass wall. His eyes grew bigger than his mouth. And yet no matter how hard he peered at the ones outside, he could find no face that resembled his own.

THREE DOORS IN A DOUBLE ROOM
by
Craig Shaw Gardner

There was something wrong with his hands. There was no dirt lodged in the lines of the knuckles. It had been scrubbed away a long time ago. The skin was far smoother than it should have been, his fingers showing nothing but the traces of a few old scars. And they were wounds he could barely remember, self-inflicted for the most part, the legacy of too many late nights at the work bench. Those sort of nights were over now. Sally had seen to that.

"Ooh," his wife breathed. "Look at that, Sammy!"

Sam Copper looked up from his too-clean knuckles, looked out of the window of the taxi at the immense structure the cab approached. It was a huge, wooden place, four stories tall and twice as wide. But what made the place look even larger was the weird decoration everywhere. Strips and spirals of wood surrounded every door and window and ran between each floor, like a mountain of icing dripping from an enormous, melting cake. Sam had done a little building in his time, but this was like nothing he'd ever seen.

"I knew Greystone Bay would be a special place!" Sally giggled, forgetting for the moment the small crystal she held between her palms. "Look at all that gingerbread!"

Sam smiled at his wife and nodded, glad she was paying attention to him for a change rather than her damn crystal gewgaws. Even inside the cab, her blonde hair shone in the late afternoon sun, framing dark eyes, full lips, and those pale freckles across her nose; freckles that she always wished she didn't have. She was awfully pretty when she got excited. It made Sam even sadder than before. Sally might be even prettier than the day he married her. He turned away from her, surprised that his too-clean hands had rolled themselves into fists.

He let his eyes focus on the hotel; no use punishing himself. Gingerbread. So that's what you called it. The whole front of the place was covered with the stuff; far too much of it, as if whoever put it up there was trying to hide something underneath. But it was like a fat man wearing stripes; the riot of diamonds and curlicues covering everything made the place look even larger and more garish, the slopes and angles of the nailed-on wood conflicting crazily with the windows and doors beneath. It hurt his eyes to look at it.

"This is it, folks," the cabbie announced as he pulled the taxi up to the front steps. "The SeaHarp Hotel."

One glance at Sally told Sam the whole story. His wife loved it.

"It's so quaint!"

"Nah." The cabbie laughed. "It's too big to be quaint. You'll see, once you get inside." He got out of the cab to get the luggage.

Sally scrambled out of the car next, moving quickly away. Sam sat there and watched her go. Once, a couple of years ago, she would have squeezed Sam's arm, kissed his cheek.

She would have wanted to share the excitement, to make Sam a part of it. And Sam would have touched her back. He would have taken her in his arms and half hugged the life from her.

He looked back down at his hands, far too pale against his charcoal gray slacks. Once, these hands had stroked Sally's hair, caressed her shoulders, touched her everywhere. These once-rough hands had become gentle with Sally, and he had discovered new strengths in the movement of his fingers or the way he turned his wrist.

Sam closed his eyes. A noise came from deep in his throat, half sigh, half groan. Where had that strength gone? He wondered now if those things in his lap were able to move at all. Once, his hands had been his life. Now it seemed that Sam hardly knew those hands at all.

"Sam? Where are you?"

He started. He had forgotten where he was, had begun to drift off. He looked around. Sally stood between the cab and the steps to the hotel. Now that she had summoned him, she had gone back to talking to the cabbie as he hauled out their luggage.

Sam opened the door on his side and pulled himself from the cab, exhaling with the effort. Marry a younger woman, they told him. It'll keep you young, too. These days, being with Sally only made him feel older. He pulled out his wallet and paid the cab driver. He turned to his wife, but she was halfway up the stairs, keeping pace with a bellman laden down with their bags.

This was so different from the way they had started out. Sam sighed again. Had it only been two years? He wished, somehow, that they could change it all back. But then, that's why he'd agreed to come to this old resort hotel in Greystone Bay. A second honeymoon, his wife had called it. But it didn't feel like a honeymoon; it just felt like the rest of their lives, just going on because there was nothing better to do. Sam started up the stairs after his wife. Maybe things would be different, maybe everything would slow down a little bit, when they made it up to the room.

He was already breathing a little heavily when he made it to the top of the steps. But his wife had crossed the porch a moment before, following the bellman through a huge set of double doors, disappearing into the hotel. Sam hurried to catch up, ignoring the stitch in his side. He walked inside. He expected to step into the lobby, but found some sort of large, empty sitting room instead. There was a huge dining room off to his left. Another set of doors opened to the right. Sam heard muffled voices coming from that direction. He was sure the woman speaking was his wife.

He walked into a room more immense than any of those he had seen before. It was the lobby at last; he could see the reception desk tucked into the far corner. His wife was over there, too, talking to a man in a raincoat.

Sam realized as he approached that he recognized the man she was speaking to. Henry something. Henry Fields, that was it, an electronics salesman. Sam recalled that Henry didn't much like his first name, preferred to be called Hank. They had seen each other once or twice a month before Sam got promoted. Hank Fields. He didn't remember ever introducing him to Sally. But he must have, at one of those trade shows or office cocktail parties they were always going to. Even from here, he could tell that Sally and Hank knew each other.

Hank took a step away from Sally as Sam approached. The salesman smiled and waved.

"Hey, stranger." Hank's deep voice always sounded slightly amused, as if he was in the middle of telling some never-ending joke. "Long time, no see."

"It has been a while," Sam agreed. He thrust out his hand and the two shook.

Sally stepped up to her husband and took his arm. "Imagine!'' she said rapidly. ''Running into somebody from the city way out here. And somebody in the same business, too.''

''Well,'' Hank replied. ''We all have to take a vacation somewhere. It was nice talking to you.'' He nodded to both of them, but his eyes remained on Sally. ''Remember what I told you.''

''How could I forget?'' Sally replied with a little laugh. ''Perhaps we'll see you around later.''

''Maybe you will.'' Fields waved a final time and turned away, marching quickly toward the front door.

''What did he mean?'' Sam said with a frown.

''Pardon?'' Sally replied as she looked around the room. ''We should get a bellboy to take our things.''

But Sam wouldn't let it go that easily. ''He told you not to forget something.''

''Oh.'' Sally turned and waved at a porter. ''I don't know. It was mostly things to stay away from. You know, any place like this has its tourist traps. Hank knows about that sort of thing.''

''Oh?'' Sam's eyebrows rose of their own accord. It sounded like Fields and his wife had talked for a while. ''Does he do some selling around here?''

''What?'' Sally looked back up at her husband, blinking for a moment as if she had forgotten what they were talking about. ''Oh, I guess he must. Why else would he be in some-place like Greystone Bay?'' She let go of Sam's arm. ''I've checked in, dear. Why don't we got up to the room?''

The porter arrived and placed their luggage on a small cart. Sam let his wife take the lead, following both her and the luggage to the distant elevator.

The bellman was gone. Sam had tipped him quickly and generously. Sam wanted to be alone with his wife.

Sally had already begun unpacking. He admired the quiet efficiency with which she worked. He liked to watch her slim fingers from behind, the way her hips moved beneath the thin fabric of her summer skirt. Sally had always been careful about staying trim.

Sam rubbed the spot on his arm where she had held him. That sudden contact had felt good, like old times. He wanted to feel that contact again.

It was their second honeymoon, after all. Just because things had changed didn't mean they couldn't change back. Sam walked up behind Sally and put his large hands on her delicate shoulders. His thumbs dug gently into the spaces beneath her shoulder blades, massaging her back the way he used to, when they had first been married.

"Sam?" she asked, surprise in her voice.

"Yes, honey?" he replied. "I thought this might help you relax."

"Please, Sam!" She stepped forward, pulling free from his grip. "Not now." She began to turn, as if to look him in the eye, but then thought better of it and returned to her unpacking.

"I'm not in the mood," she murmured after a minute. "I guess I'm just tired from the trip. I need to think a little."

"To think?" Sam replied, feeling the old anger rising up in him again. "That wasn't why we came here."

"Wasn't it?" She turned around at last to look at him. "Oh, Sam! There's too much wrong—" She cut herself off and looked away again. "No, that's too easy. I just have to concentrate. Everything will be fine once I calm down."

She reached in her purse and pulled out the crystal. Her goddamned crystal! Sam turned away this time, before he said something he'd regret. He wasn't being realistic. You couldn't change two years overnight. He had to give her a little time, that was all.

She had finished unpacking the suitcase, having hung up half the clothes in the closet on what was "her" side of the large double bed. She proceeded to put the remaining folded piles in various dresser drawers, working with deliberate speed, as if she had had this unpacking planned for months.

Sam decided he might as well make himself useful. He flipped the suitcase closed and hauled it from the bed. There was a door on his side as well. Maybe it was a second closet. In these big old hotels, anything was possible.

Sam tried the door, but it was locked. It probably led into the next room, to make this place into some kind of suite. Then again, it could lead nowhere at all. Looking at the walls and ceiling of this room, he could see signs of an ill-advised renovation, half-completed, then abandoned.

They probably tried to modernize this floor in the fifties. Sam smiled to himself, remembering what it had been like to be a teen-ager back then. They tried to modernize everything in the fifties, to bring it up to their current antiseptic standards. At least, here in the SeaHarp Hotel, either good taste or lack of money had won out, and the only signs left over were a few missing pieces of molding, and an indentation where they'd tried to put in a dropped ceiling. Besides that, and the addition of electricity, this room looked pretty much the same as it would have when it was built maybe a hundred years ago.

Sam ended up sticking the suitcase under the bed. When he stood up again, Sally was sitting on the bed, staring at her crystal.

"Please, Sam," she said before he could object. He turned away. He didn't want to get into an argument. Not now, when there might be some way to make their marriage what it used to be. He walked over to the window. They had a decent view, but not a great one, mostly filled with the roofs of the town, with the ocean sparkling off to the far right.

Sally hummed to herself behind him. He didn't have to turn around to know she was rocking back and forth on the bed, staring at that damn crystal. It helped her to think, she said, to look inside herself to find the answer that was really right. Sam thought she should talk to him about her problems, instead. But what did he know? They didn't have god damned crystals when he was a kid.

He looked down at the lawn that surrounded the hotel. Another man's eyes gazed straight into his own for an instant, then looked away. The man walked rapidly toward the hotel, out of Sam's view. But Sam had recognized the other man. It was Hank Fields.

Sam turned around to look at his wife.

"What's going on here?"

Sally blinked and frowned, still staring intently at her crystal. "Sam. Please."

"Please, nothing!" Sam felt the anger building in him once again. This time, he knew he couldn't stop it. "I saw Hank Fields watching us. It's no coincidence that he's here. What's going on?"

"Sam?" Sally put down her crystal to gaze at her husband. "What do you mean?"

"There's something between you and Hank."

"What?" she said, her voice slightly slurred, as if she was waking from a dream. "What do you—" She reached clumsily for the purse, lying beside her on the bed. Sam reached forward and roughly grabbed her shoulders. This time, she was going to tell him the truth!

The purse fell to the floor with a thump.

For once, Sally looked right at him. And she looked afraid.

"I didn't mean for it to happen," she whispered. "You'd be gone all week some times. And Hank was always there." She clutched the crystal in her fist. "Oh, I told him not to come here!"

She started to cry. She picked her purse up off the floor and clumsily tried to open it, her fingers slipping off the clasp.

"Here," Sam said. "Give it to me." He found himself both infuriated at and sorry for his wife at the same time. When she cried like that, she looked even younger than usual.

"The clasp sticks—sometimes," Sally managed as she handed him her bag. "There's—some tissues—"

Sam tilted the purse on its side so that he could get a better grip on it. He wrenched the bag open with a single pull. Something shiny fell to the rug.

Sally made a tiny, mewling sound in the back of her throat. Sam looked down at what had fallen.

It was a small revolver. Silver-plated, maybe. A woman's gun.

"What is this?" he asked, not bothering to pick up the gun.

Sally looked at the bed, away from both him and the gun. "Hank gave it to me. For protection."

"What?" Sam exploded. The anger was coming back again, fast and hot. "What business has he—? Who does he think—?"

He looked down at his hands. They had clenched into fists again.

Someone was pounding at the door. Sam turned around to look.

"Sally?" a voice yelled through the wood. "Are you all right? Sally?"

Sam was not even aware of his feet moving. But he felt his hand encircle the doorknob, and he jerked the door toward him with all his strength. He looked into Hank Fields' startled face. But the surprise lasted only for an instant, replaced by a mask of anger and defiance.

"What are you doing to her?" Fields demanded. "If you've hurt her in any way—"

Sam punched the other man in the face, knuckles connecting with teeth and cartilage. Fields crumpled, falling to the floor like a rag doll whose parts had been badly sewn together.

Sam let the door close on the fallen man. He looked back at Sally.

"What have you done to him?" she demanded.

"Nothing he didn't deserve," Sam replied, moving quickly toward the bed.

"Who are you to say that?" Sally retorted. The tears were gone, but her angry face was red and puffy. "What do you know about him? What do you know about me?"

"I know that you're my wife."

Sally laughed. "Oh, that means a whole hell of a lot. Especially with somebody like you!"

"Stop talking like that." He was almost on top of her. His hands reached for her.

"Keep away from me!" she screamed. "Keep away!"

She held the crystal in front of her, like you would hold a crucifix to ward off a vampire. Did she think he was some sort of monster? He'd show her just what kind of monster he was.

"You'll listen to me," he growled. "And you'll do what I want."

He swatted her hand out of the way. The crystal flew from her fingers, sailing against the locked door by the bed, shattering into a dozen pieces. The sound reverberated around the room, much louder than it should have been. Sam looked at the shards of glass glittering on the rug. He heard another noise, a high, whistling sigh, like the sound the wind made when it found its way inside old houses. Or old hotels, Sam thought. He looked up from the splinters of glass, and saw what had made the noise.

The locked door was opening.

He looked down at his wife, but she seemed frozen, staring at the shattered crystal. The once locked door swung wider, showing a space of half a foot. Sam turned to the door. An instant later his hand was on the knob. It had seemed before as if he had been sleepwalking. Now even that was gone, and he was farther still from the world around him, as if that sleepwalking self was dreaming, and he moved through that dream within a dream.

He stood in the doorway, staring into light. He squinted, trying to make out what stood on the other side, but could see nothing more than vague, shifting shapes. Voices spoke; voices that were somehow familiar. Someone was laughing.

He heard the sound of shattering glass.

Sam blinked. He had almost blacked out there for an instant. He didn't know what was happening anymore. He took a deep breath. The anger was making him crazy.

"You're not going to see him anymore," he said to his wife.

"What are you talking about? Hank understands me."

How could he understand her? 'Cause they slept together a couple times? "But you're my wife!"

"What does that mean? A piece of paper that I was stupid enough to sign?"

"Stupid?" What was she saying? "How can you—"

Her face twisted into a strange, cruel smile. "You don't understand at all, do you? Hank's real! Hank's alive! He's so much better than an old man like you!"

"Old man?" Sam screamed. "I'll show you what an old man can do. You'll be sorry you ever met met!"

But she wasn't sorry, she wasn't even frightened. She was laughing, laughing at the poor old man who sometimes couldn't get it up, the poor old man who foolishly thought he could keep his young and pretty wife happy. It was a real joke.

"Stop it!" he hissed.

She laughed even harder. She tried to talk, but her laughter kept the words from making any sense. Tears of mirth rolled down her cheeks.

"I will not have you laughing at me!" he shouted. "Nobody laughs at me!"

Sally found that even more hilarious. He couldn't stand it anymore. He would make her stop laughing if it was the last thing he ever did. He clamped a hand over her mouth, pushing her head back against the mattress. She struggled under the pressure, still making muffled noises beneath his grip. Laughing noises. She squirmed. He shifted his weight, struggling to keep on top of her. She was small but strong. If he wasn't careful, she'd get herself free and start laughing all over again.

He grabbed her shoulder, but she wrenched it free. Then he grabbed her neck.

He let go when she stopped moving. She wasn't breathing, either.

He had killed her.

He heard the sound of breaking glass.

The other door was open, the one that had been locked before. And Sam realized he had already passed through that door once.

What had happened? Nothing seemed quite real. But he remembered the soft feel of his wife's flesh under his fingers. He looked down at his hands, the hands he had trusted, the hands with which he had killed his wife. He hadn't meant to— If he could only—

He stood in the other doorway, looking into the light. He didn't remember walking here, either. The light still hurt his eyes, but he could see the shapes more clearly now. He thought he could distinguish three of them. Their voices were louder too, and rose and fell as if they were arguing. He couldn't make out the words yet, though, and the figures didn't seem to notice him at all.

He blinked. Here he was, standing in a doorway staring like an idiot, when he had just killed his wife.

But what should he do? Give himself up? Try to run away?

The voices murmured something in the other room. He couldn't quite make out the words. Were they talking to him?

She was going to leave him. He had heard her say it. It had been what led to his anger—that, and the taunting. It was only now, though, that he really thought about it. How dare she? Hadn't she loved him at all?

Maybe she deserved what had happened to her! She was going to leave him, and for that pantywaist salesman! She had taunted him, laughed at him, and had even brought a gun to kill him! She wasn't worth worrying about, or crying over. A woman like that was worthless!

The murmuring increased in the other room. The voices seemed to agree with him. Sam almost laughed—*agree* with him? Where had that come from? He stared out into the light. Why weren't his eyes getting used to it? Crazy things had happened. He was bound to have crazy thoughts. But if he could think, really think, about what had really happened, there might be a way out of here.

His wife's dead body was in the room behind him. Her lover's unconscious body was there, too. What would happen if he disappeared, and left the two of them for the police? Especially if he left the room through a locked door?

He looked back into the light. He didn't understand why this door had opened, and still couldn't quite make out what was on the other side. But now that it was here, he'd be a fool not to use it. Maybe he could lock the door behind him, as if he had never been here. Maybe then he could slip away from Greystone Bay, and start a brand new life.

He took a step into the other room.

He heard the sound of glass as it shattered.

He opened his eyes. He was sitting up in bed.

Something was wrong.

A balding man, in his fifties, slightly overweight, was glaring at him. But it couldn't be.

Sam realized he was looking at himself.

What was happening? The last thing he remembered was leaving. He had been running away.

He looked down at a delicate hand wearing a diamond engagement ring. Sally's hand. When he flexed his fingers, Sally's hand moved.

He no longer knew what was happening. He realized now that he didn't understand anything at all. Maybe it was all a dream. Maybe everything that he thought had happened in this room was a dream. But why did everything feel so real?

He stared up at the man that he should have been, the man angrily approaching the bed. Somehow, his mind was in Sally's body, and he was looking through Sally's eyes.

"You're not going to see him anymore," the Sam-thing declared.

But his present form was speaking, too. The lips of this new body were moving, forming words. "What are you talking about?" It was a woman's voice, almost like his wife's. "Hank understands me."

"But you're my wife!" The man that should have been him towered overhead, his hands gathered into fists the size of sledgehammers. He had never realized how massive he looked up close.

"What does that mean?" the woman's voice said, and he felt the lips move once again.

But if he was in Sally's mind, couldn't he control her muscles, too? Maybe he could stop what was happening, make some sense out of it. He tried to close her mouth.

"A piece of paper that I—" her voice stopped for a minute, then continued. "—was stupid enough to sign?"

The words had made the Sam-thing livid. He leaned over Sally, his face red and puffy. "Stupid? How can you—"

More words poured from Sally's mouth.

"You don't understand at all, do you?"

He had to stop this, to make his other self realize what was going on.

"Hank's real!"

He had to speak with Sally's voice, using her lips, her vocal chords. If he didn't, he knew what the other Sam would do.

"Hank's alive!"

He had to stop this now! No! I don't mean what I'm saying! He tried to make her voice work. No! he thought, I don't mean what I'm saying!

"Na—" Sally grunted. "Na—"

Sally's lips formed words of their own:

"He's so much better than an old man like you!"

"Old man?" the Sam-thing screamed. "I'll show you what an old man can do. You'll be sorry you ever met me!" His huge fists opened as he reached for his wife.

But the real Sam was trapped in Sally's head. He was going to kill himself. He'd strangle his brand new neck with his original pair of hands, and there seemed to be nothing either of them could do about it.

He started to laugh, and Sally laughed with him.

But, no, he couldn't give up yet. He had used Sally's eyes, had turned Sally's head and lifted her arm. If he tried hard enough, he could learn to use her voice as well. He struggled to form words, actually spoke one or two. If only his new form wasn't laughing so hard. But he knew it was his laughter as well as Sally's. The situation was too horrible. It was too funny for words.

The Sam-thing covered his new mouth. He couldn't breathe. The other Sam was like an animal, pushing against him until he pressed the life out of this new body. He had to free himself. Everything was repeating itself from what had happened before—with one difference. Last time, he had been the killer. This time, he would be killed.

He saw movement, past Sam's shoulder. Hank had somehow managed to stand up. He was leaning heavily against the door frame. He looked wildly through Sally's eyes at the other man, willing him to look his way. Sally was being crushed by the Sam-thing's weight. In a minute she would be choked as well, choked to death. He willed her muscles to push, to free her of the huge bulk on top of her, but she didn't have the strength. She would die, unless he could get Hank to pull the Sam-thing off.

Sam's other hand reached for this throat! No! He wouldn't let this happen! Sally's left hand reached over the side of the bed, searching for the gun.

Sam's weight lifted off this new body for an instant, and then was back again. But it had been long enough. He felt the cool metal beneath his newfound fingers. He grabbed the gun with Sally's hand and lifted it toward the Sam-thing's head. The person who used to be him would have to see it. He would have to stop.

The other Sam pressed into his new windpipe. Sally's body couldn't breathe at all. Her hand brought the gun up so that the muzzle rested on Sam's forehead. He didn't stop. If anything, the pressure on her neck increased. Deep within her brain, Sam could feel the lack of oxygen. He was blacking out. In a minute, he would be dead.

He had to use her fingers again to pull the trigger.

He concentrated again, using every bit of strength left to him. He was not going to die. He would survive.

Sally's hand pulled the trigger.

Instead of a gunshot, he heard the sound of breaking glass.

He stood in the doorway to the other room.

He looked down at his hands. Sam's hands. Or at least he thought they were his hands. He didn't know anymore. He tried to make sense out of what had happened. There was something about this room, or this hotel, or Sally's broken crystal, maybe all three, something that made you dream. Or was it a dream? He was afraid to turn around, to look in the room behind him. He was afraid he would see Sally's body. But more than that, he was afraid he would be dead as well.

Instead, he looked up into the light. Yes, he definitely saw the outlines of three figures now, endlessly moving and talking. But he thought he saw others in the distance, on the edge of his vision, moving closer. What were they? Should he try to get them to look at him, or should he try to sneak by them and escape? There had to be some way out of this. Somehow, he would find it.

He moved his hand beyond the door, feeling for a wall in the brightness. Somewhere, in this too-bright room, someone was laughing.

He heard the sound of smashing glass.

At first he heard the voices from a long way away.

"Stupid? How can you—"

"You don't understand at all, do you? Hank's real! Hank's alive! Na—na—he's so much better than an old man like you!"

"Old man? I'll show you what an old man can do. You'll be sorry you ever met me!"

He opened his eyes to a woman laughing. He shook his head, trying to clear the fog from his brain. The whole lower half of his face ached, like he had walked into a door. Or a fist.

What had happened now?

It had to be. He looked down at a pair of unfamiliar hands, with fingers far longer than Sam's, fingers that ended with manicured nails. He knew these hands, this suit, these shoes. He knew what he'd see if he looked in the mirror. Whatever was going on here had happened again.

He was Hank now. And, in the room beyond him, the scene was playing out all over again. He wondered for an instant if it would repeat forever.

He used the door frame to pull himself upright. In the room beyond, Sam stood over Sally, strangling her. She flung her hand wildly across the carpet on the side of the bed, searching for her revolver. It would all happen again. He had to stop them, had to get them free of whatever had caught them in its web. He knew now that that was the only way he could free himself.

He saw Sally's eyes look beseechingly into his own. Sam shifted his weight, pressing hard down on her throat.

His balance wasn't too good, but the body he was in was young and well muscled, and he managed to make it to the bed, to get his hands around Sam's shoulders. He pulled Sam back for an instant.

Sally gasped for air. Her fingers curled around the gun.

Sam shrugged off his grip, like a grown man turning away from a three-year-old. But Sally had the gun up against Sam's head. She pulled the trigger. The bullet went in through the forehead and out through the base of the skull, spewing blood and bits of brain. Sam crashed forward heavily, his chest connecting with Sally's chin, pushing it back sharply. She stopped struggling.

It took Hank a minute to push the body off Sally. He already knew it was too late. They were both dead.

He heard the sound of the wind again, the sound of the open door to the other room. He didn't turn around, though, not yet.

He knew who the three people were on the other side of the door. It had come to him all at once. They were Sally, and Sam, and Hank. Something had happened; maybe it was the broken crystal, maybe it was the first murder, maybe it was only the intensity of their emotions, let loose in this strange place. But, whatever it was, something here wanted it, and would not let them go. They were trapped here, to play out their little drama over and over.

Sam thought suddenly of the outside of this place, with its

mass of useless ornamentation growing everywhere, like a fungus out of control. There were endless designs out there, and variations on designs piled on top of each other, so that all sense of any individual piece was lost.

Was that what was happening in this room as well? Was whatever had trapped him and Sally and Hank in this moment in time going to show him that moment over and over again? It was a crazy thought, but crazy things were happening. Or maybe none of this was happening at all. Maybe it was just a recurring dream, his imagination playing tricks on him. Or maybe he'd gone over the edge when he killed his wife.

He heard soft voices coming from the other room. Sally's voice, Hank's voice, his voice. It was as if this old hotel was haunted. Except there hadn't been any ghosts here, before the three of them arrived. Now, maybe they would be haunting it, forever.

Or would they? He looked down at his new body. Hank Fields. Two people were dead on the bed, but he was still here. There was nothing to stop him from walking away from here, in a body twenty years younger than the one he had come here with. And, if he could get away from here, there'd be nothing to connect him with the two dead bodies on the bed. A domestic quarrel that ended tragically; that's what the police would call it.

He started to laugh. Whatever had held him here had slipped up. He was still alive, and in a fitter, younger body. He would get out of here and start his life all over again.

But why was he still alive? Maybe this game he was in didn't go on forever. Maybe there were only three variations after all. Poor Sally. Poor Hank. Poor everybody but him. He was going to get away scot free. He laughed even louder.

Someone banged on the door. He spun around. It was the door to the hallway, which had somehow gotten closed again. Someone rattled the handle. Apparently, it had gotten locked as well.

"Open up!" a man's voice called. "We heard the gunshot. Open up or we'll have to kick it down!"

No! Not when he was so close to getting away. He would get implicated; his fingerprints were all over the room, on Sam's coat and Sally's dress. For all he knew, they were on Sally's gun as well.

The other door opened. Laughter came from the other room. Hank's laughter.

"What, are you crazy in there?" the man's voice called from the hallway. "Stand away from the door. We're going to shoot off the lock."

They were coming for him with guns! He had to find another way out of here.

The door to the other room opened wider still, bright light spilling across the floor at his feet.

He heard the sound of glass, shattering.

REVELATIONS
by
Melissa Mia Hall

Neddy Jones is a lightning rod, a sensitive of such insecurity and fear he scares himself when he gets up in the morning and looks in the mirror. Especially when he sleeps on his hair wrong and it stands up funny. He blames it on Laura, Laura of the stricken blue eyes, dyed blonde hair and chipped fingernail polish, concave chest and clumsy limbs. Laura was one of the neediest women he'd ever met, a bird with two broken wings (a bird flew into his front window one day as she came onto his porch). He tried to help her with his Tarot readings, done at cut-rate prices because Laura never had a lot of money in her life. Money flew from her hands, seldom resting in her skinny palms. Neddy never gave palm readings but the lines on those palms always seemed unfinished, like a doll's palms. He should've known what was going to happen to her the first moment he held her nervous hand in his.

Poor Laura. Poor Neddy. Outwardly he just looked overworked and overtired. Certainly no one at work seems to notice how shaken he is, ever since Laura's suicide.

Neddy knew she would probably do it by the third visit. He thought he could avert it somehow. He told himself he couldn't actually *see* death. No one knows when a person is going to die. Only God. Neddy just saw the restlessness, the sorrow, the doom, the great unhappiness pulling her away from the ground. He thought he could change her mind about life. Readings change. People change. Good things happen that are not foreseen. It broke his heart when they did not, with Laura.

She was such a mess. Maybe he loved her. Looking back over things past is a hopeless task, like drifting in tea leaves. Like drifting through these income tax records scattered across his desk. He likes his quiet accounting job. Normally, he even enjoys the challenge of the new tax laws. But not today. Today all he sees is the vaguely distracted features of Laura's lost face.

The cards were just a hobby, something he did to charm his friends.

Laura just got hooked. Neddy read her cards every week, using them to lure her into his life, empty as hell after he broke up with his last girlfriend. She was cute, if a little off-center.

He needs to get away. Even the Tarot has told him that. At least he thinks that's what it said. Things will get better if he goes away. Since Laura's death he's not so sure about things anymore. Psychic blindness has descended upon him like a white blizzard. He still feels things, though, and he feels he has to go away. He must. He brushes back his hair and wishes he'd had it cut but his barber's an old buddy and he might ask him to do another reading and he can't. He won't.

Checking into a hotel at night is a surreptitious ordeal. The dark cloaks your actions. The approach to the building of endless windows like so many eyes, watching you. Neddy stumbles out of the cab and the driver starts to get out to help him with his bag. Neddy says he doesn't need any help and stuffs a wad of bills in his hand. The driver grins and thanks him loudly. Neddy is embarrassed. He's acting like a country bumpkin out on his first vacation. The driver roars away, his cab belching smoke. Bad gas. Neddy clutches his bag and stares at the SeaHarp Hotel, listening to the faint sound of ocean and whistling night wind.

Two mammoth stone dogs flank the entrance to this hotel, surely not ancient, but certainly old enough to have known countless visitors. Neddy takes an apprehensive breath and steps forward, then stops again. A porter comes towards him, frowning. Neddy feels embarrassed again, naughty, terribly young and foolish, like he's been caught running away from home by his dad. An especially strong ray of moonlight illuminates the porter's gloomy face. He holds out his hand for Neddy's weathered Samsonite. Neddy shakes his head and the porter looks offended. Belatedly, Neddy hands it over to him. The porter nods his head and the frown relaxes slightly. "Sir," he says, "welcome to Greystone Bay."

Neddy follows him past the dogs—he almost thinks he hears a muffled animal noise, a snuffling, pawing sound and imagines that they must come alive at midnight. He peeks at his watch and feels curiously satisfied that it's only nine-thirty.

The hotel is austerely handsome and alarmingly empty. Neddy feels like he's blundered onto a film set waiting for the crew to arrive. A vague movement catches his eye, a newspaper flapping on a sofa—a newspaper held in front of two crossed legs. Someone. Neddy lets out a sigh of relief and the porter glares at him. He's stopped in the middle of the lobby. The porter wants him to check in at the desk. Flushing hotly, Neddy does as expected and a woman appears seemingly out of nowhere, also frowning. Neddy grins and greets her with a flashing American Express card. She keeps frowning and Neddy's spirit continues the descent it had begun the morning he'd decided to leave Cedar Bridge and come here to Greystone Bay, Laura's native stomping grounds. He thought the sea air would do him good. Shit. He thought her spirit would find him here. If it exists.

"Reservation?" the woman asks, the frown lifting as her fingers close over the card.

"No—"

"Well, we're rather full up—"

Neddy's mouth drops open slightly. Unbelievable.

"But I think we can handle it—"

She's joking? Years drop away from her face as a smile leaks out.

"Great. My name's Ned Jones—"

She taps her nameplate, "Lana Cates, at your service. Fill this out please and sign there—if you will. Here's your room key—enjoy your stay."

"I think I'll stay a week—if there's any problem—"

She turns her back on Neddy, rudely oblivious.

"I mean, there won't be any problem, will there be, do you think?" Neddy insists on seeing her face again, to see her smile just one more time. He needs a smile. She turns back around and smiles brightly. She's very tan and very blonde, a natural blonde, of sand, of sun, of blue ocean sky. The way Laura wanted to be, what she called "one of them Malibu blondes." Oh, she's young, Neddy discovers. She wears a senior class ring for '85. High school. When he walked in she seemed so much older.

"No problem at all, this is actually the off-season. The water's getting too cold for swimming. We do have a heated swimming pool here, of course—but the ocean and the wind's getting nippy." She toys with a gold nugget-type pendant on a chain around her neck. "The bar's still open. The coffee shop's open—" she looks at the wall clock, "for thirty more minutes. And of course, our room service is excellent. Have a nice stay—''

The porter's been waiting all this time. As Lana Cates turns away again, with a determined whip of her hips, Neddy faces the man apologetically. ''Really, I can handle my bag, thanks—'' He reaches out for his bag and the porter relinquishes it with a disapproving grunt. Neddy hands him a five and he fades away into the shadows. Neddy heads for the elevators, glancing at his doorkey.

His room stuns him. It's a corner room with an incredible view. He pulls back the curtains and lets the full impact take his breath away. Full moonlight on water, crashing breakers, and pale shape of unlittered rocks and beach. He hears the waves. He turns off the light next to the huge king-size bed and savors the silvery light faintly tainted by a couple of manmade lights on the pier. He shakes with a sudden chill. It's just September but it feels like January. He remembers Laura's last kiss, a kiss fleeting and sweet, sweeping across his forehead and haphazardly down his cheek. ''I gotta go, Neds, I gotta go.'' She called him that—Neds, rhymes with Keds. She always made him feel about fifteen. He tried to make her stay that night. She was a walking tower of destruction, that girl. ''Hey, stay over, kiddo, I'll sleep on the sofa, really.'' Her vacant eyes considered his words. She chewed on a thumb nail and spat out flecks of metallic red. ''Naw, I gotta go, Neds.''

She gotta go, Neds. She gotta slit her wrists and watch the blood go across the tiles. She gotta go.

Why was she so sad, so beaten and unhappy? Something about her family. She hated her father. She hated her life. She didn't have a direction, a focus. She couldn't keep a job. She got bored, she said. She seldom paid her rent on time. One impulsive night he told her she could move in with him for a while. She just laughed and Neddy felt a secret relief. For a while they slept together but one evening she told him

she didn't care for all that sex crap and then had cried because
she was afraid she'd hurt his feelings (maybe his ego).
"You're my only friend now, Neds, my only one and I mean
that." If only he could've reached her somehow. She was
always so distant and disconnected. God, it hurts. Suddenly
the moon's too bright, too knowing. He shuts the curtains,
turns on the TV and every light in the room.

He'll order room service hamburger and chips. And a cup
of hot tea. No booze. No dope. He's going to sit in this room
and come clean. And let go to let her in. But the room feels
so opaque and withholding. He feels in the grip of something. Or no, he doesn't feel, he doesn't feel at all. It scares
him.

He fumbles in his pocket for his lucky penny. As he flips
it into the air, he thinks, heads the sun won't come up in the
morning, tails, it will. Heads. He groans. Laura wasn't so
great. He'd just gotten used to her slinging herself down on
his sofa, draping her legs with artful clumsiness across the
side. Used to her popping bubble gum and pulling on a strand
of her stringy worn-out hair. Used to her saying, "So how
am I gonna handle this week, Neds?" and roaming in his
refrigerator for her diet Dr Peppers.

Of course, it doesn't matter now.

He opens his suitcase and starts rooting around for his
cards. At first he had thought he wouldn't bring them along.
But they reassure him of his sanity (or insanity?). He holds
the box to his chest for a moment and then takes out the
cards. He wants to look at their dear familiar faces, especially
number nineteen, Mr. Sun. He uses the deck illustrated by
David Palladini and the sun's face is so gentle and humor-
ously benign that seeing it always soothes and calms his spirit.
Neddy turns the first card over, hoping it will be Mr. Sun
and is shocked by a blank card. He shuts his eyes and rubs
them. He looks back down at the card in his hand. Blank
white paper face. Face of nothing Arcanum number minus

zero. He turns over another and another. All blank. The Tarot deck, composed of his beloved friends. all gone. Replaced by nothing. A prank by one of his disappointed friends? He thinks back over recent readings and recalls nothing particularly disturbing, other than Laura's consistently morose readings.

Doesn't seem fair. Neddy wants to cry, would love to let go and let the tears fall, but can't. He doesn't think he's ever cried. Once, maybe when he was at his mother's funeral. He was only ten. It was okay. His dad didn't say a word, just held him. Maybe he could just visualize Mr. Sun, that round white face of orange-red and orange-yellow, the book below him open before the loving rays. It's probably the Bible, Neddy thinks and feels himself praying. The sun represents God, he thinks. He needs God right now real bad. He grips the deck of blank cards too tightly and suddenly they burst out of his hands, spraying across the floor. Who'd do a mean trick like that, stealing his cards? At least he has his lucky penny. He put it on the night table. At least he thought he did. It's gone now. Probably on the floor. It'll turn up somewhere. And he's got change. Nowhere is it written that you can't use a nickel or a quarter. Besides, he's a sensitive and he doesn't need help when it comes to feeling things. Except all he feels now is a curious blankness, a numbness. What is it they call it in broadcasting—dead air? The future just seems to have no purchase here, no substance. Even the past seems too distant. At this moment when he tries to recall Laura's face, there are no features, just a pink oval with two dark smudges for eyes. Her voice is indistinct, as well, a strangled whisper.

Dead air. He calls room service finally and stammers out his request for food. He concentrates on the flickering TV screen and turns up the volume. At least he'll dream tonight, maybe have a nice old reassuring nightmare. And what's he griping for? He needs a rest. He'll sit here and watch *Enter-*

tainment Tonight or Carson, chow down on a cheeseburger
with lots of ketchup. Did he ask them to bring plenty of
ketchup? Hope they'll remember, Neddy prays. Neddy prays
a lot.

He slept deeply for a couple of hours but now he's wide
awake and restless. He's gone to the bathroom five times.
There's no pee left but he keeps checking to make sure. He
stares in the mirror over the clean hotel sink. He drinks water
so he'll make more pee. He goes back to bed. He needs
answers. His dreams usually help him, illuminating his problems and giving answers to inner dilemmas. Sometimes they
give clues to the future. Tonight they give nothing. He recalls
nothing but loss, emptiness. If he feels anything at all in this
hotel it's the sensation of emptiness. A glass drained of water, dry, and that water he just drank—tasteless. He licks his
lips and goes back to bed. Or starts to go to bed and stops,
shocked by a white apparition sitting on his bed in apparent
agony, a woman beating her face with her own hands, then
stopping to look at him as if seeking his approval. At least
this is something. He moves quietly to the drapery pull and
lets the moonlight in. The ghost turns toward the window
and continues to cry silently. Neddy creeps closer, trying to
recognize her.

"Who are you? What do you want with me?" He sounds
like an actor in a B-movie. He feels like he should know her.
The ghost tears at her stringy hair (that's very familiar) and
opens her mouth to scream. Automatically, Neddy puts his
hand over his ears but there's no sound and the apparition
disappears, leaving no trace, not even a chilliness in the air.
Sighing, Neddy crawls back into bed and curls into a fetal
position. He used to read Tarot cards for a woman named
Laura. Then she died.

People die. He came here to get away from death and
death's not something you can escape. The ghost who just

left, maybe it was Laura and he ran her off because he didn't want to hear her scream.

His body grows pleasingly lax. He stretches out and snuggles into the plump pillow. ''I want to dream about what I should do tomorrow'' he whispers to himself. Sleep steals over his features and feeds him pictures he won't remember when he wakes up, an odd event for a man who normally experiences over fifty percent complete dream recall.

Morning slides into the room pearly grey and still. He stares at the ocean view bathed in mist. He has to do something. Go to the bathroom. Take a shower. Go get something to eat. Get out of here. He does just that, with an urgency to his movements that surprises him. There's no hurry. He doesn't have to go to work. He's on vacation. Neddy Jones has all the time in the world.

After a rushed breakfast in the coffee shop, Neddy buys an overpriced umbrella in the gift shop and goes out into the morning air. The minute he leaves the hotel, tension seems to lift from his body and he breathes easier. Images of Laura rush into his brain and guilt mixes with the now familiar pain. Why is it becoming so easy to forget her? It's probably just a normal reaction to bereavement. Certainly it's a selfish grief. He's just gotten used to having her around, loved her needing him because she was feeling so badly. He didn't have to see it in her cards because any fool could read her eyes and her crooked, sliding mouth, the way she used to try to smile and could never quite pull it off convincingly. Still, he couldn't head the reaper off at the pass. He couldn't even get her a time-out.

Good old Neds heads for the beach, heading into the wind, using his umbrella like a medieval shield. He turns the pain over and over in his head, examining it with relentless curiosity. The pain's like a lump of fool's gold, fascinating but monetarily worthless. He finds a bench to sit on. The rain's let up; he closes the umbrella carefully and puts it beside him. The bench is wet but his raincoat protects the seat of his trousers.

"Have you ever fed seagulls? I used to feed pigeons, now I feed seagulls."

The abrupt, scratchy voice astonishes him. To the left, right beside him, a burly black-haired man studies him with a jovial but oddly menacing smile. "Excuse me?"

"Barney's the name, Jake Barney, retired Air Force man. And you are—?"

Suddenly, Neddy's ashamed of his nickname. It's not tough enough. "Ned, Ned Jones. I'm an accountant."

Jake Barney mulls over this bit of news, obviously not very impressed. "I'm from Texas."

"I'm from New Jersey," Ned says, not exactly proud of the fact, but not exactly ashamed either. But it is time he stopped letting people call him "Neddy." He no longer feels worthy enough to be a "Neddy." Neddys don't let friends kill themselves. Neddys are good and brave and kind.

Jake slings himself down on the bench and it wobbles for a second from the impact. "Passing through?"

"Just visiting."

"I'm passing through. I've been passing through for about five years. The Bay's that sort of place. You just never want to leave. I've been meaning to. Lord knows I love Texas— I'm from a little town called Weatherford. You know Mary Martin and old mean J.R. on T.V.—from *Dallas*, he's from there, too." Jake wads a paper sack and aims for a trash can a good distance away. He makes the basket, hits his thigh, whoops and then looks at Ned with a sudden seriousness. "You come here to get away and whatever it was you was getting away from, well, you find it's here, too and you either look it in the face or die."

Ned feels a little strange to be having such a conversation with a stranger. He avoids Jake's eyes. They're dark eyes, stern, knowing. He nudges Ned. "Running away from a disappointment in love or what you thought was love?"

That offends Ned. "No, somebody died. A friend."

"I'm sorry." Jake glances at the water. "Looks like the rain's gonna start up again any second. Say, do you know what a mockingbird is? It's the state bird of Texas. I like them, clever sonsabitches—they imitate sounds. Mainly other bird sounds and such. Puts me in mind of people, you know, tricking themselves with their feelings." The Texan punches Ned in the side. "Say, you don't do that—you're not one of them birds, are you? Just kidding." He laughs to himself, then punches Ned again. "It ain't the end of the world yet, old buddy. Lighten up."

Ned finds Jake offensive. Where does he get off talking to him that way?

"Yep, sure am sorry about your loss, young sir, but what's dead is dead. Don't ever try to bring the dead back and don't kid yourself about how come they're dead and you ain't." He won't look at Ned. He searches the water for a lighthouse, a ship, a shark. Ned feels something. Maybe Jake is a psychic? Jake finally seems to feel Ned's glance and he greets it with a lazy half-smile. "You know what I mean, Ned, sure you do."

"Who are you?"

"Nobody in particular, I guess. I've gotten to that point in life where only inner names matter, the ones between you and God."

"Spare me, mister," Ned's got to get away from this weirdo. Who needs that kind of crap from an absolute stranger? It takes all kinds—

Laura told him she didn't like her family. She told him she hated growing up here. Ned stands outside the house she used to live in. It's a small white frame house with prim green shutters and an overgrown rose garden out front. Her Aunt

Harriet brought her up. Her dad, a man she professed to hate, lived there off and on, a man named Frederick Petersen who had married Harriet's sister, Judith Campbell, Laura's mother. Judith had died giving birth to Laura.

Someone looks out the front door. Someone leaves the front porch, someone old and bent, a soft prune of a woman.

"You there—what do you want? Stop staring! Stop staring!"

Ned can't move. The tiny woman all dressed in black carries a walking stick with a brass tip. She points the stick at him and hobbles down the walk. "Can't you leave a body alone? Haven't you any common courtesy—"

"Harriet?"

"I don't know you—"

"I'm one of Laura's friends. I thought I'd pay my respects—"

She radiates a pain much greater than his. Ned comes face to face with her, or rather, her face to his chest. He lowers his gaze to see her better. The old woman fights back tears. "I'm sorry; I'm sorry. My neighbors don't like me and they're always gawking, nosing around, making fun of me. Maybe they don't even know about Laura. Lord knows I'm getting on. I take everything to heart, you see. You knew Laura, did you? How can you know Laura? Didn't think anyone could, she was so crazy. I loved her but she was crazy, poor soul."

"I'm sorry I missed the funeral."

"Wasn't much of one. Her father was such a bastard. Still is. He didn't come either. He's off farting around New York or somesuch pit of evil. He drove her out of Greystone Bay, then he left right behind her. Good riddance to bad rubbish I say. But not Laura. Poor Laura."

"Nana?" A sweet sound from the porch from a woman with long brown hair and sad blue eyes, eyes like Laura's, large and deep-set. "You want some tea? Do you want to invite him in?"

* * *

She looks very much like Laura without her hair dyed blonde. She looks enough like her to be related and she is, she's Laura's cousin, Anne.

"I was named after *Anne of Green Gables*. My mother thought my hair would turn out red like hers but it turned out just plain brown," she explains over tea and sandwiches. She sounds very much like Laura, only her grammar is better and her clothes far more elegant. Anne finished high school and two years of college. She works at the local newspaper, or what passes for one. "I've been intending to finish up my degree, but you know how it is. Things cost."

She lives with Harriet in the tiny white house. She's over thirty and has a peace about her that Laura never had.

Ned wants peace. He feels something very wonderful. He holds her hand for a moment before he leaves and asks her if she'll have dinner with him that night. Amazingly, she accepts his invitation and they make plans to meet at a sea-food restaurant, the Dinner Bell, at seven.

Going back to the hotel, Ned notices that the closer he gets, the more he dreads entering his room with the big windows. It's so lonely. He thinks about Laura and then about Anne. She's similar to Laura but their eyes, though the same color, are very different.

The stone dogs greet him with a silent snarl.

Her eyes are not lost. They laugh with light. He holds her hand tightly. He feels corny, like a butterfly in a sun-dappled meadow. He feels drunk, but not too drunk. She talks about all the things he likes to talk about but he has no idea at all what they're talking about. He thinks they're eating lobster. She's telling a terrible joke. Over dessert (key lime pie or lemon chiffon?) she brings the talk around to Laura. He doesn't want to talk about her but she insists.

"Were you her boyfriend? She mentioned someone in her

last letter, a friend who was trying to help her get straight. Was that you?''

"Maybe.'' His fork makes swirls in the creamy pie.

"Were you in love with her?''

Hands seem to encircle his throat, choking out the air. He coughs into his napkin and shrugs non-committally.

"I know about Laura. I was always fascinated by her when I was growing up. She was three years older than me, glamorous. She was always the bad girl and I was the boring little Miss Goody Two-Shoes, not that I really wanted it that way. I was too shy to be anything else or too scared, I don't know. I wanted to be more like her. She did anything she wanted, wore fake eyelashes, dyed her hair, always had a boyfriend.'' Anne pushes her pie away. "But she was never satisfied, never happy. She hated her father—they had awful fights. She used to come to my house—my parents were alive then—they died in a car accident up in Maine two summers ago—when they'd have some real knock-down-drag-outs. Aunt Harriet coldn't go anything with either of them. Always fighting. I think her father was angry that Laura lived and her mother died. I guess he held her responsible. It's sad.'' Anne stops, reaches her hand across the table and touches his hand.

"I wish I could've stopped her.''

"Stopped her from killing herself?''

"Well, it seems you ought to be able to do something like that. I wanted to. I knew she was going to do it—I *knew* it— it's my hobby, see, you might think it's crazy but I *see* things sometimes. I *know* things sometimes—it's a responsibility— a gift—''

"A curse. I know.''

"What do you know?''

"Things.'' They stare at each other with surprise. Thoughts leak out and inter-mix.

* * *

"You mean you're a psychic?" His voice is low and incredulous.

"I don't know. Tea leaves, Tarot cards, palms, crystal balls and dreams? I think you're fooling yourself when you use those sort of things to predict the future. You can't predict the future. All you can do is know your habits, predilections, yearnings and sometimes only half-vaguely. You can know what you really think and that predicts what's likely to happen if you follow what you think is going to happen. All those things are just tools to open your subconscious. Do we see the future or only what you want to see? I don't think anyone can bear it. Even if you know it you don't recognize it usually because you're never strong enough. You know?" Anne sips her cold coffee and frowns. "Is that waiter staring at us? Do they want to close or something?"

"Let's get out of here."

He leaves another enormous tip with his bill, wondering what the hell he's doing it for. He'll be broke by the time he returns to Cedar Bridge.

They continue their conversation along the boardwalk, holding hands tightly. "So, basically, you don't believe people can see the future?"

"You might feel something, a hint, maybe, but it's important not to base your life around it. We have the ability to say yes and no, remember—"

"I think I use the Tarot like therapy—self-therapy—"

"Yeah." Anne smiles in the dark. He pulls her closer. The silence entwines them for a few minutes, sheltering. Ned's loath to break it but can't stop his next words from bubbling out. "I brought my deck, or thought I had—to the hotel with me—and I got them out the other night and someone had switched them. The cards were absolutely blank."

"That's funny. Who'd do that to you?" They're coming to the hotel. Ned's afraid to ask her up, so he's just going to kind of lead her there, hoping she won't protest. They don't have to make love or anything, Lord knows one must be careful these days, but he wants the night to last forever, or at least a few hours more.

"I don't know, but it sure got to me. It seemed so cruel somehow. My cards are important to me. I miss them when they're not there, especially the sun card."

"Why?" They're going past the dogs now. Are they smiling? Is one dog letting his tongue hang out like he's thirsty? She's not saying a word. She wants to be with him, too. Astonishing.

"He always makes me feel better." That's an understatement. He won't tell her about the time he kept getting the Tower of Destruction, the Death card, and the Devil card and how he got so mad he threw the whole deck across the room, then stomped and yelled at them like they were alive and how later, after he thought he'd picked them all up, there was the Sun card smiling up at him from the closet floor. He'd practically wept with joy he was so glad to see it.

They went straight to his room, still holding hands. They went to his bed and sat down.

"Why don't you show me those cards," she whispers.

He's afraid to but he's getting the fake deck out. She's cross-legged on the bed, arms crossed too, head down, her curly hair obscuring her features. "Why do you think of the Sun card as masculine? Isn't it odd how people think the sun is male and the moon is female. I've always thought that was strange."

He sits beside her, hands her the deck of cards in its worn box. She unties the bandana around it and opens the box. She turns the first card over. The Sun card smiles up at her. Ned screams.

"Maybe you were dreaming or maybe you were just worn out from grieving about Laura." He's resting against her breasts, soft and gentle against his cheek. He wants to cry but he can't. He's too tired.

"Yeah, probably."

"You want me to stay?"

"I want you to stay," he says, kissing her.

"You know I feel I've known you for a hundred years."

"Me, too," he says, "but we don't have to—you know—"

"Really?" she laughs.

He laughs, shuts his eyes and kisses her, thinking of those damn blank cards. He could've sworn they were all blank. Is he going to die? Is that what his vision meant? He's frightened. She moves away from him, goes to open one of the windows to let fresh air in. It's cool but refreshing. She left the box open and the Sun's been blown off the top, now a page stares face up at the ceiling. It should be face down. It annoys him. He gets up to shut the box and tie the red bandana around it, tightly, securely.

Anne's in bed, wrapped in the coverlet. Her bare shoulders shine in the darkness, softly. He joins her, pulling back the coverlet, he stares at her pale belly. It has a face.

"Ned, what's wrong?"

"I don't know—the cards—me—who knows." He doesn't remember undressing. He doesn't remember the lights going off. Things happen so fast.

"Be still," she whispers and they curl into each other. "Let's go to sleep."

His arms encircle her, fingers brushing the side of her torso. The belly's right there. It's smiling, probably. Ned knows he is.

He watches her pack. He's stayed three weeks in Greystone Bay and now Anne's going to return with him to Cedar Bridge for a visit. Maybe he can convince her to stay. He thinks she's going to stay. She's quit her job. He sometimes sees Laura's image faintly stamped across Anne's features but every day they grow fainter. He feels like some magical gift has been bestowed upon him.

"I really knew it, though," he suddenly says, holding a pair of Anne's panties. The material is pink and lacy. Anne snatches them away, smiling. "Knew what?"

"That Laura was going to kill herself."

Anne flinches like he's just slapped her. "I'm sorry but when you get right down to it I can't believe that."

"I didn't mean to know. Maybe I was hit on the head when I was a kid."

Anne closes the suitcase, zips it up and starts going through her cosmetics bag. "I guess I'd better take my electric curlers, just in case."

"You said you knew things sometimes, back at the restaurant, remember?"

"I know what I said!" She slams a hairbrush down and holds a rat-tail comb like a weapon. "Can't you just drop it? It was just talk. Maybe I know things, but just general stuff, like how I really feel. God, can't you just drop it? Does it do any good—just tell me if it does any good? I mean, Laura died. I knew something bad was going to happen to her just because of the way she lived her damned life. Her daddy beat up on her all the time and Laura did it all, drugs, bad sex, booze—you name it, she did it. Maybe not drugs—you never knew for sure. She talked a lot. She was tough. Oh God, she liked to play like she was. But I liked her. But she was mean, too. When we were kids she used to pull the heads off my Barbie dolls and bury them out in Aunt Harriet's flower bed. She'd tell me and I'd go digging up the flower bed and never find them. She'd just laugh." She drops the comb, searches Ned's face earnestly. "You say you think you could've stopped her. Well you didn't. Some things you can't change."

He thinks of all his readings. Some hobby. His serene pose of Mr. Know-It-All Magic Counselor telling everyone how to take care of their lives when his own was such a joke. "I'd like *not* to know."

Her face is like that of the Queen of Cups. "Well, just do that." She takes a tube of mascara off her dresser. She waves it through the air like a scepter. "I think we both spend too much time thinking."

He checks out of the hotel at noon. The young girl has been replaced by a white-haired woman with arthritic hands and a genuine smile. The porter who takes his bag out to his car, however, is the same dour soul. His expression refuses to change even after Ned gives him quite a decent tip, considering he's running low on funds and will have to stop by a cash machine before he picks up Anne.

He leaves all the cards, except for Mr. Sun, back in the hotel room. He clips that card to his sun-visor.

Anne greets him with a bear hug and they throw her gear into the back of his Toyota with gleeful abandon. Ned feels great. It's an Indian summer sort of day; even Aunt Harriet brims over with sincere joy as she waves them down the road.

Ned feels like something's been pressing down upon him the entire time he's been in the Bay. Even when he was with Anne, there had been such pressure. As they go past the city limits sign, the release continues to grow. He's almost giddy with the freedom surging through his bones.

"Do you think we'll ever go back?" Anne says, putting her window down to let the wind in. The sun's hot.

Ned sinks down into himself, searching for a premonition, a feeling, a clue. Shockingly, he finds he has no earthly idea. Panic wells up inside as he studies this newfound blankness. He thought his gift of second sight was a birthright, an attribute forever his and unchangeable.

He slows down. Anne gazes at him apprehensively. "What's wrong?"

"I don't know."

"Did you eat breakfast? We'll eat a big lunch. I can't wait to see Cedar Bridge. You do still want me to come, don't you? You could take me back to the Bay if you have reservations suddenly. I mean, I don't blame you—it's okay." Her voice sputters out; she ducks her head.

"No, no, I'm glad you're coming. I asked you to come." Blank cards spinning through his universe. Dreams of nothing. Just living day to day without knowing anything—without *thinking* you know anything. Accepting not knowing anything. It's so enormous. You could get lost. The face on the belly. Someone's taken away my pacifier, Ned thinks. "I've just entered a foreign country," Ned says softly.

"No, it's just Fannin county. There's a place that makes incredible hamburgers—"

"Anne—"

She pulls her hair back into a wide tortoise-shell comb. He loves how curls escape down the nape of her neck. "What's wrong, Neds?"

"Don't do that," he says sharply. Only Laura can call him Neds and she's dead. He remembers Laura. He must not forget her even though it hurts like a wound whose scab has been torn off too soon. The face on the belly, Laura's face, blemished, flushed with dread. And then another face, a child's face. And then another. Face after face, unknown faces, known faces. He didn't love her. He doesn't love them. He doesn't love. He can't love. It's too dangerous to love. Especially when you know what will happen. Or even if you think you know.

"Okay." She spies Mr. Sun clipped to his sunvisor. "Hey, what's this for?" She grabs it and grins. "You don't need this—"

In frozen horror, Ned watches her roll down the window and toss it out into the rushing air. He hits the brakes and the car squeals to a spinning stop, throwing Anne against the dashboard. They've made violent contact with a concrete wall, crumpling the bumper. Anne's seatbelt had not been of much use, being improperly fastened. He stares at her. She gingerly touches her bleeding forehead.

"You okay?"

"I'm okay," she whimpers, avoiding his eyes.

"You had no right to do that," he says. He opens his door and gets out to assess the damage and to retrieve Mr. Sun.

Laura was like Anne, self-absorbed and presumptuous, always putting her needs before his. She always expected him to read her cards, make him say that everything was going to be glorious, fabulous, wonderful. Well, life's not like that. It's hard, horrible, lonely, cruel.

He searches the ground like a bloodhound. He finds weeds, dirt, glass, beer cans, newspaper, condoms, and a bluejay's feather. His eyes burn from all the looking, but finally he finds the card caught haphazardly in a barbed wire fence. He disentangles it gently. How warm it feels in his hands. He tucks it into a pocket and turns back towards the car.

He has to make this woman understand he's not responsible for her life nor is she responsible for his. The car door remains open, the tip of it gouging a hole in the ground. A tree spills golden leaves upon the hood of the car. The concrete wall bears a huge crack in its gray façade. Surely his car didn't do that. He marvels at how lucky they were not to have been seriously hurt. His reckless driving should've drawn the attention of someone. He looks across his shoulder, expecting a policeman and flashing red lights. The highway is empty.

"Anne?" He gets in the car and looks for her but she's not there, the front seat curiously vacant. Maybe she had to pee. He laughs. Pee-pee. He feels suddenly child-like and happy, breathlessly young. He hadn't realized how much the card meant to him. He pats his pocket lovingly. *Means* to him.

"Anne—sweetie—Anne?" He gets out, walks around the

car, searching the landscape. A breeze showers more autumn leaves; he brushes a few from his hair. It's getting late. He'll get into the car and wait. She'll come back. He has to be patient.

The seat's still warm. He sits quietly. He turns the key in the ignition to make sure the engine's not dead. The motor hums. He'll listen to the radio. She'll come back very soon. The sun begins to set and Ned reaches up to move the visor. Mr. Sun smiles down at him. Neddy gapes in astonishment. He fumbles in his pocket for what he rescued from the fence. He pulls it out and stares at white cardboard.

Expect nothing.

Ned begins to cry.

Nothing.

ROOM SERVICE
by
Les Daniels

Geoffrey Darling needed a rest, as he would have been the first to tell you. He might not have been so quick to tell you that he only hoped a rest would be enough.

It really wasn't his fault. If his nerves were frayed, it was because he feared that soon his collars might be frayed as well. And why shouldn't he be afraid? Why shouldn't he be frayed? He was fifty-three years old, and he was down to his last half-million.

The way his stocks had been behaving, it had begun to look like he might last longer than his inheritance. This thought had been so unpleasant that it had summoned up its opposite: the idea that he might die with some of the family fortune still unspent. He was evidently doomed to be a pauper or a corpse, and with this realization had come the revelation that the cosmos was conspiring against him.

If brokers could not be trusted then it followed, as taxes follow capital gains, that bankers were no better. And it was in his bank, when he converted all his assets into a briefcase filled with cash, that Geoffrey Darling first noticed how unpleasant people's faces really were. The looks he received were furtive, greedy, and suspicious, and sometimes worse than that. For just an instant he thought he saw something in the bank manager's features that simply should not have been there. Darling made a determined decision that he would never put what he had seen into words, but he had difficulty in keeping the picture out of his mind.

He would have been obliged to dismiss his household help even if their faces hadn't started acting funny too; the expense of their wages was enough to make them intolerable, and of course they menaced the briefcase by their very presence. Having the money at home proved less comforting than Darling had hoped; now that he was safe from swindlers he began to feel threatened by thieves.

He cut himself off from his few acquaintances without much sense of loss and sat alone in his house. Going out meant either abandoning his fortune or else carrying it through streets clogged with twisting forms and faces. Instead he wandered through his empty rooms, often with the briefcase clutched in his hand. He thought of his past. He did not feed himself. He began to think that he would lose his reason.

Something had to be done.

His memory finally offered him a way out. Standing in his cheerless dining room, his mind drifting, he suddenly recalled a place he had not seen for almost half a century. He had been happy there one summer with his mother and his father, both long dead. He had been a boy.

The place he remembered was the SeaHarp Hotel, in Greystone Bay.

He was not surprised, somehow, to discover that the hotel still existed; he was not even surprised when he was able to book a room for that very night. He put down the phone and began to pack.

And so it was that Geoffrey Darling came to the SeaHarp Hotel. The bus trip would have been hell for a man of his background even at the best of times, but he hardly dared to drive when things were so likely to change in front of his eyes without a moment's notice. So he sat rigidly in a public conveyance, directly behind the driver, holding the briefcase in his lap, his eyes squeezed tightly shut. Hours dragged by.

The driver, who half-believed that his passenger must be blind, announced their arrival with unnecessary heartiness, and even helped Darling to step down from the bus. Darling swallowed hard, took a deep breath, and opened his eyes.

He was saved. The breeze at his back had the nostalgic, heady bite of ocean air, and the view through the opening in the hotel's high stone wall beckoned him like a dream from a happy and secure boyhood. He ran up the six stone steps toward the broad expanse of perfectly trimmed lawn, inhaling the aroma of freshly cut grass. He stepped off the walk onto the springy turf and whirled around like the central figure of some arcane child's game, his outstretched arms swinging suitcase and briefcase, his eyes wide as the brightness of the bay spun past them. He stopped to stare at the SeaHarp, and he saw that it was good. In fact, it was perfect. Somewhere in the back of his mind he might have realized that the sight which gladdened his heart was surely the product of painstaking restoration, yet the conviction remained that he had been transported into the world of nearly fifty years ago. The peaked and gabled whiteness of the old hotel, topped by countless chimneys and surrounded at its base by a cool, shaded porch, looked to him like the shrine at the end of a pilgrimage.

Not even the figures strolling on the lawn or relaxing on the porch furniture seemed threatening to him: they had the easy elegance that only wealth and leisure bring, an utter absence of vulgarity and avarice. He felt that he could empty out his briefcase and spread its green bounty on the endless stretches of green grass without the slightest apprehension, the money camouflaged not by its color but by the grace of people who would doubtless make their way among the bills as if they were no more than fallen leaves.

Still, it was best to be prudent.

He ambled in a blissful trance toward the building, passing a handsome woman in a flowered print who smiled at him pleasantly. A bird was singing somewhere, and the sun on Darling's bald spot was just precisely warm enough. Four distinguished old gentlemen were playing cards on the porch, with four glasses of what must have been very distinguished old whiskey on the table in front of them. Despite their occupation, each one of them looked up and nodded to him as he passed, acknowledging him as one of their own. A waiter hovering discreetly behind a potted plant bowed slightly, one eyebrow raised a millimeter in a silent offer of assistance.

"I know the way, thank you," said Geoffrey Darling.

He found the entrance, the glass-panelled doors that he remembered, and paused in front of them for a moment, beaming with anticipation. Then he stepped inside, and his happiness in what greeted him there caused his joyful view of the SeaHarp's exterior to fade into insignificance.

Now he was truly home. He hurried through the foyer and turned right toward the huge and elegantly appointed lobby, the soles of his shoes gliding noiselessly over oriental carpets whose intricate patterns he swore he could remember. He recalled lying on them, beside his father's chair, and studying the designs with great delight. It might have been yesterday.

Of course it would not do for him to lie on the carpets now, or to roll on the grass, but there was no reason why he could not take his father's place in one of those deep, dully gleaming leather chairs, a glass in one hand and a fine cigar in the other. Those would be more pleasant burdens than the ones he carried now, ones which he could soon lay down with perfect safety. Every face that he saw here was as it should be. No unsuitable guests would be permitted at the SeaHarp Hotel. A blessed mantle of peace descended upon his shoulders as he made his way toward the registration desk. Even the woman who greeted him there, despite her harsh face and severe clothing, was clearly one of the better sort, reminding him somehow of his maiden aunt, Martha.

"My name is Darling," he said. "Geoffrey Darling."

"Oh, yes. Mr. Darling. Welcome back."

"Thank you," said Darling, pleased and then slightly puzzled. "Did I mention when I called that I'd been here before?"

"There's no need to mention it, Mr. Darling. The SeaHarp never forgets its friends."

Darling smiled for the first time in months. He actually felt himself blushing. "I haven't been here since I was a boy," he said. "With my parents. Coming back here now makes me feel as if I'm coming home."

"The SeaHarp is my home, too. It's been in our family since 1903. My name is Noreen Montgomery."

It never occurred to Geoffrey Darling that he was breaking precedent when he reached across the counter to shake the hand of someone who, to one way of thinking, was really no more than a desk clerk. He was no longer thinking that way.

"I've given you room 403," she said. "It overlooks the Bay."

Darling was catapulted back in time. He could not have remembered his old room number if his life had depended on it, but what he heard rang with undeniable truth. Room 403. His parents had been settled in more elaborate quarters on the second floor, but he remembered what a proud little fellow he had been, at the age of seven, to have a room of his own, with his own key. And he was proud again as Noreen Montgomery handed him the old-fashioned key with its sea-green tag. 403.

"I hope you'll be happy here again," she said.

"I'm sure I will be."

"Then I hope your stay will be a long one."

She punctuated her remark by rapping sharply on the small bell beside the stack of registration cards. Darling turned to gaze expansively at his fellow guests. He was delighted by their dignity and decorum. Their noses did not writhe into obscene configurations, their eyes did not slither from their sockets, their mouths did not stretch unspeakably wide. Of course not. He was safe at home. He did not even realize that he had left his briefcase on the carpet while shaking the hand of his hostess.

He did realize it, however, when a sea-green arm reached out and snatched the briefcase from the floor. Darling was too shocked to speak. He reeled, and then he realized that the arm belonged to the bellboy. He was sorely tempted to snatch the bag back anyway, but he didn't want to draw attention to himself, and he didn't want to embarrass his hostess. Offering a sheepish grin in her direction, he surrendered his suitcase as well.

"Room 403, Harold," she said.

Still somewhat befuddled, Darling followed the bellboy, resplendent in his smart sea-green uniform with its gold braid. The uniform might have been smart, and indistinguishable from the ones in Darling's memory, but its fit was not exactly perfect. The boy was just a little bit too fat. This was the first touch of the tawdry that Darling had observed in what was otherwise a perfect setting. It was hardly worth noticing, of course.

When they reached the elevators, the boy pushed a button and turned to face the man he served. The smile he offered was somewhat lopsided, and his face was faintly sunburned. There was a pimple on his forehead. Just an adolescent hoping to shed his puppy fat, thought Darling, but still not quite up to SeaHarp standards. The elevator door slid open.

Inside they were alone, and as the elevator lurched upward Darling kept his eyes on the ceiling. It was more pleasant than gazing on the unfortunate Harold, who, with his round pink face, pug nose, and straw-colored hair, really did look something like a pig. Not the boy's fault, of course, but he did nothing for the decor. The Montgomerys shouldn't have hired him. Then again, perhaps he was a poor relation. Darling decided he could afford to be charitable. He would tip the boy a dollar.

Room 403 was just a few steps from the elevator, and the chubby bellboy scurried toward it, beating Darling by several lengths. He had the suitcase under his left arm, and the briefcase in the same hand. With his right hand, he reached out.

"May I have your key, please, sir?" The cracked voice, evidently in the midst of changing, was no more pleasing than its owner's appearance. Darling dropped the key into the expectant, pudgy palm.

The lock clicked, and the sight of 403 as the door swung open was enough to dissipate Darling's vague feeling of distaste. The room was perfect, from the elegantly faded carpet to the swirled plaster of the ceiling. The furniture was far from new, but it was solid, substantial oak, each piece worth a furlong of formica. Darling would not have changed a thing, and he had a feeling that for forty-seven years the owners had been of the same opinion. It was his room. He was in heaven, and soon he would be there alone.

"Just put the bags anywhere," he said as he reached for his billfold. "That will be all, thank you."

He didn't like the feel of the damp, puffy hand when he put the dollar into it, but a moment later the boy was gone. Darling locked the door. He also used the chain. Then he let out a sigh and sank into his overstuffed armchair.

He experienced only a few minutes of blissful thoughtlessness before something began to nag at him. The briefcase had been out of his hands, and out of his sight as well. Could that plump youth Harold, with his round, self-indulgent face, have played some sort of trick with the Darling fortune?

Darling sprang from his chair and dashed across the room. In an instant the briefcase was on the bed and he was fumbling in his pocket for the key. He issued a whistling sigh when the top swung open to reveal undisturbed stacks of grayish green, but nonetheless he rifled through each separate one to make absolutely sure that the inner bills had not been replaced by clippings from *The Greystone Bay Gazette*. Everything seemed to be in order. He manfully resisted the temptation to count the money. After all, he was here for a rest.

He stepped into the bathroom with its sturdy, old-fashioned fixtures and washed his face and hands in ice-cold water. He carefully unpacked his clothes, then decided that a celebratory drink was in order. He left the briefcase under the bed, carefully locked the door behind him, and tried the knob twice to make quite certain. Surely everything was as it should be?

Moments later in the first-floor bar, Darling perched on a padded stool and ordered a double Chivas regal with a splash of soda. He rarely drank, but when he did, he fancied himself a connoisseur. The smoky liquid soothed him, as did the clink of ice against his chilly glass. The bar was dark, and cool, and quiet. No obtrusive music played. Even the bartender was perfect, right down to his waxed and twirled mustache. They exchanged pleasant remarks about the weather, but the man was too well-trained to be intrusive. Two young fellows who virtually exuded cleverness came in and, over vodka gimlets, made what seemed to be informed observations about the stock market. Darling eavesdropped unobtrusively, his pulse quickening ever so slightly. While he wondered if he might have acquired a useful piece of inside information, he naturally began to think about his money, alone and unguarded on the fourth floor. He signed his bill and sauntered toward the elevators, determined to display no panic, but he broke into an ungainly run when he saw the door of one car sliding shut in front of him. He managed to thrust an arm into the opening, and triumphantly got aboard.

The only other passenger was the bellboy, Harold. It hardly seemed possible, but in less than an hour the creature's face seemed even pinker, and had definitely sprouted another pimple. The bellboy, whose hands were empty, stared straight ahead as if he were alone. Darling found this behavior suspicious. Might this porcine peasant have been on his way to 403? It was certainly possible. The fact that he got off on the third floor did nothing to alleviate Darling's anxiety, for it was just what a criminal under observation might be expected to do. In fact, it was as good as a confession.

Darling dashed from the elevator toward his door and fumbled for his key. He continued to fumble. In a state of mounting hysteria, he went through all his pockets twice. His key was gone. Somehow, in the elevator, the bellboy must have picked his pocket.

Darling moaned, and then recalled an incident downstairs when the bartender had asked to see his key, a commonplace enough occurrence when a hotel guest sought to sign for services. Incredibly, Darling had left his room key on the bar.

He couldn't wait for the elevators. Instead, he hurried down the stairs, all three flights, then staggered across the foyer to arrive, puffing and palpitating, at the precise spot where he had sat only a short time before.

"My key," he gasped. "What have you done with my key?"

The mustached bartender looked at him and smiled. He held the precious key up, but Darling hardly noticed it. Instead, he was staring in horror at the ends of the fellow's mustache, which were twisting and twirling into knots that

resembled nothing so much as the tails of pigs. The bartender's cheeks were swelling into ham-like buttocks when Darling snatched for his key and turned away shuddering.

He stumbled back up the three flights of stairs, his head
throbbing. He would not stop to consider what he had seen
until he had reached the security of 403. He swayed, wheez-
ing, on the fourth-floor landing, and as he started toward his
door he caught a glimpse of something sea-green disappearing around the corner of the corridor. He paused for a moment, then set out in hot pursuit, but when he stumbled into
the next section of hallway he found it empty. He heard an
elevator door open and close, ran for the noise, but was too
late. He rushed twice around the entire length of the floor's
square of corridors, and then collapsed against his own door,
the key still held in his cramped fist. He turned it in the lock
and all but fell into his sanctuary, crawling across the carpet
and feeling desperately under his bed.

The money was still there. This time, he counted all of it.
Somehow the ritual soothed him, especially when he discovered that he had not lost a cent.

He locked and chained his door and took a cold shower
with the bathroom door locked too, the briefcase resting on
the toilet top. Then he lay down naked on the bed, the money
right beside him. He cuddled the leather case like a pillow.

Nobody could blame him for being upset when he was
locked out of his own room. It was only natural. And it was
only natural (well, almost) that the bartender's face had
changed. It had only happened for a second; in fact, it probably hadn't happened at all. Just imagination. And somehow
Darling knew that it was all the fault of that damned bellboy.

He dozed fitfully.

When he opened his eyes the room was dark, and for an
instant he had no idea where he might be, but when he realized he occupied Room 403 of the SeaHarp Hotel he was
content. He was also very hungry, and a little ashamed of

himself for making such a fuss about his own forgetfulness. It was after nine. He dressed himself (just like a big boy), and to make a point he left the briefcase on top of the bed when he went downstairs for a late supper. But he did lock the door. After all.

The huge dining room had emptied out by this late hour, and Darling dined alone, accompanied only by the one waiter who was still on duty. Was there just a trace of resentment on the waiter's face at being called back to work when he might otherwise have gone home early? Surely not. Not on his face.

Darling dined on an elegant filet of sole stuffed with crabmeat, and he drank two glasses of the white wine his waiter recommended. He went without dessert, partly out of sympathy with the patient waiter, and partly because he wanted to get back to the room. He paid the check in cash so that he could keep his key in his pocket.

Room 403 was apparently untouched, but Darling counted the money again anyway, and when things didn't come out right he counted it again to reassure himself. Twice was enough. Enough was enough. He wished he had something else to do. There was no television in the room, and he hadn't thought to bring something to read. To alleviate his boredom he read through the notices and pamphlets by the telephone, discovering in the process that he still had fifteen minutes before room service closed down for the night. He didn't feel sleepy and he didn't want to stay up all night counting, so he called room service and ordered a double scotch and soda. After hanging up he realized that he hadn't asked for any special brand, but he decided it didn't really matter.

He put the briefcase under the bed and sat staring at the wall until he heard a knock. He opened the door and saw Harold.

"Just leave it here let me sign for it here's a dollar good night," rattled Darling, keeping his head down as he grabbed the tray and wrote his name in one jittery gesture. This time he was careful not to let his hand touch the bellboy's while the tip was exchanged.

Darling shut the door. He locked and chained it. He heard a noise from out in the corridor that might have been a cough or a sneeze or even a laugh, but in truth was none of these. It was a grunt.

And even in the dim light of the hallway, even with the brief glimpse Darling had allowed himself, there could be no doubt that the bellboy's turned-up nose had transformed itself into the hideous pink snout of a full-grown hog.

Darling downed the drink in one long gulp and almost choked, but the scotch did not relax him. He counted out the five hundred thousand dollars once and then again before his eyes grew so blurry that he had to close them.

When he slept, he dreamed.

He dreamed of Harold, Harold with a snout and blue bib overalls, Harold wading up to his ankles through an endless field of mud, Harold approaching a crudely constructed pen and slopping his brother hogs with hundred dollar bills, Harold ripping off his clothes and crawling naked through the fence to join the feast.

Darling sat up with a start. He saw his little room filled with summer sunlight, and experienced such deep relief that his fears were forgotten almost at once. He had been dreaming, nothing more. He leaned back against the pillows, and within a minute was aware of no emotion save a growing appetite. He reached for the phone and had almost punched the number for room service when suddenly his finger stopped short in mid-air. He had forgotten about the bellboy.

Darling considered this point carefully. He knew without a doubt that the loathsome Harold was the cause of his distress, the one discordant note in the soothing symphony that the SeaHarp had promised him. He refused to be the wretched lad's prisoner, yet discretion was advisable for his own sanity's sake. Surely, though, an employee who had worked from afternoon to midnight would have the morning off? He might even have the entire day off! Darling decided to take a chance. He picked up the phone again and ordered soft-boiled eggs, sausages, and whole wheat toast. He also requested a copy of the local paper, which he learned to his dismay was the only reading matter in the entire hotel. Still, it was better than nothing. There was a bookshop nearby, room service said, but Darling didn't think he would be ready to leave the hotel for some time.

He got up to unlock the door and put on his robe, then settled back into bed, under the covers and over the briefcase. It seemed hardly any time at all before the knock came. Despite his best intentions he felt a tightening in his chest that choked his voice as he blurted out "Come in!"

What came, of course, was Harold, but at least it was Harold in disguise. He was still ugly as sin, yet he was in his human form. Perhaps he only changed at night, thought Darling.

"Good morning, sir," said Harold as he put down the tray.

Darling decided to play along.

"Are you the only bellboy working here?" he asked.

"Oh, no sir. I just always seem to be the one on call when you want something, sir."

Darling didn't believe a word he said. There was an awkward moment of silence.

"There's a dollar for you on the dresser," Darling said at last. "You shouldn't work such long hours. It isn't good for your health."

"I like it," said the wretched boy. "I'm saving up." He pocketed his tip and backed away. He was half out of the room when he stopped. He looked apologetic. "Is everything all right, sir?"

"Yes. Whatever do you mean?"

Harold hesitated. "I don't know. You look kind of pale.

Like you might be sick or something.'' He paused again. ''And don't tell anyone downstairs I told you this, but you really shouldn't eat eggs and sausages. They're not that good for you.''

Then he was gone.

Darling was defiant. He clambered out of bed, pulled away the dish cover and prepared to devour his steaming breakfast. Deftly slicing off the top of one soft-boiled egg, he was about to attack the second when he heard a small sound that might have been a squeal. He stared at his opened egg and saw something moving inside it. Something small and pink and shiny, dripping with transparent fluid. The embryo of some misbegotten swine poked forth its quivering snout.

The second egg cracked open by itself, and mucus dribbled from its shattered shell. The sausages began to squirm, blood spurting from their crisp brown hides. They emitted cries of sheer brute agony.

Darling leaped to his feet, painfully aware that they were naked and that liquids were dripping onto them. He had just enough sense to thank God that he had not upset the tray; if he had, the things might be loose in the room. With the steely desperation of a man determined to save his own life at any cost, he picked up the tray, holding it as far away from himself as possible, and rushed to the door. He dropped the tray in the dim hallway with a crash, then slammed the door against invaders. He had torn off his clothes and thrown himself under a shower to wash away the filth before he began to shake and then to scream.

''You really shouldn't eat eggs and sausages. They're not that good for you.''

He stood under the scalding shower for so long that his skin became quite pink, then stared at it in deep dismay. Could he be changing too? He was afraid to look into the mirror, but inadvertantly caught a glimpse of something pink and indistinct behind its steamy surface.

He fled from the bathroom, as naked as a pig, then leaped into the air with a strangled shout when he heard a frantic rattling and saw the door to the hallway being pushed ajar.

He was locked in the bathroom, whimpering and huddled on the floor, before he realized that the figure he had seen was only an old woman with a vacuum cleaner.

"Go away," he moaned. "We don't want any. Don't clean. Just go."

A quavering voice came from the other side of the bathroom door. "Please, sir. I thought there weren't nobody here. Please don't tell Miss Montgomery what I done. I gotta straighten up."

"Don't straighten up," said Darling cleverly, "and I won't tell her anything. Just go now, please."

"Yes, sir. Thank you sir."

Darling thought he heard her go, but he knew that it might be another trick. He also knew that she might have taken the money, but several hours passed before he could bring himself to creep out into his room.

He squatted naked on the floor and counted his money again and again for most of the afternoon. He was ravenous.

He thought almost longingly of the tray outside in the hall. The toast might have been all right. He thought of it, cold and soggy as it might now be, but he realized that it was only bait. As soon as he opened up his door the ghastly bellboy would be there, pretending to retrieve the tray but actually bent on perpetrating some new horror. It was safer to stay inside.

He slipped the briefcase back under the bed, and as he did he noticed something that brought tears to his eyes. It was a newspaper. Some saint from room service had remembered him, and some angel had knocked this one precious item from the tray.

The Greystone Bay Gazette was a typical small-town paper, only twenty-four pages long, but Darling devoured it.

He savored every sentence, every syllable. He blessed the missing child and the unsolved murder. He pored over high school sports statistics. He looked forward to a festival sponsored by a church whose denomination he did not recognize. He laughed at a comic strip he did not understand. And when he was finished, he did it all again.

Night had fallen while he read, and by the time he had memorized the paper Darling felt almost sane again. He was also unbelievably hungry. He had never gone a day in his life without food, and now he knew why. His stomach made its anguish audible. His predicament was terrible enough, but this hollowness only made it worse. He would never be able to think of a way out while he was starving to death.

He stared at the telephone, and desperation gave birth to a plan. It was risky, but he knew what the bellboy wanted.

Darling ordered prime rib, two baked potatoes, a chef's salad, blueberry pie, a glass of milk, two cups of coffee, and a bottle of Chivas regal with a bucket of ice. He put on his robe, opened the door to the hallway, and locked himself in the bathroom.

The wait seemed endless.

Finally the knock came, and then a grunt, and then a rustle. Darling quivered on the edge of the tub. "Room service!" the voice squealed.

Darling took a deep breath. "I'm in the bathroom," he shouted, and his voice was squealing too. "Just leave it on the desk. Your tip is on the dresser."

"All right, sir. Good night, and thank you!"

Darling controlled himself for almost a minute. He was actually drooling when he slipped gingerly out of the bathroom and approached the desk. Everything he had ordered had been delivered. It was too wonderful to be believed.

He approached the meal cautiously, but nothing seemed amiss. He cut himself a tiny piece of hot, red, juicy beef and slipped it tentatively into his mouth. Nothing had ever tasted better. He swallowed and sighed. He sliced himself a more substantial chunk, and had just dropped it onto his tongue when the door to the hallway burst open.

Harold the Hog stood there.

His tiny eyes gleamed scarlet, and his mottled flesh quivered with coarse bristles. His filthy snout dribbled over yellow, discolored tusks. His sea-green uniform was daubed with mud. His mouth fell open, and it was huge.

"Mr. Darling," the bellboy said.

Darling gasped. He felt his heart skip and his throat constrict. He couldn't breathe. He tried to speak, but all he could produce were grunts. He waved his arms ineffectually to ward off the apparition and fell out of his chair. The monstrous bellboy waddled toward him. Darling crawled away. He felt its arms around his waist, its rancid breath on his neck. Both its black hands were clutching at his chest, and he knew they meant to rip his heart out.

Darling was growing weak, his vision blurred, but he reached back and grasped the creature by its tender snout. The thing roared and released its grip, and Darling dragged himself toward his fortress in the bathroom, but in an instant it was on his back again, its arms encircling him. He shrugged it off once more, but felt that it had crushed something inside his chest.

He was dizzy, and the room was dim. He wanted to vomit, but something blocked the way. He felt his bowels loosen. He died disgraced.

Tears dripped down Harold's chubby, pimply, pug-nosed, innocent face.

"You did the right thing to call me first," Noreen Montgomery said. "We mustn't alarm the other guests."

"I did what they taught us," said the blubbering boy. "In Boy Scouts. I did the right thing."

"I'm sure you did, Harold."

"I could see he was choking, so I put my arms around him and I squeezed, just like it says to on the charts. The Heimlich Maneuver."

"That's right, Harold.

"But he fought me. He pushed me away. He even scratched me. Here. Right on the nose. And then he died."

"You did everything you could, Harold. It wasn't your fault. And I know how upset you are. Don't you think it would be best if we say that you weren't here at all, and that Mr. Darling died alone?"

Harold sniffed and looked ecstatic.

"Yes," she reassured him. "That would be the best thing. You just run along home now, Harold, and take tomorrow off. With pay. And don't let this spoil your summer. I'll take care of everything.

"Thank you, Miss Montgomery. It really could be like I never came back, couldn't it? And I never would've, either, but my folks raised me up honest, and when I saw the tip he'd left on the dresser I knew he'd made a big mistake. It should've been a dollar. He never would have given me a thousand dollar bill!"

The boy backed out of Room 403.

And when she was quite certain he was gone, Miss Montgomery reached down under the bed and pulled out Mr. Darling's briefcase.

EVIL THOUGHTS
by
Suzy McKee Charnas

"Oh, Jeff, I didn't mean to be grouchy," Fran said contritely. "It's just that the crazy lady's goddamn dogs were barking again all morning back at the house. What a racket, on and on! I'm afraid it really got to me."

Jeff, hovering, escorted her through the immense dining room of the SeaHarp Hotel. Around them the warm air stirred with a muted murmuring of voices and the occasional chiming of china and crystal. "You're not upset over something about the dinner?"

"God, no, the dinner was wonderful!" she said. "I have to admit, I didn't expect anything this elegant in Greystone Bay."

He squeezed her hand. "Didn't I promise you something better than Wong's?"

Better, and more: a pleasing surprise. The faintly worn luxury of the place reminded her of similar settings in Boston. How strange it was to be so close to her home city, in a place fitted to an old Boston hotel, and yet to feel so far away.

This wistfulness and unease was wrong for tonight. They were celebrating, marking forever in expensive indulgence their first month together in the house he had inherited from his parents, and his first job after accountancy school—working in the business office of this same hotel.

"Actually, Wong's is fine," she said, not wanting to put down the local Chinese joint near the house. "But this is great. A little pampering doesn't bother me, you know that. I'm all overcome to be taken to this—this institution by my very handsome, very poised, very beautifully dressed lover."

Young lover, her thoughts added inevitably. Were those grayhaired people over there staring at them? Did they perhaps know Jeff from his youth here in Greystone Bay, or were they just noticing the tall young man and his older companion?

Oh, stop it, she scolded herself silently. As if anybody gave a damn about that in this day and age!

While he stepped aside to retrieve her coat from the cloakroom, Fran looked out past the tables at the high, dark windows over Harbor Road. Beyond the blurred reflections of people bent to their meals and conversation (*not* watching her and Jeff), she could see the silvered darkness of evening fog, and the smeary lights of the traffic. The sea beyond was invisible. Suddenly the hotel seemed a safe and cosy place, and she wished they didn't have to head home.

But she had work, and he had work. People like them only rented a few hours of this kind of extravagant living anyway. It wasn't really theirs until they had earned it—if they were lucky.

Her mind shied away from the thought of Jeff, richer, but also older, and herself older still.

Jeff held her coat for her. "Sorry about the wine, though," he said as she shrugged it on and walked out with him into the spacious lobby. "I've had some great Merlots in other places."

"Don't worry about it," she said, patting his arm. "I shouldn't have said anything about it. Who cares?"

"You don't, not usually," he said, lightly hugging her shoulders and smiling down at her. "Anyway, are you glad we came here for dinner tonight?"

"Of course," she said. His need to be reassured was endearing.

"Me too," he said. "It was time to get you out of the house anyway, before you grew roots through the floor."

"The house is fine," she said quickly. "It's the neighbors that are the problem. No, just one neighbor."

They walked out into the cool autumn night and down the stone steps at the front of the hotel. A light, tangy wind had been blowing fog in from seaward all afternoon. Now the breeze had a real bite to it.

Fran hugged her coat tighter around her neck.

"I thought it was her dogs that bothered you," Jeff said absently, tucking her arm warmly against him. They walked quickly toward the parking lot.

"Her *and* her dogs," Fran said. "I wish somebody would run over those damn dogs of hers. Save me, Lord, from little dogs! Everybody knows little dogs are crazy, from being so small and scared all the time. And in this case their owner is crazy too."

"Who, Whatsername next door?" Jeffrey said. "I thought she was a nurse. Do they let crazy people be nurses?"

Dear Jeffrey, who so charmingly lived in his youthful mind and was so tolerant even when you pointed out to him the things that should be driving him nuts the way they drove you nuts, even though you weren't an old married couple, only live-togethers, slightly mismatched. By age, anyway.

"No, dummy, not that one. I mean Whatsername across

the street and up two houses," Fran said. "That's where the dogs are. God, Jeff, don't you hear them?"

"Oh, you mean those two mutts of Mrs. Deaken's," he said equably. "Heck, they're probably the only company she's got if she's as daffy as you think."

"Nuttier. No kidding. Did I tell you? She yelled at me for walking back from the park through the lane behind her house. Around twilight yesterday, while the oven was heating up to make dinner, I took a stroll up to that little park. Then I thought I'd come back the long way, through the lane. It looked nice—hidden and a little wild, with all the weeds and the trees hanging out into it from people's back yards.

"All of a sudden her dogs started yapping and a floodlight came on, if you can believe that, at the corner of her house; and she started screaming from inside the house. It was the damnedest thing."

They turned the corner of the long white hotel façade at last and crossed the dark but sheltered expanse of the parking lot behind it.

"Screaming what?" he said. "What did she say?"

"I don't know, exactly, I could only catch a few words. Mostly it was about 'goddamn burglars.' As if a plain ordinary woman walking along a public lane in broad daylight would be a burglar."

"Thought you said twilight," he observed mildly, bending to unlock the red Tercel.

"All right, twilight, but good grief, Jeff, it was ridiculous! I could hear her shrieking, and those damn little dogs of hers yipping, all the way down to the other end of the lane."

"Maybe she's been burgled a lot," Jeffrey said. "Things have changed a lot since I grew up here."

He was probably right. His parents' house had been equipped at some recent point with a fancy burglar-alarm (much too complex, a nuisance to use), which indicated something. Hell, give the crazy lady up the street the benefit of the doubt.

Though crime could hardly be as bad here as in Boston!

Swinging the car out past the parking kiosk onto the street, Jeff said shyly, "Well, as long as dinner was okay."

"It was great, Jeff. Really."

"Good," he said. "For a minute there, I thought Mrs. Deaken's dogs had sort of outweighed everything else tonight. I want you to really like it here, Fran. . . . You know . . ."

"Yes, sweetie, I do," she said, patting his thigh. "That's what I want, too."

The crazy lady's house was dark when they drove past. Her dogs were quiet. They usually were, at night. Thank God for small mercies: there probably weren't any noise ordinances here, and anyway, who was Fran, a newcomer, to make complaints against someone with what she already knew to be the old name of "Deaken" in Greystone Bay?

Jeff opened the car door for her, clearly enjoying the old-fashioned courtesy that she accepted happily only from him. She heard him humming and jingling his keys in his pocket as he followed her up the shallow concrete steps that led up the sloping front lawn.

She turned, under the porch light, and watched him, the gangly height of him, the lively tumble of his auburn hair, his intent young face. How did I get so lucky? she thought. Oh, how did I get so lucky, to have this lovely boy love me?

He had paused on one of the steps, frowning at the lawn.

"Fran?" he said. "How often are you watering the grass? Look. There's a bunch of mushrooms sprouting in the middle of it."

She went back to him to look. Squinting, she could clearly see by the light leaking out through the curtains of the front room a group of pale, striated bubbles clustered on a little rise in the grass. The raised place was a writhe of half-buried

root from the thick-trunked shade tree that one of Jeff's fore-
bears had planted. Roots had surfaced like gnarled dolphins
all over the lawn, making the mowing a chore.

"I water it three times a week," she said. "The handyman
said to, because it's been warm for September."

Not tonight, it wasn't. She felt silly saying it.

"But it's been drizzling, nights," Jeffrey pointed out. "All
that moisture could be bad. Try cutting down a little."

"Sure," she said.

"That's more like it. Now you sound like your agreeable
self," he said.

"I'll agree to anything to get in out of this chill."

"Oh, we can fix that," he said, giving her a kiss on the
neck, and she told him to stop that, not out in the street
please, and he said well let's find a better place then, and
they did.

A perfect end to a perfect day.

The perfection held over to the next morning. She came to
the curb with him as he left for work in the Tercel. They
giggled and made a minor spectacle of themselves, and then
he drove away down the quiet suburban street, back to the
SeaHarp for the day.

Take that, neighbors, Fran thought, palming the hair back
from her cheeks. She almost regretted her youthful looks,
which kept it from being obvious (at any distance, anyway)
that she was older than Jeffrey. "Older woman kisses accountant lover goodbye." Yum.

Never mind, she would show any watching neighbors that
she was a worthy householder. She would tend to her lawn.

The smooth slope of grass from the front wall of the house
down to the sidewalk really was a source of pleasure. The
sprinkler system itself was a thrill—all that control, at the
turn of a handle. All that grass, under the high, dappled can-
opy of one large tree. It was a far cry from the little apart-

ment with the tiny brick patio in Boston, where they had started living together.

She picked her way across the wet grass (alert for deposits left by wandering neighborhood dogs) and inspected the little stand of mushrooms.

They must have popped up overnight. How nice if they should prove to be edible: sauteed mushrooms, fresh picked, some rare type stuffed with healthful and exotic vitamins, no doubt. They wouldn't be indulging in meals at the SeaHarp very often. It would be nice to have some really special, delicious dishes that she could make at home.

But the mushrooms didn't look edible. Each mushroom was about as big as a knuckle, round, and of a particularly unattractive greasy pallor that made her wrinkle her nose. They looked—well, *fungoid*, anything but fresh and whole-some, alien. Alien to the dinner table, anyway, unless it was some French dinner table regularly graced with sauced ani-mal glands.

Well, the daylight would no doubt kill the pallid little knobs. People grew mushroom in cellars, didn't they? Fog or no fog, the lawn was hardly a dark cellar. She was a city girl, not a gardener, but this much she could figure out by logic.

However, there was no more perfection that day.

She typed medical transcripts from her tape machine until the dishwasher made a weird sound and vomited greasy water on the floor. A session with an outrageously expensive plumber, plus his doltish (also expensive) apprentice fol-lowed. She contained her temper with difficulty (who knew when she might need them again, and how many plumbers were there in town?).

At least the ancient and rusted Volks she had brought with her from Boston started without fuss. But when Fran deliv-ered the transcript pages she had finished, Carmella, her sup-plier, informed her that two of the doctors were going on vacation (at the same time, of course). There would be less work for a while.

Fran cursed all the way home (including the stop at the nearest supermarket). If only Carmella had told her at the outset that this was coming!

What could she have done about it, though? Not bought that little rug for the front hallway at the flea market, that's what.

A package had been left for her with her neighbor on the north, a skinny girl who brought it over and introduced herself as Betsy. As Jeff had mentioned, she was a nurse with a late shift at Bay Memorial Hospital, though to Fran she seemed awfully young and feather-headed to be a nurse.

Betsy wandered around admiring the rather scanty furniture and the posters Fran had hung on the walls while she answered Fran's delicate soundings about the neighborhood here on the lower slopes of North Hill.

The "convenience" store down on Woodbane Street was a rip-off joint, but the shoemaker next door to it was okay, if the work wasn't anything complicated. And it was a good idea to keep your car doors locked when parked in your own yard. They had burglaries, which was why so many people had dogs. Not that they did much good. No, Betsy didn't have dogs herself, and neither did her housemates, one an elementary school teacher, one in social work, all three renters from the older couple (now in Florida) who owned the house.

"Anyway," she said, "those two little monsters of Mrs. Deaken's are more than enough for a whole block of the neighborhood."

Fran put aside the totally inappropriate blouse her sister had sent her for her birthday (a birthday which Fran would have preferred to forget) and offered Betsy tea. "What about that woman?" she said, sitting down across the kitchen table from her. "Mrs. Deaken, I mean."

"Oh, she's weird," Betsy said with enthusiasm. "Nutty as a fruitcake, if you ask me. I hear her screaming in her place all the time, just yelling like—well, like my mother used to yell at me when I was giving her a really hard time. At first I thought there was a kid in there with her, and me and my roommates seriously considered calling the cops, in case the old loon was abusing a child or something. It always sounds so violent."

She sat back, shrugging in the oversize shirt that hung flatteringly on her slim frame. "But I've never seen anybody else but Mrs. Deaken herself go in or out, not in a year and a half. So I guess she's just screaming at the dogs, or the TV. I bet she drinks. Female alkies are thin. They drink instead of eating."

Fran admitted that she hadn't seen the crazy lady yet, only heard her.

"Oh, she looks okay, sort of, I guess," Betsy said airily. "But boy, is she nuts."

Fran laughed. "Then it's lucky that Jeff didn't wind up with the place right across from her."

"I'll say," Betsy said vehemently. "She's craziest of all about men, and if that guy I saw leaving this morning was Jeff, she'd be after him in a minute."

"Then she'd have a fight on her hands," Fran retorted. "Jeffrey is mine, as in significant other, or whatever they say these days."

Was it Fran's imagination, or was Betsy surprised at this news? At least she didn't blurt out something like, oh, I thought he was your son.

In the evening before dinner, while the stew simmered, Fran and Jeffrey walked up the block toward the uneven triangle of green that was the tiny local park. It was really just a couple of oddly-shaped lots that had been left green, Jeff said, for some reason. Officially they called it North Hill

Park, but nobody used that large name because it seemed absurd for such a small patch of land.

Passing the crazy lady's house on the stroll back, Fran looked across the street and saw the bluish glimmer of a TV screen inside the front window. The house itself was pretty, with a shapely front porch framing the doorway within, and two jauntily nautical porthole-shaped windows flanking the doorway as well.

Suddenly a report like a gunshot rang from the porch: the screen door banging. Two little dogs came skittering down the bricked walk, barking wildly, and skidded to a dancing halt at the edge of the crazy lady's lawn.

"Jeez," Jeffrey said, protectively clutching Fran's arm. "What did she do, sic them on us? We're not even on her side of the street!"

"I told you," Fran said. "The woman is bonkers."

"Funny, I don't remember her being like that when I was a kid," Jeff said speculatively. "I barely remember her at all, except she was married then, I think. Must have had a tough life since."

"So what?" Fran said. "Everybody's life is tough, but not everybody sics their dogs on innocent passers-by."

"Well, at least they're not Dobermans," he said, looking back at the two bouncing, shrieking animals.

"Shh," Fran said, "you don't want to give her any ideas."

Secretly, she was relieved to have the little dogs come after her and Jeff instead of the crazy lady herself coming out, after what Betsy had said.

She cut the grass the next day with the old hand-mower they had found in the toolshed at the back of the house. The mower stuck a bit on the roots that veined the turf, and she gave up with the job half-done (it was a lot harder than she'd imagined).

But she made sure to drag the machine back and forth a couple of times over the bubbly clot of white mushrooms, like greasy blisters, which had expanded rather than drying up and blowing away. Under the blades, the mushrooms disintegrated with satisfying ease.

The tape she transcribed after lunch was from Doctor Reeves, a plastic surgeon who specialized in burn patients. His dry, dispassionate notes on two children who had been caught in a burning trailer out on the west edge of town made her feel sick.

She quit (there was no rush, with the volume of work slowed to an impoverishing trickle) and went for a walk, hands jammed in her jeans pockets.

This part of lower North Hill was occupied by curving streets of sturdy, solid houses, of modest but comfortable size, in a mixture of styles. Some showed odd and endearing turns of fantasy, like the two with roofs of layered tiling cut like thatched English cottages, and a white house with a miniature fairy-tale tower for a front hallway.

Out of sheer devilment—and to see what would happen—on the way home she walked up the lane again, toward the park.

The sandy wheel-track was choked with weeds, vines, and branches hanging over from the adjacent yards. The lanes, she knew, had once been used for garbage pickup. Then the city had bought a whole new fleet of garbage trucks that were only afterward discovered to be too wide for the lanes, which now served the purposes of kids, gas men who read your meter with binoculars as they cruised slowly through, the occasional pair of parked lovers, and (to judge by the crazy lady, anyway) burglars.

As Fran swung boldly toward the head of the lane, a sharp rapping sound snapped at her from the back of the crazy lady's house. A lean figure in a flowered housecoat glared murderously at her through the closed kitchen window: the crazy lady herself, presumably, in a beehive hairdo, banging her fist on the glass in a kind of maniac aggression.

Fran smiled and waved as if merely returning a friendly greeting and walked on, managing not to flinch from the incredible racket of the little dogs shrilling at her back. The crazy lady must have let the dogs into the side yard just to bark at Fran.

Jesus, Fran thought, striding quickly around the corner and back down the street toward Jeff's house. I shouldn't have waved at her, I should have tossed a rock through her window! Who the hell does she think she is, the witch? The lanes are city property, I can walk in them if I like.

What if she has a gun in there? A paranoid like that, she probably does. Hell, she could shoot me and say she thought I was a burglar.

People like that shouldn't be allowed to live on their own. Tough life or no tough life, Mrs. Crazy Deaken should be in an institution.

The mushrooms were back the next morning, but they were different; Fran couldn't help noticing them when she went out on the porch to look for the mail (it hadn't come yet). They were brown and flat, growing in overlapping layers along the shaggy arm of root that seemed to be the seat of the infestation.

She squatted down and stared at them. They were wet from the overnight rain and their frilled edges glistened a pallid pink.

"Yuch," she said aloud. "What evil-looking mushrooms!" She prodded them gingerly with a twig dropped by the old tree.

"They're your evil thoughts."

It was a hoarse voice from the sidewalk, the voice of the crazy lady.

There she stood, disconcertingly thin and slight in a pastel pants-suit, a cigarette smouldering between two of her sharp-knuckled fingers. She had enough lipstick on for six mouths, and she wasn't smiling.

Fran gaped at her, at a loss for words. The woman looked like a bona fide witch out of a modern fairy tale, and what do you say to a witch who comes calling? With intense pleasure Fran said to herself, She's older than I am. She's older. Old, like a witch is supposed to be!

The crazy lady said, "Have you seen a little dog? He's about a foot high, with black and white spots."

"Uh, no, sorry." Fran said with forced amiability. "I spend most of my time at the back of my house, at my typewriter."

"He got out this morning," the crazy lady said, looking around with a frown. Did she think the dog might pop up at any moment from under Fran's lawn?

Fran said, "If I do see him, I'll be sure and let you know."

"Thank you," the crazy lady said, as if she had never banged on the window or screamed at Fran—maybe she didn't recognize her? She walked away, holding her cigarette hand out from her side at an elegant angle that she must have picked up from Bette Davis in an old black-and-white movie.

Fran stared at the mushrooms. "Those are your evil thoughts?" What kind of a thing was that to say to her?

The woman was a total crackpot, one step short of being a bag-lady. She must be living on an inheritance or the pension left by a dead husband, so she didn't have to wander the streets.

But the mushrooms really did look evil, old and wrinkled and evil. They looked like—

Fran sat back on her heels, blushing. What an idea! They looked like an exaggerated parody of the folds of her vagina, that was what they looked like. No, not hers, some old hag's swollen and discolored sex.

She scrambled up muttering, "Don't be an idiot, you idiot," and with the back of the straight rake she whacked the new crop of fungus to flying fragments.

Over pizza that night with a few of Jeffrey's friends from

the hotel office, she didn't mention the conversation with the crazy lady. She didn't feel altogether comfortable with Jeffrey's friends, except for a woman a little older than herself who was working at the SeaHarp after a divorce.

On her way the next day to pick up some tapes from a back-up source who sometimes gave her work, Fran saw the crazy lady's dog, or anyway it might have been the crazy lady's dog, jittering back and forth on the far side of Woodbane Street. It made one mad dash to cross, was honked at by an approaching car, and dodged back again to the far side where it hopped on its stiff little legs and barked at the traffic.

She considered driving back to tell the crazy lady, but she had lost time over the pizza and beer last night and was in a hurry. And when she got back, Mrs. Deaken was occupied.

She was having an altercation with a jogger, from the safety of her porch. Fran parked and sat in the Volks and watched.

The jogger marked time at the curb, his head turned toward the house with its two round windows flanking the porch. "I'm not doing anything in your yard, lady. I didn't touch your yard."

On the porch the crazy lady stood with her hips shot to one side in an aggressive slouch and shouted furiously, "I saw you on my grass! You ran over my grass!"

"I don't run on grass," he said. "It's slippery, and you can't see your footing." He was middle-aged and a bit flabby around the middle, but he held his ground, running in place while he argued.

"I saw you!" the crazy lady yelled. Her remaining dog shot past her, barking. It made mad little dashes in the direction of the jogger, none of which carried it more than halfway across the lawn. "This is private property! You stay off it!"

"Gladly," the jogger retorted. "Lady, you're nuts, you know that?" He went on toward the park, shaking his head, elbows pumping, pursued by the barking of the dog. The crazy lady began screaming at the dog, which finally gave up barking and sulked back into the house, whereupon the screen door gave another mighty bang and all grew quiet.

Oh the hell with it, Fran thought, I'm not going to say a thing about the damn other dog. Someone like that shouldn't even have pets. The little beast is probably better off in the traffic.

She padded up onto her own patch of grass, where she automatically checked the mushroom site. A new crop, and a different type again, seemed to have sprouted overnight.

There were six of them, tallish, on spindly stalks, and they had elongated, domed caps with dark, spidery markings along their lower sides. Like odd, tiny lampshades trimmed with black lace, or six otherworldly missiles waiting to be launched.

Evil thoughts.

Oh bull, Fran thought, looking up the street at the crazy lady's house. What about her evil thoughts, where are they displayed?

She didn't touch the new crop. She was tired of beating them to bits and then having them show up again. It was too much like losing some kind of struggle, which was ridiculous, because there was no struggle. You don't have a struggle with a bunch of mushrooms.

She blew up at Jeffrey about the records he brought home that night. She hated salsa, and there was the expense, and it didn't help when he showed her that they were second-hand, very cheap, from the used bookstore down near the harbor.

Of course they made up. They made love. But Fran couldn't sleep right away afterward. She lay on her back and amused herself wondering which of her evil thoughts of the day those slender, silvery mushrooms represented.

She paid for the sleepless hours, as usual. In the morning, she looked hagged-out. She always checked herself in the mirror when she woke up, searching for the dry skin and branching wrinkles that Jeffrey was bound to remark on someday.

Not yet, though.

She crawled back into bed and stayed there while he made himself breakfast, so that he wouldn't see her without the repairs of makeup. She knew she looked awful, sagging and bruised around the eyes.

To her gratification, the overnight chill seemed to have killed some of the damned mushrooms. Four of the six had withered so that their caps hung upside-down from stalks that looked as if they had been pinched hard in the middle. The flattened caps drooped inside-out, the blue-black slits of their undersides exposed to the sky. She thought of the gills of strange fish, dead and decaying in the cool morning air, fossil remains of ancient forms from prehistoric seas.

On the other hand, several new growths had come up.

It hadn't rained for two nights. The grass looked a little dry, but she didn't use the sprinklers.

That afternoon Fran took a welcome break from unpacking books and organizing them on the glowing, polished shelves that Jeff's father had built into the walls flanking the front room fireplace. She stepped outside on the porch for a breath of the nippy, sea-scented air, and observed the crazy lady in what seemed at last like civilized conversation with a man out in front of her place.

He was a heavy guy in gray work clothes, and he stood with his head bent, listening to her. Then he would crouch down and examine something in the grass, and stand up and talk, and listen some more, and then they would move over a little and do it all again. For a moment Fran thought, my God, she's got mushrooms too. She felt a tilt of vertigo (evil thoughts, out on show—hers? Or mine, on some kind of northward mushroom-migration? The Thoughts That Ate North Hill Park).

Then she realized that the man was examining the heads of the crazy lady's sprinkler system. You would never have guessed this from the way Mrs. Deaken minced and preened and waved her cigarette. Her voice, if not her words, carried: a high, artificial, mewling tone like the voice of Betty Boop, while her red mouth twisted in a parody of a fetching smile.

She was positively grotesque. Fran watched from her own porch, fascinated and repelled, until the crazy lady sashayed back up to her front steps, trilling over her shoulder in an impossibly arch manner, and opened her screen door. Then came a flurry of screams, presumably at the little dog which must be trying to get out, and finally the customary door-slam.

The man in gray headed for a truck parked in front of Betsy's house.

"Excuse me!" Fran waved.

He ambled over.

"You're a lawn expert, right?" she said. God, he was massive as a steer and she caught a whiff of stale tobacco and beer on his breath. This was what the crazy lady had been flirting with?

She felt a sudden stab of deep, embarrassed pity. After all, mad Mrs. Deaken couldn't be all that much older than Fran was herself, and Fran only had Jeffrey by sheer, wild, undeserved, and unpredictable chance.

"Maybe you could advise me about this mess that keeps coming up over here." She showed the man the mushrooms.

He squatted and stared at them. "I only do sprinklers," he said. "Don't know much about grass. But it's been wet this fall, and it look like you got a dead root running along under here. Mushrooms like to grow on old dead wood."

Strange: the mushroom cluster had changed again. There was a grayish round one, a small gourd, trailing a snaky little stalk like a withered umbilical cord. She preferred the silvery ones with their inky hems, which by comparison at least had a sort of gleaming style about them, the polished perfection of bullets aimed up at her out of the crooked elbow of the exposed root.

"That's a dead root?" she said uncertainly. "I thought all these roots belonged to the big tree, there."

He shook his head and looked around. "Nope. This one's dead, that root there looks dead too. Must have been another tree here once that got took out."

"Oh," she said. "I've never had a lawn before, I don't know a thing about this. The mushrooms aren't likely to spread, then, and crowd out the grass?"

"What, these fellers?" he said, drawing a fingertip along the edge of one of the silvery ones. "Heck, no, they're real fragile. Soon as it gets a little colder you won't see no more of them."

Fran suddenly saw the similarity of the silver mushrooms to penises, polished metal phalluses with veins etched under their skins in delicate black. The lawn man's heavy finger touching one of them made her skin prickle.

"Oh right, sure, I noticed that myself," she stammered, staightening up quickly. "They only last a day or two, and then they just sort of wilt and shrivel up—"

Like an old man's cock, she thought, though the words didn't escape her. Worse and worse. She stood there smiling sickly and thinking, I'm as moronic a spectacle as the crazy lady herself, in my own way.

As the sprinkler man drove off, Fran saw smoke from a cigarette curling up from the shadows under the porch of the Deaken place.

Jeffrey only had time for a short stroll that night, up to and around the park where a couple of dogs were chasing each other, no owners in sight. He remarked that people didn't take care of their pets around here, letting them run loose like that. Fran thought about having seen the crazy lady's other dog and not saying anything to her. She drew Jeffrey home along a parallel street off the park two blocks away, so as not to pass the Deaken house.

"Too bad we can't eat those mushrooms," Jeffrey said as they walked back up toward their front door. "We've sure got a lot of them."

The uplifted caps shone like old silver in the lofty radiance of the corner street light. Fran found herself oddly relieved that Jeffrey noticed them too, that he *saw* them. What would he say if she told him he was seeing her evil thoughts?

"What are you smiling about?" he said.

"Nothing," she said. "A secret joke too dumb to say out loud." She dug her keys out of her pocket and let them into the house. "I hate those damned mushrooms. I think I'll see if I can buy something somewhere, some kind of poison I can use to get rid of them once and for all."

Jeffrey laughed. "You want to poison some mushrooms? That's cute. Speaking of food, by the way, my aunt wants us to come for Thanksgiving."

"What, already?" Fran said. They stood in the dark little hall. "It's still September, for God's sake."

Jeff held her hand, thumbing the knuckles with sensuous pleasure. "She just wants to make sure we don't make other plans first."

"But I want to make other plans," Fran said, shrinking from the prospect of an evening of being delicately put down by Jeff's blue-haired and protective aunt for being an "older woman" instead of some fresh young thing. Jeff's aunt lived higher up on North Hill, in a much bigger house, and it was plain that she didn't think much of people from out of town.

"She's not going to be around forever, you know," Jeffrey said, "and I've only gotten to be, well, friends with her in the past year." He turned on the light, and they trailed through the house getting ready for bed and quarreling in fits and starts.

I look like shit, Fran thought, staring despairingly at her

haggard reflection in the cabinet mirror as she brushed her teeth and got ready for bed. *He's getting fed up with me.*

Had that vein been there before, a bluish-gray pathway under the thin skin of her neck? *Just wait till Aunty sees that!*

In a wave of guilt and self-disgust Fran pushed him away when he touched her breast. They slept with their backs to each other that night.

Two more of the rounded, gourd-like things lay among the dangling corpses of the silver bullets next morning. Fran interrupted her work several times that day to go look at them, sullenly walking around and around the small, cursed spot in the lawn.

Last night she had dreamed of Jeffrey sleeping splayed on his back, a bullet-shaped metallic mushroom growing between his legs.

And these roundish ones, moored to their twisted scrap of vine and showing faint tracery designs under their pale, greenish skin: were they her evil thoughts about Jeffrey's aunt?

The crazy lady must see the mushrooms when she minced down the street with her one dog from time to time, smoking and throwing her hips from side to side like a cartoon whore. No doubt she looks and tells herself, goodness me, look at that—my new neighbor has some very evil thoughts.

"What's the matter?" Jeffrey said at dinner. "I've got restaurant accounts to work on from the hotel, and you're pacing around like a panther. I can't concentrate."

"Carmella returned some of my work today," Fran said bitterly. "Too sloppy, the doc said. Do it better! He should try making out all that slurred garbage he talks!"

"Why don't you go watch TV for a little while?" Jeffrey said.

"Thanks," she snapped, "have you looked at what's on? Just because I didn't finish college, that doesn't mean I'm an idiot, you know, to sit glazed-out in front of an endless parade of sit-coms and cop shows."

"Jeez, I never said—"

He stared up at her, open-mouthed, and for a second she stared back in blazing contempt! God, what a whiny, moon-faced kid he was! No wonder he clung so hard to his aunty's apron strings!

Then the hurt in his expression melted her into a shuddering confusion of fear and contrition—what in the world *was* wrong with her?—and she hugged him and apologized. They ended up in front of the TV together, murmuring and kissing on the couch and neither of them watching the screen.

"I think moving here was harder on you than you realize," he said. "You look tired. I wish I could have been around more, to help you with the details."

She wished he hadn't noticed the marks of strain in her face, the ones she noticed every morning.

Age, real age, so soon? She was only thirty-four, for Christ's sake! It had to be just strain. And he was so sweet about it, how could she resent his remark? But she did.

It turned really cold that night. Leaves covered much of the lawn in the morning, and all of the mushrooms had withered and vanished, except for one of the ovoid ones. Its sibling on the same dessicated vine had shrunk to a wrinkled brown nut, but the other one was now the size of a tennis ball and shone a glassy, livid white.

Like an egg, Fran thought uneasily, studying it. A giant, monstrous egg—a bad egg (naturally). Already a dark veining of decay was visible, like crazing in old porcelain.

No other growths had appeared. Pretty soon the frost would kill this one too, and Fran's evil thoughts would be private again, invisible even to the greedy, burning gaze of the crazy lady up the street.

Fran asked Betsy and her housemates to a Thanksgiving party, and Carmella. Jeffrey said he didn't know what Fran was doing, but he meant to go to his aunt's house on Thanksgiving. Fran had a lot of evil thoughts about that, but no more mushrooms came up.

The next time she looked, the one remaining fungus was as big and white as a baseball, and marbled all over with black. There was a delicacy as of great age about it now, an almost ethereal look, as if the bluish-white and shining shell glowed coldly from within, silhouetting the dark design that veined it.

"I've had enough of this," she muttered and she gave the thing a sharp kick.

The pale shell disintegrated without a sound, releasing a puff of thick black dust. In the instant wreckage stood a sooty stub, a carbonized yoke, which yielded, moist and pulpy, when she kicked at it frantically in a rush of horror and disgust.

The shrunken black knob emitted another breath of inky powder under the impact of her shoe, but clung to its twist of vine. She had to trample it for long moments before she was able to flatten the whole mess into a dark stain on the earth, through which splinters of the rotten root beneath protruded palely like shards of bone.

She gasped and realized that she had been holding her breath to keep from inhaling the spores, or whatever the black dust was that had been packed between the decayed center and the shell.

Who was watching, who had seen her mad dance?

No one. Betsy's house was quiet, the people across the street were doing whatever they did, and the crazy lady's driveway was empty, her old gray Pontiac absent.

How ridiculous, that a person as crazy as that was allowed to drive!

No more mushrooms sprouted.

"It's too cold for them," Jeffrey said. "Don't tell me you miss the ugly things! A while ago you wanted to poison them."

No, Fran didn't miss them. But she found herself wondering, in a nagging, anxious way, where her evil thoughts were growing now that they weren't showing up on the lawn.

After all, the thoughts didn't stop.

Like when she saw Jeffrey chatting with Betsy one evening while he was setting out the bagged garbage that the new trucks were too wide to pick up in the lanes behind the houses. The two of them stood chatting on the curb, and Fran saw a spark of easy warmth between them and she cursed it.

He said, "Maybe we should drive south somewhere over the Thanksgiving break, to hell with your party and dinner at my aunt's and the whole thing. Things are a little hairy in the hotel right now, with this drain on the restaurant income that nobody can explain. I'm frazzled. You don't seem to be in the best of shape yourself, Frannie. Look in the mirror. I'm afraid you're getting sick."

She did look, and she knew it wasn't that she was getting sick. She was worrying too much.

She was becoming more sensitive to noise, too. She woke up at night now. She would get up alone, careful not to disturb Jeffrey, and go look at herself in the bathroom mirror, sipping wine from a glass until she'd drunk enough to put her back to sleep.

Carmella said, "You better pull yourself together, Fran. I'm getting complaints from the docs you type for."

The docs who mumbled, the docs who paid too little out of their immense incomes, the docs who rattled along about burned kids and dying old people and all the rest as if the sufferers were sides of meat. The docs should feel the pain their patients felt.

That was an evil thought, wasn't it?

Fran ordered a turkey at the supermarket, for the Thanksgiving party. Jeffrey wasn't going to his aunt's for Thanksgiving dinner. His aunt had had a fall and was in Bay Memorial with a broken hip. Jeffrey spent a lot of time at the hospital with her now, which Fran resented, with dark imaginings of death and endings between Jeffrey and his aunt, once and for all.

But where were these evil thoughts? The dead roots in the lawn stayed bare, like bones worked to the surface of an old battlefield.

The turkey was ready to pick up. She hoped it would fit; she had only the freezer compartment of the mid-sized fridge that had come with the house.

On the way back from the supermarket, Fran pulled up in the street. The crazy lady was on the steps of her porch, screeching dementedly, "Get back here, you hear me? You get right in here this minute!"

The little dog was down at the edge of the ragged brown lawn, alternately turning its rear to the questing nose of a brisk gray poodle, and sitting down to avoid being sniffed. The poodle pranced and wagged with delight, its back legs bowed. It darted at the smaller dog with stiffened front legs, trying to pin it, mount it, hump it there in the gutter.

"Get away, get away from her!" shrieked the crazy lady, waving her hands wildly, but apparently she was afraid to run down and chase the poodle away. She thrust her head forward and screamed at the poodle from a rage-distended mouth, "Don't even think about it!"

Fran knew she would explode if she had to hear that raw, mad voice for another second. She leaned out of the window of the Volks and yelled, "For Christ's sake, lady, will you shut up? Let them screw if they want to screw, they're just dogs, that's what they do!"

The crazy lady stood still and lifted one bony hand to shield her eyes from the bright sunlight. Her other hand stayed at her hip, cocked at an angle, a butt smoking between the bony fingers.

Fran recoiled from the unseen glare of those shadowed eyes. She drove quickly on to her own carport, where she sat afraid to move. She watched in her rear-view mirror until the crazy lady, trailed by the little dog (in whom the poodle had lost interest), withdrew into her own house without another word.

Jeffrey said, "We got the accounts straightened out. One of the under-chefs was stealing stuff, meat, lobsters, it's amazing! I finally found the point where the figures were being faked by his boyfriend in the administration office. You've brought me luck. I love you."

They were up late, kissing and sighing and stretching against each other's warm skins. A steady breeze blew all night, hissing and seething like surf. Fran listened and drowsed, lulled by the sound.

Jeff left early for work, bouncing with energy. Fran lay in bed late, luxuriating in the languor of their long loving and heartened by the shimmer of pale sunshine glowing through the drapes. No fog, at last, a clear, bright morning!

After a steamy shower, she stationed herself in front of the mirror to rub moisturizer into her dampened skin. And stopped, staring, frozen by the hammering recognition of something that could not be.

Her skin was an unearthly pearly color, moist and shining, like the skin of a soprano made up to die in Act Three of consumption, like the skin of a delicate Victorian lady vampire, like the skin of a guest made up for a Halloween party. But Halloween was past.

The lines and smudges the mirror had been showing her for days had spread and joined each other in a flowing network of tributaries that covered her features from her throat upward and spread away past her hairline, into her scalp. The lines were mauve and blue and gray, and when she turned her agonized face so that daylight fell on her cheek, there was a slightly greenish tinge of iridescence to these shadows under the thin, thin surface of her porcelain-pale skin.

She ran to the mirror in the bedroom, and the one in the

little bathroom near the kitchen, her eyes glaring in disbelief and horror out of smoky pits in the mask. Her voice creaked and wheezed desperate protests in her throat, her hands fluttered helplessly—her own pink-knuckled, flesh-tinted, youthful hands that didn't dare touch the ancient marbled pallor of her face.

This was where the evil thoughts had been growing, in their home, their seat, their place of origin. Nothing lay ahead but inevitable disintegration of the outer shell, exposing the blackened, shrunken ruin of the brain still damp and clinging with feeble persistence to the quivering stem, the living body.

On the wild winds of her panic she tossed to and fro in the sunlit rooms of the house, screams dammed in her throat by her own terror of what the force of them would do to her fragile shell of a face.

Stifling, she flung open the front door and plunged outside into the chill, bright morning. She stumbled across the lawns, past the big tree, and flung herself down at the dead root on which her evil thoughts had first appeared.

As soon as her forehead touched the bleached bare wood, she felt the eggshell of her face soundlessly break and fall away. A swirl of sooty powder choked her breath as darkness broke in her and from her and bore her down into bottomless night.

BLOOD LILIES
by
Robert E. Vardeman

Alan Mitchell had come to the SeaHarp Hotel to die.

He leaned back in the sleek, comfortable, white Lincoln Towncar the hotel had sent for him, too tired to even look out the smoked-glass window. The driver opened the door. Mitchell heaved himself out and smiled wanly.

"I'll see to your bags, sir," the driver said. Mitchell thanked him with a vague wave of his hand. He found it increasingly difficult to concentrate. The doctors said it was his imagination, that the real ordeal lay ahead.

Mitchell refused to linger for months or even years. He had chosen the SeaHarp Hotel as the most luxurious spot he could find for his last week. Then he would take his life. Mitchell was nothing if not thorough. He had researched poison to find the best, and had rejected it as an alternative. All involved risk and the possibility of lingering or outright failure. He shuddered at the notion of the pain when some virulent poison ate away at his stomach. The slightest gastric upset put him into such a state.

Asphyxiation. That was his researched choice. He would put a clear plastic bag over his head and securely fasten it. To keep the carbon dioxide level from rising in his blood and giving him even a moment's distress, he would pump helium into the bag. His lungs would be tricked into thinking all was well.

He had brought a small green-painted cylinder of the inert gas, with appropriate valves and regulator, in his larger suitcase.

Mitchell closed his eyes and imagined the event. The plastic bag fastened with a length of duct tape around his neck. Inelegant, undignified, but necessary. The rubber hose. The hissing tank of helium. A few barbiturates to prevent him from backing out when the moment came, but not so many that it would nauseate him. A soft and gentle death, slipping off into eternal peace without pain.

He winced as he moved. Something pulled loose inside him. Again, Mitchell pushed it out of his mind. The doctors said it was nothing. Kaposi's sarcoma didn't have symptoms like this. At least, he didn't believe so. He would have to look it up in his medical encyclopedia when he got to his room. Or perhaps in the most recent issue of *Morbidity and Mortality Weekly* he had sent to him from the CDC in Atlanta.

The driver fussed behind him, getting the luggage from the trunk. Mitchell stretched and looked out over Greystone Bay. The sunlight fought a heavy fog and won by slow inches. Here and there whitecaps danced on the bay, but it seemed too sullen to interest him. He had never enjoyed water or water sports.

He turned his attention to the six-foot-high fieldstone wall that ran along Harbor Road. He smiled. The top of the wall had been adorned with more varieties of flowers than he could identify. Dying in the spring had advantages. The beauty of the flower-and-hedge arrangement pleased him.

He stopped along the stone walk leading to the hotel's porch and drank in the beauty of the grounds. The SeaHarp's grounds keeper had not littered the fine lawn with the usual icons. Mitchell saw only neatly kept grass, not swing sets and chairs and boccie ball courts or even the ridiculous bent wire wicks of a croquet field. Just green, lush, well-tended grass. Mitchell liked the hotel more and more.

"I'll have the bags sent up to your room, if you want to look around first," the driver said.

"Um, yes, thank you." Mitchell hadn't realized it. He *did* want to explore. The SeaHarp's four stories of gingerbread front needed paint. The sea air tore away at the wood constantly. Mitchell wondered what riding out a storm inside the grand old hotel would be like. He wished he would live long enough to discover the mysteries of creaking boards and howling wind and hard-driving water against bulging windowpanes. He had lived too long in the dirty hustle of the big city.

"Don't go walking there," came an irritated voice. "You'll disturb the plants. They don't like it."

"Sorry," Mitchell said, stepping back. In his reverie he had walked across the lawn and blundered into a flower bed. The gardener pushed back thick glasses with a dirty, calloused finger. He stared up in what Mitchell considered a belligerent manner unbecoming to the hired help of a resort hotel.

"Didn't mean to sound so brusque," the gardener apologized. "I take care of the flowers and hate to see them bothered." Almost as an afterthought, the small, sun-browned man added, "You wouldn't want to get your shoes dirty."

"You aren't from this area, are you?" asked Mitchell. He had always prided himself on identifying accents. Even if the gardener had spoken with the same clipped tones the others in the Greystone Bay area did, the suntan set this man apart. The heavy fog and winter storms didn't permit any native to get this tanned.

"From down South," the man said. His eyes looked like giant brown fried eggs behind the thick lenses. Pushing back and getting off his knees, he struggled to his feet. Mitchell saw his first impression was right. The man stood a head shorter than he.

The accent didn't match any Mitchell had heard. Wherever the man did come from, it wasn't the South. Yet the tan suggested as much. And the gardener had no reason to lie.

"What kind of flowers are these? They look familiar but . . ."

"All kinds," the gardener said hurriedly. "These are a strain of marigolds. And those, the ones with the light red centers, are daisies."

"I've never seen daisies with such pale pink petals and red middles."

"My hybrid. I developed them myself."

"And those?" asked Mitchell, curious in spite of himself. He had the city dweller's love-hate relationship with flowers. They were pretty to look at but too much trouble to bother with.

"Those are Byzantine Roses."

Mitchell bent over and examined the delicate, involuted petals. They had fine red etching like veins inside pure white.

"They're lovely. You must be very proud of your garden."

The man nodded and smiled almost shyly. "They aren't the best I have to offer. The lilies are better. Want to see?"

Mitchell followed silently as the gardener led him to the rear of the hotel. He had thought the other flowers were gorgeous. These defied description.

"These are prize-winners. I don't know much about horticulture but from an artistic standpoint, they're unparaleled.'' Mitchell sighed. The world had so much to offer. He would miss it after he killed himself.

The lilies thrust up bold yellow trumpets. Tiny crimson spots decorated their interior. He blinked. They seemed to follow him heliotropically as if he were the sun. He reached out. The trumpet flared and the bloom dipped toward his hand. The image of jaws opening flashed across his mind. He jerked back, embarrassed at his reaction. It was only a flower, after all.

''The insects like them,'' the gardener said.

''How do you grow them?''

''That's a secret.'' The gardener turned furtive and scuttled away. Mitchell shrugged. The flowers were as spectacular as the SeaHarp Hotel itself. Following a small path around the side of the building, Mitchell returned to the front stone steps. He passed between two large stone vases with more of the gardener's handiwork inside.

Mitchell opened the French doors leading into the hotel lobby, wondering why they didn't leave them open to catch the cooling, fresh breeze off the bay. He stopped and stared. If he had entered another world, the feeling couldn't have been much different.

Quiet fell over him like a blanket. He couldn't imagine what would shake the sense of serenity inherent in the room. A tear came to Alan Mitchell's eyes. This hotel would provide a fitting final week for him. He went to the registration desk to his left.

''Welcome to the SeaHarp, Mr. Mitchell,'' the clerk greeted.

He started to ask how the man knew his name, then remembered the driver had already brought his luggage in. A good hotel—a first class one—hired a friendly, intelligent staff. Of course the clerk knew his name. How many others would be arriving in the span of a few minutes?

''Thank you. I'd like a room on the second floor, please.''

"That's been arranged. Your luggage is in suite 207."

"How did you know I'd want a room on the second floor?" Mitchell disliked the notion of being trapped in a burning building higher than he could safely jump out. It had been difficult living and working in New York with such a phobia, but he had managed.

"The lady told me." The clerk lifted a pen and pointed discreetly toward a writing desk with a Tiffany lamp. Mitchell tried to penetrate the darkness caused by the light.

"Hello, Alan."

He knew the voice instantly.

"It's been six years, Elizabeth." His heart almost exploded when she rose and moved around the writing desk and came fully into the cone of light from the lamp. Elizabeth Morgenthal hadn't aged a day, an hour, even a second, in the years since he had seen her last.

She took both of his hands in hers and pulled him close. The fragrance of her perfume was as he remembered. He closed his eyes and inhaled deeply, savoring the moment. Transported back to happier times, the spell was broken when she kissed him. He recoiled slightly, unable to stop himself.

"What's wrong, Alan? Still angry with me?" Eyes so green they made emeralds envious stared up at him. He sought the tiny gold speck in her left eye and found it. The cute upturn of her nose and the pixy smile that quivered on her lips, threatening to break out into a laugh at any instant—he remembered them all.

"You *have* forgiven me?"

"I . . ." He had no answer. He had seldom thought of her in the intervening years. Seeing her, feeling the heat from her nearness, he wondered why he hadn't. "How did you know I'd be here?" he asked, trying to change the subject.

"You haven't forgiven me." She let out a deep sigh of mock regret. "Let me buy you dinner. You always did enjoy good meal. The SeaHarp has the finest chef, not only in Greystone Bay but anywhere within a hundred-mile radius.''

"No, no," he said, "the meal is on me. I insist. And you didn't answer the question. Did you peek at the reservations?"

"Nothing so elaborate. I saw you coming up the walk. I wondered what happened to you when you didn't come in."

"The gardener . . ."

"I saw. I decided to play a little prank on you." She stared at him with those fabulous green eyes. "You still don't like upper stories?"

"You remember my foibles. I hope you remember my better points, too."

She hesitated. Then her face broke out in a sunshiny smile. "I do, Alan. Thoughts of you have never been too far from my mind."

He swallowed, suddenly uncomfortable. "What brings you to this particular hotel?"

"My best friend got married last year and came here on her honeymoon. She made it sound so pleasant I decided to take my vacation here. I've been here a week."

"Are you staying on?" He fought down the memories—and Elizabeth's presence. He had a mission. He had decided. He would kill himself in one week. He would!

"For another week. It is expensive but restful. I've found it has restored my faith in the world. I was getting a little burned out and other things weren't going well."

"Personal?" he asked.

"Naturally. The agency grossed two million dollars last year and will double that this year."

"You always were a fine businessman."

"Businesswoman," she said. "You always were such a fine sexist man." Elizabeth gave another of the deep, almost shuddering sighs. "Business is fine. Personally, I'm a wreck."

"What was his name?"

"You always saw through to my soul, Alan. I hated that and loved it at the same time." She took a step back and swayed.

"Are you all right?" His arm went around her waist. He was still strong enough to support her. He got a chair and guided her into it. A ray of light slanted through a beveled glass window, sending gentle rainbows across her pale cheek. For the first time he noticed how peaked she was.

"It's why I came here. I work twenty-hour days. The doctor said I was killing myself and needed a vacation."

"After a week you're still faint?"

"Always the hypochondriac. When you can't fuss over yourself, you fuss over me," she said. In a low voice, she added, "I always enjoyed the attention."

"I have something in my suitcase . . ."

"I'm fine, Alan. Please. And the fainting spells only started a day or two ago. Stress. Or the relief of stress. Have you seen the porch? It stretches completely around the hotel. I enjoy sitting and watching the sunset."

"Do they serve a decent drink?"

"The SeaHarp? You've got to be kidding," she said, looking stronger. The paleness in her face remained. "The best, just like everything else in the hotel."

"Let me get settled, and I'll join you in an hour," he said.

"Not one second later," Elizabeth warned with mock severity.

"I'm always prompt."

"It's nice seeing you again, Alan. Really. And don't be mad at me."

"I'm not," he said, meaning it. What had drawn them together seven years ago was gone. Those days could never be recaptured. Mitchell felt a bleakness inside when he re-

alized he would never see Elizabeth again after the end of the
week. She would leave, return to the city and her job, find a
new lover, and repeat endlessly the same drama she had written for herself.

And he would be dead.

Mitchell considered using the elevators to one side of the
lobby, then decided to take the stairs. The sweep of the stairway reminded him of old movies about grander times, more
elegant times. When he reached the head of the stairs, he
was out of breath and had to rest.

He leaned against the highly polished mahogany railing
and stared out over the lobby. Elizabeth still sat in the chair.
The clerk had brought her a glass of water. From this distance, he wasn't hypnotized by her personal energy. She
seemed frail, as if wasting away.

Immediately, he pushed such nonsense from his mind. *He*
was the one who was dying, not Elizabeth Morgenthal. She
had always been the health fanatic, working at exercise the
way she worked at her job. That had been part of her problem, he remembered. She met muscle-bound jocks in the
health spas who invariably loved themselves more than they
ever could her.

Rested, he sought out Room 207. The key given him by
the clerk turned quietly in the well-oiled lock. The suite on
the other side was everything he had hoped for. He could die
peacefully in such a room.

Mitchell heaved his suitcases onto the bed and worked at
the intricate locks he had put on them. Minutes later, he
opened one and decided what needed hanging and what
could be put in the wardrobe's single bottom drawer. Only
then did he open the larger suitcase. Fastened inside was
the bottle of helium, a thick plastic bag, the roll of sticky
gray duct tape, the brass fittings he needed, and a long,
single-spaced typewritten letter explaining his suicide. He

leafed through the document, his eyes dancing over the will he had appended.

"How times change," he muttered. He considered finding a lawyer in Greystone Bay and changing the will to include Elizabeth. She would share his last days, just as she had already shared fourteen months of his life. She deserved more than his company. "No," he told himself firmly. He had carefully weighed what to do. Altering his plans now would only introduce error.

He took a long, hot bath that relaxed the tension knotting his shoulders and upper back. Dressing carefully, wanting to impress Elizabeth, he studied himself in the full-length mirror. The light wool jacket and shirt collar hung loose. The weight loss would continue, but only this small hint betrayed his secret. He pressed out nonexistent wrinkles in his chocolate-colored slacks and studied himself even more critically. He decided he would pass all but the most penetrating of inspections.

He took the elevator to the lobby, saying nothing to the elevator starter as he tried to remember when he had last seen a human operator. The elevators in the Port Authority had men who sat on their stools in make-work projects, but he had no need to go to the rooftop parking garages.

The sun was dipping down over the high wall with its foliage when he walked onto the porch. Elizabeth had staked out a spot with a small table and two comfortable chairs. She waved to him. He couldn't restrain the smile that came to his lips. He *had* missed her and hadn't known it.

"You are right on time. You're a constant in the universe, Alan. Never a second late."

"Some people call that a compulsion. Or is it properly an obsession?"

"You haven't changed in other ways, either," she said in exasperation. "Don't try to be so precise. It doesn't matter if you're not in complete control. Really."

"Is this the New Age philosophy? Let previous lives intrude on the here-and-now?" He ordered a dry Gibson when the waiter came and silently stood beside his chair. "Never mind," he went on. "Let's just enjoy the sunset."

"Such beauty," Elizabeth said, sighing. "I've come out here every night for a week and it still awes me."

They sat and chatted about old times, the people they knew together and apart, the threads that had bound them. After a while, they fell silent, content to watch the stars turning into hard diamond points in the velvet black sky.

Mitchell turned slightly in his chair and stared down the length of the long porch. Twin lights flared. He cocked his head to one side and got a better look. The gardener stood at the end of the porch. His thick glasses reflected pale yellow light coming from inside the SeaHarp's lobby. The man studied them. When he saw Mitchell returning the stare, he stepped back and vanished into the shadows.

"Let me buy you dinner. Anything you want."

"No, Alan. I'm the one with the successful business." Elizabeth's thin hand shot to her lips. "I'm sorry. I don't know what's happened in the past six years."

"The bookstore isn't grossing four million this year," he said, with a laugh. "But I'm comfortable. I can afford a brief vacation here."

"This is so nice running into you here," she said. "And you may buy me dinner."

"Only if you have a steak. You need the protein." He reached out and touched her cheek. The flesh was porcelain-cold.

She laughed and held his hand close, giving the palm a quick kiss. "Whatever you say, Alan."

After dinner, they had another drink in the bar. They entered their own private world when they sat in the high-backed booths.

"It's nice finding a bar without loud music. I hate shouting to make myself heard,'' she said. She giggled, then belched. ''Sorry. Too much to drink.''

''You've only had two glasses of wine, unless you had more before we watched the sunset.''

''I just had a Perrier. I can't hold my liquor like I used to. I hate to break it off. This has been so nice seeing you again, but I'm too tired.''

''I'm a bit sleepy myself. It was a long trip down on the train. May I see you to your door?''

''Always the gentleman. Of course you may.'' Arm in arm they left the bar and took the elevator to the top floor.

Mitchell's heart raced when Elizabeth stopped outside the door and handed him her key. He opened the door.

''Thank you,'' she said. She stood, head slightly tilted and eyes closed. The kiss he gave her was hardly more than a quick peck. She hid her disappointment well.

''Good night,'' Mitchell said.

''Breakfast?''

''Not too early,'' he said. ''Let's say nine?''

She nodded. He saw the sadness in her eyes—and a curious haunted expression. She spun around and closed the door behind her. The click of the deadbolt sliding home started him on his way back to his room.

He was drowsy, but he couldn't sleep. Rather than returning to his room, he went back outside onto the porch. A few other guests sat about in twos and threes, talking quietly. He didn't want their company, even if they had desired his. He walked across the dark, dew-damp lawn until he found the high wall. From here he started pacing slowly, intending to circumnavigate the SeaHarp's grounds.

He stopped and found Elizabeth's room on the fourth floor. He watched until the light went out. Six years ago there might have been more between them. Now, it was impossible. He started on his lonely walk again when the light in her room came on again.

He frowned when he saw that it wasn't the room light. A beam bounced and bobbed against the windowpane, as if someone with a flashlight had entered. He considered alerting the room clerk to the possibility of a sneak thief in the hotel. The light snapped off. He found himself unsure if he had seen anything important or if his active imagination played tricks on him.

Starting for the lobby, he paused when he heard a door at the rear of the SeaHarp open and close. He walked on cat-quiet feet until he saw the circular yellow disk of a flashlight moving on the ground. He stood beside a tree, invisible from a distance.

The gardener hurried toward his flower bed. In one hand he held the flashlight. In the other he carried a small capped jar. He dropped to his knees beside the bed of lilies and carefully unscrewed the lid. Mumbling to himself, he poured the liquid onto the flowers, being sure each got a measured amount. A lewd sucking noise echoed through the stillness of the night.

Finished, he stood and tucked the jar under his arm. The gardener left, whistling off-key.

Mitchell waited several minutes after the man had gone before approaching the flower bed. The lilies tracked him like radar. Kneeling, he avoided their questing stalks and ran his finger along the damp soil, then lifted and sniffed what he had found.

"Blood," he said, startled. In the past few months he had come to loathe the sharp, coppery smell. Involuntarily he rubbed his left arm where so much had been removed for tests. Oh, yes, he knew blood. And he knew why the gardener's lilies and other flowers grew so lushly.

The Egyptians had used slave's blood to fertilize their crops.

Mitchell wondered how many other guests beside Elizabeth Morgenthal contributed their lifeblood to the SeaHarp's thirsty flowers.

He returned to his room but sleep wouldn't come. He sat in an overstuffed chair staring at his opened suitcase holding the paraphernalia of his death.

At breakfast he watched Elizabeth eat double portions. "You're hungry," he said, knowing the reason. Blood loss would do it. His real questions were how the gardener had entered her room when she had thrown the deadbolt and how he had drawn the blood without waking her.

"The past few days I've been famished." Her cheeks burned with a fever. The paleness was greater this morning than it had been. Mitchell wondered how much blood the gardener had sucked from his victim.

"Did you sleep well?"

"I have since I got here." Elizabeth said, smearing home-made preserves on her fifth piece of toast. "That's odd, really. I have insomnia. That's one reason I work such long hours."

"It might be the other way around," he pointed out.

"The doctor said that, too. It doesn't matter. Not at the moment, Alan. I'm sleeping like a log." Her green eyes locked on his. She didn't have to add that she wished he had been with her.

They spent the day walking along the shore of the bay, skipping stones like small children, examining sea shells and discarding them, finding a peacefulness that hadn't existed for either in many years. They returned to the SeaHarp Hotel at sunset.

"It's been a wonderful day, Alan," Elizabeth said almost wistfully. She reached across the small table in the bar and touched his hand. His fingers twined with hers.

"It doesn't have to end," he said. Her eyes glowed with an inner light.

"I hoped you'd say that." She smiled almost shyly. "Your room or mine?"

"Yours," he said without hesitation, remembering the suitcase he had so carefully stored in his wardrobe. Even being in the same room with the implements of his destruction seemed wrong now.

They took the elevator to the fourth floor and entered her room, arms around each other. She flipped on the light switch. Mitchell noticed her room was much smaller than his, but still larger than the standard hotel room. He studied the room as she fussed about, dropping purse and kicking off shoes. He saw nothing to indicate how the gardener had entered.

"Aren't they thoughtful, Alan?" she asked. "They leave a fresh flower for me each night." She lifted the bud vase from the dresser top and sniffed at the delicate blossom. He watched as she weaved slightly. Her eyelids drooped the barest amount. She took another deep whiff. "I so love fresh flowers."

"You're giving your life for them," he said in a low voice, understanding one part of the riddle.

"What?" She sank to the bed and tried to unfasten her blouse. She fell to one side, sleeping deeply. The combined exertion of the day-long walk and the potent effect of the flower's narcotic perfume had caused her to fall into a light coma.

Mitchell struggled to get her off the bed and into the bathroom. He put a blanket down in the tub and rolled her onto it, hoping she would be comfortable. He didn't want her to awaken in the morning with a kink in her neck. It took longer than he'd thought it would. His strength had been taxed, too. That was the progressive nature of his disease. The T-cells in his blood turned traitor. Infections took hold more easily and conquered with little struggle.

His entire auto-immune system had betrayed him. AIDS.

Tears formed at the corners of his eyes at the outrageous fortune that had visited him. He pushed the knowledge of a lingering, painful, ugly death from his mind and concentrated.

Mitchell went to Elizabeth's wardrobe and opened the door. At one end of the fragrant, redwood-lined cabinet hung a frilly nightgown. He stripped off his clothing and donned the gown. It was too tight across the shoulders but should pass in the dark. It hid the different flow of his muscles—what remained of them—and gave him a hope of stopping the gardener.

Before he lay down in the bed, he returned to the bathroom to check on Elizabeth. Her deep, regular breathing showed she was all right. He took a few minutes to shave the hair from his left arm. Even in the dark the gardener might notice the hirsute difference. No longer. Mitchell thrust out his thin arm and knew it might pass for a woman's.

He returned to the bedroom and turned out the light. Crawling under the covers, his needle-marked left arm dangling over the edge of the bed, he waited.

The light going out gave the gardener his cue. From the ceiling came scurrying sounds, as if rats had infested the century-old hotel. From half-closed eyes Mitchell watched as a piece of the intricate plasterwork turned into utter blackness. The gardener dropped down to a chair from the exposed crawlspace. The flashlight's beam darted around, checking. The gardener hummed to himself as he came over and gripped Mitchell's arm.

A thin rubber hose circled Mitchell's upper arm. The needle sank into veins almost collapsed from too much blood being drawn. The gardener didn't notice. He had been milking Elizabeth heavily. Mitchell almost protested the amount of his blood taken. Even lying down and feigning sleep, he felt dizzy from the loss. To have taken this much from Elizabeth would have killed her.

Only when the jar was filled to the brim did the gardener remove the rubber constrictor hose and retreat. Mitchell watched openly as the gardener jumped from the chair and into the dark square overhead. Like a monkey, the man vanished. Seconds later, the ceiling was again whole.

Mitchell had to fight to sit up. The bloodletting had taken too much from him. An hour later he had wrestled Elizabeth into bed and left quietly. In two he had made his calls. In four his phone jangled for long minutes. He didn't answer it. He knew he would eat breakfast alone.

He slept fitfully, nightmares of grotesquely twisted blood cells chasing him. The sound effects accompanying the nightmares were worse. The sucking noise, the awful obscene sucking.

As Mitchell went into the dining room, a bellman stopped him. "Sir, the lady left this for you."

"Thank you," Mitchell said, knowing what Elizabeth had put in the note. He opened it and read anyway.

"Darling Alan," it began. "I'm so embarrassed about last night. I remember nothing—but do know it had to be as wonderful as you. I wish we could have spent more time together, but it's not possible. I received a call last night. There was a fire in my office and my manager was severely burned and is in critical condition. The quickest way back to New York was the 5:10 train. I tried to call your room but you didn't answer. Please, Alan, call me when you get back to the city. With all love, Elizabeth."

He tucked the note in his pocket. She would be angry and confused when she learned there hadn't been a fire and that none of her staff had been hurt.

Mitchell sat in the main dining room and stared out at the blooming flowers.

As he sipped his tea, white-uniformed men rushed past the window. Mitchell turned in his chair and craned his neck. They went to the bed of lilies the gardener had tended so carefully. In a few minutes, they returned, pushing a gurney laden with a black plastic bag large enough to hold a body. A body the size of the gardener.

Mitchell felt no triumph. What the lilies had become, he didn't care to know. He shuddered, thinking of them propagating. But that was no worry of his. He finished his Earl Grey, put the cup down with a steady hand and returned to his room.

The suitcase opened, and Alan Mitchell began his journey.

INTERLUDE
by
Wendy Webb

It was her first night at the SeaHarp Hotel in seventy years. And her last. That is, if all went well. And of course it would.

She had planned this night since the last kiss on her grandmother's cold cheek. Thought it out as the shadow of a heavy oak lid darkened the old face. Saw it while the locks were thrown, and her grandmother's almost weightless body was slowly lowered into the soft, damp earth.

She threw the first clump of dirt, heard the empty sobs of family and friends fall around her like shards of broken glass ready to cut and bleed her of all that was left. If she let it. But she wouldn't. Not then.

Not now.

Now it was her turn. Her time to face the closing. End the interlude of what was. She smiled, looked around the lobby of the old hotel. The SeaHarp knew her. Knew her almost as well as her grandmother did. Maybe even better.

She had come home.

"Room 209, Ms. Claire Smythe. Just as you requested. Sign here, if you will." He pushed a leather-bound registration book towards her.

She peered at his nametag, saw "V. Montgomery, Owner" etched in brass. "I knew your father."

"Ma'am?"

"Simon Montgomery. He is your father, isn't he?"

"Yes ma'am. He passed on a few years ago. I run the place now. Have been ever since he retired."

"And Elinor?"

"Aunt Elinor died four years before him."

"I'm sorry to hear that," Claire said. "We, the three of us, used to play together when we were children. Simon could play quite a game of croquet. Elinor wasn't so bad herself, a bit temperamental mind you, but not bad with a mallet."

"So I heard." He flipped through a pile of embossed papers, pulled one out, and scrutinized it. "The private dining room will be ready for you at eight. Place settings for six. Are there any changes?"

"No." She hesitated. "On second thought . . . yes. If possible could you add two more to the list?"

"I don't see any problem with that. We always do an overage to cover potential changes anyway. We'll take care of it." He made a quick addition to the note, tucked it away among another stack of papers. "Are any of your guests staying the night with us? We'll be glad to leave a message reminding them of the dinner time."

"No, thank-you. None is staying." Claire reached into her pocketbook, produced a roll of bills, and pushed them towards the owner.

"We'll bill you at the end of your stay, Ms. Smythe. No need to worry about it until then."

"I'll pay for it now, please." Montgomery shrugged, took the money, gave her a receipt and the room key. "Has my package arrived yet?'' she said. ''It should have come a day or two ago.''

''Let me check.'' Another rustle of papers, a raised eyebrow, then the found information. ''Yes. It arrived and is waiting in your room.'' A quick flick of his wrist and a bellhop appeared next to her elbow. ''Danny will help you with your luggage.''

''This way, Ms. Smythe. Room 209 is one floor up.'' He gave her a quick appraisal, then made a decision. ''The elevators are right around the corner.''

She bristled at the slight. ''Young man, I may be old, but I'm not dead. I'll walk.''

Confusion crossed his face. ''I'm sorry. . . .''

''That you are. Besides, I only have one bag. I can carry it by myself for that matter.''

''No, please.'' The young man looked to his boss, then to Claire. ''Really. I'll be glad to carry your bag.''

''No need. But thank-you anyway.'' She picked up the small bag and walked to the stairs. ''209 still sits over the gardens I suppose.''

''Yes, ma'am.''

''Good.'' She hoisted the luggage and started up the steps. The broad, thickly carpeted stairs were just as she had remembered them those long years ago. A little worn perhaps, but still holding their elegance in the subdued pastels and floral patterns. How many times had her grandmother walked those steps on the way to the reading room, the dining room, to the front porch for a view of the ocean, or to the gardens to inhale the deep, full scent of summer flowers in bloom? And how many times had she walked the steps to room 209? What did she feel, think about, when she went to that room for the last time?

How often had she gone with her grandmother, together, hand-in-hand, to share the special times? And they were special times. Moments that only the two of them had shared. Could share.

Until her parents took her away. Forced her into private school. ''To learn some discipline,'' they had said. And tore her away from the only family member she loved.

She never saw her grandmother again.

Until the kiss on the cold cheek.

Just before the heavy oak lid darkened her face.

And on her tenth birthday.

Claire reached the landing of the great staircase, paused to catch her breath. Maybe she should have let the young man carry her bag. And maybe she should have taken the elevator. But it was the principle of the thing. And her stubbornness, she supposed. Whatever it was, it didn't matter now anyway. Tonight was special. She would enjoy every minute of the plans that she had so carefully made.

She rubbed her swollen, painful knee with the bent, arthritic fingers of her hand, took a deep breath, and headed up the final stretch of stairs to the second floor. She stopped at the top for a quick look down over the edge of the balcony. How had they done it, she wondered? The races up and down the stairs always left she, Simon and Elinor in a pile of breathless laughter at the bottom. Now the breathlessness came all too easily. And with little exertion, if any.

She waited while her eyes adjusted to the darkness, then turned into the hallway. Small, candle-shaped lights mounted in brass cast her silhouette in distorted gray shadows on worn, somber wallpaper as she passed by. She stopped then.

Room 209.

Grandmother's room.

Her room.

The brass numbers mounted on the solid wood of the door reflected dancing light from a sconce on a near wall. She hesitated, wondered if she were ready. Knew that she was.

She fumbled with the large key in her pocket, then slid it into the lock. It turned easily, the door opened.

She dropped her bag in the sitting-room and went to the window. She pushed open the heavy drapes, blinked at the bright sunlight that filtered in through the glass of the French doors, and looked out over the back lawn and the little garden. It was still there. Still as beautiful as she remembered. She looked as far to the right as she could see. Smiled. The croquet lawn was there too. She wondered if children played croquet anymore. Decided that they did. At the SeaHarp they would play croquet.

At the SeaHarp they would be happy.

She turned back to the room, looked at the couch, the arm chairs, the tea service. The TV. It wasn't all the same as it used to be. An edge of disappointment nagged her. Not all of it was the same anyway.

She reached for her bag, went through the door to the bedroom. Gasped. A body? No. An imprint. An outline. Only a human shape would make that kind of an impression on a down comforter. Someone that would have been bedridden for weeks. Months. A small body, frail. Weak. She blinked, looked again. The cover was smooth. Newly made and pulled taut. She shook her head, tried to recover the image.

Grandmother.

No. Grandmother was gone. It was a trick of the light. A game on tired, old eyes. She smoothed the comforter, tucked in the edges, smiled. Growing old wasn't so bad. Not if you didn't let it bother you. And what could you do about it anyway? There was no fountain of youth that she knew about. She wouldn't want one. Age was a special gift. It gave time to think, to remember, to make plans, and follow through on them.

She sat down on the edge of the four-poster bed. Ran her hand over the deep grain of the mahogany, then opened her suitcase. The framed photographs, yellowed with age, lay on top. Graying, tissue-thin paper rustled like dry leaves as she unwrapped the pictures. She softly stroked the faces of her Grandmother, Christopher, and the others before placing the pictures on the bedside table. She sighed, then hung the dress that she would wear to the dinner party in one of the cedar-scented wardrobes.

She went into the large, marble bathroom, and unpacked her makeup, moisturizer, and toothbrush, then placed them carefully, in order, by the sink, next to the claw-footed bath-tub. A glance at her watch told her there was no time for a relaxing bath now. Maybe later, she decided. After all her guests had left the dinner party.

She returned to the bedroom, unpacked her nightgown, and brushed away the wrinkles. She breathed deep to catch the scent of rose sachet imbedded in the splitting threads of the once-white, cotton material. She smiled at the hint of her past, then draped the gown gently over the bed. Looked at it with longing. Later, she told herself. Later.

The brown paper-wrapped box was recovered from the sit-ting room coffee table and placed on the bedside table next to her photographs.

Just where it should be.

Just where it had been before.

She patted the boxes, toyed with the idea of opening it, decided against it. Opening it now would spoil the moment. And nothing would take away from this night. Nothing. Not even her own impatience.

It was all coming together. Finally. The years of planning had been worth the wait. She could tell. She patted the box one more time, then got dressed for dinner.

The guests would be waiting.

She walked the hall back to the stairs, considered the ele-vator, changed her mind. No, she would make a sweeping entrance—like her grandmother always did. And they always looked, always admired her beauty, her confidence. Her total control over her life. Men and women alike, the activity of the lobby stopped when she came down these stairs. The men, souls bared in their appreciative stare, watched her every move. The women looked at her in admiration, and wondered what was missing in themselves.

"Beauty comes from within, my love," she had told little Claire. "It comes from being happy. Always happy."

And Claire was happy. Then. Even at her grandmother's death, with the woman's whispered last words ringing in her ears, she was happy.

Through the scarring pain of inflicted wounds that never healed.

Always happy.

But never happier than right now.

She held her head up high, and walked across the hall to the dining room. A uniformed man snapped his heels, nodded and opened the door for her. She thanked him graciously and greeted her guests.

Mother and father sat at the end of the table. But they would, she knew. Always as far away from her as they could get. Even in a small room . . . especially in a small room, until they could send her away. This time leaving was her decision. She nodded to them, saw the coldness in their eyes. They only tolerated this situation because they had to. Because she made them come. Wouldn't let them rest until they listened to what she had to say. She nodded again, curtly this time. They responded in kind.

A waiter wearing a white tuxedo pulled out her chair, waved her into it with a small bow, then leaned with an air of conspiracy towards her. "Just nod and I'll have the meal served immediately."

"Thank you kindly, sir. I think now would be just right."

"Now, ma'am?"

"Yes. Now please."

He looked around the room, raised an eyebrow. "As you wish."

"And please, leave me to my guests after they've been served."

Another nod, and he was gone. Within minutes a parade of staff converged on the room placing plates of steaming food on starched linen-covered tables, decorated with bright, cut-flower arrangements. From the garden, she knew.

"And the dessert?"

A pause from the waiter, then a snap of his fingers. The staff reappeared, placed sampling of desserts at each place setting.

"Thank you, sir. That'll do quite nicely."

He bowed at the waist, and pulled the door closed with a barely audible "click."

"Now then," she said, raising her wine glass to the guests, "a toast." She looked about the room for compliance, frowned at her parents' refusal to participate, then spoke. "To what was. To what will be." She drank deeply, smiled at her company, then waved them to their meal.

She winked at Christopher over another sip of the wine. Admired his looks in his black tux and brilliant red cummerbund. He was just as handsome as she remembered. Just like the photograph. He winked back, then smiled with approval. She felt a hot flush redden her cheeks at his attention, then smoothed an imagined wrinkle in her dress. She looked back, and followed his gaze to her two old friends.

Rose and Constance were using the dinner opportunity to bicker over the last bridge hand they played as partners. "I led with hearts," she knew Rose was saying. "That was not the signal I gave you," Constance would argue, "You never read my signals right. No decent bridge player leads with hearts when I give them a signal. I should have partnered with Claire." Claire stifled a laugh at the look of disgust on Rose's face, then saddened at the thought.

It never ends for them. Not even when it's over.

But it wasn't going to be like that for her. It would be different.

She tapped a salad fork on her wine glass for their attention, and stood. Nervousness tightened her throat. She cleared it, and looked around the room. "Thank you, all of you, for being here. This last time together means a lot to me." She saw her parents turn away. After tonight she'd let them go. Let all of them go. But only after they heard what she had to say. She raised her voice. "Each one of you touched my life in an important way. It took a lifetime to understand how these events, both joyous and tragic, molded me into what I am." Her voice faltered, stopped. She looked around the room at her invited guests. Looked closely at their faces, as she remembered them, and saw them clearly for the first time.

The anger in her parents at a child they never wanted.

Emptiness, filled only by a bridge hand, in Rose and Constance.

Unresolved confusion at events unforeseen, and unexplained, in young Christopher.

And the two guests added at the last minute. Their coercion by inheritance of a life they never chose. His bitterness at his responsibility to his father, to the hotel. Her lonely spinster life.

The faces. All memories that she clung to, savored, as one long day on her tenth birthday turned to a week, a year, a lifetime, of unanswered questions. And now it was time to let them go. All of them. Time to meet what she had planned for all these years.

The faces shimmered in the dim light. She reached out to touch them once more, to feel again what they had given her, then hesitated. It didn't matter anymore. Not now.

She sighed. Stood to leave. She pushed open the door that led to the hallway, looked back over her shoulder one last time, then closed the door silently behind her.

She took her time going up the staircase. Wanted to feel her every step deepen the thick carpet—wanted to touch the worn, thick wood of the balcony. She sorted the various smells of the hotel as she climbed. Dinner being served to the other hotel guests. Perfume. Furniture polish. The deep scent of rose buds opening to reveal their deep reds and yellows. Salt from the bay seeped deep yet subtle in every pore of the SeaHarp.

Down the hall to her room, she tried to imagine the activity of the place as she had once known it.

The stately gentlemen in the Club Room sipping their brandy and breathing deep the aroma of imported cigars.

The smack of billiard balls as they touched, then formed intricate patterns on the tables.

Beautiful women and their men moving to orchestral music in the Ball Room. Their eyes sparkling from the light of overhead chandeliers. Their fluid movements whispered on the walls in shadows of dance.

She unlocked the door, walked through to the bedroom and stood in front of the vanity mirror. She pulled the pins that held her hair, and let the long, thinning gray strands fall about her face and shoulders. She leaned into the mirror, smiled and remembered.

It had been a deep auburn once, full and beautiful—like her Grandmother's hair had once been—and pinned up, always pinned up in a braid around her head so that it wouldn't get in the way. Mother wouldn't have it hanging down like some street urchin, she always said. But this time it was down. The soft, late summer breeze tousled it, set it free to capture the sun's rays. Christopher had noticed. More than noticed. He fell in love with her that day, she knew. And what a marriage it would be. Full of life and happiness. Until the accident.

She stroked the brittle gray of her hair, stared at the mirror that showed an old, wrinkled woman where seconds ago it was a young girl.

But there would be no sadness. She wouldn't allow it. There was only that to come.

Her hands went to her face, pulled back the loose skin until it was taut and forced an affect of a grin. She reached for the wisp of Kleenex, contained in a little brass box on the vanity, and dabbed away her makeup. A stroke across her forehead, down the side of her face.

She never bothered anyone. Couldn't they see that? So why did the neighborhood children play practical jokes on her? Call her an "old maid"? She chose the life she wanted. Made it comfortable.

Another tissue rubbed over her chin, the other side of her face.

It wasn't a punishment was it—what happened to Christopher? The horse bucked, threw him. His neck was broken like a dry twig. Her parents had claimed it was her fault. But it wasn't.

Was it?

No, she decided, closed her eyes tight at the thought, at the sound. Of course not. She loved Christopher, and he loved her. Her parents had no right to blame her, to force her to carry that burden over the years. But she had. Until now.

A final brush to her face, a final layer of unresolved questions removed. She stared at her own pale skin, saw faint blue veins traverse the surface. Saw the face of her grandmother on yet another night, a face of calm, a look to the future. Finally.

She slid out of her dress and into the white, cotton gown. It crinkled with her movement and fit just as she knew it would. Just as it was meant to be on the night celebrating her wedding. A wedding that never came. But tonight was a celebration as well.

She stroked the material. Turned this way and that to catch herself in the mirror as if she were a young girl again, felt her long hair brush against her face.

It was time.

The brown paper-wrapped package opened easily at her touch. She pulled out the wooden box, ran a finger around its smooth, polished edges. It glistened a deep rosewood red at her touch. The music inside waited for her. Waited for her touch that would open the box and free it. Free her.

Just like it had freed Grandmother.

It was the music of a thousand bedtimes as a young child nestled in the loving arms of her Grandmother.

Warm.

The music of a willing end to what was. A closure to a life.

Safe.

Music of souls that traveled as she did. Clung to an expectation of what would be.

Happy.

She lay down in the soft folds of the comforter. Turned her head for a last look at the photographs, at her friends and family. Faces caught for eternity on paper behind glass. Caught unwilling when it was time to say goodbye. She would say goodbye to them. For them.

To her parents. To Rose and Constance. To Christopher.

To her two added dinner guests, Simon and Elinor.

All taken away from her before they were ready. Before she was ready.

She could let them go now. On to the paths that they had chosen for themselves. They had kept her company long enough, had pushed away the loneliness until it had become a dim light in the distance. Now it was time to set them free as well. She rubbed a hand, swollen and bent with disease, across her moist eyes, and mouthed a silent farewell to them.

The whisper from Grandmother came to her then. A whisper as quiet as the bay breeze, as soft as rain on the garden flowers.

Claire opened the box, closed her eyes, lay still on the four-poster bed. And waited to meet her grandmother.

The sound poured out of the box, surrounded her. Covered her. Caressed. The music of generations past, stroked her gray hair and turned it auburn with the touch. Smoothed the wrinkled skin. Massaged bent joints.

She sighed deeply, felt her life slip into darkness. Into happiness.

Some felt them as a gentle wind in a still room. Others heard the small, light sound of children's laughter in the distance, yet somehow near. Still others caught a flicker of movement from the corner of their eyes, but dismissed it as a trick of the light from brass sconces.

But those who looked closely into the shadows of the old hallways, around the corners, and deep into the heart of the SeaHarp Hotel saw more. They alone saw the figures hidden by darkness.

Two little girls, their auburn hair loose about their face and shoulders, held hands.

And smiled.

A MUSE FOR MR. KALISH
by
Leslie Alan Horvitz

I

When it became clear that Kalish was never going to get the script done in time if he remained any longer among the fleshpots of New York City the three of us laid down the law and told him that he would have no choice but to come along with us. We gave him no notice because we feared with good reason (the drinking, the women, etc.) that he'd bolt and we'd waste God knows how much time searching high and low for him. And it was time we couldn't afford, not with the deadline for production looming so close. We simply walked into his room at the Wyndham unannounced and told him he had half an hour to pack, and the hell with him if he didn't like it. He was ours—an indentured servant if you will—at least until he finished the damn script.

Kalish was a incandescent writer, a masterful stylist. More importantly, he was bankable. It was his track record that had convinced my partners and me to hire him in the first place. I admit that his best work was probably behind him and that his personal life was a catastrophe. But he understood what we needed, he caught on quickly, I must say that for him. The idea that Kalish, after so many years churning out scripts in Burbank and Century City (many of them uncredited), would finally agree to sit down and write a play inspired excitement even among some top Hollywood stars who held his work, if not him personally, in high regard. Top Hollywood agents wrote us letters of intent, assuring us of their clients' interest. There followed some very serious negotiations and a line of credit from the First Boston Bank.

Kalish, however, was an alcoholic and inclined to medicate himself with alarming amounts of chemicals. Worse, he was also a manic-depressive (a condition which the alcohol didn't help, of course) with suicidal tendencies. In those lucid intervals when he wasn't in the throes of despair, he really turned into a terror, making such impossible demands that we were in danger of becoming just as unhinged as he was.

While he'd plunged right into the script, knocking off twenty-five pages in the first few days, he soon became unable to keep up the momentum. We weren't worried; even if he turned out a few good pages a day we'd be happy. But then he ground to a halt entirely. We still weren't worried, we'd factored in some down time, assuming there'd be unforeseen periods of paralysis, days when he needed to revitalize his juices. But the block persisted, the bottle beckoned, and soon our worst fears were being realized. We talked of bringing in a new writer but that would force us to start from scratch. Certainly nobody could run with the pages Kalish had completed; even the most brilliant playwright would be hard put to discern where he was taking his story, much less attempt to duplicate his ineluctable style or his unique vision.

So we were stuck with him. But it was clear that we had to get him away from New York; there was no way we could control or watch over him in a city where he had so many friends and connections. Even behind the innocently boyish faces of bellboys I was seeing dopedealers and pimps.

It was Paul's idea to spirit him away to Greystone Bay. Paul Dresser is—was—the money man, the financial wizard, a multimillionaire in his own right. He had the enviable knack of coaxing money out of the nooks and crannies where it had gone into hiding. He was in his early fifties, a few years older than Marty and myself, but like us, this was his first big commercial venture. It was important to all our careers.

"Listen, Jack," he said to me over coffee one early summer day at Wolf's, "Kalish's always saying how he loves the sea, how it inspires and relaxes him. I've got just the place for him to finish the script."

"Where is this place?" I asked dubiously.

"It's called Greystone Bay. I used to summer there when I was a kid. But what I like about it is that it hasn't been discovered yet. Not like the Vineyard and the Hamptons, overrun with tourists. There's no big scene happening there is what I'm saying, Jack. It'll take us only a couple of hours to get there. One of us can always keep an eye on him—maybe we can work out some kind of rotation—and the rest of us can just lay back, take it easy. Hell, we could all use the break."

I was unsure whether a forced relocation would accomplish what we wanted but I was willing to go along with Paul and see what developed. We'd just have to okay it with Marty, who was acting as our producer. "You have any idea about accommodations?" I asked Paul.

"I'll have to check and see if it's still in business but I remember this big hotel, one of those wonderful Victorian places, called the SeaHarp. I know you're going to love it."

Not only did the SeaHarp still exist but even though it was the height of summer Paul had no trouble securing reservations.

Dealing with Kalish went better than we could have ever imagined. True, Kalish protested, his gray eyes flashing with anger at the thought of being taken away from the seductive pleasures of Manhattan. But I'd witnessed him in rages far worse and in the end he capitulated. He knew on which side his bread was buttered. "You're going to love it, Sam," Paul told him, echoing his words to me. "Some of that fresh sea air will do you—and the script—a world of good."

We didn't arrive until after dark. Greystone Bay appeared to be sound asleep. Even along what I took to be the main road few lights were burning. It was difficult to get a sense of what the town might look like. Not that it mattered; I would have plenty of time to explore it in the days that followed.

But I didn't doubt that the SeaHarp had to be one of the more imposing buildings in town. The gables and turrets that composed the top of it, and the colonnaded porch that wrapped itself around the structure, gave it a look of importance and solidity. Not that it had mattered to Kalish, who surveyed our surroundings with a melancholy expression on his face. "I don't know why you dragged me here, Paul," he muttered. "It's not going to do a damn bit of good."

"Come on, Kalish, cheer up, it'll work out, you'll see."

But, like Kalish, I wondered.

Walking through the glass-paneled doors we found ourselves in a lobby that was almost entirely empty save for an intriguing, if somewhat incongruous, couple—a man of about seventy with thin matted gray hair, dressed somberly in suit and tie, and a lovely young woman, decked out almost entirely in black: black wide-brim hat with a complicated veil, black dress scooped low in front to reveal an enticing view of her breasts, and ankle-length black boots. They were sitting on a sofa with ample distance between them, sipping from snifters of brandy, staring straight ahead, as if transfixed. Our appearance elicited little interest from them; they scarcely raised their eyes to us.

We continued up a fan-shaped staircase to the main lobby where we located the registration desk. A man materialized from behind the desk, smiling broadly, saying, "Welcome, welcome to the SeaHarp." He was a trim little middle-aged man with a fine gray moustache. Stray hair, untended, grew conspicuously from his ears, the same color as his moustache. "You must be the Dresser party," he said.

Paul introduced us and signed all our names in a voluminous registration book that gave off a smell of must.

The clerk assigned us our rooms—Kalish in 210, Paul and Marty next door in 208, while I was installed in 309. My room, it turned out, was located directly above Kalish's.

I had expected the invigorating ocean air to narcotize me into a deep untroubled sleep. This didn't happen. It may have had something to do with the bed, although it was certainly comfortable enough, and grander than any I was accustomed to in other hotels I'd stayed at. Whatever the reason, sleep didn't come for hours.

Gradually I became aware of a rhythmic clacking sound that I realized must be coming from Kalish's battered Royal. Lucky for us Kalish was oldfashioned; contemptuous of word processors and even suspicious of electric typewriters, he stuck resolutely to the same manual he'd used for decades. I say lucky because we could always tell when he was working.

So he's already begun, I thought; if the sea air wasn't helping him sleep any more than it was me, at least he might be drawing inspiration from it. For the first time it struck me that we'd made a good move by bringing him there.

The next morning the three of us—Paul, Marty and myself—met for breakfast. Kalish was still asleep. In the vastness of the dining room we were nearly lost. There were only half a dozen other people, mostly solitary diners whose attention was concentrated entirely on their eggs and toast. It

as a dazzling day; the sun spilling in through the windows
made everything lustrous and gold with its promiscuous light.

Expecting to find Paul in good spirits I was surprised to
see him looking so low. "What's wrong? I heard our friend
working until four or five this morning, whenever it was that
he finally dropped off. He must have gotten out half a dozen
pages at least."

"That's what I thought too but when I checked in with him
this morning, just before he went to bed, he told me he'd
thrown everything away. He says that he can't make it work,
he says he can't do shit in this place and if we want him to
produce anything at all we'd better get him back to New York
today."

Marty looked nearly as gloomy as Paul. "Of course he
promised us that if we did take him back he'd reform, cut out
the drinking and the wenching. But we know what would
happen. It'd be back to the same old tricks."

"Well, I think it would be a mistake to give up now," Paul
said. "Once he sees that we're serious and that we're not
about to release him until he finishes then I think he'll come
round."

"But we have to keep in mind that he might not come
round," I pointed out. "If three or four days go by and he's
still unhappy we might have to reconsider."

"Just give it a chance, Jack," Paul said. "What do you
think, Marty?"

"Jesus, I don't know, Paul. Sure, let's give it a chance.
Sounds good to me."

That first day in Greystone Bay turned out to be the last
one where the weather obliged us. I spent it seeing the sights,
what sights there were to see, getting as far as the North Hill
area, stumbling on it almost by accident. Beyond neatly
clipped hedges and ancient oaks I spied immaculately kept
lawns and rambling white Victorian houses, summer homes

for those with wealth and probably the pedigree to go along with it. But aside from a caretaker or two I saw no one.

When I walked into the SeaHarp late in the afternoon I was astonished to see Kalish sitting in the lobby holding an animated conversation with the young woman in black I'd noticed the previous evening. Today she was in white, wearing no hat. Her neckline, however, was just as dangerous.

"Sally Porter, please meet Jack Stowe," Kalish said expansively on seeing me. "Jack is my keeper and slavemaster." He laughed mirthlessly. "I was just telling Sally all about your diabolical plan to keep me chained to my typewriter." Without pausing to take a breath he said, "Sally is fascinated by artists and exotic places."

Keeping her eyes locked on Kalish she just smiled.

"Is Greystone Bay considered an exotic place, Miss Porter?" I asked.

"Oh it was my husband's choice to come here, not that I mind it. It's really quite an interesting little town if you take the time to get to know it."

"And where is your husband now, Mrs. Porter?" It was my job to see that Kalish didn't become too distracted, after all.

"Oh, I'm afraid that Charles is indisposed. And please call me Sally."

"Nothing serious, I hope?"

"It's just something that comes and goes," she replied evasively.

"Sally has been all around the world with him," Kalish said. "Her husband is an archaeologist, he's constantly on the move."

She smiled her agreement.

"That's very interesting," I said. "Do you go everywhere your husband goes?"

"Everywhere." Then she looked up at me. There was a

wild light in her eyes. "Except of course to where he's going next."

"And where would that be?"

"The grave," she said calmly.

That night, listening for the reassuring clacking of Kalish's Royal, I heard instead laughter and the throb of music that I couldn't quite identify but which sounded vaguely Middle Eastern. A monotonous rhythmic chanting went on all night long, seeming to penetrate into my dreams. It was just what I was afraid of: Kalish was seizing upon any distraction he could to escape work. In this case the distraction was very likely a woman. And not just any woman at that, I was certain, but a woman with the beauty and wiles of Sally Porter.

The following morning over breakfast I asked Paul if he'd heard the music and he said no, he'd heard nothing at all, having sacked out early. "What about Marty?"

"Ask him when he comes down."

But Marty evidently had slept as soundly as Paul.

When I began to voice my apprehensions both my partners looked at me with bafflement. "I think you must be imagining things," Paul said.

"You didn't have a chance to sit and talk with her like I did. She has considerable charm and what's worse, knows how to exercise it—to diabolical effect."

"Look, all I know is that this morning, when I spoke to him, Kalish said he was beginning to enjoy Greystone Bay and that maybe we had the right idea after all," Paul said. He and Marty exchanged a glance as if to suggest that they were both in on some little secret.

"But what about the work?" I said.

"He says it's coming along fine now, that maybe the first night he had trouble getting into his rhythm but now it's terrific—better than anything he'd done in New York."

I looked at him in astonishment. "You of all people should know better than to believe that shit, Paul."

His eyebrows shot up. "Tell him, Marty."

"It's true, Jack. He showed us what he's written just in the last twelve hours. It's amazing stuff."

"Believe me, it's extraordinary, Jack, you'll have to ask him to show it to you when he gets up. As far as I'm concerned, it's equal to anything Kalish ever wrote in his salad days."

"Better really," Marty said.

"If this woman's to account for this then so much the better," Paul added. Then he directed his gaze back at me. "Why looked so worried, Jack? Everything's going to be fine."

That second day the skies were low, the air close, and with the novelty of Greystone Bay fading, I fell into a funk deep enough that there was little chance of drinking mitigating it. Yet I began to drink anyway—and at an earlier hour than was advisable. Other guests of the hotel were gathering in the lobby, driven inside by gusts of wind off the water, apparently with the same idea in mind. The waiters, however, exhibited no hurry in carrying out their chores; it was some while before one got around to me.

"Pardon me, sir, but would you mind if I join you?"

Lifting my eyes, I took in an older grayhaired man with high color in his face. It wasn't a waiter.

Noting the puzzlement in my expression he said, extending his hand, "We haven't met, my name is Charles Porter."

Now I recognized him. "Jack Stowe."

"Yes, I know who you are," he said, seating himself. "You are in the company of Mr. Kalish."

"You could put it that way."

He signaled the waiter, who seemed more responsive to

him than he had been to me, and ordered a Corvoisier. "You have met my wife?"

"We spoke briefly."

"She's a remarkable woman," he said.

I had a feeling, though, that this wasn't necessarily meant as a compliment.

"Your friend Mr. Kalish is a writer, is he not?"

I confirmed this.

"What I am about to ask you, Mr. Stowe, may strike you as an unusual request and if you refuse I will certainly understand. However, I don't believe it would be wise to refuse."

My curiosity was naturally piqued. "What is it, Mr. Porter?"

"I would be greatly appreciative if you could spend some time with me tonight. You see, I have been watching you—from afar. And instinctively I have the feeling that you would understand."

"Understand?"

Refusing to elaborate he went on, "Also, I thought that since my wife has taken such a pronounced interest in your friend you might benefit from what I have to tell you."

I was more mystified—and intrigued. "What would that be?"

"Be patient, Mr. Stowe, be patient. You have a great deal more time remaining than I do."

"What do you mean?"

"I mean that by tomorrow morning I may well be dead."

Looking at him, still vigorous and showing no sign of illness, I found it difficult to take his dire prognostication any more seriously than I did his wife's. Unless of course he was contemplating suicide. It occurred to me that the two were engaged in an obscure game which required the coopting of outsiders for its success.

He read my thoughts. "Please wait to hear me out before you jump to any conclusions." And then he told me his story.

On the face of it, his tale was preposterous. Sober, I should never have sat and listened to it. But with drink to sustain me I didn't move.

Many years ago, he said, he was an indifferent student of archaeology. Even after obtaining his doctorate he still could find no work in his field. He'd always burned with the desire to be Heinrich Schliemann and discover a legendary city like Troy or be Howard Carter and be the first to open up a tomb as fabulous as King Tut's. But even after acquiring a teaching position at a college—one so obscure and inconsequential that he was embarrassed to name it—his future looked bleak. "I was in such despair that I even considered forgetting archaeology and going into business," he said. "I had an offer from a friend to join his radio parts business. If I'd done that it would have been death."

One summer, in his fortieth year, he managed to scrape together the money to go abroad. Since he'd written his thesis on the ancient Near East he could think of no better destination. He stayed in cheap, decrepit hotels or in the homes of people good enough to put him up. As his journey was drawing to an end he still felt dissatisfied; it seemed to him that he'd missed something essential, that what he was searching for was right there in front of his eyes, only that he lacked the ability to perceive it.

It was in the middle of that summer while he was staying in a Turkish village that he met Sally. She was travelling alone. While it seemed that she was married her husband was nowhere in evidence. She told Porter that they were used to taking separate vacations and that she had no idea when she'd see him again.

When he asked her what she was doing in such a remote region in Turkey, where it wasn't very safe for a man to travel by himself, let alone a beautiful woman, she said that she was hunting for antiquities. She was convinced that there were few finds worth buying in places where safety could be guaranteed. But that wasn't what he found so intriguing. "She claimed to have learned the whereabouts of Elaeus which once stood on the heights above Morto Bay, beyond Sedd-el-Bahr."

I had no idea where these places might be but for fear of interrupting him I let him continue.

"It may be difficult for a layman to imagine it but for me her words were a revelation. Elaeus was a vanished city, its discovery would be of enormous importance. Perhaps not on the order of Troy or Macchu Picchu but important enough. I asked her if she could use her contacts to take us to the site. She agreed immediately. It seemed to me that she was thoroughly delighted to find someone who shared her enthusiasm for the ancient world.

"In short, we fell in love," Porter said as if this inevitably followed from what he'd just told me. "I'd had women before but there was no one in my experience to compare with her. I was completely smitten, I was ready to give up everything for her."

"But from what you've told me it doesn't seem as if you had anything to give up to begin with."

He smiled. "You have forgotten my life."

They agreed to get married as soon as Sally could settle her divorce. Sally assured him that there'd be no problem, no complications or legal entanglements; she wasn't a woman to allow anything to stand in her way. He realized from the start that she was the stronger of the two, that he was a fool to believe that he would be able to hold onto her. He was grateful for every day he had with her, certain that one morning he would wake to find her gone.

Strange things began to happen to him—good things. His career, which had been stymied for so many years, began to flourish. It got so that he could walk out into a desert of rocks and scrub brush and pinpoint with uncanny accuracy the location of ruins no one had any idea were there at all.

"I achieved everything I could have hoped for," he said. "I won grants, honors, prizes. And all the time I knew that it was because of her." Then his eyes narrowed. "Would you mind coming up to my room? There's something I'd like to show you."

This was all getting too bizarre and outlandish for me but it was nothing compared to what would come.

The Porters' room—206, located just down the hallway from Kalish's—was crowded with her belongings, her dresses, her shoes, her toiletries, her perfumes. It even smelled like her. Porter then did an extraordinary thing; after rummaging through his effects he produced a gleaming dagger. It was beautifully crafted, its gold handle, though blackened with age, was still intact, with intricately mythical figures set in jewels on either side of it.

"It's very nice," I said. "How old is it?"

"It is of great age, this is possibly the only knife like it extant."

"You got this in your travels?"

"Yes, yes, I did. It is a ceremonial knife, you see—a sacrificial knife. I would like you to give it to your friend the writer, Mr. Kalish."

I was bewildered. "I'm sure he'd be delighted to receive such a gift but really I think you're better off keeping it. Kalish, I'm afraid, doesn't go in big for antiquities. If you're going to give it away give it to somebody who'd appreciate it more."

"No," he said firmly, "it must be given to Mr. Kalish. Do you recall what I said to you before about Sally's husband?"

"You said that she divorced him."

"I'm sorry to say that I wasn't telling you the truth. You

see, Mr. Stowe, I killed him. With that knife you're holding.''

Gently I placed the knife down on the table. ''I don't think I understand.''

He smiled wanly. ''Of course, you don't. Here, let me show you something else.'' He reached into one of his suitcases and produced a small black figurine which he held up for my inspection. ''It's a moon goddess,'' he said. ''She must be at least five thousand years old.''

Whoever had sculpted her had done a competent but by no means exceptional job: the figurine was ripe, the breasts heavy, the pubis exaggerated, the belly engorged by pregnancy.

''Note the face.''

The features were eroded by time and abuse but from what I can see there was little beauty there.

''What do you see?''

I shrugged.

''That is my wife.''

I looked up at him, more confirmed in my impression that he was mad. ''I'm sorry to say, Mr. Porter, I can't see much of a resemblance.''

''The resemblance is irrelevant, it doesn't matter.'' He made a dismissive gesture with his hand, his expression betraying his impatience with me, my failure to understand.

''You must give this dagger to Mr. Kalish.'' His voice was more insistent now.

''But why? He won't know what to do with it, I'm telling you.''

''Listen to me, Mr. Stowe, my wife is enraptured by him, I don't know why, I don't know why she should be attracted to him anymore than I know what many years ago led her to pick me. But the fact is that she did and now she has chosen Mr. Kalish.''

Thinking that I would play his game, at least until I could

conveniently excuse myself and flee his room, I said, "All right, so she's chosen Kalish." Not for one moment did I believe that there was anything to it, at the most it was a brief dalliance. I couldn't believe that it would turn into a full-fledged affair.

"No, listen to me, Mr. Stowe, it is not so simple. If she has chosen him it means that he must kill me."

"Wait a minute now, I'm sorry but this is a little too crazy for me." As I was saying this I was backing towards the door.

Porter, however, sensing my alarm, turned suddenly apologetic. "You must pardon me for not explaining first. I didn't think. Please don't leave like this, Mr. Stowe. If you go now grave consequences might ensue which you could have prevented. You must give this knife to Mr. Kalish and instruct him to kill me just as twenty-five years ago I killed Mr. Barnard."

"If you want to die, you'll have to do it yourself. I don't think that Kalish is at all disposed to killing anybody, especially people he doesn't know." It was on my tongue to make some cruel reference to cuckolded husbands but I refrained—wisely I think. I merely said, "It's not in his nature." I was hoping that by keeping my voice level and cool that somehow I might break through to him and make him see reason.

"It's no longer a matter of what Mr. Kalish wants or what I want. It is Sally who makes the decision. Once she has chosen there is no longer a choice. Either he must kill me or else, failing that, I am sorry to say I will have no choice but to kill him. I'm imploring you, Mr. Stowe."

"There's nothing I can do," I said. "I don't want any part of this."

"I know that you think me mad. You can't imagine what it was like when Sally told me what I must do to Mr. Barnard. But it is worth it. No court of law will ever find your friend guilty, Sally will see to that. And she will inspire him beyond his wildest dreams. Already, I think, he is producing excellent work. It will only get better, believe me. He will produce a great hit for you, I guarantee it."

"Until the next man comes along," I said.

"It may take years, decades, who knows? It's worth it. It was worth it to me. But now I am all used up, there's nothing left I can give her. In bed you see . . ." He let his words hang there in awkward silence. "But if Mr. Kalish will not win her . . ."

"By killing you?"

He smiled as if I were a dullwitted child who'd finally grasped the most fundamental of concepts. "Exactly." He gave a shrug. "Then I will be obliged to kill him and remain with Sally until such time as she discovers another man to whom she is equally attracted. Take a look at this if you don't believe me."

From out of his battered wallet he extracted a photo. It was worn from handling through the years and smudged. It was a photo of Sally. "That was taken when we first met. Tell me the truth, Mr. Stowe, does she look any different to you now?"

Except that she wore her hair shorter then, I had to admit that I couldn't distinguish any difference.

"You see, she is ageless, it is just what I am telling you."

I said I wasn't convinced. Photographs could be deceptive even if this one was in fact taken a quarter of a century ago. My words pained him. He grew more imploring. "Please, Mr. Stowe, take the dagger. It has to be done tonight."

"Tonight?" I was almost on the verge of believing him, such was the conviction in his voice.

"Yes, tonight." His gaze found the dagger, then returned to me. "What will it be, Mr. Stowe? It's your choice."

II

Following my unpleasant meeting with Charles Porter I went back to the lobby, desperate for a drink. Only with a fortifying brace of whiskey did it seem possible for me to determine what I should do about this business. Uncertain how Kalish would react, particularly if he really was in the throes of an infatuation for Sally Porter, I decided not to say anything to him, not until I'd had an opportunity to discuss the situation with my partners.

Before I could summon the energy to go find them Marty appeared. From the troubled expression on his face I had a feeling that word of Porter's sinister proposition must have reached him too.

It turned out that after my rebuff Porter had indeed solicited Marty's help, using—I gathered—some of the same blandishments on him that he'd used on me. Like a Silas Marner who never tired of telling his tale, he'd repeated it in detail for Marty's benefit. If anything, Marty was more agitated and distressed than I had been.

"What do you think we should do?" he asked. "Drag Kalish away from his girlfriend and go back to New York? This guy Porter's a lunatic, nothing good can come of this."

"I don't know. If we try to separate Kalish from Sally he may go on strike, refuse to write another work for us. As it is, he's going great guns. I'd hate to do anything to gum up the works."

"I don't want to sound mercenary, Jack, but if this bastard kills him then we're really going to be stuck."

Somehow I couldn't believe that Porter, for all the passion with which he'd invested his words, would actually attack Kalish. "Besides," I reminded Marty, "Kalish is several years younger than Porter and physically much stronger."

"So long as he isn't three sheets to the wind," Marty said ruefully, "Then a five-year-old kid could knock him down."

"My feeling is that if we warn Kalish and tell him to take adequate precautions we really don't have much to worry about. Tell you what, why don't we wait to talk to Paul, see what he says?"

"By the way, where the hell is Paul?"

"Isn't he upstairs in the room?"

"Haven't seen him since this morning." We both looked at each other. We had a good idea where he must be.

About twenty minutes later Paul appeared. Unlike the two of us he seemed in excellent spirits. An inexplicable smile was on his lips. "Well, hello there!" he said. "Why so glum?"

"Porter," I said.

"What about him?"

As Marty began to explain he cut him off. "I know all about the dagger and that goddess crap, I was with him just now."

"You told him to take his dagger and shove it, I hope," Marty said.

Paul looked startled. "Are you kidding? I figured what the hell? He wants Kalish to have it, let him have it. What's the big deal? Better it's in Kalish's hands than his, right?"

"I can't believe you did that, Paul," I said. "You're playing his goddamn game, it's crazy. What did Kalish say when you gave it to him?"

"He was a little puzzled I guess, but he took it and told me to say thank you to Porter and then went back to his work. His work, by the way, is proceeding by leaps and bounds— nine pages so far today, a record."

At that moment I wasn't concerned about Kalish's output or his sudden fecundity. "I think you're not going to like what happens, Paul," I said.

He just looked at me as if I were just saying that to aggravate him and didn't reply.

That night I couldn't sleep, nor did I want to. Instead, my attention was concentrated on the room below mine as I strained to pick up any sound that might signal the start of violence. I even went so far as to prowl the second floor hallway late at night, surreptitiously pressing my ear to Kalish's door and then to the Porters'. But I heard nothing alarming, in fact I barely heard anything at all. No laughter, no music, no strange chanting, not even the fitful clacking of Kalish's aged typewriter; the terrifying scenario I'd begun to envision after listening to Porter's fearsome tale seemed to exist solely in my head.

Sometime before dawn I must have dozed off. When I came awake there was no telling from looking out the window what hour of the day it was; the skies were leaden gray, it could have been the middle of the morning or twilight. It was actually a little past ten a.m. My frayed nerves hadn't allowed me much sleep after all.

I knocked on the door to Paul and Marty's room, anxious to discover whether anything untoward had occurred during the night, but there was no response. With a great deal of hesitancy I rapped on Kalish's door but again my knocking was met with silence.

They'd stopped serving breakfast in the dining room by this time and all I could procure for myself was the brioche and coffee a waiter found for me in the kitchen.

Later when I went outside on the porch the maddening screech of seagulls filled my ears; they were making such a racket that no other sound could get through. Glancing to my left I caught sight of a solitary figure sitting in a rocker chair staring out to sea. It was Porter.

My heart lurched, I couldn't suppress the lurid tableau that immediately sprang to my mind: Kalish lying in a heap on the floor of his room, blood trickling from the fatal wound in his chest. I was almost about to duck back into the hotel, afraid of having to confront Porter, but it was too late. From where he was sitting there was no way he wouldn't have spotted me. I was sure to find out what had happened (if anything) sooner or later, I thought, it was better I get it over with now.

Steeling myself for what was to come I approached him. He was a study in white—hat, jacket, slacks, shoes—his hands clasped together, his legs crossed at his ankles. "Mr. Porter," I said, "How are you this morning?" I tried to sound casual but I doubt whether I came across that way.

Porter didn't stir, the direction of his gaze remained unwavering. I was now standing right in front of him so that there was no possibility of his ignoring me. Though he might be angry with me I wasn't prepared to be shunned so absolutely. "Mr. Porter!" I said a second time.

Now when he didn't respond I drew closer to him. Then I reached out and lowered my hand to his. It was cold. I felt for a pulse. There was none. Though I could see no dagger nor any trace of blood, the fact was that Charles Porter was dead.

III

It was nearly ten years before I saw Kalish again. We met for drinks in the lobby of the SeaHarp, which was little changed from what I remembered. Kalish had noticeably aged but renewed prosperity and fame had kept him invigorated—though probably not nearly as much as his wife had. Sally looked as lovely as ever, with those glorious dark eyes of hers that caused an unsettling sensation in my chest whenever she focused them on me. If Kalish found it strange that the last decade had failed to add even a slight wrinkle to her face or put an extra pound on her miraculous body he certainly didn't let on to me about it.

Mostly what he talked about was the new wing they were building onto the house that they'd bought in the North Hill. It was my impression that Kalish still had a hankering for the city but nonetheless had settled in rather agreeably to life with Sally in Greystone Bay. She said that from the first moment she'd laid eyes on the town she'd felt at home. There was something about the people who lived here, she said, that she could identify with.

There was no mention—by any of us—of Charles Porter. Talk of his unhappy end, attributed by the local coroner to a stroke, would only have put a damper on our reunion. In any case, there were more pressing concerns on my mind.

When Kalish's play *Sleep With Their Fathers* had opened we were prepared for a certain critical and financial success but nothing like what happened. Within six months the play moved from its original Off-Broadway venue to Broadway, where it played for almost three years, reaping substantial rewards for all of us—Kalish, Paul, Marty, and myself.

Only, as often happens in such cases, success ultimately proved more devastating for us than failure and uncertainty had been. An acrimonious dispute that began in a drunken exchange of words at a dinner party culminated in a long and bitter legal battle, one which ended in tragedy—Paul died of a heart attack which his family blamed on us. They maintained that if Marty and I hadn't repeatedly dragged him into court he'd still be alive. Even after a settlement was reached, Marty refused to speak to me again because he thought I should have held out for more. Kalish meanwhile was never really a part of the dispute; he had the good fortune to be able to bank his royalty money without having to spend it all on lawyers.

Only desperation would have driven me to seek Kalish out

r a favor. But there was no getting around it: my situation as desperate. Because of legal expenses and unexpected usiness reverses I was now staring into the abyss of bankptcy with no way out. There were no longer many people could tap for loans to tide me over until something finally orked out—if something finally worked out. But Kalish had he money, his name counted for a lot in the entertainment usiness, and besides, I believed he owed me a favor. Surely e wouldn't be where he was today, in a grand house with a eautiful wife, if it weren't for the efforts of my partners and yself.

His home in the exclusive North Hill section of Greystone ay proved to be a stately Victorian mansion which, with its stive gingerbread style, might have been designed by the ame architect responsible for the SeaHarp. It turned out that alish had a lawn party planned for the evening which he rged me to stay for. "You don't have to get back to the city o soon," he said, "I'm having over some interesting people om around here, you'll have a ball."

He was so preoccupied by the preparations for this affair aat he scarcely seemed to hear what I had to say. My plight iiled to elicit much interest or sympathy from him; maybe e believed it too nice a day to discuss indebtedness. The ay he said he'd think about it caused me to suspect that othing would happen; no money would be forthcoming nor ould I expect him to agree to let me use his name or his ontacts. I noticed that after I'd made my pitch he began to eep a certain distance from me as if I bore the mark of Cain n my brow. I had become one of them. He probably regret-ed having invited me to his party.

Sally, however, seemed more interested in my unhappy le. Was I mistaken to think that there was even a measure f sympathy in her eyes for me?

About half an hour before the party was to begin the house vas swarming with caterers and servants, a small army taking their orders from Kalish. A big buffet table was being set up on the lawn. The gardener was raking the gravel in the driveway to make it neater for the limousines that would shortly be parking in it. Everywhere there was an air of excitement and intoxication that had nothing to do with me.

Drunk already and disgusted with myself for not handling Kalish's rebuff better than I had, I went in search of a bathroom. Somehow I found myself in a room with mirrors—a dressing room. In one of the mirrors the half-naked form of Sally Kalish took shape. She caught a glimpse of me in the mirror; an enigmatic smile slowly formed on her newly reddened lips. A moment later I felt her touch on my arm. I looked around, dazzled by the sight of her, unable to speak.

"It's time," she said. "You can have what you want—everything you want." She paused, the smile vanished. "You can have me too. It is much simpler than you imagine."

"What is?" My voice sounded unnatural and foreign to me.

"You know what," she said solemnly. "The blade only has to break the skin, the poison on the tip does the rest. He won't even feel it—it's that easy." She was standing so close that I could almost feel her lustrous skin, her warmth. I had difficulty keeping my gaze on her face. "But of course if you refuse . . . you know what happens then. It will be you. I will have to tell him, he'll have no choice."

"When . . . ?" In my nervousness it was all I could manage to get out.

"Now, this evening." She pressed the dagger into my hand before I realized what she was doing. Then she closed my fingers around the handle.

When I joined the party it was in full swing. Somebody pointed out to me that I had lipstick on my face but by then that was the least of my worries.

NO PAIN, NO GAIN
by
Thomas F. Monteleone

"Excuse me, sir, but aren't you forgetting something?" asked Roger Easton, chief bell-boy at the SeaHarp.

"What's that?" said the thin, dishevelled guest who was walking toward the door with two arm-loads of baggage.

"That other box," said Roger, pointing to a fairly large container in the corner of the room. It looked like one of those thin-slatted crates they shipped bottled water in.

The guest stopped at the door, eased his bags to the carpet, and looked back over a bony shoulder at Roger. "Oh, that . . ."

"Yeah," said Roger. "Want me to get it for you? I can carry it out on the dolly."

The guest looked at Roger for a moment, then tried to enact a small smile. "Actually, no, I don't."

Roger was taken aback. What the heck was going on here? From the minute he first saw this guy, he figured he was a weirdo—what with the trimmed goatee and the thick horn-rimmed glasses and the baggy suit. The guest looked like one of those jazz musicians or French painters you always saw in cartoons. Of course, Roger made it his business to know as much as possible about all of the SeaHarp's guests, and he already knew this guy was a professor from Miskatonic University, and he'd been in Greystone Bay to give one of those weekend self-help seminars to all the yuppies.

"Is everything all right?" asked the guest. Roger had apparently been staring at him mutely. He did that sometimes without even realizing it. He'd start having some interesting thought, and bang, there he'd be—staring off with his mouth hanging open like he was trying to catch flies with it. He closed his mouth and gathered in his thoughts like a pile of crumpled-up laundry.

"Oh, it's just that we don't usually allow people to leave stuff behind," said Roger. "If you lose somethin' or forget somethin', that's one thing. But people don't usually leave stuff on purpose."

"*I* am," said the professor.

The abruptness of the man's answer surprised him, but Roger could only say: "And why's that?"

The tall man paused and looked at Roger. "What's your name, son?"

Roger told him.

"Do you make good tips here?"

"It's okay, I guess . . . why?"

The professor reached into his pocket, pulled out a roll of bills. "I make out pretty good with my seminars," he muttered. "Here, take this and do me a favor, all right?"

Roger accepted the bill, not wanting to steal a glance at the number in the corner, but when you were getting a big tip, bell-hops had this sort of sixth sense about it. Roger just *knew* it was a good one and he had to check it out. Once a guy from Texas had given him ten bucks, then there was that woman from New York who promised him a twenty if he'd—he looked down into his hand—My God! A hundred bucks!

"Something wrong?" asked the professor, still looming over him.

"Jeez, no, but I . . . I never got a tip like this before!"

"Nor will you probably ever again. No matter, you have one now. I want you to do me a favor, all right?"

"Yeah! Just name it!" Roger stuffed the bill into his pants pocket. It seemed to glow with its own heat, radiating wealth up and down his leg. A hundred bucks!

"As I said before, I intend to leave that small crate behind. It isn't necessary for it to remain in this room, however." The professor cleared his throat, stared at Roger intently.

"Yeah, okay. So?"

"So I want you to do this for me: put the crate somewhere safe and secure within this hotel. Hide it, if you think it necessary, but remember, it must remain within the walls of this building. Is that clear?"

Boy, this guy was sounding pretty weird, thought Roger. 'Course, there was nothing weird about the hundred-dollar bill warming up his pants pocket.

"Is that clear, Roger?"

"Huh? Oh yeah, sure. I can find a place to keep it. No problem."

The professor nodded. "Very good. Now, here, take my card. There's my phone number on it. I want you to call me at the University if you have any problems. I will be stopping back once a week to check on the bottle. Understood?"

Roger accepted the card. "Yeah, but why?"

"Well, it's quite simple really—I want to know what things look like in a month or so."

Jeez, that reminded him. "Hey, I meant to ask you. Just what is it you got in that crate, anyway?"

"It is none of your concern." The professor's voice was flat and stern, reminding Roger of his dead father's.

"Jeez, I don't know . . . I don't want to do anything that's gonna get me in trouble."

A large, bony hand suddenly vised down on his shoulder. "If you don't want to help me out, I'm sure I can find someone else who *can . . . especially* for a hundred-dollar tip."

The thought of losing his tip sent a bolt of electric juice through Roger like he'd stuck his finger in a light socket. Jeez, this guy was serious.

"Oh, no sir! You don't have to worry about that. Listen, I was just tryin' to make conversation. I don't really care what's in the crate, honest. And I'll hide it for you, no problem."

The man stared at him, as though evaluating the proposition, then nodded slowly. "Very well. Keep my card. You shall call me if anything untoward occurs between my visits. Now, let's go. I have a long drive ahead of me."

"Yes sir!" said Roger, grabbing the handle of the dolly. As he walked down the hall toward the elevator bay, he could almost hear the crackle of that crisp bill against his right thigh, and he began thinking of ways he could spend so much extra cash.

"I can't believe you wanted to stay in this goddamned place," said Angela in her whining, yet still acidic tone of voice. It was a voice Daniel Rosenthal had grown to despise in a surprisingly short amount of time.

"Jesus Christ, we just got here," he said softly, trying to keep from sounding shitty. He really wanted to make a sincere effort. "What's wrong with it? Let's give it a chance, okay?"

Angela preened in the mirror, fingering this curl and that. Daniel wondered why she just didn't get her hair exactly right, get it encased in lucite, and forget about it.

"The SeaHarp Hotel!" she muttered. "Didn't this town ever hear of a Holiday Inn?"

"They're all the same. This place has character." Daniel

opened his parachute luggage, started hanging up his shirts and pants.

"But there's nothing to *do* here, Danny-Boy. No sauna, no pool. They don't even have a night-club."

He walked over to her, put his arms around her while she continued looking at herself in the mirror. She was not the most beautiful woman he'd ever been with, and her body was just average, but there had always been something about her that attracted him.

"If you recall, honey, we're supposed to be 'doing' each other. Isn't that was this little vacation is all about?"

He'd felt her tense up as soon as he touched her. Six years of marriage and there was about as much warmth between them as ice cubes in a tray. He'd truly loved her, but she did not love him. It was that simple, and he was having a hell of a time accepting it. They'd read countless books, been to counselors and therapists, and nothing had essentially changed. Angela resented him. She was intimidated by him, threatened intellectually by him. His list of accomplishments (Daniel Rosenthal was a nationally renowned orthodontic specialist, the author of several definitive textbooks, a wildly successful public speaker, and the holder of sixteen patents) made her feel inadequate, stupid, and hopelessly inferior. Since marrying him, Angela had learned to *loathe* Trivial Pursuit. She felt powerless and inept in his presence in all things but one—and it was from this single thing that she fashioned a most terrible weapon.

Daniel had always been a naturally affectionate man. He gave his love freely and he craved it in return. And when Angela finally learned this, she lunged for her newfound power with a vengeance. Her rejection ate him up like the cruelest of cancers. When he would tell her he loved her, and only a cold, black silence welled up out of her in reply, the bottomless pain and naked fear in his heart ranged outward like a beacon of loneliness.

Only Angela had the power to hurt him so exquisitely and she wielded her special weapon with the skill of a neurosurgeon. If he made no overtures, she could let them live like brother and sister for months at a time, and then almost whimsically deign to open her legs for him when she *felt* like it. Like a dumb mutt, he would sit up and get ready for her, waiting for her to toss him a doggie-treat.

She turned and slipped out of his embrace, walked to the window, stared out at the manicured hedges and lawns of the grand old hotel. Keeping her back to him, she spoke to the leaded glass panes. "Oh yes, I keep forgetting. This is our 'second honeymoon,' isn't it?"

Daniel couldn't ignore the sarcasm in her voice. "Well, we didn't have much of a first one now, did we?"

He was referring to her wrenching a disc in her back as she picked a heavy suitcase from the airport's luggage carousel. He was referring to ten days at Lake Tahoe with her complaining of increasingly intolerable lumbar pain and avoiding even a comforting touch from him the whole time. He was referring to her answer when he suggested they substitute with mutual oral sex until her back healed: *I guess I should tell you now, Dan—I've always hated doing that to you, and honestly I don't think I could ever do it again.*

He remembered wondering back then what her definition of love might be (since it obviously didn't include giving to your lover because it made him feel good. Or deriving pleasure from simply *knowing* that you made him feel good.)

Angela whirled angrily from the window, her face twisted with a special loathing. "You prick! You always bring that up when you have nothing else to say!"

"Well I guess it's a measure of my pain, Angela. The memory won't go away."

"You bastard! You act like it was my fault! Like I hurt my back on purpose . . . !"

"You mean *if* you hurt it at all." The words came out of

him without aforethought. He knew immediately how much they would hurt her. He didn't really want that, did he?

She rushed him, raising her long fingernails at him like talons, going for his face. "You bastard!" she cried out, again and again.

This was not going well at all, thought Daniel, as he fended her off.

Roger ended up stashing the crate on the fourth floor, at the end of the wainscotted hall, in Room 434. The smaller rooms up there were practically never used, especially in the off-season. And now that November was only a couple of weeks away, nobody would be checking that room very often, if at all.

After he'd carefully hidden it behind the valenced draperies, and had turned to leave, Roger had decided that, damn it, he *did* need to know what was in that crate. Its size and weight indicated something substantial, and if it was something like a safe, then maybe he should know about it. A fantasy of the professor being a secret embezzler or bank-robber made him smile. Roger could confront him with his hidden cache of loot, and make him split the money. Yeah. . . .

But his get-rich-easy dreams faded quickly when he pried back one of the thin, wood slats of the crate to discover one of those big bottled-water bottles in there. Just like he'd first imagined. Now what the hell was going on here? Looking closer, Roger noted that the water was not clear like bottled water. Rather, it had a murky, greenish cast. Peering in through the single open slat, he could see nothing in the water, but his instincts told him the bottle could not be empty. After prying the top of the crate loose, he carefully eased the thick-walled glass container from the crate. It was bulky and probably more than three feet high. He carried the bottle closer to the window and even then, at first glance, he couldn't see a damn thing. Now why the hell was he hiding a bottle of creek-water for?

It wasn't until he started to roll it back under the draperies that he saw it.

Just for an instant, then it was gone. A flash of color and reflected light, like a polished fish-lure spinning through the water. Roger stopped moving the big bottle, again peered into the aquarium depths.

There it was. The little bastard. Jeez, it was *small*, but it was there.

The light had to hit it just right or he couldn't even see it, but once he knew what he was looking for, he kept relocating it every time it would disappear. It reminded him of that tropical fish they called a *neon*—not because of its shape, just its colors, which kept changing like an electric rainbow. Its shape was hard to figure. Definitely not a fish-shape, though. It was more like a *blob*. No shape at all, really. Roger wondered if he could see arms or legs or eyes in that tiny shapeless mass, and decided that he couldn't really see much of anything.

But that had been more than a week ago . . .

True to his word, the professor came by to check on things. Roger was very courteous to the man and persuaded him to let him tag along for the inspection.

"All right," said the professor. "Let's have a look."

Roger nodded and uncovered the bottle, then jumped back away from it instinctively when he saw the shape within its brackish depths.

"Damn!" he said automatically, his breath hitching up in his throat. He hadn't been prepared for what he now saw behind the glass.

The tiny sliver of colored tissue had been replaced by something a little larger than a softball. No, that wasn't right.

hadn't been replaced . . . whatever it was in there had grown. The little bastard was growing, Jeez . . .

The professor calmly went about observing the thing and making notes on a little pad he'd pulled from his coat. Roger peered down at the pulpy mass and winced. It was uglier than anything he'd ever seen. Essentially shapeless, it reminded him of a freshly excised organ like maybe a spleen or a brain or something. There were convolutions and folds of tissue; there were tendrils and other streamers of meat hanging off it; there were objects that might have been the beginnings of eyes and tiny clawed appendages. Roger remembered once as a kid his mother cracked open an egg and it had a half-developed chicken in it, and this thing in the bottle almost reminded him of that. It was the weirdest thing he'd ever seen, no doubt.

But calling it weird didn't cover all the bases. No way.

As Roger stared into the dark green liquid, the creature moved toward him, flattening somewhat against the glass. He sensed the thing would have liked to have grabbed onto him, and he didn't like that feeling even a little bit.

He also sensed something else about the creature: that maybe it was *evil*.

The professor continued to write something hastily in his notebook, not standing until he was finished. "All right, son, you can cover it up again."

As Roger followed his instruction, a question occurred to him—if that thing had grown so much, just what the hell was it *eating*? He decided he'd ask the professor.

"A good question," said the man. "But I'm afraid it's a bit too early to tell. Let's wait another week or so."

Melanie Cantrell checked the lock on the door to her hotel room. She'd already put the *Do Not Disturb* sign on the knob, but goodness knew she didn't want any maids coming in while she in the middle of . . . of what she was here to do.

The last phrase stuck in her mind like a line of lyrics on a scratched record. Here she was ready to do it, and she couldn't even bring herself to mention the word. She turned away from the door, passed a small mirror on the wall—something to afford a guest a last-second check of hair or clothing before leaving the room—and stole a look at her own face.

Bloodshot and red-rimmed from all the tears, her eyes looked like some zombie's from a bad movie. The muscles in her jaw, taut and corded, had contorted her normally pretty features into a mask of tense pain. Oh God, what was she doing here? She turned away from the mirror and began to unpack her suitcase. She carried several changes of clothes, extra towels and dressings, a few books, and her diary. After she emptied her bag, her gaze fell upon the telephone, squatting like some kind of dark creature by the side of the bed.

She still had a chance to call Teddy and tell him where she'd gone . . . and why.

But no, she wasn't going to involve him in any of it. She'd already decided that she would go through it alone. Besides Teddy would've went *crazy* if he ever found out she'd let herself get pregnant. He was like that when she did something he didn't like, screaming and yelling, and even hitting her once in a while. She looked away from the phone, wishing just for a moment that Teddy was the kind of guy who could be gentle sometimes. She'd never known a man who could be gentle, and her mother had always told her there was no such thing. She figured it must be true.

Well, she told herself bravely, it was time.

Melanie opened her little travel-bag and dug through till she found the vial of pills her friend Cathy had given her. Cathy was the only person in the world who knew she was spending the weekend at the SeaHarp. Melanie didn't want *anyone* to know, but Cathy had been the one who got her the drugs that would make her miscarriage (it was easy with

Cathy's older sister going to pharmacy school!). And besides, if anything happened to her, she wanted *somebody* to know where to look for her.

Melanie walked into the bathroom and shook out three of the pinkish pills, washed them down with water just the way Cathy said she should. It would take a few hours before her body would begin to rebel against the intruder in her womb; it would be best if she went to sleep for a while. Walking from the bathroom, she passed an open closet harboring several coat-hangers.

Pausing, Melanie looked into the darkness at the triangles of wire, and the memory of old horror stories rose up in her mind. She wondered what she would do if the pills didn't work.

Oh Teddy, she thought, as tears stained her cheeks. *I love you.*

When Roger and the professor checked the bottle the following week, he hesitated in pulling back the draperies.

"Go on, son," said the professor, notepad already in hand.

Roger did it and looked into the water. What he saw made his stomach churn. The professor started writing like crazy.

What was going on here? thought Roger. The damned thing was disgusting. A fuckin' monster—that's what they were growing in there.

Jeez, it looked worse than ever. The image of the undeveloped egg-embryo needed to be revised; it had changed, warped into something really alien, something *bad*. And it had been doing some *serious* growing—the bulk of it barely fit within the confines of the bottle. The thing had grown not only larger, but *darker*. Its dissected-organ appearance glistened with pulsating life. There was a sac-life thing which almost glowed with orange movement. There was something that could have been an eye. A tendril-like arm. Was that a claw? Seaweed-like stuff flowed and wavered in self-contained currents. The amorphous body constantly in ebbing motion, Roger was unable to recognize what was really growing in there. But whatever it was, he knew two things for sure: it was a nasty motherfucker and it couldn't get a whole hell of a lot bigger without busting the glass bottle.

"You didn't tell me it was gonna get so big," he said.

"I didn't know *what* it was going to do. This was an experiment, remember?" The professor's voice was calm, even. In control.

"Yeah, I guess you're right," said Roger. "But, man, it looks bad, doesn't it? It's getting crowded in there."

"No, I still think there's plenty of room."

"What is it? You never told me?"

The professor rubbed his chin pensively. "I'm not sure."

"Well, listen, is it dangerous?" Roger figured it was—no matter what the professor said.

"Probably. I don't know yet."

Roger swallowed hard. Now there was an honest answer if he ever heard one.

"Where'd you get it anyway? Are you a biology-guy?"

The man smiled thinly. "No, I'm an archeologist—I found the, ah, spores of this thing in a stoppered vial thousands of years old."

"Really? Where?"

The professor shrugged. "The ruins of a building dating back to early Mycenaean times. I brought it back from my last dig."

"Yeah, I got you." Roger didn't know from mice an' eons, but he figured the professor was onto something pretty weird, so he figured he oughta just play along.

"There were writings, too," said the professor. "They spoke of this as a *deimophage*. Fascinating, don't you think? I tried controlled experiments at the university with laboratory animals, but I didn't have much heart for the torturing necessary, you see."

Roger frankly *didn't* see at all, but he nodded his head solemnly as the professor rambled on.

"Besides, it wasn't working. None of the spores did anything. I decided they required spontaneously generated human emotion, so I thought of the most suitable test environment—hence the SeaHarp!"

"Yeah . . . right," said Roger, having lost the thread way back there somewhere. "Hey, is it okay to cover it up now?"

The professor nodded. "Till next week."

"You sure it's gonna be okay. If it grows as much this week as it did last—"

The professor waved off his protest. "Everything will be just fine, Roger. Let's be off."

"Yeah?" said Bobby Kaminski, grabbing the receiver from its cradle. He'd been pacing about the hotel room, waiting for the call for what seemed like an eternity.

"Okay, man, we're in the lobby. What room you in?"

"Two-O-Five," said Bobby. "You got the money?"

"Hey, man . . . sure we do. You got the shit?"

Bobby nodded, rubbed his nose. "Yeah, I got it." He was getting bad feelings about all this, but there was no turning back now.

"Okay, keep it stiff, man. We'll be right up."

Bobby hung up the phone and began pacing the hotel room again. How did he ever get involved in this crazy bullshit? If he wasn't such a goddamned cokehead . . .

He didn't much like himself, but he didn't like dealing with this guy, Andy, a lot worse. Sherry'd hooked him up, but Bobby didn't like the looks of Andy, didn't like his scent. The Good Fathers of Greystone Bay didn't have much compassion for dealers and Bobby was feeling pretty paranoid. Either this guy Andy was a narc, or he was just bad news. Either way, Bobby didn't dig the set up—that's why he kept his jacket on; that's why he kept his snub-nose .38 in his shoulder holster.

Hard knocks at the door broke up his thoughts. He opened the door after checking the peep-hole.

"Hey, dude, how's it hangin'?"

Andy was standing there in his leather gear, punctuated now and then by chrome studding and chains. He smelled of grease and road-grime. Behind him were two other bikers who looked like they could have been tag-team members from a World Federation Wrestling bout. One of them carried a small nylon Nike sportsbag.

"I thought I told you to come alone," said Bobby.

"Hey, I don't go nowhere without my stick-men," said Andy, who remained standing in the hallway. "So, are we comin' in, or what?"

Bobby stood aside and the trio entered—the two goons immediately casing things out like good goons should. He didn't like this situation at all. His nose was itching and burning. He'd love to take a toot right about now, but he needed to be clear, to be ready for anything.

"Okay, where is it?" asked Andy.

Bobby opened the top dresser drawer and pulled out the kilo, nicely wrapped and sanitized for their protection. "You got the money?" he asked. His voice sound weak, reedy. Scared.

Andy smiled and nodded to the goon with the Nike bag, who threw it on the bed. Unzipping it, Bobby wasn't really surprised to see it was filled with cut-up newspapers. So it was going down like this . . .

Swinging around, he reached for his gun. Better to take out Andy, then maybe reason with the other two.

But before he could complete the turn, something stunned him, creating a stinging halo around the back of his head. His knees jellied up on him and huge arms caught him as he started to go down. Bobby was dazed as they frisked him.

"You were right, Andy—he was hot," said the goon, stripping out his piece.

"So you were going to shoot me?" asked Andy.

Bobby was too numb to respond. He knew it wouldn't do any good anyway. One of them ripped open his shirt. Then somebody was fumbling with his belt and zipper.

"Just for that," said Andy, "I'm gonna let my boys have a little fun before they ex you out, man."

The pain in the back of his head bloomed like a miniature nova, but it proved to be only a sweet prelude . . .

Roger was getting very freaked out when the professor didn't show up for his weekly visit. It had been a bad week at the SeaHarp anyway—Mr. Montgomery had been highly upset by the murdered drug dealer they found in 205's bathtub. Roger was just glad he hadn't been the one to find the poor bastard.

He waited all day on Saturday, and still no professor. Roger called at the University on Sunday, but nobody was answering any of the phones. On Monday, he spoke to a woman who gave him the bad news: the professor had slipped in the shower and fractured his skull. He was now at the Miskatonic University Hospital, comatose.

Great. Just great.

That night Roger decided he'd better check on the thing in the bottle, but he didn't know what the hell he'd do if he got himself up to the fourth floor and it had already broken loose.

When he pulled back the heavy draperies and saw the bottle still intact, Roger exhaled—only then realizing he'd been holding his breath. His luck was holding, but just barely, it seemed.

The thing had grown horribly. It didn't look like there was any water left in the bottle at all. Just this bloated, sickly-green tumorous *thing*. Its amorphous shape pulsed with life like a giant, beating heart. Jeez, it looked like it was growing larger as he watched it, like it would break the glass any second.

He *had* to get it out of there. Like right away. No way it was going to make it through another night. Just get it out. Dump it somewhere.

Roger told himself he'd worry about the details later as he hefted the bottle into his arms and slipped into the deserted hallway. It had to be at least three times as heavy as it had been before and he wondered how that could even be possible. Roger kept wondering what he would say if he saw any of the Montgomerys coming down from their apartments on the fifth floor. All he needed was to get caught by them before he reached the service elevator.

The old service elevator creaked and groaned its way to the musty basement, where Roger eased the bottle past the doors and across the cluttered floor. Lawn furniture, croquet sets, umbrellas, and other seasonal equipment littered the path to the exit doors. The bottle seemed to getting heavier with each step and Roger prayed that he didn't stumble on something or lose his grip.

It wasn't until he'd carried it out to his four-year old Camaro that he'd thought of what to do with it. Placing it carefully in the back seat, Roger tried to avoid looking into the dark center of its mass. There was something very much like an eye looking back at him. Its whole body, now pressed against the glass, heaved like a beating heart. He couldn't wait to get rid of the ugly son-of-a-bitch.

Turning off Harbor Road onto Port Boulevard, Roger drove carefully through the center of Greystone Bay. It was getting late in the evening and things were quiet. Lightning flashed in the northern skies and he wondered if a storm might be descending on the coast.

With the bottle wedged into the floor-well behind the shot-gun seat, he headed straight out of town on Western Road, past the industrial parks and the other new development in some of the farmlands. There was a place up in the hills off Western Road where the government had operated a toxic waste dump. Public outcry had it closed down about fifteen years ago and since then it had become a favorite spot for adventurous kids who wanted to do some make-believe exploring and teen-agers who wanted to do some *real* exploring in the back-seats of their cars.

As Roger drove up the abandoned road with his headlights off, past the battered chain-link fence and gate, memories of evenings spent up here with Diana wafted back to him like a subtle perfume. He wished they'd been able to work things out. He still missed her sometimes, he thought wistfully as he pulled up and killed the engine.

Carefully, Roger slipped from behind the wheel, went around and pulled the bottle out from behind the passenger seat. When he reached down to pick it up, the thing inside lurched and churned, like it had tried to get at him through the glass. God, he hated it! He couldn't wait to dump it into the well and be done with the whole mess.

He'd found the well years ago when he'd been kicking around the site. The wooden well-cover had half-rotted away and somebody had tried to batten it down with a piece of corrugated steel. It was a half-assed job, and Roger had pulled back the metal and peered down into the shaft in the earth. He couldn't see any bottom and a stone dropped unto the darkness fell for what seemed like a very long time before splooshing into the water.

The perfect place to dump this thing, thought Roger as he carried the bottle the remaining few feet to the lip of the well. The circumference of the opening looked narrow, but it wasn't—certainly wide enough to swallow up the water-fountain bottle. Sucking in his breath, he wrapped his arms around it and prepared to lift it over the opening.

The timing was flawless.

The thing must have sensed its fate because as soon as he

embraced the glass, the creature inside heaved upward. With a smart little *snick!* the neck of the bottle just snapped off, pushed out and up by a thick tendril-like arm. It happened so fast, Roger didn't have time to react. All of a sudden this piece of fleshy tuber shot up past his face.

Instantly he was stunned by the overpowering stench of it. The inside of his nose stung, actually burned from the acid-stink of decay, of swamps. It was a batrachian smell, a hideous smell of something impossibly old. He staggered backwards, then spun around, still holding the bottle. And then the glass was cracking, fracturing in all directions. The thing, once free, seemed to be expanding like a balloon being filled with air. Roger was awash in the foul bath of its prison, smelling like the grave. More tendrils shot out embracing him like clinging seaweed. He screamed and a long tuberous finger leaped into his mouth, forcing its way down his throat. He gagged, heaving and puking, but still the appendage wormed its way into the depths of his stomach. He could feel it wriggling about and he puked again.

Reeling from the shock, locked in a death-dance with the thing, he staggered forward and tripped over the lip of the well. Head-first, he pitched downward into the shaft. The opening was just large enough to accept the width of his shoulders, pinning his arms to his sides. He plummeted into the darkness, picking up speed. His mind threatened to blank out from the sheer panic, and then suddenly he was jerked to a jolting stop. Reaching a more narrow spot in the wall, his body was wedged vise-like in the shaft.

And still the creature clung to him, wriggling and sliding about, appearing to assume a more comfortable position.

His thoughts were short-circuiting as he realized there was no getting out, that he was going to *die* suspended upside down and being slowly eaten from the inside out by the monster from the bottle. He wanted to scream, to cry out, but the tendril stuffed into his mouth wouldn't allow it.

Slowly the creature kept adjusting its position, rearranging itself, moving and exploring his body with its many arms, leaving a vicious trail of slime everywhere it touched his flesh. He was almost numb from shock and exposure as it moved against him, sending lancets and pincers and thorns into him.

Under his fingernails, in his ears and up his nose, through his armpits and groin, the thing shot him through with a raging inferno of pain. All his nerve endings *sang* with torment. His brain threatened to buzz away into the idiot hum of white noise, of absolute pain.

And the thing surged with pleasure and satiety.

Time lost all meaning in the dank confines of the well. The constant symphony of pain precluded any serious thinking, and all he wanted to do was die.

But Roger Easton *didn't* die.

He had no idea how long he lay wedged in the well before he realized the thing was keeping him alive in the white-pain darkness. The thing was *feeding* him parts of itself, as Roger in turn fed it.

It was the perfect relationship, and he knew it would last for a very long time.

OLD FRIENDS NEVER DIE
by
Bob Booth

Mike Condon knew he was going to die on the night of November seventh. He had seen it in a dream, not once, but many times. Mike wasn't the kind of guy who believed in psychic foretelling any more than he believed in the Loch Ness Monster, Bigfoot, or nine-inch aliens who kidnapped people. He was like the old English lady he had read about who'd said: "I don't believe in ghosts, but I AM afraid of them."

Mike Condon was a successful musician. His band, the Snappers, had been big in the sixties; producing hit singles with regularity and garnering two glorious platinum albums. In the early seventies they split. Mike and Keith Packer, who between them had written all the songs and sung all the leads, went to work for various groups as back-up singers and opened for others as a two-man band called Barney and Clyde. They never made a lot of money during those years, but they developed a cult following and they worked steadily.

Marriage, kids, houses in the suburbs, private schools—all the trappings of moderately successful businessmen in their thirties. They supplied the singing voices for animated characters big with the pre-school set and once in a while played a local club to stay sharp. Then the eighties came. An entire generation of rock & roll fans had come and gone and suddenly they were getting air play. An army of adolescents curious about the sixties, about Vietnam, about the drug culture, the civil rights movement and all that history that Mike and his friends had lived through were searching used record stores for Hendrix, the Doors, Big Brother and, amazingly enough, the Snappers.

The phone started to ring again. Various promoters were packaging groups from the sixties to tour again. The Snappers were in demand again. Except there weren't any Snappers. The drummer had bought into an Audi dealership, the bass player had become a commercial artist, and the keyboard man worked in a factory in Bakersfield. They were all out of shape, out of practice, and not the least bit interested in touring. No matter. Mike and Keith were the heart of the band. They recruited two kids and an old session man who were familiar with their style and in a matter of months the Snappers were as tight as they had ever been. Keith was a little chunkier and a lot grayer, but that was all right. He could still write, and play, and sing. Most of all, he wanted it. He hadn't given up the dream.

The dreams. The dreams started when the tour started. At first he thought it was life on the road. He wasn't, after all, as young as he used to be. Six nights a week in six different towns hundreds of miles apart were bound to take their toll. *The schedule was always the same. Rehearse in the afternoon after the roadies had set up the equipment . . . munch on the lousy buffet the promoter sent over . . . nap or meet with local acquaintances until show time . . . smile, laugh, jump around, flirt with the girls in the front row, joke with the stage hands, sing and play as hard as you could for forty-five minutes . . . go back to a converted house trailer that was home on the road for the five of them . . . live in cramped quarters . . . drink lousy local beer . . . sign a few autographs and listen for the thousandth time as some middle-aged guy with a paunch tells you he's got all your records and is, in fact, your biggest fan . . . a few hours of fitful sleep, listening to the eighteen-wheelers roll down the highway that inevitably ran past the parking lot of the arena you had played that night . . . up at dawn for the trek to the next town, the sound checks, the rehearsals . . . appearing on the radio stations that were partially sponsoring the tour . . . lunch with the councilman's sister—she had all your records, was in fact your biggest fan, and her brother did pull some strings so the promoter could get his permit, after all.*

The dreams always featured dead friends. They weren't dead in the dreams, but he was, or was about to be. He was lying on a beach or a lawn staring up at a brightly lit building. His dead friends, Janis with her bottle of Southern Comfort, Jim with his little volume of Rimbaud, or Jimi with some wildly colored scarf slung haphazardly around his neck would cluck and shake their heads, turn away from his hardening body and walk off towards some stately old place he had never seen before, not even in dreams. It looked like it might be an unusually long hotel, or a big casino on the boardwalk. It was several stories high and over the stone wall that surrounded the place he could see white clapboard with gingerbread trim and a roofline that was truly unusual. It had many more than seven gables and Mike always thought when he awoke that the architect must have been a big Hawthorne fan.

Some nights he favored the casino—there was no pool, no tables or chairs on the large expanse of lawn, nothing that would give the impression of a hotel. Other nights he thought about the lack of neon signs every casino would have, or the unpaved nature of the surrounding area—casinos need lots of parking. In desperation he thought it might be some exclusive country club, but there were too many buildings and trees around it. Behind his body he could hear the ocean so he knew it was on the coast. Probably, judging from the architecture, the East Coast or maybe somewhere in England. He wasn't sure. What he was sure of was that it was a better place. When his friends left the grisly scene of his death they always headed for it to soothe their injured emotions. He could not move his head as they walked away, but out of his glassy eyes he could see smaller figures in the distance; sitting quietly on the porch that surrounded the building, reading books or papers, or simply strolling the vast lawn that spread out in front of the building like a lush green carpet.

Then the scene would dissolve like one of those shots in old movies that indicated the passage of time. Sometimes the pages of a calendar riffled quickly only to come to a screeching halt on his forty-fifth birthday—November seventh, nineteen eighty-eight. Sometimes it would be a twirling newspaper that would land with a thud on the floor of his vision revealing the date, November 7, 1988; and his obituary, complete with picture.

Mike Condon didn't believe in psychic foretelling. Not until about two weeks before his forty-fifth birthday when he saw the flyer for the SeaHarp Hotel in an information booth at the Old Slater Mill in Pawtucket, Rhode Island.

It was the hotel of his dreams. Everything matched—the gingerbread trim, the long porch, the pounding waves of the ocean in front and the seeming lack of civilization around the place. The Snappers had come to Rhode Island to play The Tent in Warwick, and Mike had gone in the afternoon to a few of the state's historical landmarks. He had been curious to see the first factory in the United States, and no doubt the first sweat shop. It wasn't much of a place but in his mind's eye he could picture the women weaving against the sound of the waterwheel outside, perhaps reciting some puritan prayer to themselves as they worked their sixteen-hour shifts amongst the flax and under the watchful eye of Samuel Slater, the world's first industrial spy.

It was a real place, this hotel of his dreams, pictured on a yellowing brochure he found in the Chamber of Commerce rack. The strange thing was that all the other flyers were bright and printed in the recent past. The rack looked like it was straightened every day. The SeaHarp brochure was out of place not only because it had apparently been gathering dust for some time, but also because it was the only promotional flyer not about an attraction in Rhode Island.

There was only one way to look at it. His friends were trying to save him. He wasn't young any more and he was pushing himself like he had when he was eighteen. Touring was rough. Just a few months ago Ray Davies of the Kinks had a heart attack and he had been in better shape than Mike. In his dreams his friends were always walking toward this place as if toward sanctuary. It looked comfortable, safe, peaceful, quiet. November 7th loomed like a giant balloon pressuring his skull from the inside and he knew he had to get there before that day arrived. If he didn't make it, they'd find him on the beach like in the dream—stiff, glassy-eyed, short of his goal.

There was a bus from New York that stopped in Greystone Bay on its way to somewhere else. As soon as he got off it he felt at peace. It was a quiet place and even in late October the weather was warm enough for just a light windbreaker. He left his suitcase in a locker at the bus station and wandered around the town. He looked in shop windows as he strolled down a divided boulevard. He stopped for a cup of coffee and talked with the waitress about the SeaHarp.

"Is it quiet?" he asked her, trying to dissolve the Sanka in the not-quite-boiled water.

"Don't know much about it," she said. "It seems quiet to me, but why shouldn't it—Greystone Bay is a quiet town."

"Not many customers?"

"Oh no. There always seem to be a lot of people staying out there. It's just . . . it's not the sort of hotel I'd want to stay at."

"They charge by the hour?"

"No," she said laughing. "Nothing like that."

"What then."

"No tennis courts."

"Tennis courts?"

"They've got a huge lawn in the back, but no tennis courts. No swimming pool, no jacuzzi, no video games, nothing . . . that would bother anybody."

"What do they have?" he asked. He was intrigued. It sounded like the kind of spa he had read about in all those interminably long Henry James novels.

"They got a goddamn croquet patch, or whatever you call it. Inside they got some pool tables."

Mike laughed.

"No disco? No punk band on Friday nights?"

"No rockers," she said, retreating towards the kitchen in answer to an angry bark by the short order cook.

"Maybe one," he said to himself. He left a five-dollar bill on the counter and went looking for a cab. As he left he could hear the Snappers hit from 1970 blasting from the radio in the kitchen. "Sad All Alone" had made them a lot of money once. It was getting air play again because it was being used as part of the soundtrack for a movie about yuppies and menses.

The desk clerk gave him a room facing the sea and he felt strangely at home right away. There was a tang in the air; a damp saltiness that was not unpleasant for those who had grown up close to the ocean. It was almost a religious feeling. He stood at his window and watched the whitecaps rush toward the rocky shore. He felt weak all over. The sea always made him feel that way. It was a very sensual feeling of weakness, much the way he had felt the first time he had known that he was in love. It was a secret that made you strong and vulnerable at the same time. The SeaHarp would be a comfortable place to stay for a few weeks. He would get renewed. He would be rested. He would not dream.

Later he wandered around the first floor of the hotel and found himself gravitating towards the reading room. The function rooms were all well-appointed and he glanced into several of them during his wanderings. There were two game-rooms across from the reading room and like the waitress said—no video games, no pinball, just card tables and billiard tables. What struck him most was the number of people he saw. The hotel was quiet and did not "bustle" like most hotels. Yet wherever he looked he saw people quietly going about their business. Their business seemed to be relaxing. There were men relaxing in stuffed chairs with newspapers and magazines. There were women and children strolling quietly through the halls the way you would stroll through a museum or an art gallery, glancing at the exhibits quietly as if art would crumble in a lively environment. There was much of the museum about the SeaHarp. There were Tiffany lamp-shades everywhere and the oils that lined the hallways above the hand-rubbed wainscotting all seemed to be originals. No photographs or art prints in glitzy metal frames here, but solid-looking oils in massive darkwood frames with brass plates for the title and the artist's name.

Even the selection of books in the mahogany cases that lined the reading room was solid and functional. There were lots of volumes of James, Hawthorne, Melville, and the like. Not much Twain, no Hemingway. The bottom shelves were inconveniently low and filled with current bestsellers by people like Kathryn Atwood, Felicia Andrews, Lionel Fenn, Les Simon, and Geoffrey Marsh. Mike wondered if the management had put them there on purpose, making the patron uncomfortable who read anything but the classics. At eye level, on the shelf an average sized person would normally see first, were the collected works of John Updike.

On first reflection Mike felt like a Geoffrey Marsh thriller. Marsh had entertained him on many a lonely night on the road. Then he thought he ought to take the opportunity to read one of those tomes he'd been promising himself to look into for many years. Everybody's list of unread masterpieces is about the same—*War and Peace, Ulysses, Remembrance of Things Past, The Brothers Karamazov, Moby-Dick*—and Mike Condon was no different. He chose Thomas Mann's *The Magic Mountain*. The book must have meant a great deal to someone in management as there were several copies of it scattered throughout the shelves.

He was halfway through the first chapter, traveling to the sanitorium with Hans Castorp, when he fell asleep. Sleeping in the afternoon was something Mike rarely did, but the description of the snow-covered journey up the Swiss Alps to the place where tuberculars went to die before the invention of tine tests and wonder drugs depressed him and made him tired.

"Getting to be an old man," he mumbled as he got up and headed for the bathroom. He did not feel rested. His back ached and his knees creaked as he moved across the room. It took three glasses of cold water to wash the velvet out of his mouth and he promised himself to quit smoking. He was patting his pockets for cigarettes before he got out of the bathroom.

When he finished freshening up he decided it was time to get something to eat. He wasn't hungry really. He just knew he hadn't eaten in a long time.

He decided to forgo the dining room and eat in the bar instead. It was dark in there. He sat at the brass-railed bar with his elbows resting on the leather trim and his head resting on his hands, which were cathedraled beneath his chin. He ordered a Bloody Mary and a corned beef sandwich (with mustard, on rye) and waited silently to be served. There were two other customers in the room, sitting in a darkened booth in the corner. They were quiet when he first came in but soon laughter smoked its way across the room and distracted him from his sandwich. He listened intently and chewed slowly. The sandwich was tasteless. It was the kind of sandwich that normally would taste either good or bad. But never tasteless. Never bland. As he chewed he marvelled at the lack of sensation. The food in his mouth tasted gray. It was a mass of fiber about as appetizing as polyester. The laughter grew louder, more frequent, and finally almost raucous. One of the revelers was throaty and loud. Her laughter conquered the bar's darkness and he could have sworn he had heard it before. He tried to place it and failed. If she reminded him of anyone, it was someone he hadn't thought about in a long time. He had half made up his mind to approach them and ask if he could buy them a drink, but by the time he turned around to make his move they had gone.

At first he thought they had just moved further into the booth, sliding across the brown leather to make room for him. But no, the booth was empty. On the table were two old-fashioned glasses thick with melting ice and a half empty bottle of Southern Comfort. One of them had left behind a scarf. He thought maybe it was like dropping a handkerchief, someone's way of inviting him to the pursuit. He decided to take it with him in the hopes of returning it to her when their paths crossed again. When he got into the corridor, which was better lit, he noticed that it was purple paisley. When was the last time he had seen paisley. It had to have been over twenty years ago.

Mike walked around the bottom floor aimlessly, searching for he knew not what. Finally he came to a set of French doors that led to the back porch and the spacious lawn spread out before it. There were benches where couples sat and he could see four middle-aged men playing croquet. He sat to watch the competition and was surprised to discover that there was none.

At first it seemed like any other game of croquet that he had ever seen, though truth to tell he hadn't seen that many. They played by the rules, smoothly stroking the wooden balls through wicket after wicket, but there seemed to be no competitive fire. The players were all men, middle-aged, well-dressed, slightly paunchy. They possessed the aura of successful businessmen yet there was none of the spirit that successful people bring to all of life's activities. They played too politely. They never tried to smash another player's ball away from a wicket. They never raised a fist in triumph after a good shot or slapped a back in admiration or derision. Though he was at a distance he could have sworn they never even smiled. It was spooky.

Not spooky enough to investigate any further, however. Instead he felt like reading for a bit so he got up and headed back to his room. His sandwich and his drink hadn't been that appetizing yet he felt full, like the aftermath of Thanksgiving dinner. He thought he might order an Alka Seltzer from room service.

When he got back to the room he didn't order anything. He thought it would be too much trouble. It wasn't just going to the phone and calling in his order. He'd have to get up again to open the door, then walk to the dresser for his billfold . . . he was just simply too tired. He tried to read *The Magic Mountain* but Castorp had only been at the Sanatorium for an afternoon when Mike drifted off to sleep to the sounds of a guitar playing.

He could see where the music came from without getting out of his chair. There was a room at the opposite end of the corridor from his and he could tell that the player was using a Stratocaster with a small practice amp. Still, the sound was fantastic. The player had a feel for the music that was nothing short of extraordinary. He bent the notes torturously and produced the feel of some of the great old blues players—a sense of proficiency without the sloppy headlong rush for speed à la Jimmy Page. He placed the style right away. It was Hendrix. Only Jimi could get that soul-wrenching emotion out of a guitar in a style as distinct as any since Django Reinhardt; but the song was a new tune, written and played not three years ago by Stevie Ray Vaughan. The man played and played and Mike knew he couldn't wake up until the song was over. On the surface it was a pleasant enough fantasy. He was comfortable and he enjoyed the music. Still, he wished for the beach, the blood, the glassy stare. . . .

When he awoke it was dark. He hadn't turned on the lights, as the sun had been bright in the afternoon sky when he fell asleep. He was tired. No, that wasn't it. Listless maybe, or "logy" as his mother used to say when he was in grade school.

He began to wonder if he had been drugged. Whatever drug it was it was not one he had taken before. It felt a little like being on massive doses of Valium or Librium in that he wasn't bothered by all the little aches and pains and annoyances that the average aware person is heir to. Yet unlike the downers he was used to, it also robbed him of any sense of being alive. He remembered the gray taste of the corned beef, the listless way the other guests played croquet, and the lack of any noise about the place. Everyone seemed to be living in slow motion, like a ward full of first-time heart attack victims suddenly aware of their own fragility.

He was frightened. He wanted to get out of the hotel as fast as he could, but where would he run to? Back to his family? The Road? His Fans? November 7?

He went down the corridor and into an elevator. The elevator paused for a second and began its descent with a slow, smooth, lifeless motion. When he got to the bottom floor, he walked into the lobby (though in his mind he was bursting into the lobby). He wanted to confront somebody. He wanted to grab somebody by the goddamned throat and demand an explanation. He wanted to make his presence felt.

He did nothing. The manager, a Mr. Montgomery, stood in the lobby right in front of the elevator, rocking back and forth on his heels with his hands clasped behind his back.

"Is everything all right, Mr. Condon?" he said, grinning.

"Fine," Mike heard himself say, though it wasn't. He nodded in return of Mr. Montgomery's nod and walked past him toward the bar. He couldn't understand why he hadn't asked the man, who was the most likely person to know the truth, what the story was with the SeaHarp Hotel. It just didn't seem like the right thing to do.

The bar was empty. He had hoped to meet the couple that had been there in the afternoon, but it was not to be. The bartender was absentmindedly wiping down the bar and he didn't appear to be the kind of guy who would tell him anything, though no doubt he could if he wanted to—bartenders know everything.

He went across the hall to the library where there was a middle-aged man sitting in an overstuffed chair reading a slim volume, probably poetry. The man had close-cropped dark brown hair and was going to seed around the waistline, though he was about the same age as Mike. He laid the book face down on the arm of the chair and Mike could see the title—*The Drunken Boat* by Arthur Rimbaud. Mike knew

the book and he had a vague memory of a friend who used
to live by it, but the details were fuzzy. Still, the more he
looked at the man and the more he thought about the book
a certain connection sparked in his consciousness. It was a
dim flickering like a flashlight whose batteries have lost their
potency.

"Have we met?" he said. "My name is Mike."

"We haven't met that I know of," the man said. "My
name is Jim. Maybe we've run across each other on the
grounds."

"Jim?" Mike heard himself say. "No, I don't know any
Jim."

Mike turned away from the man and began to look at the
shelves. He was looking for something to read. He remembered reading something in the morning but he couldn't remember what it had been. It must not have made much of an
impression. He knew he had looked at the bookshelves before
but remembered nothing that he specifically wanted to look
for.

He saw lots of Kafka, Proust, Sartre, and Dostoyevski.
Some of the titles he was familiar with: *The Nothing Man,
Nausea, The Stranger, The Trial, They Shoot Horses, Don't
They?, Shoot The Piano Player*, and *The Magic Mountain*.
The last title attracted him. It seemed light, airy, and fantas-
tic compared to the other depressing titles. He took it off the
shelf and held it in his hands while he looked further.

"Nothing a little more uplifting than these?" he said to no
one in particular. He saw Henry James, Herman Melville,
Nathaniel Hawthorne, and John Updike ad infinitum. But
nothing with a little spirit, a little zing.

"Hmm," the man called Jim mumbled from behind his
Rimbaud.

"No best-sellers? No romance? No adventure?"

"Life's an adventure," the man said quietly, staring over

the top of the glasses Mike hadn't seen before. "Haven't you had enough of that on the outside?"

"I could have sworn I saw some paperbacks here earlier." Mike said ignoring the man's question. "Geoffrey Marsh was one of them. There were a few of his titles I haven't read in here this afternoon. Someone must have taken them."

"Geoffrey Marsh?" the man said. "I doubt it."

"Why is that?"

"Does this look like the kind of place that would carry paperbacks?"

He had to admit that it didn't. It was almost as if the memory of the books was something he had carried in with him from some previous life, some leftover from a past existence.

"Art is that which lets you escape the existence you're most fearful of," the man said philosophically. It was the kind of general statement someone he used to know was fond of making—sweeping generalities so broad they could not be effectively argued against. In some circles it passed for profundity.

Mike didn't answer. He was staring down at *The Magic Mountain,* doubting now that it was the fantasy its title promised.

"When you were . . . 'younger' . . . you lived a pretty mundane existence and read exotic books to help you escape; rocket ships, tropical·islands, willing women, solvable cases. It was the same with the music, art, cinema."

"And now?" Mike said, afraid of the answer he was going to get.

"Now you need quiet. You need rest. Life has stimulated you enough. You need the literature of the condemned, the damned. You need to know that the castle is unreachable, that monsters lurk outside your door—down your street, that life is a bad joke of which you are the butt; you need the literature of disease."

Mike didn't answer. He had a headache. The man's words made no sense to him on one level, but he had not the energy to argue against him. He felt neither like reading, arguing, playing croquet, or anything that would make him expend energy. He just wanted to go back up to his room and sleep.

"Let's go and get some food," the man said.

Mike shrugged and waited for him to lead the way. It was funny. He wasn't hungry and he didn't have fond memories of the hotel's food, though it was true he had only eaten once. Even the finest restaurants occasionally served bad meals. It was curious that Jim hadn't said 'let's go get something to eat' or 'let's go for a pizza.' No, he had said, 'let's get some food' the same way you would say 'do you have to go to the bathroom?' Like something to be gotten through but not enjoyed.

The restaurant was well-lit but not bright. A man and a woman sat up front near the French doors that led out to the ubiquitous porch. Jim nodded at them and headed their way. The woman laughed as they approached and Mike recognized it as the laugh he had heard in the bar that afternoon.

She was short and pleasant-looking, with red hair and a face full of freckles. She said hello in a gruff voice that had apparently been abused.

"Name's Janis," she said. "Port Arthur, Texas."

"Mike," he said. "L.A."

"Spent some time in L.A." she said. "Never going back."

Mike nodded and sat down. Her partner was a thin black man with sleepy eyes and extraordinarily long fingers that he ceaselessly drummed on the table top while they waited for service. His name was Jimi.

The food was priced steeply and totally bland. Nothing with tomato sauce or spices of any kind. Lots of beef, some fish but no shellfish. No ethnic food. Strictly British.

Mike ordered the filet along with the others. It was small but he had trouble finishing it. So did the others. They ate enough to satisfy their need for food. A potato, some carrots, a little steak, bread pudding and decaffeinated coffee.

The conversation seemed pointless. When Mike asked what they did for a living they seemed to ignore the question, as if they didn't need to do anything. They didn't ask him what he did. He didn't volunteer it. They talked about neither money, politics, sex, art, or religion; the staples of conversation among strangers since the beginning of civilization. They talked about disease, death, the pointlessness of existence, the undiscoverability of the cosmos, and the fickleness of human relationships. Mike did not enjoy himself, but the time passed and eventually it was time to head for his room and get some sleep. The waiter didn't bring a check. Neither did he ask for their room numbers so he could put it on a tab. Instead they all just got up when enough time had passed and went their separate ways.

When he had washed, changed and got into bed he began to read. *The Magic Mountain* had an interesting if slow-moving beginning but he despaired of ever finishing it.

He decided after a while to go to sleep. As a child he had always had to have a night light. As an adult he had to have a television or radio on in the room. It was what got him through the night.

There was no television, but there was a marvelous old radio on the nightstand next to the bed. It was an old Philco from the thirties, made of wood with a cathedral top. The speakers felt like real cloth instead of plastic and the radio had that mellow sound only a wooden box can give. The on/off knob was a small brown affair, discreet and functional. No digital display on this radio, just a small window with a yellow light—just AM. The local stations played classical or soft rock mostly. Finally he found a station from New York that played the music he liked though he had to listen to it through the screeching and fading of a faraway source. The last song he heard before he fell asleep was called "Sad All Alone" by the Snappers. He liked it. If he ever got up the energy to go into town he would have to look for the album. The group showed promise. Maybe he could get the bellman to get him a copy.

AMI AMET DELI PENCET
by
Nancy Holder

April is not the cruelest month in the town of Greystone Bay; in March the slate-grey fog congeals into a siege of rain that pounds the rooftops and hurtles through the streets. Raingutters burst with greywater pressure; storm drains clog and regurgitate. Rivers tumble down the hills, north and south, and plummet into Greystone Bay itself.

The bay waters churn; long-lost objects materialize on shore. In ancient yellow sou'westers, the old men come out with metal detectors and prowl like sandpipers through the wreckage. Children whoop among the kelp and decayed gumboots, rotted lobster traps, eyeless dolls, the remains of luckless fish.

Behind the scavengers, the SeaHarp Hotel stretches the length of Harbor Road like an immense white sea serpent, gables and chimneys the spines along its back. The ornate gingerbread trim flares into magnificent scales and barnacles. It is caged by a high stone wall; and in March, the geraniums in the pots along the top of this wall sag from the ferocity of the rain. They bob and flail like drowning creatures.

From a taxi, the hotel's lighted windows glow murkily, monstrous eyes staring underwater. The dark windows of unoccupied rooms are caves that harbor voracious sharks, eager to dart out, to bite, and grab, and pull one down beneath the surface. . . .

Or so it seemed to Rachel Unger, as the cab floated to a stop and the driver turned to her with a question in his eyes, as if to ask if the hotel was really her final destination.

He was a young man, good-looking in a back-East sort of way, and that had made her feel uneasy ever since he'd picked her up at the bus station. Whenever he looked at her she flinched, as she usually did when strangers looked at her; as she always did when young men looked at her; and wondered if everything were completely concealed. Just in case, she adjusted the fold of her turtleneck sweater and smoothed her hair over the side of her face.

He swung out of the car into the deluge and raced around to open her door. Rachel took a deep breath, climbed out, and moved out of his way while he slammed the door shut. Rain pelted her. Her panty-hose clung to her legs and the wind whipped her black wool coat, purchased for the trip. The salty gale slapped her face and she plastered her hair over her jaw line, wishing she'd worn a scarf.

"I'll get your bags," the man said. "Go on up."

Rachel bobbed her head and dashed to the steps cut into the center of the wall. She was defenseless; hadn't remembered to pack an umbrella. No one used them in Southern California. If it rained they just stayed inside their cars.

But in Greystone Bay, people swam down the streets, wrapped in coats and gloves, slickers and rain boots, dots of light grey or dark grey with a bouncing slice of black held over their heads. They slogged through their flat-slate weather, existed in it, went on with things. They were a different kind of people, these grey Eastern fishermen of grey Greystone Bay. She wasn't sure if they were her kind of people; she'd thought to stay, but perhaps she'd just unload the house and go back.

To what?

On top of the wall, the geraniums sagged, puddles of crimson blossoms ringing the bases of their pots. The presence of the ragged plants gave the hotel a sense of having been caught unawares by the storm; as she had been caught by the simultaneous arrival of her fifty-fifth birthday, her forced retirement, and the notification that she'd inherited a house in some podunk town on the Eastern seaboard. From a man unrelated to her, and apparently unrelated to anyone in town.

Else, how to explain the condition of the property on North Hill, of the pools of foul-smelling water on the parquet floors; of all the windows, not one spared? Who was he, the owner of the mildewed raincoat in the coat closet, which hung plaintive as a loyal and lonely dog, that no one had looked after his house after his death?

Hartfield Croome Simpson. Rachel knew little more than his name: that he was wealthy; that he had traveled much of his life; that no one had mixed much with him for vague reasons Mr. Mordicott, his lawyer, had been unable, or unwilling, to make clear when he flew to Los Angeles to meet with her.

Mr. Mordicott did explain that her benefactor's middle name, Croome, betrayed his relationship to an old Greystone Bay family who had fled the town shortly after the Civil War. The Croomes, apparently, were shunned by everyone in Greystone Bay. Local legends concerning them abounded, most of them centering around their graveyard. They ranged from tales that the family vaults were filled with vampires or zombies or some other sort of monster, to the story that nothing at all—no bodies, no skeletons—was discovered when the coffins were removed from the Croome graveyard to make way for the railroad.

"The usual sort of nonsense you hear in a small town," Mr. Mordicott had concluded, as he notarized Rachel's signature on the title transfer of Mr. Simpson's house. "He wasn't even sure how he was related to the Croomes. Poor Harry. He had a streak of melancholy in him that the rest of *them* mistook for snobbery. Never could make friends. Lonely. No one went to his funeral. Except me, of course."

Mr. Mordicott could offer no clue as to why his client chose Rachel from all the living souls in the world—and so far from Greystone Bay—to receive his once-magnificent mansion. The lawyer had drawn the will up thirty days before Mr. Simpson's death. The man had gone night sailing; in the morning, the boat washed to shore; four days later, Annie, one of the employees of the SeaHarp, found his body on the beach.

So now the circular stairway, the cupola of stained glass, recently smashed; the kitchen, knee-deep in water, painted red as in the olden times to keep out cockroaches, were Rachel's. Pantries, dumbwaiters, bay windows, a basement—all the civilized accoutrements, like umbrellas, that Californians did without. She had, at first, thought to claim them; but after seeing the extent of the damage, she was no longer sure.

And frankly, after giving the town below the mansion a good look, she was even less sure. Mr. Mordicott said this was the worst time of year to visit; that summer was lovely and fall and winter like Currier and Ives. She supposed this was all to the good, catching Greystone Bay at its most cantankerous; but heavens, a few months of this rain and one could turn positively . . . suicidal.

Rachel was short of breath by the time she reached the top of the steps in front of the hotel. Though it had been a short distance, and not steep, fighting the rain had tired her. She paused for a moment, which probably looked ridiculous to anyone who was watching. But she was already soaked through; what was the point of hurrying any longer?

On either side of her, two huge vases of more downtrodden geraniums splashed with rainwater; twin stone cisterns, with streamers of color floating in them and spreading out in fine tendrils, like the brilliant red hair of someone bobbing beneath the surface.

Rachel blinked. The streamers undulated and for a flash of an instant, she saw the texture of flesh, a silhouette of a long, narrow nose and sharp chin, a gaping mouth, open as if in a scream, and no teeth, none—

Gasping, she jumped away from the vase, and collided with the cabbie, who had come up behind her with her luggage.

"My god!" she cried, looking from him to the vase.

"What?" He stepped around her and peered in. "Drop something?"

Rachel swallowed hard and looked, too.

Flowers, stems, leaves. Rainwater.

"I thought I saw something."

He said nothing, shrugged. She moved aside and he bounded up the steps—he was so young—along a path, and up another set of steps before landing on the porch.

Rachel followed. Tasseled draperies hung in the windows; she was so eager to reach the promise of warmth—

—perhaps, too, to put some distance between her and the vase—

so eager that she slipped and almost fell. The cabbie grabbed her arm and said, "Careful. You go down here, you're likely to drown."

Startled, she glanced at him. There was no smile on his face, no hint of any kind that he'd been joking. He stood in the rain, holding onto her arm, in his thick leather jacket and leather cap and she had the silly thought that he *had* seen the head in the vase, but pretended not to.

"What an odd thing to say," she blurted, and still he didn't smile, only held the door open for her. She went past him, thinking how grey he looked. How vacant. How could she ever have thought him good-looking? It was a sign of her age; god, fifty-five. Out to pasture, wasn't that the saying? Old maid, spinster. A man was distinguished, even young, at fifty-five. A woman was simply old. Christ, if she'd known how depressing Greystone Bay would be, she would have waited until—

"Oh, my," she said, as she stepped through the doors and into the lobby.

The room was leagues long and leagues high, with vast expanses of oriental carpets in blue-grey and sea-green, and flocked Victorian wallpaper in a faded shade of midnight blue. Chandeliers bobbed in the overcast light and glowed faintly on a gallery of armchairs and small tables; a wide, fluted staircase carpeted like the lobby floor; lamps of brass with green shades; and everywhere, rammed between tables and secretaries and cocktail arrangements, pillars of marble, white and cold as icebergs.

The rhythm of the rain increased, then ebbed; Rachel had a sense of standing in the rooms of a sunken ocean liner. She touched the neck of her sweater and said, purely in jest, "Since I didn't drown out there, maybe I can drown in here."

The cabbie's features remained expressionless.

"How much do I owe you?" she asked to cover her confusion. She knew the SeaHarp was Greystone Bay's showpiece; perhaps she'd insulted him with her remark.

"Ten bucks. With the luggage and all," he added, as if she might think he was trying to cheat her.

She pulled out a ten and dug around for a couple dollars.

The cabbie pocketed the bill. "It's fine." He raised a finger to someone across the room and walked back into the rain.

A bell dinged and a man in a burgundy uniform appeared

from a door behind the registration desk and headed toward her. Rachel's attention rested on him briefly before she did a double-take and stared at the girl who had rung for him, her palm still poised over the bell.

It was her head Rachel had seen in the vase.

Rachel staggered backward, covering her mouth; and was further shocked when the girl mirrored her movements, looking as startled and perhaps as white as she must. They stared at each other while the man grabbed up Rachel's bags and said, "Staying with us, ma'am?"

Rachel lowered her hand. How ridiculous. Of course she hadn't seen the girl's head in that vase. She was tired from the plane and then the train, and the bus. She should have rented a car. What a backwater place this was. Rachel pondered again her plan for moving here. It seemed less pleasing a prospect with every moment she spent in Greystone Bay.

Behind the desk, the girl also composed herself. She was quite lovely, very Scottish looking, with masses of long red hair, though not too well brushed nor too clean, and big— huge—blue eyes. Against the burgundy jacket of her uniform her skin was pale, as most people back East seemed to be; and short, perhaps no taller than five feet. She didn't seem old enough to be working a job. Perhaps she was related to the family who owned the SeaHarp: the Montgomerys, Mr. Mordicott had told her.

The girl mustered a smile as Rachel drew near and said, "Good evening. Welcome to the SeaHarp." She wore a little bow tie that matched the jacket, with small navy polka dots on it. Very—what did the kids call it?—preppie. Perhaps if she wore some makeup or tied her hair back, she would look more adult—

—*less like the head in the vase, with its sensuous, Art-Nouveau hair*

"I don't have a reservation," Rachel said, then realized

that might sound rude and backtracked. "Thank you. Good evening to you."

"You don't need a reservation. We're nearly empty," the girl said artlessly. "This time of year." She gestured with her head toward the entrance doors. "There's nothing to do in the rain."

She pushed a leather-bound guest book toward Rachel as if it were a distasteful thing to be gotten rid of as soon as possible.

"Please sign this." A tone of pleading accompanied the request. She dropped her gaze to Rachel's hands and folded her own on the gleaming wood of the reception desk like an obedient child about to receive a reprimand. Her fingers were long and thin, her nails ragged from biting. There was blood crusted on her cuticles.

Wincing at the sight of the tortured fingertips, Rachel signed her name, then hesitated at the space for her payment address. "I'm the new—"

"Single or double?" The girl whirled around and faced a brass plate from which hung rows of brass keys with numbers stamped on them.

"Single."

The girl nodded and moved her hand over the rows. "We have 303. It has a nice view of the bay."

"That'll be fine," Rachel replied, but privately wondered if she were serious. The rain was coming down harder now; she'd be lucky to see her own hand through it, much less enjoy any kind of scenery.

The girl held the key out with the same eagerness to be rid of it as the guest book. Rachel took it with her left hand and tapped the book with the pen in her right.

"Actually, I'm in transit. You see, I'm the new owner of Mr. Simpson's house. On North Hill?"

The girl dipped her head and mumbled something. Her forefinger flew to her mouth and she nipped at the flesh on the right side of the nail. She took another nip, then looked up.

"I'm Annie. I usually work in the dining room. But the desk clerk is sick and I had to fill in."

"Well, you're doing a fine job," Rachel assured her, but the girl—Annie—showed no sign that she'd heard.

"You don't need to write down anything. I—we all know where that house is."

"Oh." Rachel laid down the pen.

"I'll take you to your room," Annie said, and grew even paler, as if the prospect terrified her.

"I'm sure I can find my way. The bellman—"

"He's already gone," Annie murmured dismally. "He went up right away."

Annie moved from behind the desk. The polyester skirt that matched her jacket was baggy and too long; Rachel supposed she was wearing the uniform of the indisposed desk clerk. She looked like a waif in it, some poor, bedraggled creature someone had let in out of the rain and dressed in castoff clothing.

"But how did he know where to take my things?"

Annie pointed to the left, toward the stairs. "I don't know." She looked so agitated Rachel was afraid she might collapse.

"I think I can find it," Rachel said. "If you'll just tell me where the—"

"Oh, no, I must take you. I'll get in trouble if I don't."

"Really?"

Pursing her lips, the girl nodded.

They walked past the magnificent staircase to a row of three elevators, each with an attendant uniformed in burgundy. The three young men sat on stools, and appeared startled to have work to do.

"Hello, Annie. Evening, ma'am," said the operator whose

elevator Annie chose. He was young also, and winked at Annie before she ducked her head.

"Third," Annie snapped. She and Rachel walked into the elevator after the man slid back the gate. It was upholstered in dark blue leather, quite grand, Rachel thought. They must be losing a fortune on this place with all the vacancies.

The girl hadn't asked her for a credit card or anything. And she had forgotten to ask the rate. Well, there was no where else to go, was there? She'd take care of everything later, after she got out of these soaking clothes.

The elevator lurched, then dragged itself upward on its cables, creaking. Annie methodically began to gnaw on her cuticles, thumb first, then forefinger, then middle finger, and so on. Rachel fought the impulse to brush her hand away from her mouth and concentrated on the semicircle of numbers above the door. She wished Annie hadn't come with her; she made her nervous. She checked her turtleneck sweater and her hair; everything was all right. But still, she tensed when the young man looked at her with interest: was something showing a tiny, little bit?

He grinned. "Nice weather we're having, eh?"

He wouldn't speak so casually if he could see. Rachel relaxed a little and smiled with him.

"Liquid sunshine. That's what we call it back home."

"You must be from California."

"Yes. Los Angeles."

His dark eyes lit up. "Hollywood, eh, Annie? Do you know any movie stars?"

"Me? Oh, no."

The attendant looked excited. He was charming, really, with freckles over the bridge of his nose and flashing white teeth. Shiny hazel eyes and neatly trimmed, cocoa-colored hair.

"I'd like to meet Arnold Schwarzenegger. Or Clint Eastwood."

Rachel nodded. ''Well, Clint Eastwood's the mayor of Carmel now, so it's easy—''

''We're there,'' Annie said. She took one final chew, then pushed in front of the man and opened the gate. She stepped out and, without waiting for Rachel to follow, stomped down the hall.

''I'll wait to take you down, Annie,'' the man called. There was no reply.

Rachel found Annie standing on the threshold of a room done in soft grey and dark blue. There was a four-poster in one corner, and a window with open grey drapes beside it. It was dark outside; rain batted against the panes. The rest of the room was furnished with polished wooden antiques, a lamp with a Tiffany shade, and an old lavebo and bowl on a nightstand beside the bed.

''Why, it's charming!'' Rachel said. She came up behind Annie, who didn't move into the room. ''Much nicer than I . . well, it's nice.''

''I'm glad you like it,'' Annie said tonelessly. ''And there are your suitcases.''

Side-by-side on a low sort of a booth, her luggage awaited.

''Well,'' Rachel said again. She took an awkward step around Annie and walked into the room.

''Bathroom's in there.'' Annie waved in its direction.

Rachel opened the door. A sink, a toilet, and a huge claw-footed tub surrounded by a curtain. She pulled back the curtain and scrutinized the tub. Spotless.

''Very nice.''

''Okay.'' Annie turned on her heel.

''Wait,'' Rachel said.

Annie turned sharply around.

''Is there room service?'' Rachel laughed apologetically. 'I've gone all day without eating.''

With a look of despair, Annie sagged against the door jamb. ''I can bring you something. From the kitchen.''

"If it isn't too much trouble." Rachel checked her watch. "What time is dinner downstairs?"

"In an hour. I'll bring you some tea and a sandwich."

"No, I can wait."

Annie closed her eyes. A look of total exhaustion—or was it defeat?—stole over her features. "It's all right."

She left before Rachel could protest further.

And it wasn't until then that Rachel remembered it was Annie who'd found Mr. Simpson's body on the beach. Badly decomposed, Mr. Mordicott had said.

"Poor child," Rachel whispered, imagining the scene. She resolved to be very kind to Annie when she came back with the sandwich.

When Annie knocked on the door, Rachel met her at the transom so she wouldn't have to come into the room. But Annie bustled in as if nothing had ever bothered her, laid the tray on a small round table, and waited while Rachel seated herself and took a bite of the sandwich.

"It's wonderful," Rachel said, tasting ham. She wasn't a practicing Jew; nevertheless she rarely ate pork. But her resolution to be careful of Annie pricked at her, and she took another bite in hopes of satisfying the girl.

"I'm glad you like it." Annie stood with her hands intertwined, then hurried across the room to the bed and folded down the bedspread and sheets, puffed up the pillows.

"Oh, you needn't do that," Rachel said. "I'm sure the maid—"

"I don't mind." Annie worked around the bed, smoothing the blankets. "I know how."

"Yes, you certainly do." Rachel reached for her purse, intending to tip her.

But Annie darted out of the room and shut the door.

"Poor little mermaid," Rachel murmured after her. "Poor little Orphan Annie."

In the night, Rachel sat by the window and watched the rain. How lonely it was here. She huddled in the chair she'd dragged over and leaned her cheek on her hand. She had on a high-neck flannel nightgown and her salt-and-pepper hair was brushed over her shoulders, concealing everything, though there was no one to see. Had only been someone once, and he had recoiled—

She shook the wounding memories from her mind. Her breasts made soft pillows for her knees as she drew her legs against her chest and stared at the grey torrents. What had she expected from Greystone Bay? She was intensely disappointed that Mr. Simpson's house was in such terrible shape. She hadn't much money and it would probably take a fortune to repair all the damage. He hadn't left her any cash; there was no mention of any in his will, except for a sum of ten thousand to go to Mr. Mordicott for legal fees.

She thought again of his raincoat. That sad coat. What had he worn sailing? When he was found—when Annie found him—what did he have on?

Unless the waves had ripped him naked.

She shivered. What a frightening thing, to die alone—

—but we all die alone

To drown, then; to call for help and no one comes—

—almost as bad as screaming for help during a fire.

She dreamed the old dream that night, with a new twist: instead of the fire, a tidal wave emerged; the waves rising up and over her head—

—then fire, not water, rains down on her. Fire engulfs her, and she is screaming. She's a writhing figure of flame, drowning in more flame, and her hair burns around her face like crimson petals.

The wave crashes again, water this time, pulling her under while she's gasping and clawing to reach the surface, the breath expelled from her lungs.

Kelp wraps around her ankles and jerks. Things come at her, swimming at her, coming for her—

But she wrestles free and escapes. It's raining on shore but at the top of the hill she can see the lights of her house, her beautiful home. Panting, she thinks of the rooms, of her cat, Maxie, sitting by the stove. She reaches out to the lights, and weeps with relief.

Steam billows around her and she gropes through it, sobbing. And she runs to the house on North Hill, where she is welcomed by—

by—

Rachel's eyes flew open and she sat bolt upright; once she understood she was awake, she lay back down and pressed her fists against her chest. Her heart was thundering; had to watch that. A series of heart attacks had forced her early retirement from her secretarial job with the water district.

As she quieted, she became aware of something inside her clenched right hand. She explored it with her fingers. It was hard, and smooth, and circular.

Then she turned on the light. It was a ring, an ornate, heavy silver ring, with swirls of filigree around a large black stone. It was too big even for her thumb; she hefted it in her palm and gazed at it curiously.

It must have been on the night table. Evidently someone forgot to put it on when they'd moved out of the room. Didn't say much for the maid service, did it?

It seemed very old; there were nicks in the circular smoothness of it. There was a luster to the single black stone that seemed more a patina of age than a natural glow to the gemstone, whatever it was. Onyx? Jet?

Shrugging, Rachel set it on the nightstand and turned out the light.

If she dreamed again, she didn't remember.

* * *

In the morning, when she woke, she was cradling the ring in her hand. The bath tub was filled with water, and there were wet footprints leading from the tub to the bed and back again.

She felt terrible, as if she hadn't slept at all.

When she went down to breakfast, she saw Annie bustling in the kitchen with a huge vat of something—*head cheese*, Rachel thought perversely. She waved. Annie's eyes widened and she disappeared farther into the bowels of the kitchen, where Rachel couldn't see her.

After breakfast, Rachel went to the front desk and asked the desk clerk to call a cab. The clerk was an older girl than Annie, and more robust. It was hard to believe she'd been ill the day before. While Rachel waited, she stuffed her hand in the pocket of her coat and touched the ring.

"Oh," she began, "I forgot. Did anyone lose . . ."

And then she thought, Even if this ring does belong to someone, this girl will probably keep it. She probably wasn't sick yesterday, just wanted the day off, and made Annie fill in for her.

"Yes, ma'am?" the clerk asked, pausing as if she had a million things to do and Rachel was holding her up.

The ring didn't belong to Rachel. It looked old and valuable, and of sentimental value. Someone might miss it very much.

Then they could have phoned or written after it. If they were that careless, they didn't deserve to have it.

Rachel slipped the ring over her thumb. Without saying anything, she shook her head and walked away from the desk.

"I'll wait for the cab by the doors," she said.

The taxi took a while in coming; by the time Rachel reached North Hill, it was no longer raining. The air trembled with moisture; the house dripped with it. The damage looked worse on second inspection and she and the elderly driver traded sad, confused looks.

"Damn shame," the man said, and took her back to the hotel.

Where, she discovered, she'd been moved into a suite on the second floor.

"But I *didn't* request it," she insisted to the clerk.

The girl looked embarrassed. "I'm sorry, ma'am, but you did. When you asked for the cab. You walked back and asked me for a suite."

"That's ridiculous!"

"You stood by the doors for a while, then you came over here and said you were expecting someone, and to put you in a bigger room."

"I did *not*." Rachel leaned forward. The clerk's eyes widened.

Immediately Rachel drew back. Sure enough, the scarf she'd wrapped around her neck had fallen open. The clerk had seen.

"I'm sorry. I'll put you back in your old room," the girl said quietly, and Rachel nodded once, stiffly.

She spent the afternoon calling carpenters and painters and house inspectors and everyone else she would need to repair the house on North Hill. She made dozens of appointments and decided to buy a cheap used car rather than spend a fortune on taxis or rentals.

The next day she bought the first one she saw, an '81 Datsun compact, and drove herself to the house.

It wasn't until she was standing in the parlor, soaking up the stinking water with a mop, that she realized what she'd done.

She'd decided to stay in Greystone Bay.

In Hartfield Croome Simpson's house.

"*My* house," she said with satisfaction, continuing to mop.

That night, Rachel heard herself whimpering. She woke up and found the ring on her thumb.

The tub was full of water. Footprints traced pathways back and forth and back again.

She had a fleeting vision of Annie and thought, that girl's trying to play tricks on me! I have a mind to complain about her in the morning.

But when morning came, and she saw Annie toiling in the kitchen, she kept silent. Poor kid, she'd been through enough.

Work proceeded on the house. She stayed in the SeaHarp; and after a week, when they moved her back into the suite, she flushed but said nothing. She fretted about Alzheimer's. This was how it started, didn't it? With periods of forgetfulness? The prospect of sinking into senility terrified her. She would be taken to a home, where they would take care of her, feed her,

bathe her

She'd kill herself first. She'd drown in the bay the way poor old Hartfield Simpson had, before she'd let them do that.

But how else to explain the nightly tubfull of water and the footprints? It couldn't be Annie; Rachel now always checked the door before retiring. The chain was in place, and the lock, and the chair, which she began dragging against the door every night.

No one came in the night to fill the tub, or parade around the room with wet feet. It had to be faced: she was doing it herself.

And with that fear came a new set of nightmares: she came to one night seated in water up to her breasts with a scrub brush in her hand, and she was rubbing her flesh raw, her poor, scarred flesh:

Not just burned, but destroyed, splintered and fractured and shattered and blasted; plastic surgery might have helped, but she couldn't have endured the prodding, the staring, the horror on the faces of others.

There's a doctor in the hospital, young and sensitive and wonderful. He's treating her; she's only eighteen and she wants to die. He understands her agony. He gives her all the morphine she wants. The burns are the worst he's ever seen, he confesses to her. His nurse leaves the room to vomit in a bed pan.

A fire in a movie theater. Not an accident. No clues as to identity or motive of the perpetrator.

The doctor says Rachel has a lovely soul; that her beauty shines through.

He's seen her, damn him to hell, he's seen her lying there with those sores and the flesh that glistens and oozes worse than anything the monster movies can cook up with their special effects.

He's seen her; she trusts him, and him alone. And when she's released, he comes to her apartment to make love to her.

But he can't. He's too revolted. Even he, who knew.

She tries to kill herself after he flees, but she doesn't know they've turned off the gas for the day, to work on the streets or some such idiocy.

The scars started (ended? but there was no end to them) at her jaw line and traveled the entire length of her body. They puckered her breasts—her nipples were rivulets of dark pink flesh—mottled her private parts. She had no pubic hair. They went inside her legs and down to her ankles; she never wore skirts after the hemlines went up. In the fifties and sixties she lost jobs over her slacks, but what did she care?

No husband, no children, no real friends. Rachel ached for those things, never recovered from being cheated of them. She never grew bitter, which might have been preferable to her loneliness.

And watching her North Hill mansion take shape again after its own terrible ordeal, she figured she might as well be lonely in Greystone Bay as back in Los Angeles.

Yet her Alzheimer's—or whatever it was—grew worse. Besides taking baths (and lying back in bed without drying off?

Now the sheets were wet, too) and demanding a suite, she began to sleepwalk.

Or day walk, or whatever one might call it. She roamed the streets of Greystone Bay in a stupor, meeting people she didn't remember later, buying things she couldn't afford and had no use for—perfumes, chocolates, bouquets of tea roses and a crystal vase to put them in.

Worse yet, she told everyone in the hotel her husband had sent them to her.

And worst of all, they acted as if they believed her. In fact, occasionally someone would inquire as to when Mr. Unger was planning to arrive.

At first she had no answer for them, but quickly she devised a set of pat excuses for his delay: it was taking longer than he'd planned to finish his business; he had to sell the house in Los Angeles. She thought it would be a small matter to deflect their inquiries since they couldn't really care about the matter. But Rachel hadn't counted on the appetite of a small town for gossip with little else to do besides trudge around in the unending rain.

Particularly the appetites of the owners of the hotel: Victor, Frederick, and Noreen Montgomery.

Two brothers and a sister, they were handsome people, of the same dark-haired, fair-skinned cast as many of the inhabitants of Greystone Bay. Tall, and a little too thin, and with an abstracted air that Rachel supposed came from having to manage a hotel, they loved to chat with their guests. Of the three, Noreen had the most time for quizzing Rachel, who had avoided attention ever since the fire, found herself blooming, late in life, into a stupendous liar for the amusement—and approval—of Noreen Montgomery.

For Miss Montgomery would sit perched for hours on one of the chairs Rachel found so uncomfortable, dressed in becoming grey cashmere, and ask question after question: his birthday, his astrology sign, what cologne he wore. Rachel manufactured an answer for each question, pausing, weaving, deceiving. She told Miss Montgomery how tall he was; and how handsome—maybe not as good-looking now as when he was young; and certainly not as attractive as Miss Montgomery's own two brothers; but still, quite a good-looking man. She used her cruel doctor-lover as her pattern, which she embellished whenever it seemed necessary: he smoked a pipe; he hated the traffic in Los Angeles; he was eager to get to Greystone Bay. Of course he missed her. He was bringing their cat, Maxie.

Occasionally, Miss Montgomery would flop back in her chair and say, ''Ah!'' as if Rachel had provided her with some kind of inspiration, or clue; as if bit by bit, Miss Montgomery were piecing together a picture of Rachel's beloved Brian. (And that was, had been, his name. Brian Covey, M.D.)

Bordering this almost pathological interest, Annie often hovered on the outskirts of their conversations like a fretful lapdog, benignly ignored like same. Once she encountered Rachel in the hall on the way to her suite. She was carrying a covered dish that smelled like sea water. She cried out, then stood aside to let Rachel pass.

''Good evening, Annie,'' Rachel said kindly.

''I didn't know you were married,'' Annie retorted, making it sound like a challenge.

''Well, I am.'' Rachel frowned at her, then remembered her promise to be nice to the girl.

''You don't wear a ring.''

Rachel paled. The ring! Maybe it belonged to Annie, and she wanted it back. Perhaps she'd left it on the nightstand herself. It had come off a chain around her neck while she was fluffing up the pillows that first night—

Rachel clamped her hand around the ring, which she always carried in her pocket.

"I lost a lot of weight." Rachel licked her lips. "It's too big and I haven't had it made smaller."

Annie nodded unhappily. Just then the elevator operator came around the same corner. He was tucking his shirt into his trousers; when he saw Rachel and Annie he flushed and said, "Good evening, Mrs. Unger. Um, hi, Annie."

Annie blushed and looked guiltily down at her covered dish. Oh, they've been fooling around, Rachel thought, and was pleased for Annie's sake.

"Good evening," Rachel replied, and went into her suite.

Where she was overcome by grief; wave upon wave, like the bay that surged in a big, ugly mass across the street.

For of course there was no Mr. Unger on his way; no handsome Taurus with a pipe and a twenty-year-old London Fog raincoat. There wasn't even a cat, for the love of God; no one, no one at all was coming for her. No handsome young man tucking in his shirt; no one to make her blush and stammer like a girl. She was alone in the world; and the stories she'd been telling could only serve to isolate her further. When she moved into her house and no Mr. Unger ever showed, wouldn't tongues wag! They'd say he'd run off, or died, and they'd speculate and gossip and stare; and sooner or later, someone would see part of her she didn't want them to see—

So she cried and cried at the stupidity that was overtaking her, this awful Alzheimer's-whatever that made her act so foolish and say the dumbest things. What was wrong with her? She should move back to Los Angeles before it was too late.

She had her nightmare again, only this time there was someone in the fire with her. A man's hand, around her thigh; man's breath on her cheek. Everywhere the scent of man and then—

—of the underbelly of the sea, thick and viscous and suffocating. A smell like smothered smoke; like garbage; like death.

When she woke up, her first thought was, That *was* Annie's head in that vase.

She put the ring on her thumb, and went back to sleep.

Rachel stayed in the SeaHarp for almost three months. When she moved out, it was June, and she felt a blessed relief and an intense confusion that her bills were paid, both at the SeaHarp and for the restoration of the North Hill house. How could she have managed it all on her secretary's pension? But Noreen (they were "Noreen" and "Rachel" by then) assured her that she was square at the hotel; and all the carpenters and painters left her employ with good, signed checks.

With great joy, she moved a surplus four-poster and dresser from the hotel (Noreen was so generous) into the house. Much of the original furniture could be restored, but that would have to wait until she saved some more cash. And she certainly wouldn't pay good money to ship her old junk all the way across the United States.

Annie wept the day Rachel left the SeaHarp. Rachel was touched and told her she could visit her at her new home any time she liked. The charming young man hovered around her, but Rachel wasn't sure Annie liked him any more. She was nervous and furtive whenever he was near; she rarely looked at him. Perhaps the Montgomerys forbade fraternization among their employees, and they were keeping their romance a secret.

Rachel dismissed thoughts of Annie as she stood in the middle of her white-and-blue kitchen as her first summer fog seeped in around her; and unbidden the thought came: Here I am, in the belly of the beast.

That was an odd remark. She set the kettle on to boil and

opened the door to the thick summer air. It was heavy with summer thunderstorms and the chirping of crickets.

"Maxie," she called, then shuddered and shut the door.

Because she didn't own a cat named Maxie. She never had.

If the SeaHarp was a sea-serpent, Rachel's house was a jellyfish, floating atop the crest of North Hill. Surrounded by elder trees, it billowed in the night fog, cresting and riding the breezes, a sparkling white membrane.

In the night, as she walked along the shore of the bay and smiled up at the lights, she imagined she saw the house expand and contract as if it were breathing. She knew she was right to stay; a house like that needed life inside it.

Her eyes filled with tears, and the yearning that had been with her since she was eighteen surged inside her. She wrapped her nightgown around herself to hide the scars and looked down at her bare feet, cut by fragments of shells and the edges of sharp rocks; and thought:

What the hell am I doing here in the middle of the night?

She'd wandered so far she'd reached the outcropping of the pier where the old men and boys fished. She ran the length of the beach, pausing before the SeaHarp, poised and ready to strike. The lights were off, save for a bubbling glow above the entrance and a light in the reception area.

So it could have been her imagination that she saw Annie in the window of her old room, 303, dressed in a long, green dress, her hair rippling behind her as if suspended from dozens of wires—

—*as if she floated underwater; it was her head in the vase, it was*

She was playing a harp. The young man stood behind her, naked, caressing her breasts through her dress.

Rachel gasped and blinked.

No Annie. No boy. No harp. Just a hotel, with everyone sensibly tucked in bed.

Rachel's heart thrummed against her ribs. She panicked. Heart attack! Clenching and unclenching her fists, she took deep breaths, trying to relax.

After she grew calmer, she kept to the small sidestreets and snuck home. God, if anyone should see her, tripping through town in her nightgown like some senile old bat. She would die. Simply die.

She let herself in through the kitchen and slammed the door, leaning against it. Hastily she pulled away when she realized she was soaking wet. No doubt it was the moisture in the ocean air.

But no, the walls of the kitchen were glistening. The tile was slick.

And in the living room, the new parquet floors pooled with water.

And a strange odor wafted through the house.

"Mildew!" Rachel said disgustedly. So that was why the repairs on the house cost so little: none of the workmen had known what he was doing!

She walked through the house, touching all the walls. Wet clean through.

The bathtub was full of water.

And Rachel thought she heard the lyrical music of a harp, far away in the night breeze,

undersea.

Before Rachel could call the workmen the next day, the walls dried. The pools of water evaporated. They seemed to leave no damage, but she worried about seepage and told the carpenter so, who promised to have a look as soon as he could get out there.

During the first two weeks in the house, Noreen was Rachel's only visitor. She came for coffee and admired the repairs Rachel had effected.

"It's even better than when Harry Simpson lived here," Noreen said, and Rachel sat tall with pride.

"I've never owned my own home before. I still can't figure out why he willed it to me."

"He was an odd one." Noreen trailed her hand along the balustrade as if she were caressing the arm of a lover.

"Mr. Mordicott said he was rather reclusive."

"Oh, he got around." Noreen threw back her head and laughed. She was striking, in her white-dark way, with strong features and deepset brown eyes. "He was friends with my brothers and me. Good friends."

"Oh? I didn't know." Rachel poured more coffee. "Please, tell me what he was like. I don't know a thing about him, really. For the life of me, I don't know why—"

"Fierce. Very fierce." Noreen moved her shoulders. "A temper. Moody." She tilted her head. "Arrogant. A great one for secrets."

Noreen turned her gaze on Rachel. "He never told me about you. Giving you the house, I mean. Do you know our father left the hotel to my little brother. Cut Frederick and me out entirely. We work for Victor."

"Oh?" Rachel drew up slightly, surprised and a trifle pleased that Noreen should confide something so personal to her.

"We don't mind. The old place is a headache. It's given Victor ulcers. Unencumbered, one . . . swims more freely."

Noreen rose. "I've got to get back. It's been lovely seeing you again. Your husband—"

"Any day," Rachel said quickly.

"How nice." Noreen smiled at Rachel. "How very nice."

"Would you take these with you?" Rachel put some of her homemade brownies on a plate and covered them with a gingham napkin. "And please give one to Annie. She keeps promising me she'll come by but—"

"I'll see that she does." Noreen accepted the plate. "Goodbye, dear Rachel."

They touched cheeks; they were that close. Rachel was tempted to confess the creation of Mr. Unger but just couldn't bring herself to do it. It was too ridiculous.

And besides, she was afraid she'd blurt out the rest: the wet sheets and the baths and the sleepwalking; and the trill of the harp and the sussuration of the sea that had begun to whoosh through the walls late at night; inside the walls—

"I hope you'll come down to the hotel for a meal or some coffee. As a friend, of course. With us."

"Thank you, I will. Soon," Rachel replied, but realized as she spoke that she never wanted to step foot in the SeaHarp again.

But she had no idea why.

Gradually, neighbors introduced themselves and Rachel invited them in to view the restored mansion. The first few offered compliments and praise, though they seemed ill at ease about something. It was Barbara Parker, whose Queen Anne towered three blocks away on Sentinel, who wrinkled her nose and said, "But, Rachel! You must have terrible problems with mildew! That *smell*."

For some reason, Rachel felt a pang of fear. Safe in her pocket, she slipped her ring around her thumb and worried the black stone as she cocked her head and said, "Smell?"

"Don't tell me you don't notice it!" Barbara began opening cupboards in the kitchen. "Nope, not in here. You've got a dandy case of mildew somewhere."

She opened the coat closet. "Well, for heaven's sake!"

Harry Simpson's lonely raincoat hung like a slimy piece of decomposed seaweed. Both women stepped away from the odor and Rachel clung more fiercely to her ring.

"I'd think you'd want to toss that out," Barbara said.

Rachel was seconds away from screaming that she had. Instead, she swallowed and shook her head.

"I can't imagine why the workmen didn't."

But she had; she'd done it herself. What, had she gone and dug it back up?

She shook her head. Of course she hadn't dug it up. She'd never buried it. Just laid it on top of the piles of rotted wood for the men to cart away.

Barbara Parker didn't stay long after that. She told Rachel to get some Simple Green—"get rid of that in no time"—and invited her to dinner.

Then she was gone.

The next time, it was Rachel who noticed the smell. She was sitting at the kitchen table balancing her checkbook. There was a noise—

"Ssh, Maxie," she said without thinking.

And then a thick odor pervaded the room, all at once. A sharp, tangy, salt smell that curled under her nose, making her jump up and cry out.

Then a light tapping on the front door.

"Just a minute!" she cried. She searched the kitchen quickly to see what on earth could be making such a terrible stink; finding nothing, she walked to the door and opened it.

Annie stood on the threshold, looking solemn. She was dressed in a pair of baggy jeans and a teal sweater. Her hair was braided down her back.

"I've come." She hesitated on the threshold as if trying to peer around Rachel.

Rachel smiled kindly and opened the door wide. "Well, come in. I've been hoping to see you."

Annie glanced at her, then lowered her gaze to the floor.

"I just made some cookies." Rachel led the way into the kitchen. "Did Noreen . . . Miss Montgomery give you some of the brownies I sent?"

Annie nodded. She sat in the chair Rachel offered, took a

cursory look at the opened bank book, and folded her hands
on the table. "Thanks," she said belatedly. "They were
good."

Rachel bustled around, pouring tea and arranging cookies
on a plate. She hadn't seen anyone in four days, except when
she went to the market for the Simple Green. The people in
Greystone Bay were not a chatty lot; it wasn't like back in
Los Angeles, where people greeted strangers on the street
and exchanged a few sentences on the weather or politics or
the surf or something. Here, folks kept more to themselves.

Annie ate silently, shifting occasionally in the chair. Rachel was bursting to talk to her but didn't know how to begin.
Instead, it was Annie who started the conversation. "You
must get lonely here," she said.

"Well, my husband—"

Annie cut her off with a look. *She knew.* She didn't have
to say the words aloud; Rachel cleared her throat and tried
to say, "Do you want another cookie?"

Instead, what came out was, "You can't believe how lonely
it gets!" and she burst into tears.

Annie watched her cry for at least five minutes. She didn't
move while Rachel sobbed. She sat still as a statue and said
nothing until Rachel daubed at her eyes and blew her nose.

"I'm sorry. I just got carried away."

Annie nodded. "It will be all right, then." She stood; her
hands trembled at her sides and she scrutinized the wall behind Rachel so hard that Rachel finally turned around.

"What? Annie?"

Annie moved stiff-legged to the door. She fumbled with
the handle, threw the door open and dashed across the threshold.

"Mrs. Unger," she began. She chewed her lower lip. Her
bony chest rose, fell.

"Annie, what's wrong? Please, I know I've been silly. I
just started. I don't why I . . . invented a husband." She

ould feel her face grow hot. "Everyone was asking me ques-
ons. One thing led to another."

Annie shuffled her feet, stared down at her shoes. "I saw,"
he said.

Rachel took a step back as she touched her turtleneck
weater.

Annie looked at her. "Maxie was the name of his cat. He
ad her with her."

She flew over the driveway and disappeared down the
treet.

Rachel watched her. Her mouth worked but no words came
ut. She thought she was going to faint. She was sinking
eneath the surface, sinking downward, where it was harder
o think. She was fighting to hold on, fighting—

—and she heard a familiar voice behind her saying, "Give
: to me, you bitch! It belongs to her! It all belongs to her!"

She lay face down in a pool of water; her body ached and
he couldn't breathe. Someone was on top of her, pushing
er head under water; her eyes bulged and she was choking,
osing consciousness—

—but she wouldn't let him have the ring.

That was what he wanted, she knew, as she knew her as-
ailant's identity. It was the elevator operator, Annie's young
nan. He was going to kill her for it. Her hand was clenched
round her thumb, where the ring was; and she wondered
vhy he didn't just pull it off. Why did he have to drown her
rst?

For she was drowning. In a pool of water too shallow to
lose over her head, she was unable to breathe. There was
o air left inside her—no jellyfish, she—yet she doggedly
eld onto the ring. She was going to die for it; she was going
o die—

She came to. She was lying on her side on Woodbane
treet. It was dark.

A hundred feet from her, the boy lay unmoving. His face

was averted, as if he hid in shame; but the moon glistened on pale skin, on stiff skin, bloodless.

Rachel lurched to her hands and knees and began to crawl toward him.

Then lightning cracked through the sky. The night burst apart and through the tears rain showered the ground. Shards of grey forced Rachel onto her back and she covered her face, crying out. Thunder crescendoed around her; she sat up and wrapped her arms around her head as she got to her knees.

If I don't drown out there, I'll drown in here.

The young man's body shifted into the gutter. The rain pummeled him, ricocheting off the side of his face in silvery discs like rubbery bubbles of oil. He didn't move.

April is not the cruellest month in Greystone Bay; this was a siege of rain, a deluge that flooded the street. And would plummet into the bay.

Rachel struggled to her feet, suddenly certain that if she didn't get home, the rain would sweep her into Greystone Bay and she would drown there. She burst into tears and waded down the middle of the street, her clothes wrapped around her, impeding her steps. She wanted to go back for the boy, but there was no time for that; besides, he'd tried to kill her. Why should she waste her strength?

She thought she heard him groan; she flailed and watched as the gutter filled around him and lifted him off the ground. It occurred to Rachel that he might already be dead.

"Oh, Annie, poor Annie," she said. Nausea rose inside her and a sense of urgency propelled her to stagger on down the street to the shelter of her home. She retched as she walked, doubled over. The rain, the goddamn, unending, unendurable rain, fell harder.

She wondered if Maxie was out in the storm.

And if perhaps she were having some kind of hallucination; if she were sitting in the bathtub with the scrub brush, imagining all this because she had Alzheimer's. She remembered other things now: that a bouquet of flowers had arrived for her yesterday, with a card signed, *Ami amet deli pencet.* She knew that was what it said because she'd memorized the words, thinking them some kind of code, or puzzle, or joke. Or warning.

She remembered, too, that when she was having her nightmare last night, she awakened to the stench of wet smoke. She screamed aloud, thinking the house was on fire. She found no flames, and no sign that there had been any; but the smell persisted.

But she did discover a series of handprints on the bannister that Noreen Montgomery had caressed so lovingly: large, moldy handprints spaced at regular intervals, as if someone had used the balustrade as an aid to get up the stairs, pulling hard, dragging upward, moldy hands that smelled of smoke—

The water swirled around her calves. Then the blessed lights of Rachel's house came into view and she ran toward them, arms outstretched.

She flung herself into the house and slammed the door. The phone was ringing and she picked it up, shouting, "The boy's out there! Please, go help him. He's on—"

"Mrs. Unger, are you all right?" It was Annie. Her voice rose shrill and terrified.

"The boy—"

"Oh, my god." Annie's voice seemed to fall away from the phone. Then she came back on the line. "It's all right, Mrs. Unger. He wanted you to have it. I understand. I'm not angry."

"What are you talking about?" Rachel shouted.

"Mrs. Unger, Miss Unger—"

"Who are you?" Rachel gripped the phone with both hands and shrieked into it. "What is happening?"

"He did it because of the pain he caused you. He's so sorry.

"Who are you?"

Annie hung up. Rachel stood by the phone, screaming, "Who are you?" over and over again.

The lightning snapped; water trickled beneath the kitchen door. The trickle became a steady flow; water dripped down the walls. It fell in a waterfall from the sink onto the tiles and eddied around Rachel's ankles.

Rachel dashed from the kitchen into the parlor. Water shot down the stairs like a waterfall. Had she left the tub running?

She took the stairs two at a time. The hall was becoming a river; by the time she reached her bedroom door, the water reached her knees. She had to fight to open the door; when she pushed it back, more water crashed around her, submerging her to her waist.

She staggered back, was flung against the opposite wall. The water kept pouring out of her bedroom. She fought against it, battling toward the bathroom, though she couldn't imagine all this water coming from those two little taps.

And then she remembered something else: there was an inscription on the inside of the ring, and it said the same thing as the card that had accompanied her flowers: *Ami amet deli pencet.*

The room filled to her chest. She lost her footing and went under, opened her eyes and saw her clothes and furniture bobbing like the things beneath the surface of her dreams; beneath Greystone Bay itself. All the useless things, the junk, the wreckage.

She tried to stand up and realized the water had risen above her head. The room was filled almost to the surface; perhaps a foot of space remained. Rachel fought to reach the surface—

—a huge wave rose over her head, and something wrapped around her ankle, pulling her down—

She opened her mouth, losing her air. The thing that had her turned her around and looked into her eyes.

He was handsome, so very handsome, in his windbreaker

and sailor's cap. He had pale skin and large blue eyes, and rich, dark red hair.

He took her in his arms and pulled her clothes off her, slowly, deliberately, while she floundered, her eyes opening and closing as she began to go. All her scars were visible and he touched them with his big hands, no hint of revulsion in his manner or his look.

He opened his mouth and said, "It means, think of a friend who loves you." His voice rumbled through the water toward her; it sounded as sweet to her as the music of Annie's harp.

She began to cry; her tears drifted upward, mingled with the vast space of water around them. Her hair undulated behind her like the petals of spring blossoms.

Of course it hadn't been Annie's head—

Ami amet deli pencet.

"Oh, do you?" she tried to say, but nothing came out. Shyly, she embraced him and he held her tightly as she went, out with the surge, out with the tide, out with the undertow.

Into July, the sweetest month in Greystone Bay.

THE CHRONICLERS

CHET WILLIAMSON is a Pennsylvanian who knows about too many old, bad movies for his own good. He is the author of several highly-acclaimed novels, including ASH WEDNESDAY and DREAMTHORP.

AL SARRANTONIO, from Putnam Valley, New York, is an avid amateur astronomer and likes to fish where you can't catch anything. His latest books are MOONBANE, an sf-horror novel, and COLD NIGHT, a mystery.

ROBERT R. McCAMMON is twice winner of the Bram Stoker Award and the best-selling author of SWAN SONG and STINGER. He lives in Alabama with his wife, Sally.

BRYAN WEBB is an award-winning non-fiction writer who lives in Georgia where his electricity is constantly threatened by cows that rub up against the telephone polls. He chews gum better than anybody in the state.

STEVE RASNIC TEM lives in Colorado, and made a name for himself in short fiction before doing the same with his first novel, EXCAVATIONS. He is married to poet/short story writer Melanie Tem.

CRAIG SHAW GARDNER is the author of the best-selling six-volume Ebenezum novels; his newest is, honest to god, SLAVES OF THE VOLCANO GOD.

MELISSA MIA HALL once again proves that Texans are different from thee and me, and more weird. Her stories and poetry have appeared in just about every major magazine and anthology in the field.

LES DANIELS lives and works in Providence, Rhode Island, and is the creator of San Sebastian, a truly wonderful and vicious vampire. His latest novel is YELLOW FOG.

SUZY McKEE CHARNAS, who confines her considerable skills to no one genre, lives in Albuquerque and is the author of the landmark THE VAMPIRE TAPESTRY, and DORO-THEA DREAMS.

ROBERT E. VARDEMAN also lives in Albuquerque and is the author of dozens of fantasy, sf, and western novels, in-cluding the CENOTAPH ROAD and WORLDS OF CHAOS series.

WENDY WEBB lives in Georgia, is a full-time nurse, and has just completed her first novel. According to her, she taught her father, Bryan, all he knows about writing.

LESLIE ALAN HORVITZ, despite the numerous misspellings of his name to the contrary, is a man. His best-selling novels include THE DYING.

THOMAS F. MONTELEONE lives in Baltimore, sells cable television on the side, is the author of FANTASMA and, with Jon DeChance, of CROOKED HOUSE.

BOB BOOTH, a typesetter by trade, book collector by inclination, lives in Rhode Island, where he's trying to convince his daughter not to practice too hard for her part in *The Bad Seed*.

NANCY HOLDER has lived in Japan, studied ballet in Germany, and now lives in San Diego. She speaks fluent Californian which her two border collies, Nan and Ron, do not understand at all.